the
LAKE
HOUSE

the
LAKE
HOUSE

SARAH BETH DURST

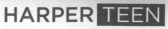

HARPER TEEN
An Imprint of HarperCollins*Publishers*

for Becca

ONE

Claire excelled at three things: ballet, homework, and identifying all the ways there were to die in any given situation. Like now, on this boat. She couldn't stop thinking about how easy it would be to be knocked off the side, hit your head as you fell, and drown.

Less likely: being guillotined by a fishing line.

Also unlikely but still possible: being pierced by shrapnel if the engine exploded.

She fidgeted with her life jacket, touching the three buckles in rapid succession, until she felt reassured they were secure.

I hate boats, she decided.

She also hated airplanes, particularly the minuscule prop planes that felt as if they'd been assembled by a five-year-old with unfettered access to glue. That had been the other option for the trip to the Lake House—itty-bitty prop plane. There were no roads.

"Not a fan of boats?" Reyva asked.

The driver started the engine.

"They're loud," Claire said, shouting to be heard. "Like a

lawn mower mated with a wood chipper and had a hideous, gargling child."

Reyva's lips twitched as if she were considering smiling but didn't want to commit. Claire wasn't certain she'd seen her smile once yet. It didn't seem to be Reyva's thing.

As they shot across the lake, the boat slapped the water again and again. Each time, Claire bounced off her seat by a half inch. She wrapped one hand around the flimsy metal rail, trying not to make it obvious that she was holding on for dear life, especially in front of the two girls she'd just met and the boy driving the boat.

It'll be fun, her parents had said, much too cheerfully. *Plus, think of how much it'll help your college applications! You'll learn new skills, have new experiences, and make new friends!* Claire glanced at the other two girls. Friends. She never knew what to say to turn a person she'd just met into one of those, but since the boy driving the boat, Jack, seemed intent on increasing their speed beyond the limits of the speedometer, it wasn't first on her list to worry about.

Across the boat, not holding on at all, the other girl—her name was Mariana, Claire remembered—took a selfie as her hair blew in the wind. Lowering her phone, she shouted what sounded like, "*Porpoise!*"

"Can't be!" Claire shouted back. "There aren't any freshwater dolphins or toothed whales in Maine. Only Asia and South America." She winced at herself. Why did she *always* sound like she'd swallowed a textbook?

Mariana shouted louder. "Not porpoise! *Porpoising!* The way

2

the boat is bouncing. It means the trim is set incorrectly. I can fix it." She tucked her phone into her back pocket as she stood up.

Claire squeezed the rail tighter.

"Sit down, please!" Jack called.

"You have to adjust the trim! Trim *up!*" Mariana called back to him, but she, to Claire's relief, sat down.

Jack adjusted the throttle, the engine changed pitch, and the boat's bouncing subsided. It sped more smoothly over the lake, and Claire relaxed her grip a little. "Hey, thanks!" he called to Mariana.

She flashed him a brilliant smile and tossed her hair, and Claire saw his eyes widen and cheeks tint pink. *Good*, she thought. *He'll be staring at her now.* One less person to notice how terrified she was.

"More useful than she looks," Reyva commented.

Claire wasn't sure what to say to that, so she nodded vaguely. She'd only known the two other girls for about an hour—due to the weather, they were all arriving a day late. She was glad it had worked out that way. It was better than arriving late alone. She couldn't be "the new girl," singled out, if there were three of them. Reyva or Mariana could take the spotlight, while she blended into the wallpaper. It was the best possible outcome, really—preferable to nearly any other Claire could currently imagine.

"Have you ever been to the Lake House?" Claire asked Reyva.

"Nope. My dad said it's been closed for years. He was so excited it reopened that he was practically giddy. He said it had always been his 'dearest wish' that I attend the beloved retreat where he forged so many precious memories and made lifelong friends—so dear that he has literally never talked about it once."

"Both my parents went," Claire offered. "They said it was a *formative experience.*"

Reyva laughed. "My dad tossed in that phrase a few times too. I told him I'm already formed."

"You didn't want to come?"

Reyva shrugged. "You?"

She'd told her parents of course she'd go. If they thought this was best, then yes, sign her up. There was nothing else to say since it was clear they'd already decided. Obviously, she would have rather stayed home for the summer, no matter how great it would look on college applications. She hadn't even arrived, and she was already out of her comfort zone. Surreptitiously, Claire touched the buckles on her life jacket again and thought longingly of her bedroom with all her books, and a door that closed everyone out. "I'm not sure 'want' is the right word. But it'll be great."

"Are you trying to convince me or yourself?"

"Both?"

"Fair enough."

Reyva fell silent.

Claire tried to enjoy the boat ride. Spray spat in her face, and it was refreshing, if she didn't think about how much bacteria could be in each drop. She made herself take a deep breath. The lake smelled like a fresh-mowed lawn, undercut with the aroma of dead fish.

The trip lasted another forty-five minutes, which officially made this the largest lake that Claire had ever been on. Finally, the boat slowed, angling itself to drift up against a dock, knocking into it. Jack hopped off, secured the lines, and waved at them all to hurry up. He held out his hand to help Mariana, but she jumped from the boat as if she hadn't noticed.

Claire waited until the other two had disembarked before she joined them, carrying her backpack, which was crammed so full that she felt unbalanced. She wouldn't have minded if Jack had offered his hand to help her, but he didn't. He was busy hauling Mariana's bags onto the dock. Reyva had a similar-sized backpack, but Mariana had a backpack plus two suitcases large enough to smuggle a couple of kindergartners inside them.

With another sunny smile at Jack, Mariana said, "I packed light."

"You and I have different definitions of that word," Reyva said.

"I only brought outfits with green in them, in honor of the woodland setting." Mariana waved her painted nails at the shore.

To Claire, Reyva said, "I can't tell if she's serious."

Following Mariana's wave, Claire confronted the forest for the first time. It was thick, populated mostly by white pine, spruce, hemlock, and sugar maples. The bark of the occasional white birch tree provided the only break in the lush, dark green. She couldn't see any hint of a house.

Jack pointed to the end of the dock, where a trail of packed dirt led in between the trees and bushes. "Follow that for a half mile, and it'll lead you right to the Lake House. The program director, Ms. Williams, will be there to greet you and introduce you to everyone."

As Jack untied the line, Mariana asked, "You're . . . not coming with us?"

"Lake House policy. Drop-off only." He hopped back onto the boat and revved the engine. "Stick to the path, and you'll be fine." To Claire, he said, "You won't need a life jacket." He held out his hand.

Feeling herself blush, Claire put down her backpack and unclipped her life jacket. She handed it back to the driver. Reyva and Mariana had already tossed theirs onto the boat. She hadn't wanted to take hers off until she was firmly on land, and technically the dock wasn't land. It was a wooden bridge to nowhere, supported by narrow poles that were continually weakened by partial submersion in water.

"Sorry," she muttered.

"Enjoy your summer," he said.

"Aw, you won't be stopping by? Even to say hi?" Mariana asked.

"Um . . . uh . . . I . . . that is, I don't . . ." A few of his words were lost as he pushed off from the dock and waved. "I'll let your parents know you made it safely. See you in August!"

He motored away from the shore.

"I think you scared him off," Reyva said.

Mariana shrugged. "Boys are fun to scare."

Reyva nodded. "It's not *not* true."

Claire stared after the girls. She wished she had that kind of confidence. Or any kind. She was fairly sure she hadn't said anything to Jack except her name and "Sorry." Oh well. He wasn't the one she'd be spending the summer with—these girls were.

All of them faced the woods.

"You know, if this were a movie, the soundtrack would shift here," Mariana said. "Something orchestral, like John Williams. I'm thinking the *Jurassic Park* entrance theme, as we begin our grand adventure."

"Can't be that grand," Reyva said. "It's summer camp."

"'An enrichment retreat,'" Mariana corrected.

"Either way, no theme song."

But Mariana started humming the *Jurassic Park* theme anyway. As she hit the climax, she marched off the dock with her suitcases and backpack, and Claire hurried after her. She caught up with her at the start of the trail. Mariana had stopped and was staring at the trees with awe on her face. "I've been to Muir Woods and seen sequoias and redwoods, but there's something about this . . ."

"It's the quantity of trees," Claire said. "In national parks like Muir, every tree is studied and treasured, visited reverently. But here, there's miles and miles of forest, and I don't think anyone's ever taken the time to pay attention to each individual tree. They're nameless. Indistinguishable. It makes it all feel . . . overwhelmingly endless." According to her parents, this was an old-growth forest, which meant it had never been logged. Some of these trees, they said, were hundreds of years old. It had been an oddly intense conversation. Before this summer, she'd had no idea her parents had such strong feelings about the woods of Maine. They'd waxed poetic about it for at least an hour, before launching into their much-more-in-character spiel in which she was made to promise that she would never leave the trails or the grounds.

"So what you mean is, you can't see the trees for the forest?" Mariana asked, laughing. "Okay, that was a really bad joke. Sorry. Couldn't resist."

Reyva brushed past them. "We'll survive. As long as there are no puns."

Mariana followed her. "The tree-o sets off on an adventure!"

Reyva gave an exaggerated groan and picked up her pace, leading the way. She liked both of these girls already, which was a good start. *Maybe*, Claire thought, *this will be okay.* Maybe she could be a new Claire here, a never-before-seen version of herself who made friends easily and didn't freak out about every little thing. She'd come home radiating confidence and calm, leaving the old Claire behind, shed like a butterfly's chrysalis or a molted snakeskin. *Hopefully more butterfly than snake*, she thought. Certainly, that was what her parents wanted.

The woods closed quickly around them. Light filtered down between the branches, casting everything in a greenish hue. This late in the day, just before dusk, the shadows were thick in the underbrush. Following Reyva, Mariana lugged her suitcases up the path. Behind her, Claire kept to the center of the trail and watched for poison ivy.

Birds chirped to one another, and the branches rustled with the weight of squirrels as they scampered from tree to tree. The trail wound around boulders, and she had to keep an eye on her footing. The dead needles on the trail were slick, and there were plenty of rocks and roots threatening to trip her. The air also tasted much more sour than she'd expected for the Great Outdoors. *Shouldn't fresh air be, well, fresh?* she thought.

"Anyone know exactly what we'll be doing here?" Claire asked. "There was no useful info online, not even a website." She'd done thorough searches, and not only was there no official website, but there was no chatter about the Lake House anywhere, which was weird—or at least bad business for a camp that was trying to reopen. Of course, it didn't help that the name was so generic.

Mariana gasped.

Claire reached out, ready to catch her if she'd tripped. "Are you okay?"

"There's no Wi-Fi," Mariana said. She'd dropped her suitcases and was holding her phone up toward the sky. "I didn't expect cell service out in the middle of nowhere, but with the house so near—I should be able to see at least the name of their network, even if it's password protected."

"It's not necessary to password protect their network out here," Reyva said. "Unless they're worried about the bears stealing their bandwidth."

I forgot to worry about bears, Claire thought. Not that she thought they'd steal Wi-Fi, but she wasn't eager to encounter one. Or a mountain lion. Or a wolf. Maine had all three.

"True," Mariana said, picking up her suitcases and continuing on, "but we should be close enough to—"

In the lead, Reyva halted.

Claire and Mariana caught up to her and also halted.

Claire felt as if she were plummeting from a plane, or what she'd imagined that would feel like. Distantly, she heard the voices of the others, the cries and the gasps, as they all stared at the clearing with the house—or what should have been the house.

Because the house was not there.

It had been consumed by fire.

Only a blackened shell remained.

TWO

Of all the potential disasters Claire had imagined, both plausible and far-fetched, this one had never entered her calculations. Yet here it was: the roof had collapsed, half the walls had crumbled to ash, and only the chimney still stood at its full height.

This was why the air on the trail had tasted so sour, she realized. Here by the Lake House, it was worse, bitter, like a wood fire mixed with battery acid. Wisps of smoke rose in tendrils off piles of ash. If there were still hints of smoke, she thought, the fire must have happened recently. She pictured the house ablaze.

"Did they get out?" Mariana asked, dropping her suitcases and backpack. "Please tell me they got out."

Claire called, "Hello! Is anyone here?"

"Lucky it didn't burn down the forest," Reyva said.

"Not lucky if they didn't get out," Claire said, but Reyva was right—if there had been any wind when the place burned, all the fallen trees, the dead brush, and the blanket of pine needles would have lit up and it would have spread. Five log-cabin-like sheds had also been destroyed by fire, but the house and the sheds had been separated from the forest by an airstrip with cracked pavement, a weed-infested tennis court, and a charred lawn as broad as a baseball field. She called again, "Is anyone here? Does anyone need help?"

A flock of birds startled from a nearby tree, but otherwise there was no movement.

Shedding her backpack, Reyva started across the lawn.

"Wait!" Mariana called. "You shouldn't go in there! It's not safe!"

Ignoring her, Reyva stepped over the crumbled remnants of the doorframe. Swearing under her breath, Claire also shed her pack, then jogged after her and stepped over the threshold.

Inside—if one could call it inside, since there was no roof anymore—was a pile of debris. Part of the roof was piled on collapsed stairs. One wall, partially standing, had bits of flowered wallpaper, which had been scorched sepia-colored. Charred electrical wires and broken pipes were exposed. A blackened mirror still hung, though several framed photos had fallen. Their glass had shattered, and the photos were shriveled like dead leaves.

"Help me with this?" Reyva asked.

Together, they tried to shift a chunk of the roof. Grunting, they maneuvered a section of shingles and then dropped it. Ash mushroomed into the air, and they fell back, coughing. Claire's eyes watered. She wiped them and blinked rapidly.

"If anyone's in here . . ." Claire let the words trail off.

To destroy the house this thoroughly, it had to have been a huge blaze. The smoke would have choked anyone who had been trapped long before the walls collapsed. Either they made it out, or . . . *Or they're beyond caring if we find them*, Claire thought.

Safely beyond the doorframe, Mariana said, "They must have escaped. See?" She pointed to the airstrip. "No plane. They could have taken it, if there was one. Or a boat."

Claire let out a yelp. "The boat! We have to get it back!" She pivoted and ran out of the house and across the singed lawn. Jack had already been speeding away when they'd begun their hike, but he might not be out of sight yet. . . .

She heard footsteps behind her. Glancing back, she saw Mariana frowning at her feet as she ran. Flying over the trail, Reyva passed her, then Claire. "He'll be too far away," Reyva said, but she didn't slow.

"We have to try."

"Obviously."

Then they didn't speak. They just ran.

Avoiding the rocks and roots, Claire half hopped and half jogged down the trail. She was acutely aware that at any moment, she could trip and twist her ankle, but she also knew that with each second, the boat was speeding farther away.

And it wouldn't return for weeks.

Don't think, she told herself. *Just run.* She forced herself to count her footsteps, every stride, to thwart the litany of *What if, what if, what if . . .*

They burst out of the woods and ran onto the dock. In the distance, the boat was still visible, but so small that it looked like a toy. Its wake was a V-shaped ripple behind it. Jumping up and down, Claire shouted and screamed, "Jack, come back! Help! Help us! Fire!"

Beside her, Mariana and Reyva yelled and waved too.

Sound traveled well over water. Maybe Jack would hear them; maybe he'd see them; maybe he'd turn the boat around and check on why they'd returned to the dock.

With the others, Claire shouted until her throat ached, but the boat vanished around the bend in the lake, beyond a granite rock face. Gone.

She dropped her arms down. They felt heavy and limp. Her heart was beating hard.

Reyva swore under her breath.

"Exactly," Claire said.

Reyva swore louder and punched at the air. "He isn't due back until *August*."

"I am aware of that."

"It's June."

"That it is."

"And there's no cell phone coverage."

"Also aware," Claire said. "And trying not to panic."

"This isn't a great situation," Reyva said.

Yeah, I noticed that too, Claire thought. She looked across the water. In every direction, the shore was choked with trees. There wasn't a single house visible. Her parents had raved about how secluded this place was, nestled within a national forest, miles and miles from any hint of civilization, but that didn't seem like a selling point anymore. She tried to clear out a corner of her mind to think through the problem logically, as if it were one of the mental puzzles she loved. Standing on the dock, listening to the lake water lick the pilings, wasn't going to change anything about the situation.

Wringing her hands, Mariana paced back and forth on the dock, as she repeated over and over, "This can't be happening. Can't be happening. It's my fault. All my fault. . . ."

"How is this your fault?" Reyva asked.

"I scared him off."

"He was supposed to leave," Reyva said. "It had nothing to do with you."

Mariana nodded, but it was more like an automatic reaction than agreement. "He'll come back. Or someone will. Eventually, the director will remember we were on our way here, and she'll send someone to pick us up."

"Assuming the director and the others got to safety," Claire said.

"You mean assuming they're not all *dead*?" Mariana said, her voice a half octave higher. She was breathing extra fast.

"Well, yeah," Claire said. She thought that was obvious. And better left unsaid. She wanted to believe that the house had had spectacular fire alarms, and everyone had vacated in plenty of time, along with all their belongings and any sentimental items, and had flown to the nearest city, where they were enjoying a stay in a hotel with lots of Wi-Fi, but they had to consider all possibilities.

"You know, I thought I was a glass-half-empty kind of person," Reyva said, "but I think you have me beat, Claire. You're talking about all of this like, I don't know, like you're informing us that you just finished brushing your teeth. You are, how do I say this? Ridiculously resigned."

Claire winced. "Sorry? I just . . . think we need to face the facts here." As she inhaled, she tasted the burnt scent that permeated the air. She didn't know how she hadn't identified it sooner. It undercut every other odor with its bitter tang. She should have been more alert when they'd docked and not assumed that the bitter scent in the air was just exhaust from the boat's motor or whatever. If she'd suspected there had been a fire, she could have called back the boat sooner. Or better, convinced Jack not to leave until they investigated. . . .

But how could she have predicted *this*?

"There's something else," she continued. "We have to assume that no one escaped."

Mariana's voice was even more shrill. "Why do we have to assume that? I don't think we *have* to assume that. Maybe they were injured. Maybe they're unconscious. Maybe they're in a hospital, recovering. Or here's a wild idea: maybe they're home with their families."

"Look, it's just . . ." Claire tried to think of the right words to explain her thoughts. Usually she tried to avoid sharing her internal monologue; it helped prevent moments like this, when people looked at her like she had three heads. But this was too serious a situation. "It's getting dark, and the boat is gone. And we have no evidence that anyone but us is here, or has any idea what happened."

Mariana gasped.

"Bingo," Reyva said. "She gets it now."

"We're on our own," Claire said.

"But someone will be expecting to hear from one of us . . . or one of them," Mariana insisted. "When they don't, they'll come.

I mean, my folks couldn't have been happier to see me go, but don't either of you have parents who care?"

Claire was certain her parents *did* care, often too much, but they also weren't expecting to hear from her immediately. Jack had said he'd let them know she'd made it safely, and her parents had told her not to worry about calling home often, since they knew she'd be having so much fun.

Hah.

So they weren't going to be waiting for a call. Sure, eventually, they'd worry. But "eventually" could be a while. *And also,* a little voice inside whispered, *I'm sure they're happy to have a break from worrying about you.*

"Key question for the moment: Will anyone worry before it's dark?" Claire asked. She pointed to the sky, which was already graying. The sun had sunk behind the granite hills, the leftover glow from sunset was fading fast, and the woods were cloaked with shadows. "We need a place to spend the night, and it should be somewhere rescuers will find us."

"Back at the house," Mariana said. "That's where the airstrip is, and that's where rescuers will come look for us, when they come."

If they come, Claire silently amended.

Reyva was looking at Claire. "You said *if* in your head, didn't you."

Claire didn't reply to that.

"I vote we camp here, near the dock," Reyva said. "That way, we can keep watch for boats. Signal them before they get away."

"I should have packed a flare," Claire said. It could have

17

worked for catching Jack's attention. Her parents usually kept one in the car, in case of emergency, but it hadn't been an item she'd thought she'd need for camp. First-aid kit, yes. Flare, no. "We could light a fire."

"I don't think more fire is the best idea." Mariana gestured in the direction of the house.

"If it's by the shore, someone might see it," Claire said.

"Or they'll just think we're toasting s'mores," Mariana said. "I really think we should go back to the house and wait for rescue there."

"If we hear an airplane, we'll have time to make it back to the airstrip," Claire reasoned. "But a boat might pass us by and if we're not down here, we'll never know."

"Stay by the dock or return to the house," Reyva said. "Now is the time to decide. Vote? All those in favor of the house, raise your hands." Mariana raised her hand. "And by the dock?" Claire raised her hand. "Deciding vote to me, then. By the dock."

"Fine," Mariana said. "Anyone know anything about camping?"

"I know I wish I'd packed a tent," Claire said. Also, sleeping bags. She'd expected to be living inside a house, sleeping in a bedroom. She'd worried about how she'd manage having a roommate and not being able to have a minute alone to compose herself when she needed to. She hadn't worried about . . . *this.* She really, really hoped all the people had made it out.

"Let's go retrieve what we did pack, and figure out how we're going to do this," Mariana said. She started up the trail, and

Reyva and Claire followed her. This time, there was no need to rush. None of them were eager to see the burnt house again.

When they reached it, they didn't linger. They picked up their packs and Mariana's suitcases and filed back onto the trail. Before it was obscured by trees, Claire shot one more look at the remnants of the Lake House. She had a feeling she'd be seeing that sight in her nightmares for a very long time.

The shadows were noticeably thicker this time through the woods. Claire turned on her phone's flashlight and held it in front of her to illuminate the trail. All of them were silent as they walked, each locked in their own thoughts, and when they reached the lakeside, Claire thought it almost looked peaceful.

The water was a glassy black, with ripples that were silvery. Above, the sky was a deepening blue. The hills still glowed with a yellowish blue to the west, but to the east, it was already dark.

"Anyone have matches for a fire?" Claire asked.

Mariana shuddered.

"For the signal fire," Claire clarified.

"No matches," Reyva said.

It wasn't a disaster, Claire told herself. There were other ways to light a flame. All they needed was a spark, and she had a Swiss Army knife. It was just a small one, but any blade would make a spark if you struck it on the right kind of rock, wouldn't it? "I've watched enough survival shows—my parents love them—that I *think* I know how to make a fire, but I've never actually done it."

Reyva shrugged. "Can't be that hard. Cavemen did it."

"First, we need tinder. Dried moss, or dried bark. Cotton

would work. Anything dry that will catch a spark." Crossing to a birch tree, Claire stripped bits of bark off. Reyva began gathering sticks and fallen branches and pulling them into a pile by the shore.

"I think I have cotton balls in my makeup kit," Mariana said. Kneeling next to her suitcases, she began rooting through them. "You know, I've never slept outside in my life. Not that I'm not fine with it. I totally am. I mean, adventure, yay!" Her voice was shaky, but Claire appreciated that she was trying. "So how do we do this? Just find a patch of dirt we like? Oh, I know! We can spread out my clothes and use them for cushioning! I have spares. As you noticed, I'm an overpacker. Everything but the kitchen sink, as my mom would say."

Mariana's babble was almost soothing.

She continued. "Speaking of kitchens, what do we do about dinner? And water? I know there's a lake, but we have to boil it, yes? I feel like I heard that. Can't drink unpurified water. Anyone pack a pot or kettle or whatever?"

"Definitely can't drink the lake water," Claire said.

"We can go back to the house in the morning and search for additional supplies," Reyva said. "There might be useful items that survived the fire."

"You want to raid the place where people have, potentially, died?" Mariana asked.

"Um, yes?" Reyva said.

"If we can find any kind of metal container," Claire said, "or anything that can withstand the heat of a fire, we can use that to boil water for drinking." She liked that idea. If she could keep solving problems, then she might be able to keep her thoughts under control.

"And what do we do if we find someone"—Mariana swallowed hard—"dead?"

Reyva scoffed. "Be glad it's not us. Practically speaking, that's all we can do."

Mariana sucked in air as if she were about to launch into some kind of speech, but Claire interrupted her. "Back to the food question. I did pack some snacks." Kneeling, she opened up her backpack: a few granola bars and dried mango slices, her favorite. Mariana and Reyva both sorted through their packs and pulled out their snacks, adding several Hershey's Kisses, a half-eaten bagel with cream cheese, a yogurt granola bar, and a snack-size bag of Cape Cod potato chips to the pile, as well as a pack of gum. It made a nice stack. Almost enough for a meal.

It won't last, Claire thought.

In fact, she doubted it would last much more than a day, split between three of them. If they were stuck here for longer . . . *We'll need to eat somehow*, she thought. Learn to fish. Or hunt.

But maybe she was getting ahead of herself, letting her pessimism take control, per usual. It was possible a boat would return for them as soon as it was light again. All they really had to do was make it through the night. They didn't have to instantly become hunter-gatherers. She had to stop catastrophizing; this wasn't hopeless.

Tomorrow they'd be able to search the house and grounds

more thoroughly. Maybe there would be something they could use. Like a spare boat to get themselves away from here. She wished she'd checked around for that. A retreat on a lake ought to have a few canoes, if not a powerboat. See, there was hope.

Worst case, she thought, *we can hike around the lake.*

Except, judging by the length of the boat ride, it would be a very, very long hike. Better if they could either be rescued or rescue themselves.

"Okay, another important survival question," Mariana said. "Bathroom."

Claire pointed to the woods. "Just don't wipe with poison ivy."

Mariana turned on her phone's flashlight and aimed it at the trees. "Great and useful advice, if I knew what poison ivy looked like."

"Three leaves with the two side leaves growing directly from the stem," Claire said. She'd once researched poisonous plants before a family picnic. Her parents hated picnics but thought the fresh air would be good for her. They were always insisting that various things were "good for her," without any interest in what she thought. She thought of how they always insisted a third of her plate held vegetables, how they limited screen time, how they signed her up for all-day ballet intensives without ever asking her, as if she were incapable of taking care of herself or making sensible decisions. Like this summer. She hadn't had any choice about coming here. They'd decided the Lake House would be good for her, and that was that. In their eyes, she was their constant renovation project, in need of continuous care and guidance. Especially lately. "Often the leaves are shiny but not always. There are some harmless vines with three leaves, but if you avoid all of them, you'll be safe."

"Right. Got it. I'll be right back." With her phone, she tromped into the woods, away from the trail. They listened to her footsteps through the underbrush for a minute.

"My parents promised new experiences," Reyva said.

"Mine did too," Claire said. "Wish they'd been wrong about that."

Kneeling, she made a circle of rocks and began preparing to light the fire. With Reyva helping her, she placed the birch bark and a couple of Mariana's cotton balls in the center as the tinder and positioned the sticks around it in a pyramid. They didn't speak while they worked.

As they finished the pyramid, Claire asked, "Have you ever fished or hunted?"

Reyva studied her. "You don't think rescue is coming."

"I think we don't know," Claire said, "and I don't think a few granola bars and Hershey's Kisses are going to last more than a couple of days."

"Never fished before. You?"

"Once or twice, when I was little. My grandfather took me." She remembered one such trip, age six or seven, when her nose had burned so badly that it started peeling by bedtime. He hadn't known how to take care of a kid. But he'd tried. She still missed him. He'd been her only relative who understood how awkward she felt 90 percent of the time, because he'd felt the same way.

She'd spent many holidays being awkwardly but pleasantly quiet with Grandpa, until her parents ferreted her out and forced her to play with the other kids. They never considered that she might not have anything in common with her cousins. One particularly terrible Thanksgiving, her cousin Emma had been teasing her to the point of tears, and Grandpa had told her to hide under the table. He'd covered for her with her parents, claiming she was off on a scavenger hunt organized by his neighbor, and he'd snuck her books and pie until the day mercifully ended. *He never once acted like there was anything wrong with me*, she thought. "He didn't like fishing," Claire told Reyva, "but he thought it was something a grandpa should do with his grandkid." The theory wasn't that complex: stick bait on a hook, lower the hook somewhere fish swam, and wait for one to bite. It helped to have a hook, line, and a fishing rod, though. And some idea how to gut the fish, which she didn't have.

"Someone will come for us," Reyva said.

"Rather not have already starved to death when they arrive," Claire said. "I think we should at least make plans for lasting a few—"

A scream tore through the woods.

Claire spun to face the forest. "Mariana?"

Reyva plunged into the woods, in the direction of the scream. Turning on her phone light, Claire hurried after her.

It wasn't hard to find Mariana. They could see the light from her phone, wobbling through the trees, and she hadn't stopped screaming.

As Reyva reached her, she clapped a hand over Mariana's mouth and shushed her. "Shh, it's okay, shh, shh, quiet." Mariana quit screaming. Instead she whimpered softly. Claire caught up a few seconds later.

"What happened? Is she okay?" Claire asked. "Mariana, are you okay?"

Reyva lowered her hand, but Mariana didn't speak. She just shook her head and aimed her phone's light at a clump of nearby pine trees.

And Claire saw the body.

It took an extra second for her brain to process what she was seeing.

It was a middle-aged woman, eyes open, mouth open, slumped against the trunk of a pine tree. Blood, black except when the light hit it directly, coated her chest, her right shoulder, and her left thigh.

Claire dropped to her hands and knees as spots danced in front of her eyes. She told herself to breathe. Just breathe. She inhaled and exhaled. In and out. Just in and out.

A person had died.

Here.

She'd thought it was possible, when she saw the husk of the Lake House, but knowing it intellectually and seeing it right in front of her—

"She's not burned," Mariana whispered.

Shakily, Claire stood up and made herself turn to face the others—and the body. She saw that Mariana was right. There was no sign of burns, scorched clothes, or singed hair, at least not that she could see. There was so very much blood. . . .

"She was shot," Reyva said flatly.

"How can you tell?" Claire asked.

Reyva just looked at her.

"It could have been . . ." Claire trailed off. She didn't know what else it could have been, but none of them were doctors or coroners, so Reyva could be wrong . . . or not. She squeezed her eyes shut, then opened them again. "You think she was shot?"

Wordlessly, Reyva pointed to the woman's right shoulder, then chest, then thigh.

"I've never seen a dead body before," Mariana said, hushed. "What are we supposed to do? Who do you think she was? Was she the program director? Ms. Williams?"

"Maybe it was an accident," Claire said.

"You don't shoot someone multiple times by accident," Reyva said. She knelt next to the body. Claire didn't know how Reyva could stand to be so close. She felt like bolting or vomiting or both.

"Who did this?" Claire asked.

"How should I know?" Reyva said.

Mariana asked, "But you think she was m-m-murdered?"

"Yes," Reyva said. "And I do think it's the program director. Or was. Jack said she was supposed to meet us."

Claire took a deep breath and then another. She couldn't taste the hint of smoke in the air anymore, which meant she'd gotten used to it. In another minute, she suspected she'd get used to the dead body here. One of the advantages, if one could call it that, of always imagining the worst-case scenario was that it didn't take her long to process all the ramifications of their situation.

And the worst part wasn't that there was a dead body here.

The worst part was that somewhere out there . . . was a killer.

THREE

Inhale.

Exhale.

Inhale.

Don't scream.

Claire had imagined what it would be like to see a dead body. Did other people—did *normal* people—do that? She suspected they didn't, at least not on a regular basis. She'd pictured one on a subway platform, one on a street, another in a hospital bed. She'd run through dozens of macabre scenarios, yet never envisioned stumbling on one in a dark wood. That kind of thing felt relegated to horror movies. Yet here she was. In real life.

Beside her, Mariana was whispering, "Oh dear God, wake up, Mariana. It's a dream. You're asleep. Wake the hell up."

"You aren't asleep," Reyva said flatly. "And this isn't the time for freaking out. We have to figure out what to do."

"I think it's *exactly* the time for freaking out!" Mariana said. "It's a tailor-made time for freaking out. How are you both taking this so calmly?"

Without changing inflection, Reyva said, "Oh no. Ahh. Eeeeee."

"Seriously?"

"I don't do performative emotions," Reyva said. "Yes, it's terrible, but we can't help her. We can't call the police. We can't call anyone. So what do we do?"

"We *don't* stay here," Claire said. Her heart was beating so fast and loud that it made it hard to think, even to breathe, but she tried to keep her voice steady and normal. The last thing she wanted was for them to notice how bad she was at holding herself together.

Reyva snorted. "Are you planning to swim home? It's miles. Even farther on foot. You saw how ridiculously far it is around the lake. We're talking *days*. Unless you're an endurance athlete—"

Claire tugged on both Reyva's and Mariana's sleeves. "I mean, we can't stay right here, right now, with *that*." She heard the shrillness in her own voice and forced it lower. "Come on." Neither of them protested as she led them back through the woods.

Her heart was hammering as she waded through the bushes, and her skin prickled as if she were being watched by dozens of unseen eyes. She thought about switching off the phone light—it had to be visible through the trees—but she couldn't make herself plunge them into darkness. She told herself they needed the light to find their way to the water, where they'd left their packs, where it wouldn't feel as if the trees were closing in on them.

Count your steps, she told herself. *Keep it together*. One, two, three . . . Twenty-six, twenty-seven, twenty-eight . . . She kept her eyes fixed on the beam of light and her mind fixed on the numbers.

Only when she saw the glassy blackness of the lake did she turn off her light.

"Mariana, turn your light off," Claire said, her voice a whisper.

"What? No. Absolutely not."

"She's right." Reyva reached over to grab Mariana's phone, and Mariana clutched it to her chest. The beam swept up and illuminated her chin and nostrils, as well as the leaves on the branches that bent over the shore.

"It's too visible," Claire whispered. "We don't know who could see it."

Mariana stared at her, then turned it off. She whispered, "Sorry."

Night folded over them. Claire was aware of the sounds: the lap of water on the shore, the wind through the trees, the loud chirping hum of crickets.

"If there's someone out there . . . ," Mariana began, again a whisper.

"We don't want them to see us," Claire said.

"But we won't see them either."

She didn't have a good response to that. But Reyva did: "We listen. One of us stays awake at all times, and we stay alert. Keep our backs to the water and face the forest. And when it's dawn . . . we figure out what to do next. One hour at a time." She sat down on the rocks.

Claire wished she could stop worrying about what would happen next, especially since the images that her brain was oh-so-helpfully conjuring were nightmarish. She gathered up the tinder they'd collected, the bark and cotton balls and so forth, and tucked it into her pack. They certainly weren't about to light a fire tonight.

"Okay, so what else?" Mariana whispered. She sat too, perched like a bird who was ready to take flight at a second's notice.

"What else what?" Reyva asked.

"What else can we do to keep from being *murdered in our sleep*? Why do I keep having to spell everything out? These are not the kinds of things I'm supposed to be worried about! I'm supposed to be worried about whether anyone will like me, whether I'll get along with my roommate, whether the food will be decent, whether the showers will have reasonable water pressure to rinse the shampoo fully out of my hair, whether I'll have a summer romance that will have me pining away for whoever and listening to sappy songs on repeat."

Claire had been thinking about that—about how else to keep them safe, not about a doomed summer romance. "Instead of sleeping exposed out here, we could hide ourselves in the woods."

"There are dead people in the woods," Mariana said.

"Only one we know of," Claire pointed out.

"That doesn't make it better," Mariana said. "I'm not going back in there."

"We could set a kind of alarm," Claire said. "Something that if a . . ." She didn't know what word to pick. Intruder? Killer? ". . . if *someone* were to approach our camp, they'd make a loud noise. Like a string of tin cans, if we had them. How about sticks they'd have to step on?" If they made the sticks unavoidable, it could give them a few seconds' warning, which was better than none.

Reyva seemed to like that idea. "Anyone have any wire? We can string it neck-high between the trunks." She pointed to the nearby trees.

Excellent idea. Except Claire hadn't packed any wire. "I don't. Mariana?"

"You people are almost scarier than whoever is out there," Mariana said. "How do you leap from seeing a dead body to instantly stringing up trip wires?"

"Technically, it's not a trip wire if it's neck height," Reyva said.

"But a trip wire might be better," Claire said, thinking about how it would work. "Less noticeable. And the sound of someone falling should alert us, and we can either run or defend ourselves."

Mariana scooted back from them toward the dock. "Seriously, who are you and why are you this way? This is not normal behavior." She was still holding her phone tightly.

Claire felt her face heat up in a blush. Her oddness. There it was, being pointed out by a relative stranger—again. But this time, unlike the other 99.9 percent of the time, the situation warranted her intense worry. Whatever way her brain was wired, her thoughts were right for this moment. She was sure of it. "I—I just worry a lot," she explained.

"I, on the other hand, am a runaway with a checkered past, used to life-or-death situations. I'm hiding out here under a false name," Reyva said. And then she gave a snort. "Seriously? I'm exactly like you. Unless *you* are hiding out here under an assumed name, in which case I am *not* like you."

Mariana scowled at her, obviously not amused. "Convince me to trust you."

"Please don't make me do trust falls," Reyva said.

"No trust falls," Mariana said. "Just . . . I don't know you. Either of you, which wasn't a problem before—when we were supposed to be at *normal* camp doing *normal camp things*. My mom insisted I'd quote-unquote 'learn new skills, have new experiences, and make new friends,' but I don't think any of this is what she meant."

Funny, that was the same phrase her parents had used— multiple times, actually, in their tag-team monologues about why she must experience a summer at the Lake House. *Learn new skills, have new experiences, make new friends.* There must have been a brochure. Claire hadn't seen one, though.

"Also, I don't like the silence."

"Might be safer if we're silent," Claire said, eyeing the shadowed trees.

They all fell quiet.

Claire listened again to the forest. With the crickets or cicadas or whatever they were, it was louder than her own house at night. There, she was used to the hum of the air conditioner, the tick of her bedroom clock, and the creak of the floorboards as her parents moved about. She wished she were home right now. She wondered what her parents were doing, if they were imagining all the fun things and great new people she was meeting at the Lake House.

She was fairly certain they weren't imagining any of those people would be dead.

For once, I wasn't pessimistic enough, she thought.

At least she could set her stick alarm, for whatever that was worth.

Using the wood they'd gathered for the fire, she laid a lattice pattern at the edge of the forest. Anyone coming out from the trees would have to step on it, and unless they were ridiculously light on their feet, they'd snap at least a few twigs. Or that was the idea.

After a few minutes, Reyva and Mariana joined her. They ventured in between the trees enough to pull out more sticks and branches until they had a moat of debris between their camp and anyone approaching.

It wouldn't, of course, do anything to help against a person with a gun if they decided to shoot from a distance. But maybe it would prevent them from being surprised by anyone who wanted to sneak closer. If anyone was out there.

Once they'd finished with the sticks, they spread out enough clothing to cushion the ground. Claire rolled up a flannel shirt to be her pillow and then brushed her teeth without water.

"It's going to be a long night," Mariana said.

"If anyone needs to pee, don't go far," Reyva warned.

"I'm never going to pee again," Mariana said.

"Okay," Reyva said. "Everyone makes choices."

"Never going in the woods either."

"Considering we're in a forest, that might be a hard promise to keep," Claire said. She knew how Mariana felt, though. Every time she blinked, she pictured the burnt house and the blood-soaked body. She tried not blinking. Lying back on her makeshift bed, she stared up at the sky.

Stars speckled the cloudless night. The three stars of Orion's belt were easy to spot, and so was the Big Dipper. She traced it to the North Star. That was the sum of her knowledge of the night sky. She hadn't spent much time outside at night. She didn't regret that. The moon was three-quarters full, but she didn't know if it was waxing or waning.

She'd never been a night owl. Or a morning bird. Her favorite time was afternoon, preferably a Saturday, with a drizzle outside—the kind of weather where any family outdoor activities or yardwork or whatever would be canceled, and she could have hours to herself. On a rainy Saturday afternoon, you weren't expected to do anything you didn't want to do, or be anyone you weren't. Extra bonus: you also usually didn't stumble upon burned-down houses or corpses.

"Did anyone make a wish on the first star they saw?" Mariana asked, her voice still a whisper.

Both Claire and Reyva turned their heads to look at her.

"What? I've done it since I was a little kid. It's nice."

"What did you wish for?" Claire asked her. She couldn't remember the last time she'd made a wish on a star. She supposed she always made a wish on her birthday candle, though, so she couldn't criticize. Usually it was simple: *no dying this year.*

Though she'd obviously lie to assembled relatives and say she'd wished for a date to the prom or world peace or something.

"You'd better have wished for a rescue," Reyva said.

"Actually I wished for an original exhaust manifold and white-wall tires," Mariana said. "I'm restoring a '55 Corvette. She's beautiful." Her voice got dreamy. "Pure white finish, red leather interior, chrome-plated valve covers. They only made seven hundred of them. She's one of the first of her kind wired with a twelve-volt system."

Claire propped herself up on her elbow to see Mariana better. She was layered in shadows, but Claire thought she could see the hint of a smile on her lips. "Do you have your license?" She'd assumed they were the same age. Her parents had only just allowed her to get her permit. They weren't sure she was "ready," they'd said. They refused to even practice with her until she finished Driver's Ed. Given her history—that was how they'd put it, her "history"—they thought it wise to be extra cautious. Driving could be stressful, after all.

"Pfft." Mariana waved her hand in the air, causing the bracelets on her wrist to clink like a wind chime. "Who needs a license when you have dreams?"

"You didn't really wish for that, did you?" Claire asked.

"Obviously not," Mariana said. "A wish won't come true if you tell. But I do want the tires. I'm expecting a text from a parts dealer with a price estimate. Maybe when I don't text him back, he'll realize something is wrong and send a rescue." Rolling onto her side to look at Claire, she asked, "What would you wish for? Aside from the obvious. Say it has to be a wish that has nothing to do with being here."

She'd wish she hadn't come to the Lake House. She'd wish it hadn't burned. She'd wish the director wasn't dead. She'd wish she had a satellite phone. She'd wish she had a boat. Or a car and a road. But if it couldn't be a relevant wish . . . Claire racked her brain. She knew that technically there was no right answer, but it still felt like a trick question. *Think of something that won't make you sound messed up*, she ordered herself. "I'd wish to have a class with George Balanchine. He's considered the father of American ballet." As an explanation, she added, "I do ballet."

"Isn't he dead?" Reyva asked.

"A class while he was alive," she clarified.

"Good, because that would be—"

Mariana cut her off. "Obviously she didn't mean that. Don't disrespect the dead." To Claire, she said, "My parents made me take ballet. I was terrible at it. Also, gymnastics, soccer, and volleyball. Only let me quit when I made a deal: I'd ace the tenth-grade geometry final, and they'd let up. I was in ninth grade and not taking geometry so they thought it was a safe bet. Showed them. Not that it mattered, as it turned out, but that's another story."

"Mine too," Reyva said. "Not the geometry thing, but forced ballet, gymnastics, and soccer. I switched to mixed martial arts in fifth grade, but it wasn't enough. They still insisted I join the school track team in junior high."

Mariana laughed. "Mixed martial arts? Like, full-contact cage fighting? Was that before or after you became a runaway with a checkered past? Rather violent for elementary school, don't you think? No one lets ten-year-olds become MMA fighters."

"My parents own a gym," Reyva said, "and they offer plenty of junior MMA classes. I was the junior league second-place champion at the Northeast Regionals, and the look of disappointment on my parents' faces was classic. They didn't raise me to be second place—their exact words."

"I'm sorry," Claire said.

"Don't actually care what they think."

Even with the moonlight, Claire couldn't see Reyva's expression well enough to guess if she was telling the truth or not. She wasn't sure Reyva would let her feelings register on her face regardless.

"I guess we all have parents who wanted to raise overachievers," Mariana said. "I suppose that's not a surprise, given that we all have parents who thought shipping their children off to an 'enrichment retreat' for the summer was a spectacular idea. Wonder if they knew each other when they were here. They probably overachieved together."

They lay quiet again.

Claire remembered the day she'd gotten her first pair of pointe shoes. She'd just turned eleven, and her mother had taken her to the dance supply store. She'd seen all the posters of ballerinas posed with the silk ribbons crisscrossing their ankles, and she'd imagined herself executing the perfect fouetté turn. Of course, she'd known it would be painful, in a theoretical kind of way, to adjust to pointe, but she hadn't expected her toes to feel as if they'd been mashed into a wooden box. After her first practice with them, she'd left specks of blood on the lamb's wool inside. After a week, she'd wanted to quit. But the look in her parents' eyes . . . At least when she danced, they saw a daughter who wasn't so broken, even while she bled into her shoes.

In retrospect, it would have been more useful if she'd picked MMA instead of ballet.

Claire broke the silence. "If you know self-defense, maybe we stand a chance."

Reyva snorted. "Against someone with a gun? I've only fought controlled bouts in a ring with referees and rules. That doesn't qualify me to protect anyone in the real world."

"You're more qualified than a ballerina and a mechanic," Claire pointed out. "You know how to throw a punch."

"You can't punch a gun," Reyva said.

There wasn't any good response to that.

Claire listened to the crickets. It was kind of comforting, the undercurrent of the chirps. It rose and fell in a rhythm, a bit like a heartbeat. The forest's heartbeat.

A twig snapped. She stiffened and held her breath.

Please let that be a squirrel.

She watched the trees, looking for a hint of movement. She saw nothing. No more twigs broke. She felt her skin prickle, certain they weren't alone.

"You two sleep," Reyva said. "I'll take first watch."

She couldn't imagine being able to sleep. Her mind felt as if it were whirring as loudly as the motorboat's engine, incessantly tossing up terrible thoughts.

"What will you do if someone comes?" Mariana asked.

"No idea. Guess I'll punch their gun."

It was going to be a very long night.

Claire hoped they survived it.

FOUR

We aren't dead yet, Claire thought. *Yay.*

With her arms wrapped around her knees, she watched the sun rise over the lake. It bled yellow over the tops of the trees first, and then the light spread, bleaching the sky until the last of the stars vanished. The moon hung on longer, fading until it nearly looked translucent. She supposed she'd appreciate the view more if her mouth didn't feel gummy, her eyes didn't feel crusty, and her hair didn't feel matted to her neck. At some point in the night, she'd slipped off her flannel-shirt pillow, and now sand coated her cheek. She'd tried wiping it off, but her skin still felt gritty.

The birds had been tweeting since predawn, at least a dozen different calls all jumbled together like an orchestra tuning up. They'd woken her, and she'd told Mariana, who was on watch, that she'd take over.

So now she was awake alone. Hopefully alone.

The lake sparkled, obnoxiously cheerful.

It had been sunny like this on the day of Grandpa's funeral, the first time her brain and body had betrayed her so badly, the first time her parents had voiced the thought that Claire had been stuffing deep inside: *There's something wrong with me.* She had managed to put on the black dress that her mother had laid out on her bed, but when it came time to clasp the pearl-drop necklace around her neck, her fingers felt as if they'd frozen into claws. She couldn't make herself do anything but gulp in air like a fish on land. Her heartbeat had sounded so loud that she couldn't hear her parents screaming at her to calm down and just breathe. She'd thrown up, then passed out. When she woke, she was covered in sweat, and her parents had never looked at her the same since. It was her least favorite memory, and she wished the sun on the lake hadn't reminded her of it.

She didn't dare have an episode like that out here, in front of Reyva and Mariana. Better to think of something—anything—else. Like what they could do to continue to avoid dying.

They were stranded on the distant shore of a very large lake, surrounded by uninhabited forest. Not great. But . . . if they hiked along the edge of the lake for long enough, they would eventually reach the dock that they'd departed from with Jack. It had had a boathouse—a shack, really. Jack had let her in to use the bathroom before they'd crossed the lake. She couldn't remember if there had been a phone inside, but it had to have one, didn't it? The dock with the boathouse had been about a two-hour drive from the nearest town, but if they could find a phone and call for help . . . The trick was the word *eventually.* As Reyva had pointed out, it would take several days to skirt the lake. And that was assuming they didn't get lost or injured. Without food . . . especially without fresh water . . . She was trying not to think about how thirsty she was already. She hadn't had anything to drink since yesterday, and her tongue felt thick and gluey. She eyed the lake as it lapped the shore. Dehydration wasn't a pleasant way to die, nor was puking out one's guts after drinking bacteria-laden lake water. In fact, if she had to rank deaths based on undesirability—

"You're thinking hard," Reyva said behind her. "I can practically hear the squeak of the hamster wheels turning in your brain."

Claire wondered how long she'd been awake, watching her, and decided not to ask. "We can't just set off into the woods and think we'll find help after a few hours," she said. "It's going to be a several-days walk around the perimeter of the lake. At the very least, we'll need to bring drinkable water." It would be best if they could each carry at least a quart . . . if they could find a way to carry it—yet another problem.

"I know it's not recommended, but given that this is an emergency . . . there *is* an entire lake full of water we can drink."

"With bacteria, viruses, and brain-eating parasites."

Reyva blinked at her. "That's not really a thing."

"Seriously *is* a thing. It's an amoeba. Lives in warm fresh water."

Reaching, Reyva dipped her fingers into the water. "The lake's cold."

"Giardia, then," Claire said. "Extremely common. Causes cramps, diarrhea, and vomiting, which leads to dehydration, which could be . . ."

"Deadly," Reyva finished the thought.

Claire nodded. Drinking untreated water was a fast way to death out in the wilderness. Plus she hated throwing up. You couldn't breathe, and she hated that feeling more than anything. No matter how thirsty she got, it was not worth the risk. "We need a way to boil water and a way to carry it."

"You still want to light a fire," Reyva said. "What about the killer in the woods? He might not just let us hang out and boil water. Or she."

"Statistically speaking, most likely he. And he won't have to shoot us if we die of dehydration or starvation." She didn't see a way around taking a few risks. "Look, we make as small a fire as possible. Only in daylight, and as soon as we've boiled the water we need, we put as many miles between us and this place as possible."

Mariana spoke. "You aren't saying we should leave here, are you?" Both of them turned. She was awake and sitting up. Her hair was poofed on one side and flat on the other, and her partially removed makeup was smudged around her eyes. "Not sure that's the best idea. When someone comes to rescue us, they'll come to the Lake House."

"You want to stay? Even with *that*?" Claire waved her hand in the general direction of the body.

"Very much not a fan of *that*, as you know," Mariana said. "But I've been thinking about it. . . . There's no reason for the killer to still be here. They did what they came to do. Sticking around the scene of the crime? Good way to get caught. They're probably miles from here, busily hiding any evidence that they were ever at the Lake House."

That . . . was possible. But should they bet their lives on a possibility?

"I think we should focus on making it easier for rescuers to find us," Mariana said. "Light your signal fire. Write SOS in the sand. Shout. Bang homemade drums. Everything we can think of to draw attention to ourselves. One of us can stay by the shore and watch for boats, while another one waits for a plane at the house—Why are you looking at me like that?" She patted her hair. "Did I sprout an extra head?"

Claire closed her mouth, suddenly aware she'd been gawking at her with her mouth dropped open and eyes wide. Had Mariana not seen a single horror movie ever? "Sorry. Just . . . We can't split up. Much too dangerous. As for the rest . . . we can't pretend it's safe here just because it's inconvenient to worry about a killer."

"If some psychopath with a gun wants to kill us, we can't stop them. So I vote we don't worry about that and instead focus on the things we *can* do."

Not . . . worry? About being murdered?

Reyva shook her head. "There might be *something* we can do about it. Like run. Or hide. Or not paint a giant target on our backs that says, 'I'm fine with dying horribly.'"

"I'm not 'fine with dying' in any way," Mariana said. "But if we're able to be rescued, that solves all our problems—murderers, dehydration, starvation, even mosquitoes." She waved her hand as if to dismiss all the myriad silly details of survival.

Claire turned over her words in her head. Maybe Mariana had a point. Or at least part of a point. "She's right," Claire said at last.

Now Reyva stared at her.

"Sort of," Claire amended. "Look, we have two goals with diametrically opposed solutions: we have to stay hidden so we don't get killed, and we have to be visible so we get rescued and don't die." She didn't like that those were the facts, but she was trying to consider the problem from as many angles as she could, given the number of unknowns. It was the only thing making her feel as if they had any control over any of this. "So we have to take whatever measures we can that fulfill each goal without torpedoing the other goal. We stick together. We take turns on lookout. We *don't* light a signal fire that could be seen by anyone in the air, on the water, or in the woods, but we *do* spell out SOS on the shore and on the airstrip so that overhead rescuers will find us. And we boil water with as small and inconspicuous a fire as we can."

Both Reyva and Mariana were nodding.

"Let's do it," Reyva said.

"Compromise for the win!" Mariana shouted.

Claire and Reyva shushed her.

"Sorry," Mariana whispered.

All of them watched the woods for a minute, but no one burst out to murder them.

Choosing a stretch of beach-like shore, they located stones and used them to spell out the letters *SOS*. Claire kept one eye on the forest as they worked. She couldn't shake the prickly feeling that they were being watched.

It's just birds, she told herself. *Or squirrels.*

Or bears. Or wolves. Or mountain lions.

When they finished, they loaded up their packs with the clothes they'd used for bedding—Mariana took the longest, stuffing her favorites into her pack and abandoning her two suitcases by the SOS in place of punctuation marks—and then they started up the trail that led to the remains of the Lake House. It felt as if even the birds were more hushed today. The wind barely rustled the leaves.

"I'm not sure I'm ready to face it again," Mariana said.

Claire definitely wasn't, even though she knew how badly they were going to need drinkable water. It was all well and good to think of plans in the abstract, but now that they were on their way to see the Lake House again, all she wanted to do was cower by the dock. She'd never been a spectacularly calm person, but this was a whole other level.

Usually when she was on the verge of losing control, her father would lob brainteasers at her, like the classic one about a farmer who had to bring a fox, a chicken, and a sack of corn across a river. . . . The solution was chicken first, then fox but bring back the chicken, then corn, then lastly chicken again. Or you put the fox in a cage, the chicken in a cage, and quit having free-range animals in your rowboat. But without her dad providing puzzles for her to solve, she was stuck trying to soothe herself on her own. She settled on silently reciting the Fibonacci sequence, each number the sum of the preceding two numbers. It escalated from zero plus one soothingly quickly. She was just about to add 196,418 to 317,811 when they reached the Lake House.

It didn't look any better in daylight. The Lake House was still burned to the ground. At least it smelled better, and there were no more wisps of smoke. They tucked their packs out of sight in the bushes and, without speaking, crossed the lawn to the remains of the structure.

A maple tree was still standing beside the collapsed walls. A few shriveled leaves still clung to the blackened branches. It must have been an old tree—it was wide enough that she couldn't have wrapped her arms around it if she tried. It could have been hundreds of years old. Seeing it destroyed was nearly as sad as seeing the house itself.

"One of us makes the SOS on the airstrip, one of us searches for useful items, and one of us keeps watch," Reyva suggested. "All of us stay in visual range."

"I vote the MMA girl keeps watch," Mariana said. "I'll make the SOS."

That left one job. "I'll . . . search," Claire said.

She stared at the ashes. If they were right about what had happened here, she wouldn't just find burnt items. Reyva clapped a hand on her shoulder. "If you find any dead bodies, try not to scream. Someone might hear."

"Very helpful," Claire quipped.

"You want me to search with you?" she offered kindly.

Claire had been the one to say they needed a pot for boiling water and canteens for carrying it. "No, thanks. My idea. I can do this. Besides, one of us does have to keep watch." She squared her shoulders. Maybe she could find other items that would be useful, like a canoe. *You can do this*, she thought. *You can be useful, instead of weak and pathetic.* She never wanted these girls to look at her the way her parents did, as if she were as fragile as glass. "If we get separated, meet up by the dock."

"Why would we get separated?" Mariana asked.

"Always good to have a plan for that," Claire said.

"You know, no offense meant, but you keep talking like you know what you're doing, and I'm not sure you do."

I definitely don't know what I'm doing, she thought.

She just hoped what they were doing wasn't going to get them all killed.

She didn't start with the house. The odds of finding bodies . . . Better to start with one of the sheds near the house. As she'd seen yesterday, all of them had burned as well—or more accurately, had been burned. She couldn't pretend it was an accident. It would be too much of a coincidence, given the body they'd discovered. Obviously the killer was an arsonist as well.

Or . . . killers?

She didn't know if it was just one person who had done all this. She didn't know whether the crimes had happened sequentially or simultaneously. Maybe she could find some sign of—

No. It didn't matter right now. What mattered was that she focused on the task at hand. Already Mariana was hauling rocks onto the airstrip, arranging them into an SOS, while Reyva patrolled the grounds. The quicker they finished, the quicker they could be away from here.

She was certain they'd be able to convince Mariana to hike to safety. Reyva was on her side, and that made it two to one. *Just need a few essential supplies, and we're off.* If she could just stay on task, she could stay okay.

Claire approached a log-cabin-style shed with a collapsed roof. Sorting through the debris, she figured out quickly it was for lawn maintenance equipment:

Lawn mowers, leaf blowers, and hedge trimmers, all damaged beyond repair.

Also a wheelbarrow, shears, rakes, and shovels.

She loaded anything that looked remotely useful into the wheelbarrow to be sorted through later, and she carted it outside.

She then raided the next shed. This one had held sports equipment. Much of it had been destroyed by fire—burnt tennis rackets, melted volleyballs, charred croquet mallets. But a set of rusted weights was unharmed. She couldn't think of a purpose for them at the moment, but anything could be useful if you were inventive about it.

It was like another little puzzle, ideal for keeping her brain from spiraling down a hole, if she didn't think too hard about *why* she was doing it: invent an alternate purpose for whatever she could salvage. She was eyeing the structural integrity of a rusted and unfortunately empty toolbox, to determine if it would work for boiling water, when she noticed the manhole cover embedded in the floor.

She wouldn't have seen it if the floor hadn't been eaten away by fire. The metal disc was beneath the floorboards, but those floorboards were half ash. She pried one back, and it crumbled in her hands. A few more, and she had it exposed.

Not a manhole cover. It looked more like a hatch on a submarine.

A trapdoor.

But a trapdoor that led to . . . what?

Odd.

Kneeling in the ashes, she located the hinges. Before she could decide whether or not to open it, she heard Reyva call her name.

Claire rushed out. She scanned the charred lawn—but she didn't see an intruder. Just Reyva, jogging across the grass to her.

"Everything okay?" Reyva asked. "You were in there awhile."

"Yeah, fine. . . ." Had Reyva been worried about her? More likely, she was just anxious about whether or not she'd find supplies. They didn't know each other well enough to really care. She glanced back at the shed. "I found a metal toolbox that might work to boil water."

"Find anything that looks like food?"

"Not unless you want to eat melted volleyballs."

"Kind of was hoping for something tastier." Reyva gestured toward the house. "It's pointless to hope anything survived in the kitchen."

"Well, the kitchen didn't survive, so I'd say you're right." Maybe if they could move the chunks of collapsed roof, they'd be able to identify which room was the kitchen, but that would take much more time and energy than they had to spare. Plus she was still hesitant to explore the house itself. "As soon as Mariana finishes with her SOS, we should head back to the lake and boil as much water as we can."

The sooner they began their hike, the sooner they'd reach civilization. She didn't have time to be distracted by little oddities like a trapdoor inside a shed.

"Trying hard not to think about water," Reyva said.

"I want to try to find some containers so we can carry it," Claire said. The toolbox could work for boiling, but it would be awkward to carry on a hike if it were full of water. "Let me know if you see anything else odd. There's something about this place that doesn't feel right."

"Hmm, could it be the fact that it was burned to the ground?" Reyva drawled.

Claire wrinkled her nose at Reyva. She couldn't put her finger on exactly what the problem was, but the place looked run-down in addition to the fire damage. She'd expected a newly renovated camp to be, well, renovated.

She crossed back to the sheds to search the third one—the last one, really, since the fourth shed had fully collapsed into ash and rubble. Poking her head inside, she saw the floor was covered in shattered glass and pottery shards. Most of the shelves had buckled and fallen, taking with them a supply of mason jars and clay flowerpots, but one shelf had survived the destruction. The other shelves had fallen at angles around it, protecting it, and there were at least ten whole glass jam jars with screw-on lids. Perfect for holding water.

Broken glass crunched under her shoes as she stepped gingerly over it. Pausing in the center of the room, she swept the glass aside with her feet. She studied the floorboards for a moment. No trapdoor in this shed. Just in the other one. It nagged at her, like an unsolved brainteaser.

Why was there a trapdoor, and where did it lead? Clearly, it had been intentionally hidden, which was a strange choice if it just led to an extra storage area. What if—

Reyva stuck her head into the shed. "Claire? Mariana's done with the SOS. Did you find—ah, jars!" Stepping over the glass, she retrieved five of them. Claire picked up another four and carried them out to the lawn.

They joined up with Mariana.

Waving one of the jars in the air, Reyva said, "Look what Claire found."

Mariana oohed and aahed over the jars appropriately, and Reyva praised her SOS, which dominated the airstrip but wasn't obvious from ground level unless you knew what you were looking at. "Since it's such a quality SOS, I think that's a vote in favor of staying," Mariana said. "There's a chance someone will see it and rescue us."

"Still two votes for hiking our way out of here," Reyva said. "Especially now that Claire has found the supplies we need to avoid dehydration."

"Actually . . . ," Claire said, her thoughts solidifying into what felt like almost a certainty. "I think we should stay a little longer."

"What? Why?" Reyva asked. "You're the one who said—"

"It's possible the others aren't all dead." She turned to face the shed with the trapdoor. "I think they could be hiding. Underground."

FIVE

Together, they tried to pry up the trapdoor.

Squatting, Claire positioned herself between Reyva and Mariana. She dug her fingers beneath the lip of the lid. "On three? One, two—"

"Love when people interrupt the countdown to ask if it's on three or after," Mariana commented. "Like, a trillion movies have noticed it's a problem, but still there's no standard."

Reyva rolled her eyes. "Seriously, Mariana?"

"It's perpetually funny."

"Actually isn't," Reyva said.

"Just trying to lighten the mood. My therapist says I hide under humor and bravado. I told her I'm just naturally this charming, and it's her issue that I intimidate her."

Claire didn't intend to laugh, but she did—it came out as a warbling squawk. She swallowed it quickly, but Mariana beamed at her. Claire gave her a tentative smile back.

If she had to be stuck in this nightmare with two strangers, at least she was with these two. Of course, she gave them about half a day before they decided they were sick of her. She was *not* good under stress. Unlike Reyva, whom nothing fazed. And Mariana, who switched from distraught to cheerful with lightning speed. "*On* three. One, two, *three*."

They lifted, but the trapdoor didn't budge.

Digging her fingers in deeper, Claire said, "Again. One, two, three." Each of them squatted deeper, braced themselves, and lifted.

The hinges groaned, but the lid shifted upward an inch. With a grunt, the three girls shoved harder and pushed the lid open. Side by side, they peered into the dark pit. A rusty ladder descended into the shadows.

"Hello?" Claire called. "Anyone down there?"

Her voice echoed, tinny, against the metal walls of the shaft. No one answered. Claire's heart sank. She'd been so sure. . . . Or at least she'd wanted to believe it was possible. She'd imagined everyone fleeing the house—taking refuge from the flames belowground, protected by a fireproof lid. She supposed it had been a foolishly optimistic idea. After all, if they'd hidden from the fire here, why hadn't they emerged when it was over?

"Guess we really are alone," Mariana said.

"Except for the murderer," Claire couldn't help saying.

Reyva snorted.

"What? It's true." Facts were facts.

Reyva smiled—fleetingly, but it still counted as a smile. It looked mismatched with her black eye shadow, smeared after a night outside, giving her a comic book supervillain look. "It's just that I've spent years cultivating a the-world-sucks-and-then-you-die attitude, but you with your wide-eyed pixie look . . .

You're an inspiration, that's all."

Claire had never been told she looked like a wide-eyed pixie. "Um, thanks?"

"So who's first?" Reyva asked.

"Excuse me?" Mariana said.

Reyva pointed toward the darkness. "Don't you want to know what's down there?"

"Let me think . . ." Mariana tapped her chin in mock thought. "No. Definitely don't care to see what's in the pitch-black hole in the ground. Come on, fainting from thirst here. Let's get that water boiling. Hydrate or die-drate!" She struck a cheerleader pose. "Team Hydration for the win!"

But Claire was already shining her phone light down the shaft. She doubted any victims of the fire were down there, but there could be useful supplies. If this was a prepper's bunker, or even just an extra storage area for the camp, it could make the difference between life and death. There could be a functional phone. Or, more likely, canned food that would help keep them alive. Better to be thorough than to starve while a crate of beans and tuna lay a few feet beneath them.

"I'm not going down there," Mariana said.

"Great," Reyva said. "You can keep watch. Shout if we're all going to die." Holding on to the top of the ladder, she hopped into the hole and landed on one of the rungs. She began to climb down. Sticking her phone in her back pocket and giving an apologetic look to Mariana, Claire followed her.

Below her, she heard the sound of Reyva's breathing and the squeak of the ladder with each step she climbed. Claire wondered how deep the shaft went—she imagined, briefly, descending miles underground—but as she completed the thought, she heard a thump.

"Made it." Reyva's voice drifted up.

She saw light splash against the metal walls of the shaft as Reyva, below, turned on her phone light. Soon after, Claire had reached the bottom too. It felt damp and cool, and the motionless air tasted rank, thick with the smell of mildew and urine. Wrinkling her nose and trying to breathe shallowly, she let go of the ladder and wiped her hands on her jeans, then again because she still felt coated in grime. After less than a second down here, she felt as if she needed the longest shower ever, but she resisted the urge to climb back up and join Mariana in the fresh, non-urine-scented air. She switched on her phone light too and swept the beam in a wide circle. It flashed against dirt and stone walls.

Reyva hissed.

Claire pivoted to face the way her beam was pointed. Both phones shone on a cage. It was large, about eight feet by eight feet, and empty, with the cage doors propped open. Clumps of dirty hay were scattered on the floor, and a bucket sat in the corner. Shackles dangled from the wall within the cage.

"Okay, that's. . . disturbing," Reyva whispered.

Shivers raced up and down Claire's arms. Coming down here began to feel like a very bad idea. She'd pictured shelves. Maybe a bunk. Old equipment. Not this.

It felt as if the cage was waiting.

For us, she thought instinctively, and then banished the thought.

There had to be an explanation. She needed to think of it as a puzzle to solve. Gulping in air, she wondered if there was less oxygen down here. Sweat popped onto her forehead. She couldn't help feeling that there was something about the stale air inside the bunker that felt like a held breath. Once, something or someone had waited in this cage.

Heart thumping, Claire inched forward, looking for clues—tracks, fur, or claw marks. She touched one of the bars and felt gashes, as if an animal had tried to bite through the iron. She spread her fingers along the gashes, trying to guess if they were from teeth or claws. "What was in it?"

"Guard dogs?" Reyva guessed.

"Kept underground?" That had to violate a half-dozen animal cruelty laws. She shuddered, imagining dogs forced together into this lightless, damp cage.

"Dogs for illegal dog fighting?"

"It's a pretty large cage. Wolves? Bears? Maybe the owners of the Lake House caught and sold wild animals illegally." Certainly nothing legal had been happening here. The only consolation was that there weren't any wolves, bears, or trained-to-be-deadly dogs currently, which begged another question. . . . "Whatever kind of animal was in here, where is it now?"

"Wish you hadn't asked that," Reyva said.

So did Claire.

Both of them turned slowly, shining their lights around the bunker and halting when they reached a break in the wall. The edges of the opening were jagged. It looked as if it had been blasted through, torn through—*or eaten through*, she thought, though when she asked herself *what* could have eaten through a cement wall, she had no answer.

This is a bad place to be with an overactive imagination, she thought. She wished she hadn't climbed down that ladder. Or boarded that boat. Or left her bedroom.

She liked how safe her room made her feel. She'd tried to explain that to a friend once—Priya had been pressuring her to come to a party. A senior's parents were out of town. Everyone was going to be there. She'd have fun, Priya had promised. All the girls from their lunch table would be spending the night at her house afterward. She hadn't understood when Claire tried to describe all the things she worried about. In fact, Priya had laughed. But every time Claire tried to spend the night at a friend's house, she had to sneak out of her sleeping bag and check every door lock, every window lock, and every knob on the stove, and then she'd lie awake worrying she'd missed one. This was a thousand times worse. There were definitely no comforting locks to check here.

Through the hole, a tunnel led into darkness, and when Claire inched forward, she saw the walls within the tunnel were rough rock, not cement like the bunker. Roots dangled down from between the rocks.

"Natural cave?" Reyva asked.

"Looks like."

"Wonder where it goes."

"Maybe whatever was in the cage went that way," Claire said. She didn't like that idea. She was hoping the cage was a remnant from an earlier, less savory time in the history of the camp. It was possible it hadn't been used in decades.

Except for the fact that it still smelled. Something had been kept here and that something had escaped.

Possibly recently.

I really don't want to meet that something, Claire thought. She thought back to the program director, dead in the woods, and wondered if she had known about this. Perhaps not, since the trapdoor had been hidden beneath floorboards. Or perhaps yes, and that's why she'd been killed. Either way, they couldn't ask.

"Want to explore?" Reyva asked.

Claire didn't even have to consider it. "Not in the slightest."

Reyva exhaled loudly. "Good."

Both of them retreated to the ladder. Reyva climbed first, and Claire followed. By unspoken agreement, they each climbed as quickly as they could. When Claire popped out into the shed, they both grabbed the lid and yanked it shut.

Looking at it, Claire shuddered.

And then Reyva asked, "Where's Mariana?"

They burst out of the shed.

Claire opened her mouth to shout for Mariana, but then clamped it shut, remembering that Mariana might not be the only one to hear her.

Outside looked exactly as they'd left it: a horrible kind of peaceful. Clouds had rolled in, blanketing the forest in a duller light. A breeze stirred the ashes of the burnt house.

She scanned the yard for Mariana. But she wasn't by the house. Or on the airstrip. Or near the tennis court. Claire felt panic start to rise into her throat as all the possibilities unspooled into her head at once: What if she'd wandered into the forest and become lost? What if she'd hurt herself? What if she'd drowned in the lake? Or the most likely: What if she'd been discovered by the killer and shot or stabbed or burned alive or buried alive or—

"Hey, guys," Mariana said behind them, "what was down there?"

Claire jumped before her brain confirmed—it was Mariana. Just Mariana. Not a murderer. Or a wild animal. Or anything that wanted to hurt her. At the same time, Reyva spun around with fists raised. Seeing it was Mariana, she exhaled too and lowered her hands.

"You scared us," Reyva said accusingly.

"Really?" Mariana said. "I didn't think anything scared you, Reyva. Isn't that what you were trying to prove by jumping into the terrifying murder pit?"

Reyva glared at her.

Claire's knees felt wobbly. She put her hands on her thighs and breathed deep. It was all too much, the constant fear, the stream of horrific images spilling into her brain that each seemed more plausible than the last. She wished she were home. She'd pull the covers over her head and never leave.

I wish I'd never come here, she thought. *I wish this were all a dream. I wish I'd wake up. I wish—*

She felt a hand on her back.

"Claire, you okay?" Reyva asked.

Mariana was there too, her hands on Claire's shoulders. "Deep breaths. Do you want to sit? You should probably sit."

"I'm fine," Claire said, sucking in air.

Not here, she ordered herself. *Not now.* She could not lose it. Not in front of them. She had to stay calm. *Stay normal. Please!*

"You don't look fine," Mariana said. "You look like you're going to faint."

She'd fainted before, and she knew what that felt like—a blackness that ate your vision from the bottom up. This wasn't like that. Not yet. She was still in control. "Just need a minute." She counted as she breathed, in and out, tapping out the seconds with her fingers until slowly, finally, she felt herself begin to calm.

They waited and didn't say anything, and Claire appreciated that more than anything they could have said or done. It was, in truth, the best thing. It gave her the space to keep breathing and keep counting until her heart was no longer galloping wildly. In a moment, she felt better.

I'm okay, she thought. *They don't know.* She'd held it together, barely. Straightening, she said in as light a voice as she could manage, "Glad you're not dead."

"Ditto," Mariana said. She was eyeing Claire as if she were expecting her to keel over, and Claire felt her face heat up bright red. She wished the others hadn't seen her like that, so close to the brink. Should she explain, or try to laugh it off? What were they going to say? But instead of saying anything about it, Mariana just apologized. "Sorry for scaring you guys. I thought I heard a noise behind the shed."

"So you went to check it out?" Reyva asked. "By yourself?"

"I'd like to sound badass and say yes, but in reality, I went in the opposite direction and hid. I figured if it was danger, I could yell and warn you two when you emerged."

"What was it?" Claire asked.

"Just a squirrel. Don't think it was even rabid, and wow, that would be a thoroughly embarrassing way to die—survive fire, murder, dehydration, starvation, but get killed by a squirrel."

"Better to be safe," Reyva said. "Also, we haven't survived yet." She met Claire's eyes, as if to say, *I said it this time, not you.* Claire managed a shaky half smile back. She took a deep breath of fresh air, grateful that the wobbly feeling had receded and doubly grateful that they weren't making a big deal out of it, like her parents would have.

They would if they knew how far it could go.

Claire shook the thought from her head.

"We didn't die by fire," Mariana pointed out. "So that's one win for us." She then winced as she glanced at the Lake House. "Sorry—that was insensitive. I didn't mean . . . I should really learn to think before I speak. Did you find anything we can use? Food? Bottled water?"

"Sadly, no," Reyva said. "In fact, I recommend never opening that again. It's beyond creepy." They described what they'd found: the bear-size cage, as well as the opening in the wall that led into a cave.

"We think it held wild animals, for sale or for illegal fights or something," Claire said.

"Or it's where they put campers who break rules," Reyva said. "Any cage large enough for a bear is large enough for a human."

Mariana shuddered. "I'm going to assume that's a joke and you have a dark sense of humor. My parents might have shoved me out the door, but I'm positive they wouldn't have approved a camp with cages." Claire agreed with that—the way her parents had gushed, she'd expected the Lake House to be a paradise of idyllic rainbows and Life-Affirming Experiences. So far, not a single arc in the sky.

"It is, and I do," Reyva said. "But there *is* something off about this place." All three of them looked at the ruins of the Lake House. "Aside from the obvious."

Claire agreed with that too. "No more splitting up," she said firmly. Best if they stuck together, no matter what. No straying from each other's line of sight, not until they were certain they were safe. They were each other's best chance of survival. "And I vote we get away from here as quickly as possible."

"Seconded," Mariana said.

"Thirded," Reyva said. "Let's move."

SIX

You could survive three weeks without food, but only three days without water. Or at least that's what survival TV shows said. Obviously, the math changed if you were hiking through the woods, expending energy without replacing it.

As they carried the toolbox and the mason jars back to the lakeshore, Claire forced her brain to focus on calculating how much water they'd need instead of how thirsty she was. She wished she knew exactly how long a hike it would be. Three days? Four? Five? If she estimated the average distance between trees and counted the number of trees on the stretch of lake they could see from the dock . . .

Wind blew in a gust through the branches, and the leaves rustled. Claire tensed.

"I can literally see you worrying," Reyva said behind her. "It's like you've got a cartoon bubble over your head with a black squiggly line in it."

"Sorry," she said automatically. "Just . . . thinking about how much water we'll need."

"We'll boil as much as we can and carry as much as we can.

Maybe Ms. Overpacker here can part with a few more outfits."

Mariana had already ditched her two suitcases by the shore and stuffed just what she'd deemed essential into her backpack, but her pack still dwarfed Reyva's and Claire's. "That's Dr. Overpacker to you," she answered. "I earned my PhD in excess."

"If we have to, we'll boil more," Reyva said. "There's an entire lake out there. And if it rains, we can catch rainwater. That'll be fresh and safe to drink. We're going to be okay."

Claire wished she felt half as certain as Reyva sounded. "I'm not going to hope for rain. We don't have any way to stay dry. And it'll be a thousand times harder to light a fire if it rains." She looked up at the strips of sky between the pine trees and was relieved to see cloudless blue. It was remarkable—and more than a bit alarming—how quickly the weather changed here. She wondered if that was typical of Maine. "You can die of exposure in summer too, especially if you're soaking wet when the temperature drops at night."

"You're full of fun facts," Reyva said.

Claire winced. Once, in kindergarten, she'd had the brilliant idea to tell her classmates about the dangers of carbon monoxide after her parents had installed a sensor. The entire class freaked out and her parents were called to the school. Just last month, at Driver's Ed, when someone had asked how likely it was they'd die in a car crash, the statistics had spilled out of her mouth before she could stop them. The other students had definitely not appreciated that. "I just . . . thought it was something we should all know."

"It is," Mariana said earnestly. "Ignore her."

"If we're going to get through this, I think we need to maintain a positive attitude," Reyva said. "My parents' favorite saying—and I cannot believe I'm quoting them, but here we are—is that attitude is what makes you a winner or a loser."

"Which explains why you're such a ray of sunshine?" Mariana asked.

Narrowing her eyes, Reyva glared at her. "I'm trying something new. There's a poster in my parents' studio: 'You can overcome anything if you believe you can.' Cheesy, yes, but that doesn't mean it's not true." She paused, then added, "Let's not tell them I said that."

"It *isn't* true," Claire couldn't help saying. "Positivity can't help if you're hit by a car. It can't stop an earthquake. Or a volcano. Or an asteroid. It can't cure cancer, or make an old person young again. Or heal a gunshot wound."

Stop talking, she told herself. *Just stop.*

"But it *can* keep you from giving up," Mariana said. "I think Reyva's right. We improve our chances if we stay positive. Totally believe that. Go, us!"

"Yeah, not doing a cheer," Reyva said. "And I prefer to flavor my positivity more as determination than perkiness, but whatever. I believe we'll succeed if we focus on succeeding."

"Of course. Yes. Sorry," Claire said. She clamped her mouth shut.

God. Why did she automatically jump to imagining the worst-case scenario in every instance? There was no formative childhood trauma that she could point to. It was just the way she was wired. In fifth grade, she'd lost her best friend, Angie, when she'd overshared. Angie's mom had ducked out to run errands, and she'd shouted upstairs to them some kind of garbled be-back-soon. Claire had been shocked that Angie hadn't asked her mom to repeat what she said. When Angie asked why it mattered, Claire had told her that she always made a point to memorize the last thing her parents said before they walked out the door, in case they died while they were out. She then detailed all the ways a parent could die: heart attack, brain aneurysm, traffic accident, drunk driver, accidental homicide . . . She'd scared Angie so badly she'd cried, and Claire hadn't been allowed back. So she'd learned to hide her pessimism from friends, family, everyone—but it still slipped out even under the best of circumstances. *And these are definitely not the best of circumstances*, she thought.

A stick snapped in the woods.

All of them froze.

Claire didn't breathe. She listened, trying to separate the sounds of birds from other sounds. She heard one three-note birdcall, then a two-note descent. Whoever had made the noise hadn't startled the birds.

She reminded herself that it was far more likely that the murderer/arsonist was miles away from the scene of the crime. He'd have no reason to stick around. She had to chill. Reyva was right—if she was convinced every second that they were going to die, she'd be an exhausted pile of twitching nerves by sundown.

Except that doesn't change the fact that any second, we could die, she thought.

Quit it, Claire. Go, us, remember?

After a few long seconds, they resumed their trek down to the lakeshore. None of them spoke again until they saw the blue peeking through the trees.

The lake surface rolled with waves. Reflecting the clouds that had cropped up during their walk, the water looked grayer than it had at dawn. All along the shore, pines, hemlocks, and maples swayed. She wondered what had happened to her blue cloudless sky from only a couple of minutes ago. The wind and clouds had sprung up fast. "The wind will make this trickier," Claire said.

"Oh, yay," Reyva said.

"We can do it," Mariana cheerleaded.

"We *will* do it," Reyva corrected. "Perseverance, not perkiness."

Climbing over the boulders that littered the shore, Claire searched for the perfect spot: flat and shielded from the wind. Away from the trapdoor and the burned-down house, out of the woods, and with a task to do, she felt a bit calmer.

All we have to do is light this fire, she thought. *Tackle one problem at a time. Don't borrow future problems.* It was the closest she could manage to Reyva's parents' motivational posters. It was good advice. Just because she'd never followed it before didn't mean this couldn't be the first time.

Locating a viable site, Claire called the others over. "How about here?"

Three weather-beaten boulders framed a patch of sand and pebbles. Assuming the wind didn't change direction radically, the rocks would act as a buffer.

"I'll fill the toolbox with water," Mariana volunteered.

"I'll find sticks," Reyva said.

Kneeling, Claire retrieved the unused wad of tinder, made of Mariana's cotton balls and bark, and began to build a pyramid of twigs over it. Every few seconds, she glanced up at the woods. Had it been a squirrel or the wind, or was someone out there? She felt as if there were dozens of eyes staring out at them.

Trying to shake the feeling, she picked up a rock and examined it. It was gray, flecked with mica, and hard—you know, a rock. "Anyone know what flint looks like?"

"When you mine a block of gravel in *Minecraft*, there's a ten percent chance it will drop flint," Reyva said. "And when you hit a rock with a sledgehammer in *Zelda*, it can give you flint, rock salt, or a precious stone."

"Did not picture you as a gamer," Mariana said.

"I'm full of surprises."

"Strike flint with a blade, and you get a spark," Claire said. But she had no idea if any of these rocks were close enough to the hardness of flint to work. She'd never paid attention to types of rocks. She could distinguish sedimentary from metamorphic and igneous, thanks to eighth-grade earth science, but that was about it.

"Actually only play at friends' houses," Reyva said. As an explanation: "Parents."

"Ah, got it," Mariana said. "Mine think any indoor activity that isn't homework is likely to cause a fatal vitamin D deficiency. Don't even get them started on the evils of TV. That's part of why I started working on cars—the garage counts as outside. Held my first wrench at age three, or so the family story goes. Apparently no one realized, or cared, that a steel tool was not an age-appropriate toy."

"Mine . . ." Reyva seemed on the verge of continuing, but settled on just: "Yeah. Parents."

Eyeing her, Claire wondered what she wasn't saying.

She wanted to ask, but she didn't dare. They might ask what *she* was keeping locked up tight. Instead, Claire chose a rock at random and took out her Swiss Army knife. It wasn't one of those knives with a million attachments plus a tiny food processor. Just two blades on opposite ends, a short one and a long one. Over her tinder bundle, she hit the rock with the longer blade.

It didn't spark.

She examined the knife. The rock had scuffed the edge, but it looked okay. She tried again.

"What if you strike faster?" Mariana suggested.

Claire noticed that both Reyva and Mariana had come closer to watch her. She felt a bit like she was onstage, about to perform a magic act that she hadn't practiced. *All that's missing is me in my underwear, and this would be a classic nightmare*, she thought. Granted, her typical nightmare tended to be less about embarrassment and more about dismemberment, but still . . . She wasn't immune to the fear. She remembered a teacher in elementary school once insisting she stand at the front of the classroom for an oral report on . . . what was it? The life cycle? She'd spent entirely too long on the decomposers and was dubbed Worm Girl for the rest of class. She'd hid in the bathroom for lunch that day, but thankfully the nickname had been forgotten by the final bell. It was funny, the things you remembered when you were busy trying not to die.

She tried again with the rock, striking harder.

"Let me try," Reyva said.

Claire passed the rock and knife to Reyva.

Leaning over the tinder, Reyva struck the rock hard. And then again. And again. Each time, Claire held her breath. Once, she thought she saw a spark—but no, it was just the glint of the blade, catching a bit of stray daylight from between the clouds.

Mariana gathered firewood, adding to Reyva's pile.

"Maybe a different kind of rock?" Casting around, Claire found a mottled rock with pink splotches. "Here, try this one."

Reyva tried and failed.

"How about this one?" She gave her a grayer rock with a rough edge, not yet worn by the lake. Reyva took it and began striking it just as hard.

"Quit staring at me," Reyva growled. "I hate failing with an audience."

"Sorry," Claire said.

"Go do something useful. Like fetch firewood. This is *going* to work."

Mumbling another apology, Claire helped Mariana haul more sticks and fallen logs to the shore. Every time she darted in between the trees, she tried to look as deep into the woods as she could. She could see a reasonable distance before the overlapping trunks blocked her view, but that didn't preclude a lurker behind a tree or a rock. These Maine woods were littered with fallen logs that had never been cleared and huge boulders left behind by glaciers. Plenty of places to hide.

Stop it, she told herself.

"At home, you can actually see more than a few feet without a tree getting in the way," Mariana said as she tugged a fallen branch out of a snarl of brambles. "I think all the greenery is making me claustrophobic."

"Where's home?" Claire asked, her eyes still on the woods.

She paused, oddly, which made Claire glance over at her. "LA," Mariana said. "Specifically, Santa Monica, the part where the beach parties start on Wednesday and pretty much don't stop until Tuesday. I'm not used to the quiet here."

Claire, on the other hand, wished it weren't so loud: the wind, the birds, the squirrels. It all made it impossible to tell if they were truly alone. "You like it there?" *Hey, look at me having a normal conversation*, she thought.

"Sunshine. Earthquakes. Mudslides. Raging wildfires. Excellent burritos. Constant selfies. It has it all. I never want to leave. Plus all our family is there. I'm an only child, but I have a plethora of aunts, uncles, and cousins. We've been there for literally generations, and no one's *ever* moved out of California."

There was a wistfulness to Mariana's voice that made Claire wonder if Mariana was worried she'd never see them again. She thought about reassuring her, but wasn't sure what to say that wouldn't sound fake. "You're close with your family?"

"We're all close—really close. Everyone's in everyone else's business all the time, you know? Which can be great, except when it's not. When I came out . . . a lot of my cousins were really supportive. One aunt was not. She made her opinion known, loudly, as if my very existence was a personal disappointment to her." Mariana fell silent for a moment, then said brightly, "One out of a gazillion isn't bad. Could've been a lot worse. Having the rest of them around me . . ." Her voice broke. She swallowed and finished with: "Yeah, I wish they were here. Not my aunt, obviously. Or my parents. But my cousins. Aunts. Uncles. Grandparents. I wish they were all here."

Claire didn't have any family besides her parents. But she would have given a lot to have had them here. Or better still, to have never come at all. They'd been so insistent, though—so very certain that this would be a great experience for her and would fix all of her personality flaws, or whatever.

Nope to that, she thought.

She wondered what it would be like to have people around you who supported you, exactly as you were. Did Mariana even know how rare that was? *I think she does,* Claire thought. *Why else would she have sounded so sad? She misses them.*

Claire wanted to ask her more: What was it like having a big family, especially one that so obviously loved her as she was, not as she could be? And why did she deliberately exclude her parents when she listed the relatives she missed? But if she asked, then Mariana might expect Claire to open up and talk about herself. . . . Yeah, she didn't want to do that.

With one more look at Mariana, Claire returned to Reyva. "Any luck?"

"Does it look like I've had any luck?"

Wordlessly, Claire handed her a new rock—a white one.

Quartz, she guessed. She wished she'd memorized the relative hardness of rocks. Geology suddenly felt a lot more important than high school science had implied. It had been more focused on volcanos and plate tectonics.

Depositing an armful of sticks next to the boulders, Mariana asked, "Anything?" She was back to sounding cheerful again, no hint of tears in her voice anymore. She was good at hiding herself, Claire thought.

Reyva shot her a glare. "Yeah, I got it blazing, but then decided to stomp it out because it was too hot."

"Keep trying," Mariana said encouragingly. "You're doing great."

Another glare, but Reyva tried again, even harder. On the third strike, a tiny spark jumped from the quartz and sizzled in the air.

Mariana cheered and—

Crash!

Reyva jumped to her feet. She was yanked down by Mariana. Crouching, Claire felt her heart beating so hard that it almost hurt. It sounded as if something—or someone—had felled a tree. A scream built in her throat but she kept it down. The three of them huddled by the rock, waiting for someone to burst out from the forest.

But no one did.

The trees continued to sway in the wind.

"Broken branch falling?" Reyva offered.

"Squirrel?" Mariana suggested.

Reyva raised her eyebrows.

"Very large squirrel?"

Whatever it was, it hadn't jumped out to kill them, so that counted as a win in Claire's mind. "Keep going," she said to Reyva. "You almost had it."

"Ooh, how about you try holding the tinder against the rock?" Mariana said. "That way, if you get a spark, it won't poof in the air before it has a chance to catch."

It was a good idea.

Hands shaking a little, Claire extracted a fluff of cotton from the tinder pile, and Reyva held it with her thumb against the quartz as she hit it with the blade. A spark jumped off. Simultaneously, the blade snapped at the base.

Crying out, Reyva dropped it.

Claire's heart fell with it. So close!

"There's a second blade," Reyva said. "I'll keep trying."

Reaching out, Claire put her hand on Reyva's wrist. "We might need it." If they had to gut a fish or . . . She tried not to finish imagining the reasons why they might wish they had a knife. She glanced again at the woods. Her mouth felt dry, and she swallowed.

Keep it together, she reminded herself. *It's a puzzle to solve. That's all.*

The trees were blowing harder now, brushing up against one another. Over the wind, it would be even harder to tell if anyone were approaching. The pines and spruces creaked and groaned as they swayed. It looked even less friendly than it had before, if that was possible.

"Now what?" Mariana asked.

"Not giving up," Reyva said. "How about rubbing sticks together?"

"It's supposed to be really hard to do," Claire said. "But we can try." She checked her phone. It was already three p.m. She'd hoped to have begun their hike hours ago. They'd wasted so much time already on the knife and rock, but what choice did they have? No matter how many times she did the math, they'd need drinkable water to survive the trek.

She spared another glance at the trees.

"How hard can it be?" Mariana said. "You just spin a stick, right?"

Claire selected the driest chunk of wood from their stack, and she used the broken blade from her Swiss Army knife to dig a small hole. She then wrapped the broken blade carefully in one of her socks and tucked it into her backpack, using a side pocket so she wouldn't accidentally slice herself. "Idea is to create enough friction. Reyva, hold the tinder bundle next to the hole."

While Reyva held the cotton steady, Claire stuck one end of the stick in the hole, held it between the palms of her hands, and rubbed her hands back and forth to twist the stick.

Watching over her shoulder, Mariana asked, "Do you actually know what you're doing?"

Continuing to twist the stick, Claire thought, *No.* Out loud, she said, "Seen it on TV. Of course, I've also seen brain surgery on TV. How to pilot a plane. And how to defeat an alien invasion. So, you know, this will probably fail."

After a few minutes, Reyva said, "My turn."

Claire sat back. Her palms felt raw. She examined them and saw they were red and indented with knots from the stick. Scooting back, she gladly let Reyva take a turn.

Kneeling, Reyva twisted the stick faster than Claire. "Distract me. Talk."

"How about we get to know each other?" Mariana suggested in a bright, sunny voice, as if they were hanging out at a Santa Monica beach instead of . . . here.

Claire tensed. This was exactly the kind of conversation she preferred to avoid. Maybe they could talk about TV shows? Or the weather? Or . . .

"Let's start simple: What's everyone's favorite color? Mine is pink. But not the kind of sweet pink that parents who are irrational about gender identity like to use to swaddle babies. I like the obnoxious neon pink that feels like a punch in the eyes."

She relaxed minutely. *That* level of getting-to-know-you she could handle.

"I like black," Reyva said.

A tendril of smoke curled up, and they crowded around it. Claire scooted the tinder bundle closer—and the smoke died. Her heart sank.

"Black is boring," Mariana said. "It's the new gray." Claire could tell she was still trying for upbeat and casual chatter, but the waver beneath her words was unmistakable. All of them were on edge.

"Everyone looks good in black," Reyva said.

"Patently untrue," Mariana said. "Look at Claire. She'd look like a corpse in black."

Both of them looked at Claire. "Can you please stop imagining me as a corpse? And I like green." Although after being stranded in the woods, she thought she might change her mind about that. She never wanted to see a tree again. She briefly fantasized about taking a chain saw to the forest, and then her brain helpfully supplied a litany of images of chain saw injuries.

Reyva resumed twisting the stick.

"All right," Mariana said. "Good start with the getting-to-know-you bonding. How about we jump a little deeper? What's your greatest secret, or your greatest fear? Speak up and don't be shy. This is what summer camp is supposed to be for."

"Oh? Stranded, hungry, thirsty, and failing to start a fire?" Reyva waved her red palm in the air for emphasis, then continued trying to twist the stick as fast as she could.

"Not *this* this, but intense emotional bonding with virtual strangers is supposed to be part of the experience. So, spill. Tell us your deepest, darkest desire."

Claire held still. She felt like an alarm siren was wailing inside her head. This was definitely *not* a conversation she wanted to have. Her deepest, darkest thoughts deserved to be buried as deep as she could bury them. The other girls didn't want her darkness. They wanted surface desires—like what normal people wished for on stars and birthday candles.

On the other hand, she couldn't help but wonder what Reyva and Mariana would answer. What kind of thoughts were they holding inside?

"I desire a spark," Reyva said. "One that stays lit and spreads."

"Okay, fine, a spark, but what's in the depths of your soul . . ."

Mariana trailed off, then slapped her forehead dramatically. "Batteries!"

Reyva stopped twisting the stick. "What?"

"I should have thought of it sooner. We can use a battery to make a spark!" She pawed through her backpack. "Here we go! Knew I packed a nail dryer."

She produced a travel-size nail dryer and held it up as if it were a grand prize.

Raising her eyebrows, Reyva said, "Okay. First, you packed a nail dryer. For summer camp. Second, when you sorted your belongings to take only the essentials . . . you *still* packed the nail dryer."

"Enrichment retreat," Mariana corrected. "And I believe in the importance of self-care. Manicures are soothing and provide the illusion of control over life. A situation can't be entirely hopeless if you're able to maintain your cuticles."

"Uh-huh."

Claire folded her hands to hide her chewed fingernails.

"Next, we need gum." Returning to her backpack, she muttered to herself. "Have to connect positive to negative . . . Ah, here it is!" She waved a pack of chewing gum in the air.

What did that . . .

Pulling out a stick of gum, Mariana unwrapped it and stuck the gum in her mouth. She chewed and hummed at the same time as she pried off the plastic back of her nail dryer and dumped out a double-A battery. "Claire, can I borrow your knife?"

Claire handed her the Swiss Army knife.

Carefully, Mariana sliced a thin strip of gum wrapper. "My

cousin did this as a party trick once. The key is you need a wrapper made of both foil and paper, and you have to cut it so it's narrow in the center. . . ." She sliced it into an hourglass shape. "Get the tinder bundle ready, Reyva. If this works, it'll go fast."

Reyva didn't hesitate. She held it out in her hands, low, to keep it out of the wind as much as possible, and Mariana knelt opposite her.

Excited, Claire inched forward to watch. *Please work*, she thought. *Please!*

Mariana pressed one end of the metallic gum wrapper to one side of the battery and one end to the other. She held it—and the center of the strip of wrapper caught fire with a bright, beautiful flame! "Quick!" Mariana yelped.

Reyva shoved the tinder bundle closer to it, and the flame hopped to the cotton. Reverently, she lowered the flaming bundle to the pyramid of twigs and tucked it within. The flames spread, hopping from dry stick to dry stick. Scrambling, the three of them fed the fire the sticks and branches they'd gathered. They placed each one carefully, so as not to smother the baby fire as it crackled and grew and spread.

"Brilliant," Claire said to Mariana. "You're brilliant."

"I am smarter than I look," Mariana said, "which, by the way, is a terrible phrase. Why should how I look have anything to do with how well my synapses fire? Do you know how many times I've had to argue with our school guidance counselor about what class I should be in? Like, every year. He'd look at me, see a teenage girl with excellent makeup skills whose fits are on point, with the name Mariana Ortiz-Rodriguez, and assume I couldn't possibly handle AP Chem. Sexism *and* racism, with a splash of biphobia, in one mustached package. Fabulous fun. And my parents are zero help when it comes to taking time from their own issues to talk to my school. Their lives and their problems always take precedence over mine. Never mind how their bad choices affect me. They never even asked me how I felt when—" She cut herself off. "They never ask me."

What bad choices? Claire wondered.

"But hey," Mariana said brightly, "I'm learning resiliency and self-reliance."

"Mine threatened a teacher with bodily harm if she placed me in too low a class," Reyva said. "So, involved parents aren't fun either. They don't trust I can do anything without their very vigilant oversight and endless constructive criticism."

Claire's parents didn't hound her about grades. Instead, they wanted her to make friends and not stay in her room all the time. *Get out and do things*, they always said. They complained she lived too much in her own head. It wasn't healthy for her to be so closed off. Not even daily ballet lessons pacified them anymore the way they used to. Whatever she did, it never seemed to be enough. They just couldn't seem to see her as anything but a problem that needed to be fixed. *Well, I'm doing things now, Mom and Dad*, Claire thought. She doubted this was what they'd had in mind.

They all stared at the fire.

It didn't matter what their parents said or didn't say. Their parents weren't here to either approve or disapprove. *We are here*, Claire thought. *And we started this fire by ourselves.*

Crackling, it danced over the wood. Yellow and orange flames so bright that they were nearly white. Sparks rose into the air with snow-like flecks of ash, and the wind stole them and blew them over the lake.

"I've never seen anything more beautiful," Mariana said. "And I've been to Malibu." She slid the battery and pack of gum into her pocket, deep so there was no chance they'd fall out. "Keeping these babies close."

"Let's get the water going," Reyva said. They positioned the toolbox full of water as close to the fire as they could. Once it boiled and then cooled, they'd transfer the water to the glass jars, seal them up, and be ready to go—after they drank, of course.

A drop of rain landed on Claire's cheek.

"No," she whispered.

It had to be spray from the lake. Or spit. Maybe one of the others had talked too enthusiastically. Or maybe she'd imagined she felt—

Rain began to patter down onto the rocks.

SEVEN

Crouching over the fire, Claire tried to shield the flames with her body. Kneeling, Reyva blew on the embers, trying to keep them alive as the drops fell faster and faster.

Mariana dug through her pack and pulled out a flannel shirt. "Here, grab the sleeve. It's not waterproof, but it'll help."

She and Claire held it over the fire like a tarp.

Claire felt the rain stream down her neck. It soaked through the back of her shirt as she bent over the dying fire. How had this storm sprung up so fast? It wasn't fair! Rain slapped the rocks faster, and the wind blew the rain sideways, beneath the shirt. It pelted their lovely pyramid of sticks.

The fire sputtered.

"It's not working!" Claire cried.

A sad tendril of smoke curled up from what had once been their tinder bundle.

"But we had it!" Reyva said. "We'd done it! It's not fair!"

Claire 100 percent agreed. It felt like the universe was laughing at them. Everything against them, and now it had to rain?

Abandoning the doomed fire and her flannel, Mariana dumped the lake water out of the toolbox and began opening the glass jars. "All we need is fresh water, right? So this should work! Catch the rain!"

She was right. Never mind that they'd worked so hard to start the fire—the result was what mattered. If they could catch the rain, they'd be fine. *Well, relatively fine,* Claire corrected herself. *Better, at least. Able to leave. As soon as it stops raining.*

If it stops raining. . . .

The rain was falling harder.

Claire joined in, helping Mariana position the glass jars against the rocks so they wouldn't fall over as they filled with rain. Reyva reluctantly abandoned the fire, and it sputtered as it died.

As soon as they'd set up the jars, they retreated beneath the trees, dragging their packs with them. Rain hit the branches and slipped down the fissures in the bark. Claire wasn't convinced it was any drier under the trees than it had been out in the open on the lakeshore. Every few minutes, the wind blew, and all the water that had collected in the branches above them splashed down.

"We need a better tree," Reyva said. The remnants of her eye makeup streaked her cheeks like black tears. She wiped half of it away with the back of her hand.

"That one?" Mariana suggested.

They hurried through the pines to an old, fat maple. Pressing against the trunk, they huddled together. Through the trees,

Claire could see the lake as it was pelted with rain. It was falling so hard now that the air looked gray. Wind whipped through the forest, carrying rain with it.

We're going to be soaked, she thought.

I'm already soaked.

All their supplies. All their clothes.

"We can't stay out here," Claire said.

"Not much choice," Reyva said.

Claire's hair was plastered to her neck, and she felt rain on her face flowing faster than tears. Her clothes stuck to her body. It wouldn't be long before everything dry they owned was saturated. All the wood would be soaked as well. They wouldn't be able to start a new fire to dry themselves.

"Maybe it'll stop soon," Mariana said.

"Or it won't," Claire said, "and the sun will set and we'll be—"

"So what do you want to do about it?" Mariana snapped. "This sucks. I hate this." She stepped out from beneath the tree and shouted at the sky. "You hear me? I hate this! Stop raining! *Stop!*"

It didn't listen.

She stepped back under the tree.

"Feel better?" Reyva asked.

"Yes. No. I don't know. There has to be somewhere we can go to get out of the rain before we're so waterlogged we develop gills."

Claire realized she was shivering, which wasn't great. *Hypothermia*, she thought. Could you get that in summer? How long did it take to set in? She looked up through the branches and flinched as rain hit her face. Squinting, she tried to guess how low the sun was. They'd spent several hours on the fire. Before that, they'd searched the house for a while. . . . "I can think of one place out of the rain, but you won't like it."

"Nope," Reyva said.

"You didn't even hear my suggestion."

"Not the murder hole."

"It will be dry," Claire pointed out. "And the cage was empty."

"We don't know what was in that cave," Reyva said.

"We don't have to find out," Claire said. "We stay in the bunker. Change into dry clothes. Dry out our wet stuff. And leave in the morning." It was a sensible plan. Certainly more sensible than spending the night in a rainstorm. She wrapped her arms around herself and tried to stop shivering. She wondered what the signs of hypothermia were. Certainly shivering.

"It can't rain this hard forever," Mariana said.

"Maybe not forever, but it can rain for hours," Claire said. "Do you want to keep standing out here when there's a nice, dry hole in the ground—"

"—with an ominous cage," Reyva added.

"—with an empty, unused, old cage that has a bucket we can use to catch additional fresh water? We dry out, we sleep, and we leave in the morning."

The wind whipped the rain into them so hard that Mariana staggered backward. "Fine! But we stick together, okay? No splitting up this time. That was profoundly stupid, like teen-in-a-horror-movie stupid, and I make it a goal to never make the same profoundly stupid mistake twice. Like not measuring the cylinder and crankshaft carefully enough when you're rebuilding your engine. Half a thousandth of an inch can matter. Never will screw that up again."

"Agreed," Claire said. She didn't know what a crankshaft was, but the sentiment . . . "We stick together."

"Let's go," Reyva said.

Clinging to one another, they tromped through the bushes, the ferns, and the muddy leaves toward the trail to the Lake House. Claire felt her sneakers squish, already soaked, and as they made their way up the trail, mud seeped in over the sides. It would be days before they dried properly.

Claire used to love the rain before she came here. Under normal circumstances, it was an excellent excuse to stay inside and escape into a book or lose herself in practice at the ballet barre in her bedroom. Her parents couldn't prod her to "get some fresh air and see some fresh faces" if the weather was lousy. That was always their solution: just go "participate in life." Put herself out there. If she managed to sequester herself in her room early enough, she could squeeze in a few hours for just herself before her parents started to wonder, loudly, what she was up to and why, if she'd finished her homework, she wasn't being social with any of her perfectly nice classmates. The rain used to be a friendly coconspirator.

But out here, it felt as if the rain was an enemy who hated them with a hateful hate.

By the time they reached the Lake House, the rain was

pummeling them. It was falling so hard that it was difficult to see more than a few feet in front of them. Shielding her eyes with her arm, Claire forded ahead.

When she reached the ruins of the shed, she squatted in the mud next to the trapdoor. "Help me!"

Together, the three of them yanked the lid open. Reyva dropped her pack down the shaft, and Mariana and Claire followed suit, then Reyva scurried down the ladder. Mariana went next.

"Shut it behind you," Mariana said.

"Absolutely not," Claire said.

"But the rain will get in."

"We'll catch it in the bucket."

"What's the point of a shelter if you leave the door wide open?"

"What if we can't open it from the inside? It takes all three of us to pry it up—only one can fit on the ladder. What if it's too heavy?"

"You're underestimating us," Mariana said. "We're stronger than we look." She paused and added with a pointed look, "You are too." But she climbed down the ladder without any further argument.

Claire pushed the lid open wider so it lay flat on the floor, and then she followed. As soon as she was partway down, she knew coming here was the right decision. The wind couldn't touch them underground. Rain still spat at her, trickling down the opening, but it wasn't anywhere near as intense as being exposed out in the storm.

She reached the bottom. Both Mariana and Reyva had already turned on their phones' flashlights. "Probably should conserve batteries," Claire said. "Just use one." They were lucky the phones still worked at all. She knew her battery was low. She'd charged it before she'd left Connecticut, but that felt like eons ago.

Mariana glared at her as if all this were her fault, but she switched off her light. Reyva left hers on, its beam casting striped shadows from the bars of the cage.

"We'll stay here until it stops, then we'll take the rainwater in the jars, bring the toolbox in case we need to boil more, and hike out of here." Claire tried to make her voice sound upbeat. She wasn't as good at that as Mariana. Even Reyva was better at positivity when she was trying.

"And what do we do if it starts raining like this when we're out in the woods, hiking around the lake?" Mariana asked.

"Hope it doesn't," Reyva said.

"Not loving that solution," Mariana said. Claire heard the edge in her voice—the fighting-not-to-cry tone. "Do you really think we're going to be able to make it out of here on foot? I'm not much of a hiker."

"I think we have to try," Claire said.

Mariana looked as if she wanted to say more, but instead she nodded.

"Or, another idea: we become wild women and live off the land," Reyva said. She was shivering so hard that her teeth were chattering. "Never return to civilization. Years later, they'll make documentaries about us."

"Only if we can order pizza," Mariana said, sounding a bit less like she was going to freak out, which in and of itself was a good thing. Claire wasn't sure what she'd do if one of the others lost it.

She also wished Mariana hadn't mentioned pizza.

So far, she'd done a decent job of not thinking about food, but once she imagined the taste of a nice thin-crust margherita pizza, her stomach began to complain. It let out a whine like an out-of-tune trumpet. Startled, Claire laughed, and the others laughed too—thin and strained, but for a moment, Claire felt better than she thought she had any right to feel. If they could still laugh, maybe they weren't totally doomed.

"Do you think any place would deliver Thai?" Mariana asked. "Give them directions to the murder hole next to the burned-down house. Can't miss it."

"We'll need to ration," Claire said. "And then . . . I don't know." Hunt? Fish? Forage? She couldn't see them taking down a deer with their bare hands. As for foraging, she didn't know how to tell poisonous berries from nonpoisonous. She knew people *could* do it, but she was fuzzy on the details as to *how.*

"We may just need to be hungry for a while," Reyva said.

"Not loving that idea either," Mariana said.

Reyva snapped, "Open to a better one."

"Sorry. That wasn't aimed at you. Just the situation in general. I mean, look at us. Can't really get any worse than this."

Claire winced. "Please don't say that."

"Seriously," Reyva said to Mariana. "I'm not superstitious, but even I think you should spit three times or whatever."

They all fell silent. Claire listened to the rain splash into the bucket at the base of the ladder. Across the bunker, Mariana began to shed her clothes, kicking off her shoes and stripping off her shirt. She pulled on new, dry clothes and transferred her phone, the battery, and the pack of gum into her new pockets.

Now wearing a hot-pink shirt, Mariana tied another flannel shirt around her waist, over her cuffed jean shorts. This one was green plaid. When she saw Claire looking, she said, "I packed for Maine. I heard flannel is, like, the required uniform. Plus, classic bi look. Couldn't resist the chance to embrace such a fashion cliché." She waved her hand at their packs. "Come on, change. You'll feel better in dry clothes."

"Did your clothes stay dry?" Reyva asked.

"You'll feel better in *drier* clothes," Mariana corrected herself.

Sitting on the floor, Claire took off her wet sneakers and socks. She wiggled her toes. They looked as pruny as if she'd soaked in the bath. She twisted and squeezed one of her socks, and water poured out of it.

That gave her an idea. She held her other sock over her open mouth and squeezed. Rainwater dribbled onto her tongue, and she drank it greedily.

"Ew," Mariana said.

"No brain-eating lake bacteria in socks."

"Fair point. But not thirsty enough for sock water. Shirt water, sure." She squeezed a few drops from her soaked shirt. "I'm not giving up. No matter what."

Rolling her eyes at both of them, Reyva scooped a handful of water from the bucket at the bottom of the ladder, as if to say she wasn't giving up either. None of it was *enough* water, of course—they needed those jars by the shore—but at least, Claire thought, her tongue no longer felt like cardboard.

"You know, my parents' insult of choice is 'quitter,'" Reyva said. "'You don't want to be a quitter.' 'We didn't raise a quitter.' As if that's the worst thing you could be."

"Our parents would make excellent friends," Mariana said. "Mine think the worst is to be seen as a failure. Above all, everyone has to understand that you're successful. Sending their daughter to an enrichment camp—they thought that was quite the power move, as if it would make up for . . ." Once again, she cut herself off. She finished: ". . . whatever else."

"Mine want me to be happy," Claire said, "but only they get to define what that looks like." She shut her mouth. She didn't want to go down that road any more than Mariana wanted to finish her sentence.

Looking away from the others, Claire changed into drier clothes. So did Reyva. They spread out their squeezed-but-still-wet clothes in one corner. Claire didn't have much faith that they'd dry, but it was better than balling them up sopping wet. She supposed they could leave them behind if they weren't dry by morning. The less they carried, the better.

In fact, it would be best if they carried as little as possible. She dumped out all but her toothbrush and toothpaste, a change of clothes in case of more rain, extra socks, the Swiss Army knife and broken blade, and her first-aid kit. Seeing her, Reyva also began to weed through her clothes, all black, leaving a small pile next to her. Mariana tossed out a hair dryer, followed by multiple outfits. Her pile was more like a large mound.

"Can't say I love the smell of this place," Mariana said as she repacked. "It's got a unique mildewed-locker-room-mixed-with-unclean-zoo odor. It would make the world's worst scented candle. But you were right, Claire—it's dry." Sealing up her pack, she cast a wistful glance at the abandoned clothes. "We'll wait out the storm and then—"

Thud.

Everything darkened. Only Reyva's phone lit the bunker.

Claire sprang to her feet. So did Reyva. "What was that?" Reyva asked.

"The trapdoor," Mariana said. "It's shut."

Both Reyva and Mariana went over to look up the shaft. Claire felt her heart beat harder and faster against her rib cage.

"There's a storm. Lots of wind. It blew shut," Reyva said.

Shivering hard, Claire could only shake her head. Her throat felt clogged, and her heart was racing. It felt difficult to suck in enough oxygen. She knew she'd pushed the lid open flat on the ground. There was absolutely no way that any wind, no matter how hard, could have blown it shut.

Someone had closed it.

EIGHT

Crossing to the ladder, Mariana craned her neck to look up at the hatch. "So, here's a delightful fear: being buried alive. Never used to be my greatest fear, but could be now." She shuddered and hugged her arms. "Six feet under, dirt pressing down, air running out."

"Don't be melodramatic," Reyva said. "This isn't like that. It just blew shut in the storm. I'll open it." She began to climb the ladder.

Louder, Claire said, "Don't."

Reyva stopped halfway up the ladder.

"It wasn't the wind."

"Of course it was the wind," Mariana said. "What else—oh."

Jumping down, Reyva backed away from the ladder. All of them stared up at the trapdoor. Claire felt as cold as if she were still soaked through. She couldn't stop shaking. "I left it open all the way. Flat on the ground. No wind could've blown it shut. Wind doesn't work that way. It wouldn't have had the leverage to flip it. A person, on the other hand . . ."

"We don't know it's the killer," Mariana whispered.

Claire raised her eyebrows, and Reyva gave a snort. No one friendly would have closed the hatch. There was no reason to do it, except to trap them down here.

"Maybe we can talk our way out of this?"

Reyva whispered, "I'm calling it: white, middle-aged male in a tank top or camo."

"So if it *is* a walking cliché who is the killer—" Mariana continued.

"A cliché for a reason," Claire said. "Eighty-eight percent of homicides are by men, with the highest rate among men ages twenty to thirty-nine."

"Okay, not going to even ask why you know that," Mariana said. "So if *he* is up there, then odds are he'll underestimate us. Everyone always underestimates and undervalues teenage girls. Especially white middle-aged men in tank tops or camo. So we use that. We act like we think he's our hero. Greet him like he's saving us. We pretend to be scared and helpless. Use sexism to keep him off-balance. If he sees us as harmless—"

"We have one Swiss Army knife between three of us," Claire pointed out. "We *are* harmless." Besides, it wasn't as if she had experience stabbing anyone. It didn't exactly come up in ballet class.

"MMA girl can throw a punch."

"I do have an excellent right hook," Reyva admitted.

"He has a *gun*, in case you've forgotten," Claire said, slightly louder than a whisper. And then quieter: "And he's already proved he's willing to use it."

He was most likely up there right now, waiting to see what

they'd do, ready to pick them off one by one as they emerged from the bunker. Or else he was waiting for the rain to stop, and he'd come down at his leisure, with his gun.

She sucked in air. It felt like there was less oxygen than there had been. She told herself to quit being absurd. There was plenty of air. Unless there wasn't. Unless the lid was airtight. Unless they really were buried alive.

Stop it, she told herself. *Just breathe.*

Taking even breaths, Claire tried to think. *Solve the puzzle.* "If he comes down the ladder . . ."

". . . then we'll have the advantage," Reyva finished, even though that wasn't what Claire had planned to say. "He'll have to hold on with at least one hand. And he'll be feetfirst, not gun-first. We'll know he's coming long before he has any angle to fire."

Mariana nodded. "Okay. Great. I like the way you think. So what do we do?"

"Hit him in the back of his knees," Reyva said. "Knock him off the ladder."

Claire pictured the possibilities. They'd hear the trapdoor—he couldn't surprise them. If they could incapacitate him before he could attack them, they might have a chance. She cast around for anything they could use: clothes, toiletries, the bucket . . . "Look for weapons. Anyone have anything we can spray in his eyes?" Kneeling next to her supplies, she pocketed the Swiss Army knife, as well as the broken blade.

"Spray-on suntan lotion." Freeing it from her pile of discarded items, Mariana held it up in the air like a trophy. "Stings like hell if it gets in your eyes, says personal experience."

"That'll work," Claire said.

"There are three of us," Reyva said. "One of him. We can do this."

With her suntan lotion, Mariana joined Reyva at the base of the ladder. Reyva stood in a fighter's stance, both hands curled into fists.

Claire paused her search through her pack to look at them. So ready. So brave. They weren't panicking or dissolving into puddles like she wanted to do. She felt tears prick the corners of her eyes. She liked these girls. A lot. She wasn't certain when that feeling had started, but she was certain about one thing: *I don't want to watch them die.*

This was a terrible, desperate plan with a high probability of failure. Odds were she wouldn't have to see them die, because she'd be dead too.

Not a reassuring thought.

"If he comes down that ladder," Reyva said, "we knock him off, pin him down, take the gun, and lock him in that nicely convenient cage. Got it?"

"Got it," Mariana said.

But Claire said, "If."

"Sorry?" Mariana said.

"*If* he comes down the ladder. He doesn't have to. He can wait us out. Eventually, we'll run out of food and water. Water first." The bucket had only gathered an inch of rainwater. If their captor had decent supplies, all he'd have to do was wait. Eventually, either they'd be forced to emerge, or they'd be too weak to fight back when he came down to finish them off.

Reyva lowered her fists. "You're right."

She knew that she was.

"I hate that you're right."

She knew that too, and she hated it too.

"So, now what?" Mariana asked. "We can't just sit here, waiting for him to decide the time is right to . . . you know." She dropped her voice even lower on the words *you know*.

Claire tapped her fingers, counting the taps as she thought. The killer had two options: come down or wait them out. And they had two options: stay or go.

Not up, though.

That was not an option.

Turning her back on the ladder, Claire faced the opening to the cave that they had all been so studiously ignoring since coming down here. "We could see where that leads."

She braced herself, expecting a round of arguments.

But Mariana just turned on her phone's light and aimed it at the hole. "Lesser of two evils."

Reyva nodded. "Sure."

Just . . . sure? Really? Claire stared at both of them and then at the hole in the wall. It looked as if the concrete had been gnawed away. The edges were rough and crumbly. Beyond it was a tunnel of rocks and dirt. Roots dangled down, squeezed between the rocks.

It wasn't impossible, she thought, that someone had used this tunnel before—for example, when fleeing the Lake House fire. They could be embarking on a well-trod escape route. Or the path could lead to a dead end. *Emphasis on* dead, she thought.

Always fearless, Reyva said, "Okay, let's do this."

Reyva climbed through the hole first, with her slimmed-down pack on her back and her phone in one hand. Mariana followed. *What makes them so brave?* Claire wondered. If she'd been asked the same question, Claire knew how she would've answered. She would have said: *I'm not.* She was just well practiced at faking it. She didn't know, though, what gave Reyva and Mariana the strength to continue.

Or why they trusted her enough to listen to her. Her friends, classmates, random acquaintances . . . most of the people she knew discounted her as the pessimist, the downer, the scaredy-cat. Once, with Priya, she'd tried to convince her to leave a party early. Don't go to the bonfire. Don't drink so much. Don't trust Zach; he doesn't care about you.

You're afraid of living, Priya had told her.

No, she'd said. *I'm afraid of dying.*

She'd been right, partially: the cops had come, but Priya had accused her of calling them, even though she hadn't. . . . Claire didn't know why she was thinking of this now. At least Zach hadn't been an arsonist/murderer.

Reyva and Mariana listen when I say we have to leave. They seemed to care what she said and what she thought. *Please don't let them find out I'm faking it.*

Claire followed them into the tunnel, also with her mostly-empty backpack and phone. She glanced back once, into the shadowy bunker. It was full of proof that they'd been there: their wet clothes, all their muddy footprints, everything they'd left behind, but there was no sense in trying to hide that. If the killer didn't know they were here already, he'd have had no reason to shut the hatch.

Of course, by leaving, they were losing their advantage if he decided to come down the ladder—it was obvious they'd been there, and it was obvious where they'd gone—but maybe he didn't know about the tunnel. Maybe he thought he'd taken care of them by trapping them in a hole without food or water, and he'd already left the area.

She kept telling herself that as they fumbled their way through the cave: this was the best out of two terrible choices. Unless it wasn't, of course. It was possible that the cave didn't have an exit. Or that it narrowed so much a person couldn't squeeze through. Or it could have pits or crevasses they could fall into, cliffs they could fall off, or underground rivers they could drown in.

"One step at a time," Reyva murmured ahead of her.

"I know," Claire whispered back.

"I can hear you panicking. You're stressing me out."

"Sorry. I'll panic quieter."

Mariana spoke up. "You can't tell me you're all chill about this, Reyva."

"I'm not chill," Reyva said. "I'm controlled. There's a difference."

Climbing over another rock, Claire kept a tight grip on her phone and hoped the battery didn't die while they were down here. The cave wasn't a nice, friendly tunnel with a flat floor for tourists to walk along. It was a jumble of boulders with roots dangling between them.

"So what *does* make you freak out?" Mariana said.

"We're back to this?" Reyva asked. "Why do you want to know what scares me?"

"Well, I don't really. Just want to get to know *you* since we're together in this." Mariana climbed over another rock and ducked beneath a root.

Claire tried not to think about all the rocks pressing in on them or how much earth and rock was above them. It felt like it wanted to squeeze them in a fist of rocks. What if it collapsed? Cave-ins happened all the time. What if they dislodged a key support and caused the cave-in? *No one would ever know how we died*, she thought. *Or even that we died. We'd be missing.* Another set of faces on TV. An unsolved case.

She thought of her parents. Maybe they'd started to worry— she hadn't checked in or texted to tell them she'd arrived safely or that she hated the food, hadn't made any friends, had poison ivy and a million mosquito bites, and could she please come home. What would they do when they realized she wasn't coming home? How long would they search for her? She wondered if they'd blame themselves, or each other, for sending her here. Truthfully, she kind of blamed them. And herself. She wished she'd told them what she really felt, that she didn't want to go, rather than assuming—like she always did and like everyone always made her feel—that what she felt was wrong or irrelevant.

"Come on," Mariana said. "Fill the silence. I hate silence. Especially this one. It's not a nice, companionable silence. It's an ominous silence. Talk to me. What's your greatest fear?"

Mariana was right about the silence, Claire thought. It pressed in on them as if it had its own weight. Like the darkness beyond their phones' lights. The darkness and the silence had a thickness to it that could smother.

"Death," Reyva said.

"Nope," Mariana said. "You barely flinched at the corpse."

"Hugs," Reyva said.

"More plausible. Keep going."

Reyva huffed as she scrambled over a boulder. "You know when you run into someone you know but don't really like and they go for a hug? You try for a wave, but no, they're just going for it, and you can't dodge, and so there you are. And it's no A-frame hug either. A full-body squeeze. You imagine drop-kicking them into the sun, but you know what your parents would say if you did that. So you're just stuck until they decide they're done. Horrifying."

"So you fear intimacy," Mariana said.

"Not exactly what I said."

She doubted that was what Reyva really feared. She'd noticed that Reyva cut herself off whenever she talked about life before the Lake House. So, for that matter, did Mariana.

Claire heard pebbles skitter, and she froze. "What was that?"

The others stopped. Listened.

"What?" Mariana asked.

She didn't hear anything else. "Must have just been loose rocks." But she shivered. The air was damp and chilled within the cave, and it smelled musty, like wet chalk. It was like crawling through a dusty refrigerator, thick with the miasma of rotten food.

"Your turn, Claire," Mariana said. "Greatest fear?"

"Me?" *So many to choose from*, she thought. They really didn't want to know the litany of things she feared. It was far better if they thought she had a normal number of ordinary fears. "Guess I'm not a fan of the dark."

"Yeah, no one is," Mariana said. "Try again. Deep down, what do you fear?"

Deep down . . . I'm afraid I'm made of fear, Claire thought. *Instead of bones: fear. Instead of blood: fear. Instead of a heart and lungs: fear. I'm afraid I am just faking being a normal person, capable of dealing with things in a normal way. And my greatest fear is that someone will see that. My greatest fear is that you'll see me for who I am.* But she obviously wasn't about to say any of that out loud. At best, she'd sound melodramatic. At worst . . . Well, they wouldn't understand regardless. No one ever did. Not her parents. Not her friends. Maybe her grandfather would have, but he was gone and she'd never asked him. "Can we not talk about this right now? In fact, probably better if we're quiet."

"Seconded," Reyva said.

Mariana huffed. "Fine."

Quiet, they focused on sliding around a boulder. Claire tried not to think about what it would be like to be underground in an earthquake, the ground shifting around them and the boulders squeezing together. Maine didn't have many earthquakes. Or any, that she knew of.

"Just to reiterate in case you missed it the first time, I hate silence," Mariana said.

Neither Claire nor Reyva replied.

As the cave narrowed, they dropped to hands and knees and crawled. The rough rock scraped like sandpaper on Claire's knees. She tried to breathe evenly. The air was motionless. She felt as if her throat was coated in dirt. She imagined her lungs filling with dirt, her muscles solidifying into stone, her body becoming a part of the cave. What if they never made it out? What if there was no out?

Her phone beeped. Low battery.

Oh no.

She glanced at it. Five percent left. And the time said 7:03 p.m. Only about an hour and a half left of daylight outside. Not that it mattered down here.

"Hey, it widens!" Reyva called.

Ahead, Reyva disappeared from view. She was followed by Mariana dropping out of sight. For an instant, Claire was alone in the narrow crawl space between the rocks. She sucked in air and forced herself to keep moving.

She crawled forward, and her hand landed on air.

Standing in the larger cave, Reyva and Mariana were shining their lights in all directions. Emerging behind them, Claire stood. She dusted dirt off her knees and breathed in. Still damp and musty. At least, though, there was room enough to stand, which made her feel slightly less as if she were going to die squeezed between rocks. Yay for that. "Which way now?"

Their beams danced over the rock. "There." Mariana aimed her phone upward. High above them, three-quarters of the way up a slope of rocks, was an opening that disappeared into darkness.

A way out?

It would be a climb to reach it, but it wasn't impossible.

"Or there." Reyva aimed her light across the cave, at another tunnel that was about six feet high and three wide. Easier to reach, but it looked as if it led farther into the earth rather than up and out. "Or . . . we could choose door number three." She pointed her phone's light at a third tunnel that looked like a mouth with rocks as teeth that would chew them up before swallowing.

"We have choices. How fabulous," Mariana said. "Any ideas how we can tell which way to go?"

Crossing the cave, Claire peered into the tunnel. Same damp air. Same musty smell. She held her hand out, trying to feel if there was any air movement. For all she could tell, it led to the center of the earth.

"Pick one at random?" Reyva suggested.

"Hate that idea," Mariana said.

All three of them stared at the cave, as if it would give them some clue. Claire studied each opening. Choice A was higher up (which meant it could lead out) but smaller (which meant it could also become too narrow for them to fit). Choice B was wider and looked smoother. Easier going, but to where? Choice C was thick with roots.

She didn't know if there was any way of knowing which was the right choice. Or if they had time to make a mistake, before the killer caught up with them. If there were even a hint of light from any of them, then they'd be able to make an intelligent decision. . . . She had an idea.

"Turn off your lights." Claire turned off her phone's light.

After a second's delay, the others turned off theirs, and the darkness closed around them. She marveled again at the fact that they listened to her and trusted her. Maybe, all this time, she'd just had the wrong friends. That was a novel thought.

"Um, why did we do that?" Mariana asked, her voice a bit shrill.

"Wait for your eyes to adjust," Claire said, "then look for any light."

She closed her eyes, trying to speed up her pupils expanding, and when she opened her eyes again, she couldn't tell that she'd raised her eyelids. She blinked and blinked again. She'd never been in a darkness so absolute. Her finger strayed over the flashlight button.

Now she was the one who wanted to fill the silence.

"So what's *your* greatest fear, Mariana?" Claire asked in a whisper.

The darkness made you feel as if you could only whisper. Even then, her voice sounded distant. Claire wished they'd been standing closer when she'd had her bright idea to turn out the lights. She heard their breathing—all three of their breaths sounded thunder-loud in the silence and stillness of the cave.

"Being vulnerable," Mariana said automatically. "Therapist nailed that in one. I have a great need to be capable. So that makes my greatest fear: being helpless, being powerless. Like, you know, now."

Claire thought about that as she stared into the darkness.

"Yeah, okay, I'm stealing your answer," Reyva said.

"Me too," Claire said.

Pivoting slowly, she strained to see any hint of light. Wait, could she see layers of grayness? Maybe to the left and up . . . Yes, there were shadows several feet above them, a hint of daylight filtering into the darkness. That had to be the way out! Up, toward the first tunnel she'd seen. She opened her mouth to tell the others, then felt a brush of wind ruffle her sleeve.

She swung around and tapped her phone's screen—

Neither the flashlight nor the screen turned on. Not even the dead-battery icon.

"Reyva? Mariana?" She couldn't help the terrible note of panic that shook her voice. She tried to breathe calmly, evenly. She'd known the battery was low. It must have finally run out. This shouldn't be a surprise. Except she'd thought it would last a little longer. It had only been a few minutes since it had beeped.

"You all right?" Reyva asked. Her voice sounded distant, almost underwater.

Another brush of wind, this time from the opposite direction. Pivoting, she strained to see, to hear. She was afraid to speak again. Whoever was there would hear her. He'd find them. She felt her heart beat faster, like a bird's wings beating against her rib cage.

It's your imagination, she told herself. *There's no one here.*

They would have heard the trapdoor. Or footsteps in the cave. Or seen another light. The killer couldn't be down here with them—they would have heard him, wouldn't they?

"Hold your breath," Claire whispered. She stopped breathing. Beside her, she heard Reyva and Mariana inhale and then not exhale. She listened.

She thought she heard breathing.

Or wind.

Maybe it's wind.

Please, let it be wind.

She exhaled. "Did you hear that?"

Very, very softly, Reyva said, "We're not alone."

NINE

Not alone.

Not alone.

Not alone.

The words ricocheted inside Claire's brain until they sounded as loud as a howl. She felt a brush of air against her cheek, and she jumped back.

Where? Which way was safe?

If we can't see him, he can't see us, she thought.

But he would hear them breathing. She felt as if her heart was thumping loud enough to be heard from the moon. Certainly he'd hear them if they moved. If they didn't move, though . . . She again imagined dirt in her throat, rocks in her veins.

The longer they stood in the dark, barely breathing, the more she thought she could see shadows: darker ones overlaying with lighter grays, but only in one direction.

Mariana whispered, "Did you feel that?"

"What?" Reyva asked.

"Wind."

"I felt it," Claire said.

Maybe it had been wind. Maybe they were alone, and it was her imagination befriending her fear. Except that Reyva had felt it too, that certainty that someone else was near.

They fell silent again, listening. Claire felt as if every hair on her arms was alert, every muscle tense. She kept turning her head, peering into the blackness, as if that would make it possible to see.

A low whistle.

Wind again? Or was it the sound from a throat?

She didn't hear any footsteps. Only her own breathing, too fast, and the thump of her heart, also too fast. Beside her, she heard Mariana and Reyva breathing in syncopated rhythm with each other.

"There's someone here," Mariana said, her voice barely louder than an exhale.

"It's the dark messing with us," Reyva said. Claire heard the click of plastic, then a rattle. Then: "My phone won't turn on. Battery must be out. Mariana?"

"Mine's not working either," Mariana reported. "Claire?"

All three phones couldn't have simultaneously died. Yet they had. "Dead," Claire said. Then amended, "The phone. Not me." *Yet*, her brain helpfully added. She felt prickles all over her skin, as if the darkness were full of hands and claws reaching for her.

"Move toward me," Mariana said, certainty in her voice. "We have to stick together."

Shuffling her feet forward, Claire felt her way toward Mariana's voice. She held out one hand in front of her, as if she could pierce the darkness. Mariana kept talking in a low murmur:

"This way, toward me, over here . . ." At last, her hand met flesh. "Got you. Okay, Claire?"

"It's me," she said. "Where's Reyva?"

A hand landed on Claire's arm, and she bit back a scream.

"I'm here," Reyva said.

Claire patted her hand. "This is you, yes?"

"Yes, obviously. Who else—" Reyva cut herself off. "Don't answer that. There's no evidence there's anyone else here. We just need to stay calm and controlled and not let our imaginations run away with our common sense. Now that we're together, which way—"

Pebbles rattled in the distance.

All three of them froze.

Claire tried to pinpoint where the sound had come from. Behind them?

She heard a grunt-like huff of air. *That was* not *wind,* she thought. *Was it?* It had come from the same direction as the pebbles. There was someone crawling through the same cave they'd used. She was sure of it. Mostly sure.

Wordlessly, she tugged on the others' arms. They needed to *move.* Stay here, and they'd be caught, or at the very least, scare themselves to death. They had to keep moving. Toward the visible shadows above them. Toward the wind, if they felt it again.

She inhaled deeply, as quietly as she could. The air still tasted musty.

She pulled them down so they could crawl—it would be safer if they felt their way forward, she thought. Together, bumping into one another, they crawled over the rocks. Claire led the way, keeping her gaze fixed upward on the lighter gray, hoping that meant the way to eventual sunlight.

She heard the others breathing beside her. Her knees scraped against the ground, but her primary goal was silence. Disturb nothing. Make no sound.

Reaching the wall of the cave, she felt for a handgrip. Her fingers touched a ledge. She gripped it. Slowly, she climbed upward, toward what she hoped was the way out. She heard the sounds of Reyva and Mariana climbing too, hand over hand, up toward the shadows.

She began to lose track of time. Had they been climbing for seconds or minutes? Had they been in this cave for hours or days? It felt as if nothing existed but the darkness and the silence. She wondered how high up they were. If they fell . . .

Keep climbing, she told herself.

Maybe she'd imagined that the shadows were grayer above. Maybe it wasn't sunlight at all. Or maybe when they reached the light, it would be a crack too small for them to squeeze through.

She could have made the wrong choice.

The others were trusting her.

They don't know me, she thought. If they knew, they'd pity her. Certainly wouldn't befriend her. They'd distance themselves, like everyone else did.

Afraid of my own shadow, that's me.

Except here she had no shadow.

A whisper of wind breathed in her face. She inhaled—it tasted cleaner, fresher. She crawled toward it. Closed her eyes. Opened them again. Her pack pulled against her shoulders, and she was glad she'd emptied so much of it.

She felt a hand touch her ankle and bit back a scream.

"Just me," Mariana whispered.

Pebbles rattled, falling down the rock wall into the cave below.

"Also me."

Claire listened for any sound that wasn't the three of them. It was difficult to differentiate who made which sound. Was that scuffle Reyva or Mariana? Was it someone else?

If the killer was in the caves with them, why hadn't he come with a flashlight or a phone light or anything? Was he feeling his way through the tunnel? How close was he? Had his light failed too? That seemed unlikely. Maybe the killer was so familiar with these caves that he didn't need it. He could be following them by sound. She wanted to freeze, like a deer that's been spotted.

Hunters shoot deer, she told herself, and kept crawling.

She inhaled, and this time there was a hint of pine beneath all the dirt and gravelly taste that coated her tongue. She thought she saw a differentiation in the degree of blackness above her, a darker rock against a lighter one. She climbed a little faster.

Reaching, her hand hit empty air. She felt around and touched the edges of a hole. A hole that led out? She definitely smelled the unmistakable tang of pine trees. She climbed toward it. Her hand landed on pebbles, and they shifted, tumbling down to the cave floor—a long way now. She froze. Behind her, she heard Reyva's and Mariana's breaths seize.

And then she heard something else.

A laugh.

Slight and breathy. A snicker. It sounded as if it came from everywhere, and then it faded. *Just the wind,* she told herself. It was a good thing, the sound. It meant they were close to an exit. She forced herself to breathe again and to keep climbing.

She saw a sliver of sunlight, a zigzag like a permanent lightning strike, above her. *Sunlight!* She climbed faster toward it, wishing she dared speak out loud to tell the others. She kept her eyes fixed on the light.

At last she saw it: the opening above her.

It was narrow, but she thought she could squeeze out. Wiggling out of her pack, she shoved it up and out, then she reached both arms through, braced herself on the other side, and then tried to lever herself up. She wiggled, hearing pebbles and dirt dislodged. Behind her, Mariana and Reyva cried out softly. "Sorry," she said. "Almost there!"

Half out.

Leaning over, she clawed her fingers into the dirt. She pulled herself up. Hips. Then knees. Last, feet. She crawled out of the hole and then half tumbled and half slid until she splatted stomach-first on the soggy, flat ground.

The rain had stopped, thankfully, and everything smelled like wet earth. She rolled onto her back and squinted up at the blue sky between the branches of the trees. It was still daylight, though judging by the shadows, the sun was low in the sky. They were lucky it was early summer, with its late sunset and early sunrise. The wet leaves soaked into her back, and she knew she should move—they had limited time before it was too dark to travel—but she didn't want to.

She breathed in. Fresh air! Closing her eyes, she breathed while listening to the others tossing their packs out, then climbing out then down to flop next to her.

They panted side by side, lying on the ground, in the silent woods.

Why was it so silent?

Opening her eyes, Claire sat up. She scanned the trees. Every second since they'd stepped foot off that boat, the forest had been thick with birdcalls: twittering, tweeting, cawing, crying, singing, in an overlapping cacophony that never stopped.

But now the birds were quiet.

"I think we should move," Claire whispered.

"Never want to move again," Mariana said.

Reyva snorted. "Never want to see a cave again. Especially that one."

Claire got to her feet. She turned slowly in a circle, looking for motion through the trees. Even the wind was silent.

But if that was so, was it wind she'd heard in the cave?

Twelve times one, twelve. Twelve times two, twenty-four. Thirty-six. Forty-eight. Sixty. Seventy-two. Eighty-four. Ninety-six. One hundred eight. . . . She didn't feel calmer. She switched to reciting the digits of pi: *Three point one four one five nine two six five three five eight . . .*

Water dripped from the leaves, steady. Everything glistened with droplets. The ground felt soggy beneath her. She should have heard sound beyond the fall of leftover rain, shaken from the trees. But there wasn't a single chirp or warble.

Reyva got up too. "What is it?"

"No birds," Claire whispered.

Reyva nudged Mariana with her foot. Groaning, she pushed herself up to standing.

In three directions there was only forest: spruce and hemlock, maple and birch. Bushes, ferns, and brambles wove a thick knee-high layer of undergrowth between them. The low sun cast long shadows over all of it.

In the fourth direction was a mound made of boulder-size rocks and packed dirt. Halfway up, on an angle, was the hole they'd climbed out of, the entrance to the cave. No green grew on the mound, not even moss or the pale gray lichen that grew in lacy patterns over the other rocks. Just a pile of rock and dirt, slick from the rain.

It made her think of a cemetery. Specifically, a freshly covered grave. She tried not to think about the fact that they could have died down there. It could have been their tomb.

Staring at the hole they'd climbed out of, she shuddered. It was unmarked and half hidden by the shadows of the rocks above it. If someone were to fall in there by accident . . . They'd climbed a long way up. It would be a deadly fall. *We won't come near here again*, she thought. She fixed the rock formation in her mind: an array of boulders with the cave opening tucked between them. She wouldn't accidentally stumble over it.

"Any idea where we are?" Mariana asked in a whisper.

"Somewhere we shouldn't be," Claire whispered back.

Out of the corner of her eye, she saw the ferns shudder.

Grabbing Reyva's and Mariana's arms, she stepped backward. They stepped with her.

It could be a squirrel. Or a bird. If they were going to flee, they had to be sure they ran in the right direction, ideally toward the lake. Once they found the water, they could follow the shoreline to civilization. Begin their trek out of here. Leave this nightmare behind.

A bony hand clamped onto Claire's arm.

She was ripped away from Reyva and spun around. She saw him in a flash: tattered jeans caked with blood, a torn shirt with a single sleeve, mud-caked beard, straggly red-streaked-with-gray hair in clumps.

She screamed.

The man screamed back at her, spittle hitting her face. "You!" He shook her, gripping her arm so hard that it felt as if he was digging his fingers into her skin. His fingers were coated in caked-on dirt and dried blood. "It's you!"

Mariana kicked him hard in the knee, while Reyva pulled her right fist back and let it fly at his face. She connected with his cheekbone, and he reeled back. Claire yanked away, falling backward as she pulled out of his grip. She landed on the ground with a thump that rattled through her bones.

Clutching the side of his face, he lunged for Mariana. "Is it you? Tell me!"

Mariana skittered sideways as he swiped at her. Shoving her hand into her pocket, she withdrew her suntan lotion. She sprayed it in his eyes, and he howled.

"Run," Reyva commanded as she yanked Claire onto her feet.

Together, the three of them sprinted away from the wild man. Claire felt her heart racing and her mind screaming so loudly that it drowned every thought but *run*. She glanced back.

Wiping at his eyes, tears streaming down his cheeks, he chased after them in loping, wolflike strides, trampling ferns and plowing through bushes. "Stop! I have to know! Am I free?"

A branch slapped Claire's cheek. She felt it sting and stumbled from the shock. Reyva pulled her forward. And then Mariana skidded to a stop, forcing Claire and Reyva to stop too.

Claire felt a sharp pain as the wild man seized a wad of her hair. Screaming, she grabbed the back of her head and lunged forward. Reyva, fists ready, stopped and faced him.

"Man! Gun!" Mariana yelled.

All of them turned to see a second man, this one in camo with a trimmed beard and a shotgun in his hand, by the cave. He stopped, raised the gun, aiming at them.

The wild man instantly released Claire.

"It's you!" He hissed like a cat and then ran, back bent, with arms swinging, toward the man with the gun. Over his shoulder, he called to the three girls, "Run! Don't let it take you!"

Unfazed, the man kept the gun leveled, aiming toward the girls as if he didn't see the other man, until the wild man barreled into him, grabbing him around the waist. His shot fired wildly toward the sky, sounding like a crack of thunder and shaking the leaves until they rained down, as the two men fell.

Claire, Reyva, and Mariana ran.

TEN

You can't run in a straight line through the Maine woods. You weave between trees. You clamber over fallen logs. You watch for rocks. Brambles grab your sleeves, your hair. They scratch your arms and your face. Any exposed skin.

You can't run quietly through the woods either. You crunch dead leaves. You crack fallen twigs. You thump down on rocks, and you squish through mud.

And you leave a trail, if you aren't careful.

It was only after they'd run wildly over roots, rocks, and dead leaves with no other goal but *away* that Claire cleared a spot in her mind to think again:

Two men in the woods.

One had scared them, then saved them. The other had tried to shoot them. And either could easily follow the track they'd left behind—a wide swath of broken twigs, crushed leaves, and trampled ferns. Even she, who had never tracked anyone in her life, could have followed the trail they were leaving.

"Stop," she panted.

The others slowed.

She leaned over, hands on her knees, and tried to catch her breath. Her side ached, and she felt coated in a sheen of sweat. She listened to the birds calling from tree to tree, like children squabbling over a toy. *They're back*, she noticed.

"We lost them," Mariana said. "Right?"

"Not for long." Claire pointed to the obvious trail behind them. With the recent rain, it was worse. She could see their footprints in the muddy ground as clear as if it were a pack of elephants tromping through the forest.

"Maybe they won't follow us," Mariana said.

Both Claire and Reyva snorted at that. Claire said, "Enormous forest, yet they just happened to be right by the cave exit?"

"You think they were waiting for us?" Mariana asked.

She hadn't fully thought it through, but— "Yes. Definitely." If you wanted to catch a mouse, you closed up one hole and then waited for it to emerge from the other hole. Someone had sealed the trapdoor shut knowing there was only one other way out.

"Why?" Mariana asked. "And what was up with the guy who hadn't showered or shaved in a millennium? Why did he attack us, and then attack the man with the gun? Did they know each other? Wait—don't answer that. Let's make sure we're safe before we do postgame analysis. Are we safe?"

Listening, Claire heard the moment the birdcalls stopped. The forest was dead quiet. "Not safe. Keep running."

The others didn't ask any questions. They just started running. In the distance, Claire heard a trickle of water and had an idea. She veered toward the sound, and Reyva and Mariana followed, like birds in a flock, again trusting her without a word.

She wondered if they had any idea how much that trust meant to her. Panting hard, she had no breath to tell them.

Soon, she spotted it: a stream, tumbling over mossy rocks. It bubbled and gushed and gurgled as if it were trying to chatter with them as it jumped and wound between the trees.

Reyva and Mariana didn't slow. They jumped over the water, their sneakers squelching in the mud on the opposite side, but Claire halted in the middle. The water soaked through her sneakers into her formerly dry socks.

"Hey," she called softly, a stage whisper.

They stopped and looked back.

"Retrace your steps, carefully," Claire said in a loud whisper. She pointed at the stream. "If we walk in the water, they won't know where we've gone." She didn't know if it would fool an expert tracker who expected tricks like this, but there was a chance that their pursuers could underestimate them.

Carefully, they walked backward. Closer to the stream, they sank a half inch into the mud, deepening their prints but not adding any new ones. They joined Claire in the brisk, bubbling water.

"Which way?" Mariana whispered.

"Downstream," Claire said. It would lead them to the lake. Eventually.

Following Claire downstream, they walked single file. They couldn't run through the water—the mossy rocks were too slick. They had to pick their way carefully, from rock to rock, but they left no footprints.

Claire continued onward relentlessly, leading them through

the bitingly cold water that varied between an inch and ankle-deep.

She tried not to think about how thirsty she was. Or how hungry. Or how low the sun was. The trees were so thick that she couldn't see it, but it had to be close to dusk.

Eventually, a bird called, and then another.

"I—I think we're okay," Claire said softly.

"My shoes aren't," Mariana said.

Reyva huffed. "Are you seriously—"

"Obviously I'm not seriously complaining about my shoes," Mariana said. "Except, yeah, my feet are wet, and that's not great."

It's not great, Claire agreed. Hypothermia. Trench foot, also known as immersion foot. Lots of issues with wet feet if they couldn't get them dry. But not being shot at was a much higher priority than that right now. She slowed, catching her breath. A moss-covered flat rock protruded from the stream, and she held her arms out for balance as she walked onto it. She sat on one end. Reyva and Mariana joined her.

"You can't possibly think I'm that shallow," Mariana said.

"I don't know you," Reyva pointed out.

"You do," Mariana said. "We've bonded. All this"—she waved her hands at the trees, the stream, and everything—"running for our lives . . . escaping psychopaths . . . very bonding."

"Rather have skipped it, thanks," Reyva said. "And it's not like you've learned anything about me. All you know is I don't like hugs, and I don't want to die."

Claire took off her shoes and socks and squeezed the water out of them. This wasn't rainwater, and she didn't dare drink it. Her feet felt pruny, and she poked the bottom of them. She wondered at what point trench foot set in and which symptom came first. Numbness? Soreness? Blisters? Smell of decay? "We also know you have an excellent right hook. Thanks for that." She thought of how the two of them had jumped to defend her. No one had ever done that. Granted, no one had ever attacked her before either. *All sorts of new experiences*, she thought.

"That's hardly all we know," Mariana said.

Reyva snorted. "Right. You know what I let you see."

Tossing her still-damp-from-the-rain hair, Mariana straightened as if posing for a photo. "Oh? You wear black because you think it makes you look tough, which it does, by the way. Your whole vibe, badass. But you wear it because you think it fits your self-image of having no emotions, and that's not true. You have plenty of them. You just squash them down. Until they erupt out and you deck a lunatic in the woods. My guess: your parents have opinions on what you're allowed to feel, as well as what you do, and so you respond by controlling what you show the world. You want us to think nothing fazes you. Fact is, you care a lot, and you're terrified that someone will realize it and use it against you. Like, you know, I'm doing right now."

Staring at her, Claire felt like she should applaud or something. That was masterful. And kind of intense. Reyva was staring at her too, an expression of near horror on her face. It was, Claire thought, the most emotion she'd seen on Reyva's face since they'd arrived.

"Or," Mariana said, "I'm off base, and your greatest fear is really just snakes."

Claire looked from Reyva to Mariana then back to Reyva. There were about sixteen emotions warring for supremacy on Reyva's voice, but in the end, she just swallowed and said, "My preschool had a boa constrictor. It was cool. I haven't been afraid of snakes since."

"It had a *what*?" Mariana said. "And the teachers thought this was a good idea?"

"Also had pet mice. I didn't make the connection between the two until years later."

Mariana blinked. "Well. Okay. Definitely don't have time to delve into that."

She was right—there wasn't time to linger. Now that they'd caught their breath, they had to keep going. Pulling her socks and shoes back on, Claire stood and stepped back into the stream. "Let's keep moving."

If they stayed on the move, it would decrease the odds that the two men would catch up to them. *And bonus,* Claire thought, *it'll decrease the odds that Mariana will decide to psychoanalyze me next.*

As the shadows stretched longer, they continued to tromp through the stream. "It would be delightful if we had a plan," Mariana said. "Any idea how we make sure the man with the shotgun and the man in desperate need of a haircut don't find us?"

"Claire, worst case?" Reyva asked.

Claire gawked at her for a second—no one had *ever* asked her that; she tried to imagine Priya or her parents ever asking her that—and then she focused on answering. She glanced up at the wiggle of sky between the branches of the trees. It had flattened to a deep gray blue with a faint smattering of stars. Well past sunset. Soon, very soon, they'd be stumbling around in the complete dark. They had to find a safe place to spend the night. But where? "Worst case, they guess we used the stream to hide our tracks. Only two choices: upstream or downstream. Since downstream heads to the lake, because gravity, and that's the only landmark we know . . . If we stay by the stream, they'll find us eventually."

"Then we move away from the stream," Reyva said. "But not so far that we can't find it again."

Looking around, Claire noted that this area was particularly rocky. If they kept to the rocks to avoid footprints, that should hide their presence. They could tuck themselves into the shadow of one of the boulders that littered the forest. And in the morning, they could continue to follow the stream to the lake, then the lake to safety.

She shared her thoughts with the other two, and they agreed: they'd spend the night away from the stream, as hidden as possible, then return at dawn. Leaving the stream, they selected a decent-size boulder to hide themselves behind.

"No fire?" Mariana said.

"No fire," Claire said.

"How about a barricade?" Mariana asked. "Like hunters use. A deer blind? Wait, that name doesn't make sense. Is that really what it's called? Never mind. Doesn't matter. Whatever it's called, we can make it out of branches and stuff."

Claire loved that idea. "Brilliant."

"Told you: I'm constantly underestimated."

"Not by me," Claire said sincerely.

Mariana stared at her.

"And never again by me," Reyva said, a bit sourly, but then she had been the one who Mariana had psychoanalyzed.

Now Mariana stared at both of them, without words for the first time since they'd arrived. At last, she said, "Thanks."

Together, they gathered fallen branches that were flush with leaves and arranged them like a wall. At Mariana's direction, they laid them haphazardly. Every few minutes, she'd check from a few feet away to make sure it looked natural. As they worked, the forest around them darkened. When it grew too dark to find additional branches, Mariana pronounced them finished. Between the rock and the branches and the darkness, even Claire thought they might survive the night undetected. *Maybe*, she amended.

Behind the blind, they laid their packs on the ground to separate them from the soggy earth. They had to choose their spots by feel, bumping into one another until they settled down side by side. Feeling around in her pack, Claire extracted a T-shirt and rolled it up to use as a pillow. She lay down in the darkness.

"And now . . . we just . . . sleep?" Mariana said.

"That's the idea," Reyva said.

"I don't know how I'm going to sleep," Mariana said.

Claire agreed.

Above, stars dotted the sky. Gray clouds skittered across them. The tree branches swayed in the breeze, creating new views of the sky and blocking old ones. Claire wondered if Mariana had made a wish on the first star.

Shifting, she wished she'd swept the acorns, twigs, and pebbles out from under her "bed." She was going to wake with a thousand inexplicable tiny bruises. But she supposed so long as she woke, that was the key thing.

"I cannot even begin to express how much I want a burrito," Mariana said. Her voice was softer than the crickets. "There was . . . There *is* a food truck across the street from my high school that has the best burritos. Fresh avocado. Carne asada that melts in your mouth. And the cheese—best cheese."

"My mom loves this cheese shop that opened up in our town," Claire said. "She buys the strangest cheeses, the kind where you scrape off the mold rind and the rest is supposed to be delicious but it smells like the inside of a gym locker."

"You're from Connecticut?" Reyva asked.

"Yes." Claire couldn't remember if she'd said it before or not. She didn't think she had. They'd leapt straight over "where are you from" to "what's your deepest fear." She thought about telling them more—about her parents, about how they pushed her to make more friends, about how she pushed everyone away for fear they'd get too close and see too much. . . . Maybe just stick with talking about where she was from. "Did I tell you that?"

"Cheese shop," Reyva said.

She grinned. It was a cute shop, and the old guy who worked there was wonderfully curmudgeonly. He never asked how anyone was doing, which meant she never had to lie. She'd just listen to whatever obscure emo music was playing while he meticulously sliced Mom's stinky cheese.

"Funny how just thinking of a taste can make you remember

everything about a place," Mariana said. "California . . . It's avo-cados and cheese to me. And it's the smell of the marine layer, which is basically just the stench of rotting seaweed and other ocean crap, but I still love it. Other places don't smell like that. When it doesn't smell right . . . makes you feel off, you know? Like you have to try extra hard to make sure the world knows exactly who you are." She let out a strained laugh. "Ugh, listen to me. One or two near-death encounters, and I get all deep."

"I think it's nice that you love your home so much," Claire said. She wasn't sure she could say the same. She felt safe there, yes, and she missed not being in danger—and having ready access to food, water, and a shower—but did she love it? Home held a constant reminder that she was not enough. "Must be a great place."

"Yeah," Mariana said.

That one syllable sounded so forlorn that Claire reached out her hand in the darkness and found Mariana's. Fingers curled around hers for a moment, and Claire thought she was going to say more—perhaps explain why she was so wistful whenever she mentioned home, or why she thought she ever had to try extra hard when she was the most together person that Claire had ever met.

But instead, Mariana released Claire's hand and said in a bright, chipper voice, "Reyva, you have a favorite food? Any-thing special a relative makes for you?"

"My parents defied their families in every way except food. They make only family recipes, mostly curries. Lots of chickpeas and lentils."

"Favorite?" Mariana persisted.

"Not chickpeas and lentils."

Mariana laughed, softly so the sound wouldn't carry through the night.

Beside her, Claire heard Reyva rustle as she shifted positions. "I have one granola bar left," Reyva said. "Split it or save it?"

"Split," Claire voted. Maybe if her stomach wasn't so empty, she'd be able to sleep. Also, they had to keep up their strength, especially if they were going to be running from wild men and dead-eyed hunters.

That was, she decided, the most disturbing thing about the man with the gun: the emptiness in his eyes. Well, that and the gun.

Reyva broke the bar into thirds.

Chewing on her share, Claire listened to the sounds of the forest at night: the crickets, the crunch and crackle of night animals moving through the dead leaves, the wind through the branches. She wished she had water to wash it down. Her mouth felt as dry as if she were chewing chalk. When she finished, she lay down again.

She listened to the others breathe. Counted their breaths, then counted the cricket chirps. At a hundred, she started over.

"You were right," Reyva said after they'd been silent for a while.

"Who was right about what?" Mariana asked.

"You about me."

"Oh. Cool."

"But I don't have to like it."

Claire smiled in the darkness.

The crickets were a steady song. She listened to them, letting the thrum-like chirp soothe her. It reminded her of the ambient music that Mom liked in the background while she worked. She'd encouraged Claire to listen to it too, especially when she felt stressed. Claire had resented being told what to listen to, but she had to admit that it did help. Especially now. She was fairly certain than if any armed man or other predator came tromping through the underbrush, the crickets would stop.

Beneath the song of the crickets, Mariana said softly, "If we're truly bonding, then I should tell you . . . I'm a liar."

The crickets chirped.

"What?" Reyva said.

"I don't live in California," Mariana said. Her voice was dull, almost too quiet to hear. "Not anymore. We picked up and moved in February. To Indiana. Away from my cousins and aunts and uncles and grandparents. All my friends. My school. I was three-quarters of the way through junior year when I had to start over. Would have been president of yearbook next year. And Pride Club. And Math Team. Instead, I had to come out all over again, to complete strangers who didn't care because by junior year, every friend group has calcified. Fun times."

It was bad enough to go to school every day without any close friends. At least everyone at Claire's high school was familiar. She would've hated to have to start over. She imagined walking in new midyear and shuddered. "I'm sorry."

"Why did you move?" Reyva asked.

"That's the kicker," Mariana said. "We had to, because Dad

131

screwed up. At work. He borrowed . . . No, he *took* money that wasn't his. Said it was just a mistake. But he stole it. Because he wanted to impress people. Because he thought we needed it. Because having it fit his self-image better. Stupid reasons. But it doesn't matter why. He stole it." Her voice broke.

She's crying, Claire thought. She couldn't see Mariana's face in the darkness, but she could hear it in her voice. She reached out her hand and took Mariana's again.

This time, Mariana didn't let go.

"He could have been arrested," Mariana said. "But they didn't press charges. It was in all the papers, though. Everyone knew. And so, my parents decided it would be better if we moved. They never asked me. They didn't care how it affected me, to uproot and leave everything and everyone. And Dad . . . he said he did it for us, for me. So I could have things like the shell of a '55 Corvette. As if I'd rather that than a life at home with all our family and all my friends."

Claire didn't know what to say. She knew what it was like to love parents who thought they were doing the right thing but kept making everything worse. You loved them, even when they messed up, but sometimes that made everything else harder.

"He sucks," Reyva said succinctly.

Mariana let out a half laugh, half cry.

"Have you tried to tell them how you feel?" Claire asked, and then winced at herself. Pathetic to give out advice that she wouldn't take herself.

"They have enough problems," Mariana said. "I didn't want to be another one."

"Noble, but stupid," Reyva said.

"Hey!" Releasing Claire's hand, Mariana rustled in the darkness. Claire heard a soft thump and then Reyva said sarcastically, "Ow."

Then Mariana said, "I'm sorry I lied to both of you. I just . . . wanted to pretend everything was okay. At least for the summer. I didn't want to think about it."

"It's okay," Claire said.

"Yeah," Reyva said. "You don't owe us every detail of your life. Especially if it doesn't help to talk about it." Claire shot a look at the shadow that was Reyva and wondered what it was that she wasn't talking about. Regardless, she knew she wasn't going to ask.

"It *does* help, though," Mariana said. "I didn't like lying to you. I mean, it was easy at first, and it didn't matter. But . . . I don't want to be like my dad. He was trying to fool everyone, to be someone he's not. I don't want to make the same mistakes he did."

"Are you planning to embezzle money from us anytime soon?" Reyva asked.

Mariana let out another startled laugh. "No."

"Then I think you'll be fine."

They talked for a while more, a lighter chatter about the differences between high school in Indiana and California, levels of snow in February, and their families, until Mariana no longer sounded as if she had tears in her voice.

Eventually, they all slept.

★ ★ ★

Claire woke at dawn as stiff and sore as if she'd slept on a pile of rocks, which was accurate. Running through a few standard ballet stretches, she blinked her crusty eyes as she listened to the birds. She peered out between the leaves of the wall of branches they'd built as she pointed and flexed her toes. She didn't see any movement in the woods around them. A woodpecker tapped in the distance.

She also heard an odd whiny rumble.

Listening to it, she wondered what—

"Boat," Mariana said. "That's the boat! Up, everyone!"

She shot to her feet, as did Reyva. Claire scrambled up, grabbing her pack. "That way." She pointed in the direction of the hum. "Yes?"

Pushing their barricade aside, they hurried through the woods. Leaves crunched under their feet, and Claire knew they were leaving footprints again, but speed mattered more.

She ran her fingers quickly over the straps of her pack, tapping them in rhythm to her feet as she ran. *A fox and a chicken need to get across a lake, but there's only one boat* . . . No, it was a fox, a chicken, and a bag of corn. The chicken and the corn can't be in the boat at the same time. The fox and the chicken can't be together. But corn and fox are fine. How far away is the boat? How close to the shore? How far away were they?

She listened for the birds, for the water, for the boat.

Her ankle twisted as her foot slipped off a rock. She hissed. Paused. Had she sprained it? Broken it? Twisted it? She couldn't afford any of that.

"You okay?" Mariana asked.

"Heel first," Reyva advised. "Rock through your foot. Keep it straight. And keep going! Never let pain define you!"

Claire tested it. In a few steps, the sharp pain faded. Just a temporary twinge. She'd overreacted. She'd hurt her ankle far worse in pointe practice and had kept dancing rather than interrupt the instructor; she could keep running. "I'm fine." She picked up her pace, catching up to Mariana and Reyva.

Reyva ran with a determination that made it look as if she'd plow through a tree trunk if it dared get in her way. She barreled through bushes. Twigs grabbed her, and they snapped beneath her resolve.

Mariana kept her hands in front of her, warding off the branches.

Claire calculated as she ran. Each step, each turn, as if she were executing choreography. She saw the layout of the trees ahead of her. Right, left, right, straight.

The boat sounded closer. Didn't it? Or was that wishful thinking?

She stared through the trees, willing herself to see the lake.

Abruptly, the hum cut off.

Reyva swore.

"Not necessarily bad," Mariana said, huffing. "It could be at the dock."

But where was the dock? Claire clutched her side. It hurt. And she felt a yawning hunger. They were using too many calories without replacing them, and it was starting to catch up with her. Her mouth felt dry. She hadn't had enough water. "I can't . . . ," she said, panting. Slowly, her legs wobbled. She saw black spots in front of her eyes. Putting her hand on a tree trunk, she gasped in air. Her throat hurt from breathing so hard.

"Got to keep going," Reyva said, coming back to her. "Come on."

She tried to wave them on. "Go ahead. Keep the boat here. I'll catch up."

"No way," Mariana said. "We stick together. That's the rule. Stick together, and we'll survive."

"Is that a promise or a hope?" Claire asked.

"Both."

Mariana and Reyva got on either side of her. Their arms around her waist, they hurried together, propelling her forward. Up ahead, Claire saw sunlight. An open area. They ran forward and saw the burnt house beyond the empty airstrip. The SOS was gone, the rocks scattered—either by wind or by human hand, Claire wasn't sure which—but beyond that it looked the same.

They crossed the cracked airstrip.

Claire felt prickles on her back. They were too exposed. Anyone could see them. She felt as if she had a target painted on her back. She didn't look at the house as they passed, but she did shoot a glance at the shed with the trapdoor.

She slowed. "Reyva. Mariana."

Both of them slowed too and stared into the shed.

Inside, rocks had been piled on top of the closed trapdoor. Multiple hundred-pound flat rocks, stacked six feet high. She doubted there was anyone in the world strong enough to push that trapdoor open from the inside.

Only someone very strong and very determined could have done that. Someone who really, really hadn't wanted them to escape.

ELEVEN

A flash of orange in between the trees.

Someone's coming, Claire thought. She grabbed Mariana and Reyva. "Hide."

Together, they sprinted to the nearest shed, which had three mostly intact walls. Crouching behind it, they flattened against the charred boards. Claire counted her breaths. She tapped her index finger on the strap of her backpack, in rhythm with her inhales. Her heart was racing again, and her head was beginning to ache.

Could you die from too much fear?

She was reasonably sure the answer was yes.

Beside her, Reyva peeked around the corner of the crumbling shed wall. Inching closer, Mariana whispered, "Who is it?"

Pulling back, Reyva shook her head.

She didn't know.

It could be a rescue—the police, coming to belatedly investigate the fire. Or another camper with no clue what was waiting for them at the Lake House. Or their parents, worried about them.

Or it could be the man with the shotgun, the wild man, or some brand-new dangerous stranger. Maybe one of the men had an accomplice who had been called in to finish the job. She thought again of the cage in the underground bunker and wondered if there was any connection.

She heard whistling, a tune that sounded vaguely like something she'd heard on the radio, but twisted to a minor key. Off pitch, it made her shiver. Again, Reyva peered around the corner.

The whistle cut off.

"Holy hell," a boy said.

"It's Jack," Mariana said with certainty. "The boat boy." Without waiting for either of them to react, she emerged from behind the shed at a jog. "Jack!"

Claire and Reyva followed.

Jack had halted at the trailhead. Staring at the burnt Lake House, he looked as stunned as if he'd been whacked in the face with a baseball bat. He was the flash of orange she'd seen—he was wearing a bright orange T-shirt with a coffee cup bearing the words *Mainely Brew*. He also wore khaki shorts and carried a small gray backpack.

Mariana barreled toward the trail, snagging his arm as she passed. "Jack! Great to see you. Thought of you often. Missed you terribly. We've got to go."

Twisting out of her grip, he didn't tear his eyes from the burned-down building. "What happened? Are you okay? Where's—"

Reyva reached him next. "Don't know. Already burned when

we got here. Dead body in the woods. Guy with gun, trying to kill us. Got to go *now*."

He held up his hands as if in surrender. "Wait. Stop. What?"

He didn't know, Claire thought. *Of course he didn't—he wouldn't have left us here if he knew any of it.* But she suddenly realized what that meant: if he hadn't heard any news about the fire . . . then the other kids—all the campers and the counselors—hadn't escaped.

Claire clutched her side as she jogged behind Reyva. She'd never run this much. Her throat hurt from too much panting and too little water. She didn't care how pathetic she looked or sounded. "Please, help us."

That got through to him.

"Of course. Are you all right? What do you need?"

"Your boat," Mariana called over her shoulder. She was already heading down the trail with long gazelle-like strides, her hair streaming behind her.

"We need to get out of here," Claire said. "Go someplace safe. Go to the police." They needed someone who could do something about the dead program director, the burned-down house, and the two dangerous men in the woods. And they needed a car, bus, train, any way home. At this point, she'd even accept a prop plane. Or, statistically worse, a motorcycle.

Jack began jogging down the trail with them. He kept shooting glances behind them, even after the view of the Lake House was blocked by trees. Claire, on the other hand, was busy watching the woods on either side of them.

It was entirely possible they weren't the only ones to have heard the boat.

She wished she hadn't had that thought.

Either man could be waiting for us, she thought. *It could be a trap.*

She had to tell the others her worry. She didn't want to. She wanted to be wrong—to be overly and unrealistically anxious, like Priya and Angie and her parents and her teachers and her doctors said she was. She wanted to believe they were running to safety, and they'd jump in the boat and motor away, leaving all this behind them.

"What if . . . ," Claire began.

Reyva sidestepped a root. "Don't say it."

"If Claire has something to say, let her say it," Mariana said. "She's been right nearly every time since we've gotten here."

I have? Claire thought. That was a first.

Jack asked plaintively, "What did you mean 'dead body in the woods'? Who? How?"

Claire saw a hint of blue water through the trees. Either they kept running full tilt to the dock and hoped that speed was enough, or . . . "Someone else could have heard the boat too."

"Yeah, thought you were going to say that." Reyva halted, put her hands on her knees, and stared through the trees as if she could clear a path with just the intensity of her gaze. "Okay, we can do this. Stay low. Sneak to the shore. As little sound as possible."

Jack said, "I don't think—"

"You don't need to think," Reyva told him. "Or talk."

Mariana took his hand and patted it. "Stick with me. We'll explain later. As soon as it's safe." She tugged him down, and they all crouched low as they walked down the trail.

"Just tell me: Who's dead?"

"We believe it was the program director, Ms. Williams," Mariana said. "Never saw a picture of her so can't be sure, but she looked the right age for—"

"Shh," Reyva said.

If it weren't so loud to walk through the forest, Claire would have suggested they leave the trail—it was the obvious way to approach the dock, and it would be watched. But with the inevitable crunch of leaves and snap of twigs . . . *We'd be heard.*

She scanned the forest in front of them.

Listened to the birds.

Kept walking quietly, as aware of every step as when she was en pointe.

The lake was ahead. She could see bits of blue in the spaces between the trees. She wanted to run to it, but she knew this slow and steady approach was smarter. They kept moving, cautiously, down the trail.

"There's about ten feet between the edge of the forest and the dock, then the dock itself," Reyva whispered as they approached. "We'll be exposed for the time it takes to cross it. Gotta move fast."

"Zigzag?" Mariana suggested.

"Good idea."

"We can jump in the water," Claire said. "Swim to the boat."

"Faster to run."

"Jack, how quickly can you restart the boat?" Reyva said.

"Um, very, I guess? But I think I really deserve to know what's going on. You can't mean *dead*—" He wasn't whispering.

Mariana clapped her hand over his mouth.

Spinning to face him, Reyva said in a furious whisper, "Yes, dead. And if we don't want to be dead too, we have to escape right now. Got it?"

"Promise we'll explain everything later," Mariana whispered in his ear.

Or at least as much as we know, Claire thought, *which admittedly isn't much.* Except that people had died, and she didn't want to join them.

A woodpecker pounded at a nearby tree, and all of them jumped. Claire spotted it high in the branches of a pine, black and white with a patch of red. It pecked again, as loud as a hammer and as rapid as her heartbeat felt.

Closer, she heard the slosh of water as the waves lapped against the shore. The wind was ruffling the surface of the lake, and it flashed as it reflected the sunlight in sparkles. So peaceful. So picturesque. It felt like a lie.

They couldn't see the dock just yet. But the boat would be tied to a cleat. One of them would need to untie the knot while Jack started the engine. The others could flatten themselves on the bottom of the boat to make themselves as small a target as possible.

It was a risk. But what choice did they have? This was their best chance of escape.

We can't screw this up, she thought.

"Anyone fast with knots?" Claire asked.

"Got a cousin who loves boats," Mariana said. "Taught me a bit. I'll untie it."

Claire shook her head. Mariana was full of surprises. "Jack, you stay low and start the boat as quickly as possible, while Mariana unties the rope—"

"Line," Jack corrected.

Claire halted mid-command. "What?"

"On a boat, it's a line, not a rope."

That . . . did not feel like a priority. Did he not understand the seriousness of the situation? He'd seen the burned-down house, and they'd told him about the corpse. "Mariana unties the *line*, while Reyva and I watch for danger."

"Or you two could just get in the boat and stay down," Mariana said.

"We'll get in *and* we'll watch for danger," Reyva insisted.

Soon, they were at the end of the trail. Crouching down behind one of the boulders on the shore, they looked out at the dock. There! She saw the boat, but a dark figure stood at the helm. Who was—

The boat's motor roared to life.

The man in camo maneuvered to the side of the boat and untied the line from the dock. He looked back at shore, scanning the edge of the forest. His shotgun lay next to the steering console, in easy reach. His face was unreadable at this distance, but Claire thought—

"Stop!" Jack roared. He burst out of their hiding place and ran toward the dock.

"Jack!" Mariana cried. At the same time, Claire yelled, "Come back!" And Reyva yelled, "Get back here!"

The man in the boat picked up his shotgun.

Mariana screamed, "Jack, watch out!"

"Get down!" Reyva yelled.

Eyes on the shore, the man kicked off from the dock with one booted foot. Gun tucked under his armpit, he shifted to the back of the boat and increased the throttle. As Jack ran onto the dock, the boat sped away.

"Come back!" Jack yelled after him. "What are you doing?"

"Stop, Jack!" Claire shouted. Reyva and Mariana joined her, shouting at him to get off the dock, to watch out—this was the same man who'd tried to shoot them and who had most likely shot Ms. Williams.

Hearing them, Jack turned toward them, away from the boat—

And a gunshot thundered.

Screaming, Claire, Reyva, and Mariana ducked behind the rock. They heard the boat motoring away, increasing in speed. Reyva rose to peek around the boulder.

Another thunderous shot.

As Reyva dived to the ground, Claire clapped her hands over her ears and closed her eyes. She felt as if the sound were echoing over and over in her head. She'd never heard a gun fired before, not outside of a TV show or a movie. It sounded like a thunderclap inside her head, and she felt its echo in the base of her stomach.

The motor grew farther and farther away.

"Jack?" Mariana whispered.

"I don't know," Reyva said.

Mariana rose to her feet, and Claire pulled her back down. "Not yet."

When the boat's hum grew more distant, she released her. Mariana popped to her feet. "Jack!" She ran toward the dock, her footsteps thudding on the wood.

As she rose to her feet, Claire saw Jack, prone on the dock, lying facedown. Mariana dropped to her knees next to him. She kept repeating his name.

No, no, no, she thought. *He's dead. And it's our fault. My fault. I knew there was danger.* If she'd warned him better . . . If they'd stopped him from running out there . . . If they'd taken another second to explain what they were afraid of . . . Sinking to the ground, she tried to focus on inhaling. She couldn't seem to get a full breath. She felt sweat bead on her forehead. Counting furiously, she tried to beat back the panic. *Not now,* she thought. *Not here. Please.*

"Not dead," Reyva said. "Claire? Breathe. He's not dead."

At Reyva's urging, she looked again to see Mariana helping Jack stand. He was clutching his head and staring out across the water at the distant boat. *Not dead,* Claire's brain repeated. *He's not dead.* She found she could breathe again.

Claire and Reyva joined them on the dock.

"Are you shot?" Reyva asked bluntly.

Wordless, Jack shook his head, then winced.

"Move your hand," Reyva ordered. "Let me see your head."

He withdrew his hand. He had a cut on his forehead. A stream of blood wiggled down his forehead to stain his eyebrow. It shone bright ketchup red in the sunlight, looking almost unreal. Or too real. "When I heard the shot, I dropped. Hit my head."

Claire shed her pack. "I've got a first-aid kit." She dug through until she found it. Her hands were shaking as she opened it. Reyva took the antibiotic cream from her, squeezed some on his cut, and then took a Band-Aid and stuck it on. "He could have a concussion."

Reyva nodded. "Do you feel dizzy? Nauseous?" She sounded so grim that Claire wondered if she had experience with concussions.

Jack shook his head after the first question, winced, and said no to the second, then he stared out at the lake again. "He shot at me."

"He missed," Mariana said. "So that's a good thing."

"He took the boat," Jack said, again stating the obvious.

"And that's a bad thing," Reyva said. "Now that we're all caught up, what do we do?"

All four of them looked out across the sparkling lake. The boat bounced over the surface of the water, smacking down in a spray of foamy water. *Porpoising,* Claire remembered. It left a V-shaped wake behind that spread out into ripples.

"On the plus side," Mariana said, "at least he can't shoot at us anymore. So we're safe? Yay? Is this 'yay'? I think it is."

"Except we lost our best escape route." Claire sank onto the dock. Her muscles felt wobbly. She'd run too much and eaten too little. She was acutely aware of how thirsty, how hungry, how tired, and how sore she was. And how close she'd come to losing it, back behind the rock. She'd held herself together by mere threads this time.

She was not in any shape to begin a days-long hike.

"You don't happen to have any cheeseburgers in your backpack?" Reyva asked Jack. At the word *cheeseburger*, Claire's stomach let out a loud rumble that felt like an ache. She wrapped her arms around her middle.

His hands closed over his backpack straps. "Um, no?"

"Fresh water?" Mariana asked.

"The lake—" He waved at the expanse of water around them.

"Bacteria, I'm told," Reyva said.

"Well, yeah, true," Jack said. He hadn't stopped staring at the boat, now tiny in the distance. In a few minutes, it would disappear around the corner, where the lake bent around granite cliffs. "I can't believe he took the boat."

I can't believe we're not all dead, Claire thought. He'd had the perfect chance to shoot them all. Instead he'd been the one to flee.

Odd, she thought.

With him in possession of the boat and the gun, he had all the advantages. She'd been certain he was hunting them before—certain he'd been the one to close the trapdoor, certain he'd waited for them by the cave exit, and certain he'd been targeting them.

So why would he leave them here?

What was he running away from?

Or who?

She tried to look on the bright side, like Mariana: at least it meant one danger was gone, whatever the reason. *So that just leaves us with the man with the wild hair, dehydration, and starvation.*

Also, hypothermia if it rains again.

She had a sudden thought: "Rain! The jars!"

Scrambling to her feet, she hurried off the dock. They'd left the jars by where they'd first attempted to make a fire. If they hadn't fallen over, they should be full of fresh rainwater—

Yes!

Grateful, Claire sank to her knees next to the jars. The pebbles dug into her skin, but she didn't care. All the jars, as well as the toolbox, had several inches of rainwater. Clean, beautiful, non-bacteria-laden water!

Reyva and Mariana joined her on either side. "Oh, bliss!" Mariana said. Picking up a glass jar, she drank a long glugging drink. So did Reyva.

Claire wrapped her hands around another jar and drank too. It was cold and sweet and perfect. She swallowed and swallowed until she remembered she should breathe. Lowering the jar, she inhaled. Even the air tasted better now.

"Bad idea if we drink it all?" Reyva asked.

Yes, it was, but . . . "We need it," Claire said firmly. Maybe now that the killer was gone, they could try for a fire again and boil more. They could even make an enormous fire and hope it worked as a signal fire to draw any hopefully-non-murderer with a boat.

Maybe things are looking up, Claire thought.

She immediately wished she hadn't had that thought. She'd probably jinxed them all. After all, they were still stranded.

And now they were four.

I'd just gotten used to the three of us, she thought. Glancing at

Jack, she wondered how their new addition was going to change their group. He certainly couldn't be happy to be stuck here with them. What would he think of her? Of them? Was he going to be a help, or a burden? Would he judge her and make the others see her the way she feared they would? She'd started to feel so close to Reyva and Mariana—was he going to break that apart?

That had happened before—a girl named Sonia, who Claire had nearly opened up to. They'd started to become friends, but then Claire had bumped into her at Starbucks while Sonia was with a group of kids from school. . . . She'd heard them whispering about her as she left, telling her about how Claire had melted down at the homecoming dance. She hadn't vomited that time, but the paramedics had come, in front of everyone. . . .

"Hey, Jack!" Mariana called. "Any chance you have a phone with you? A working phone? Like . . ." To Reyva and Claire, she said, "What do they call those phones that work anywhere?"

"Satellite phones," Claire said.

"Do you have a satellite phone?" Mariana called.

At last he left the dock and joined them by the boulders. He sank down in the wet pebbly sand and put his face in his hands. "No phone. No boat. No clue what to do."

Mariana patted him on the back. "Don't worry. We know what to do."

Claire asked, "We do?"

"We stick together, all four of us," Mariana said cheerfully. "And we try not to die."

TWELVE

Try not to die.

That was the key, wasn't it.

"He expects us to die," Claire said. "That's why he left." He could have stayed and shot them, but it would have taken time to hunt them down. And it would've meant more murdered bodies in the woods that could be discovered and investigated. If they died of natural causes, on the other hand, then he was in the clear for their deaths.

He might have even hidden or buried the program director's body by now. That would have been the logical move. Dispose of that, and then leave the three of them, plus Jack—the only ones who knew about her—to die of exposure. Neat, tidy, done.

"He knew he was taking our best, possibly only, way to escape," Claire said, "and he left us here to starve and die." She liked that theory a lot better than the other possibility: that he was running from the wild man. Especially since the wild man had been unarmed. It was much more likely the killer was seizing the opportunity to flee the scene of his crime than that he was fleeing an unarmed, unwashed, and unhinged man.

"Yeah, he's not nice," Mariana said. "Got that."

Claire winced. She wasn't saying this right. "What I meant . . . He left us to die, so you're right: all we have to do now is *not* die. He narrowed the problem. And that's good. Well, not *good*, but . . ." She trailed off. Nothing about this was *good*, but maybe it was a solvable problem?

To Jack, Reyva said, "Who knows you're here? Anyone who will send a rescue when you don't come back? Parents? Friends?"

"It's just my dad and me, and I . . . didn't tell him I was coming." Jack was still staring across the water, as if he expected the boat to reappear.

"Why did you come?" Reyva asked. "Did you know we were in trouble?"

Good question. Why was he here? Claire hadn't thought to ask. He hadn't been scheduled to return until August. Maybe she should be more suspicious of their new addition.

"I didn't . . . I . . ." He turned to look at Mariana and blushed bright red. "I came to see you. You said . . . Well, I just thought a visit . . . You asked me to . . . I had no idea the Lake House . . . I had no idea."

Okay, that's more embarrassing than suspicious, Claire thought. *He's harmless.* And maybe a little likable? He sounded as awkward as she usually felt.

Mariana flashed a smile at him, and he reddened more, the blush spreading down his neck. "Very sweet. And it was *almost* a heroic rescue. If you hadn't left the boat key in the ignition, we'd all have been cheering for you. As it is, you're cute enough that we forgive you." She patted him on the cheek.

Still blushing furiously, he faced the lake again. "I didn't expect—"

"No one did," Reyva cut him off, clearly uncomfortable with Jack's embarrassment. "Big surprise. Ahhh. Okay, let's move past it and figure out what we do next. Claire, any thoughts on how to avoid the whole dying thing?"

Happy to change the subject, Claire ticked off on her fingers. "Shelter, water, food. Solved the water problem for now, so of those, I think the most pressing is food." Her stomach squeezed as if in agreement.

"What do you have in your pack, if not a cheeseburger?" Mariana asked Jack. She walked her fingertips up his arm to his backpack strap.

He flinched, twisting his shoulder away from her fingers. "Not much. Nothing useful."

Reyva caught Mariana's wrist in her hand and lifted it away from Jack. "Quit terrorizing the boy. Claire, continue what you were saying. Food?"

Right, Claire thought, taking her eyes off Jack and Mariana. *Work the problem. If a fox and a chicken need to cross a lake* . . . "We have a lake, which I assume has fish, and we have a forest that has plants, berries, nuts, and other forest-y things, as well as squirrels, rabbits, birds, and deer." Also wolves, bears, and mountain lions, but those weren't part of this calculation.

"I'm not eating a rabbit," Mariana said.

"You will if you're hungry enough," Reyva said.

"Let's start with the lake," Claire said. "Jack, have you ever gone fishing?"

"Yeah, of course, but with tackle and rods and bait . . ." He waved his hand at the water. "You can't just catch fish bare-handed, you know. It takes equipment. Lures and line. Or if we had a gill net—that's a net you dangle in the water. Fish try to swim through the holes and get themselves tangled. Gill nets work really well. But again, don't have one in my backpack."

Unfortunately, Claire hadn't seen a net in the ruins of the sheds. Melted volleyballs, yes. Old weights, yes. A wheelbarrow. But no fishing supplies.

"The tennis court," Mariana said suddenly.

Yes! The net on the tennis court! "Brilliant," Claire said. If it was intact . . . All they needed was a net with holes the right size to tangle a fish. "So we get the tennis net, tie it to a pole, and extend it from the end of the dock out into the lake. We'll have to angle it since the dock isn't flush with the water level, but that should be doable."

"We'll need a pole as well as a net," Mariana said.

Reyva waved her hand at the trees. "Literally in a forest."

"Fair enough," Mariana said, nodding. Claire could tell the others were getting excited. "It could work. Sure. Fish for dinner!"

Jack said, "Well, it's not that easy. There's no guarantee a fish will—"

"Then we try a whole bunch of different things at once," Claire said. "How do we make fishhooks?" She thought for a moment. "Bent nails." There were bound to be nails they could extract from the ruins of the house or the sheds. "Anything we can use for a line?"

"Dental floss?" Mariana said. "I've got some of that."

"Worth a try," Reyva said.

"It'll break if the fish fights hard enough," Jack warned.

Why did he have to be so negative? *Wait*, she thought, *am I criticizing someone else for being negative?* That was a first. She grinned involuntarily. Her cheeks felt stiff, as if she hadn't smiled in days.

"And not entirely sure they'll like mint-flavored," Mariana said. "But maybe fish dislike fish breath too. We could be creating a whole new aquatic dating scene."

"What else is in the lake that we can eat?" Claire asked. "Crabs? Oysters? Snails?" It was strange how all this optimism felt. *Floaty*, she decided. She felt full of bubbles.

"Um, we've got freshwater mussels," Jack said. "They burrow in the sand and gravel near where streams dump into the lake. You don't have to worry about red tide like the saltwater ones with them." When they looked blankly at him, he clarified, "Safe to eat. But I don't think—"

"We shouldn't give up on fishing lines," Mariana said. "Whole lake out there."

"What do we have that's stronger than dental floss?" Claire asked.

"Don't look at me," Reyva said. "I'm not the overpacker."

"How about electrical wire?" Mariana suggested. "Assuming it didn't all melt, we can pry it out of the walls of the Lake House, strip off the insulation, and ta-da!"

Jack began, "Hey, I don't—"

"Okay, so we set up a net in the water off the end of the dock, Jack teaches us how to set snares, and we use nails and wire to try to fish." That was three possible avenues to food. She liked the sound of that. *It sounds like hope*, Claire thought.

"Wait, stop! Just stop! What are you all talking about?" Jack yelped. *"Fishing lines?* I don't plan on being here through dinner. We have to find a way out!"

They all stared at him, deadpan. "We've been stuck here. Without your boat. For *days*," Mariana snapped. "You really believe we didn't try to think of a way out?"

They were silent for a moment. Claire took up the thread. "Best we could come up with was heading to the boathouse. I imagine the walk takes several days. We'll need to sustain ourselves along the way."

Jack stared at each of them in turn, his eyes wide. Then he seemed to deflate. "I also know how to make snares, if we can find wire. And Paiute deadfall traps."

"What're those?" Reyva asked.

Jack knelt in the sand, demonstrating. "You take a heavy rock, prop it up with a stick. Use another stick to brace the first stick—" Using one of the sticks from their former fire, he propped up a rock. The instant he released it, the rock smacked down. He yanked his fingers back just in time. "It's a little tricky, but the idea is that you put bait underneath. When the prey comes along, it knocks on the stick and *splat.*"

"That's horrific," Mariana said.

"Like with fishing, it relies on a bit of luck," Jack said. "You can set twenty traps and get nothing. It helps if you know the areas the animals go. Find their tracks."

Maybe our luck is looking up, Claire thought. Jack lived here.

He was outdoorsy. He fished. He trapped. He camped. He was perfect.

She studied him in a way she hadn't when he'd been their boat driver or just the boy Mariana was flirting with. He had floppy blond hair, freckles on his nose from lack of sunscreen, and blue eyes that matched the lake. He reminded Claire of a golden retriever, eager and sweet, at least now that the initial shock of the last hour had passed. Maybe it was okay that they were four. Maybe Jack was exactly what they needed to change their fate. She wondered what she would have thought of him if she'd met him at school. Most likely, she would have hoped he wouldn't talk to her so she could avoid having to talk back.

"What do you know about edible plants?" Claire asked.

"I know you can eat fiddleheads," Jack said. "And dandelions. Also, there could be black raspberries, blueberries, wild strawberries, mulberries—especially blueberries. I think they're in season. Also heard you can eat pine bark, the white layer under the rough stuff, but it kind of messes with your system, if you know what I mean. Not sure that should be our first choice."

Fiddleheads, blueberries, dandelions, pine bark—she carefully cataloged all of that.

"Probably a lot more plants that are edible," Jack said, "but I'm not really a salad guy."

"You just haven't had a salad with avocado," Mariana said. "Bliss."

Jack frowned. "Avocado doesn't grow in Maine, so we won't find any of those."

Just out of sight of Jack, Reyva rolled her eyes, and Claire bit back a laugh. She felt like laughing at everything—the lake, the sky, even the man with the gun who thought they'd die. She felt, for the first time since she'd seen the burned-down house, hope. It was as potent as a shot of caffeine. "You may be our hero after all," Claire said to Jack. It was a bit galling that they'd needed him to swoop in—and kind of unforgivable that he'd clearly left the keys to the boat *in* the boat—but she wasn't about to deny his usefulness now.

He looked startled and then smiled.

Claire smiled back. She hadn't been able to say more than two words to Jack on the ride across the lake, but somehow it wasn't as hard to talk to him now, when they were all stuck here together. *Learn new skills, have new experiences, and make new friends*, she heard her parents say. She was *not* going to tell them they'd been right, in a way. "Okay. Let's do it. Step one: we loot the Lake House for whatever we need. Step two: Jack teaches us everything he knows."

Together, the four of them trooped up the trail to the Lake House.

The birds were chirping, and Claire felt more hopeful than she had in days. This time, they didn't need to be quiet because they'd all watched the man with the gun motor away. "You know how to clean a fish too, right? And how to prepare a rabbit or squirrel or whatever we catch?" she asked Jack. "You can teach us that too?"

He lit up as if she'd invited him to explain his favorite movie. "Key is not to pierce the guts. That's especially true with any rodents, but fish can have parasites too. You have to be really careful not to puncture the intestines, or you'll contaminate the meat."

"How do you identify—"

"Going to stop you right there," Mariana said. "Maybe we can save this conversation for later? Really don't want to puke on an empty stomach."

"Sorry," both Jack and Claire said.

They shared a smile.

Definitely okay that there are four of us, Claire thought. So far, Jack was proving both useful and nice. She hadn't realized how badly she'd needed something positive to happen.

"Thanks," Mariana said, slowing to step over a snarl of roots. "Appreciate it. Instead, how about you tell us what your favorite color is, Jack? Or your greatest fear?"

Reyva groaned.

"My . . . what?" He looked confused. Claire thought that was his standard expression: light befuddlement. She supposed that when he woke up this morning he hadn't expected to be in this situation. He'd expected an illicit trip to the Lake House to flirt with Mariana. All in all, she thought he was handling it well, except for the part where he'd run out onto the dock and almost gotten killed. That had been rather less than clever.

"What's your favorite color?" Mariana pressed.

"Um, I'm not sure I have one?"

"Everyone has a favorite color, in case they're asked their favorite color," Mariana said. "You learn that in preschool. Colors and farm animal sounds. For some unknown reason, we all receive intensive training early in life in farm animal noises."

"I like green?" Jack ventured.

"Good! So does Claire. See, we're bonding." She shot a triumphant look over her shoulder at Reyva, as if that proved a point that Claire didn't think anyone had really been arguing. Reyva responded with a snort. Undeterred, Mariana continued, "What about your greatest fear?"

"Ahh, I don't . . ."

"Leave the poor boy alone," Reyva said.

Claire changed the subject. "Do you see any edible plants?"

He liked that question a lot better. As they walked, he pointed out the various plants: ferns (you could eat the tightly curled tops of young ferns, called fiddleheads), poison ivy (you definitely couldn't eat that), nightshade (don't eat that), mushrooms (probably could eat some, but he didn't know which ones so don't eat them) . . .

Off the path, he spotted a blueberry bush and led them to it. Examining it, Claire memorized the leaf pattern: almond-shaped leaves that alternated along the stalks. Clusters of whitish-green waxy berries. A few had splotches of purplish blue.

"Not quite ripe."

"Ripe enough?" Mariana asked.

"Maybe? Or it could give you a stomachache."

He searched the plant and found a half dozen that were more blue than pale, less waxy too. He held them on his palm. Mariana grabbed two. So did Reyva.

Claire hesitated. "You're certain they're not poisonous."

"Positive." As proof, he ate one.

Then his eyes went wide, and he clutched his throat.

"Jack!" Mariana cried, dropping her berries. She grabbed his shoulders. "Breathe! What do we do? Breathe!"

He released his throat. "Kidding. Sorry."

Claire sucked in air and put her hands on her knees.

Mariana punched him in the shoulder. "So not funny."

"Sorry, sorry, I just thought . . . Lighten the mood, you know?"

Claire felt Reyva's hand on her back, a cool pressure that made her head spin less. "You're okay," Reyva murmured near her ear, so close that it tickled. "We're all okay. What do you need?"

She needed Reyva to punch Jack, but Mariana had already taken care of that, albeit not very hard. Claire made herself inhale steadily as she ran through ballet combinations in her head. She thought of an attack she'd had once in the supermarket, by the vegetables, and how she'd heard a little kid ask, *Mommy, what's wrong with her?* She hadn't had an answer. It wasn't as if anything had happened that day. She'd merely seen a headline, another school shooting, not anywhere nearby or anyone she'd known, but it had been enough to set her brain spiraling. She hadn't been able to stop imagining it happening in her school. Here, she couldn't stop picturing Jack convulsing at her feet. *He's fine*, she told her brain. *Look at him, he's fine. Grand port de bras forward, tendu back in fondu, close in plié, rond de jambe* . . . She took a deep breath. Straightening, she said, "Are they edible? Truth."

"Truth," Jack said. "Completely edible. Sorry again."

"And the fiddleheads?"

"You boil them," Jack said. "Otherwise they're too bitter."

"You said you can eat dandelions too," Claire said. If she focused on facts, the noise in her head retreated, at least somewhat. "How? Boil them too?"

"Or fry them. Make a tea out of them. They're supposed to be better for you than spinach or kale, at least that's what my dad said. He puts them in fish stew. Every part of a dandelion is edible."

Her parents had a constant war on dandelions in their yard. Who knew? Now that she was focused firmly on dandelions, the lack-of-oxygen feeling had retreated to just a tightness in her ribs. She very much wished her body wouldn't do that. She wondered if fiddleheads and dandelions would be enough to keep them alive. She doubted it.

"Cool, then let's get that tennis net, catch a fish, and make some dandelion-and-fish stew," Mariana said. "Wow, this is a weird summer. Imagine the postcards home we could send . . . if we had stamps."

"Lack of stamps is not the only reason we aren't sending postcards," Reyva said.

Claire picked up the blueberries that they'd dropped. She placed one on her tongue. It felt like a stab of bitter sweetness. Not quite ripe, as Jack had said. She bit, and the juice filled her mouth—she thought it might be the most violently flavorful berry she'd ever tasted. She ate a second one as they headed back to the trail.

Jack fell into step beside her. "Sorry again. I wasn't thinking about what you guys went through. Have you really not eaten anything since I dropped you off?"

"Not much," Claire said. "A few snacks."

Reyva jumped in. "You don't have to worry. We haven't yet resorted to cannibalism, if that's what you're asking."

Jack looked appalled. "That was not at all what I was asking."

Before he could say anything more, they reached the Lake House. He slowed as soon as it came into view but was swept forward by Claire, Reyva, and Mariana. Claire supposed they were becoming used to the sight, which was terrible in and of itself. You shouldn't get used to the sight of tragedy, but this time, they had a particular goal.

They beelined for the tennis court. Claire hadn't paid much attention to it before, except to notice it was cracked. Up close, it was in even worse shape than she'd thought. It was riddled with fissures, moss, and weeds. Unplayable.

A few dandelions had sprouted in the cracks. Claire yanked them out of the ground, shook the excess dirt off the roots, and shoved them into her pocket. She smiled as she imagined telling her parents that she was saved by eating their lawn's enemy, and her smile faded—she hoped she got the chance to tell them. She was getting much too carried away with all this hope. *Focus on one thing at a time*, she thought. *First, the net.*

Half torn from its posts, the net sagged. The ropes were coated in moss, with rips in certain places. But some of it was intact, and Claire guessed it was an okay size for catching fish. At least it seemed appropriately netlike.

Jack pulled a knife out of his backpack. It was about five inches long, with a handle that looked like it was made of bone.

He took off the sheath and sawed the remaining rope that connected the net to the post.

They stared at him.

"You just, like, carry that around?" Mariana asked.

"It's Maine," Reyva said. "He probably has a lobster trap in his backpack."

"That would be useful," Claire said. "You said you didn't have anything useful in there." She eyed his backpack, trying to gauge its weight from the pull on the strap. She wondered what else he carried, as well as what else he knew, that could be helpful. Was he holding out on them? Maybe he had a useful item that he didn't realize could help them. . . .

"I don't have anything edible." He held the knife up so they could see. "Dad gave it to me when I was eight. It was his father's. The handle is made of carved elk antler."

"An heirloom knife," Mariana said. "Cool. For my quinceañera, I got an heirloom tiara. Almost the same thing. Except not." Starting at one side, she began rolling up the net. "You know, you'd think they would have fixed up the tennis court before reopening. What if we'd wanted to play tennis instead of the much-more-cardio-oriented running for our lives in terror?"

"Why did the camp get shut down in the first place?" Claire asked. She'd asked her parents that question, and they hadn't known. Just waxed on about what a formative summer it had been, and then they'd stared adoringly into each other's eyes. They'd begun dating at the Lake House, which hadn't been a detail that Claire had known—she knew they were high school sweethearts, but not that it had begun at summer camp. In fact, they'd never mentioned the Lake House until they got it into their heads that she should go. After that, it was pretty much every other sentence out of their mouths, as if a light switch had been flipped. She'd never seen them so focused on anything. It was as if they'd expected this place to be the salvation for all her—and therefore all *their*—problems. But not once in their extended soliloquies about the glories of the Lake House had they ever explained why it had closed.

"Because it's in a national forest," Jack said. "They lost their permit; at least I think that was it. Also there was the kid who died."

Mariana halted with the net halfway rolled. "What kid?"

"It's one of the local legends. He haunts the lake. Every so often you get a lone hiker showing up and claiming they saw him, and it fuels a whole lot more ghost stories."

"So this place is burned down *and* haunted," Mariana said. "Yay."

Warming to the subject, Jack said, "His name was Arthur Benedict, and he was sixteen when he died. Snuck out with friends one night. The friends came back. He didn't."

Reyva rolled her eyes. "Nope, this place is definitely not haunted by a ghost named 'Arthur.' No place is haunted by a ghost named Arthur. Bloody Mary, yes. Arthur Benedict, no."

Claire laughed.

"Obviously the friends murdered him," Mariana said.

"Well, yeah, obviously," Reyva agreed.

They carried the rolled-up net off the tennis court, then

dumped it next to the charred maple tree in the middle of the lawn, near the wheelbarrow with various equipment that Claire had salvaged from the sheds. She peeked through it, looking for anything that resembled wire or fishhooks. She found a hammer. "Anyone want to pry out nails for fishhooks?"

Reyva took it.

"And we need wire for snares and the fishing line," Mariana said.

"Normal electrical wire won't work," Jack said. "It'll be too thick. Hard to bend, even stripped. Best is twenty-four gauge, if we can find it. Thinner is better too, because it's harder for the rabbits to see."

"What uses twenty-four gauge?" Reyva asked.

"Speaker wire," Mariana answered promptly, before Claire could ask what twenty-four gauge meant. "Maybe the camp had a PA system, like in a school."

Side by side, they approached the ruins of the house. Staring at it, they all fell silent. Claire felt a chill on her skin, even though the wind was still.

After a moment, Reyva went first. Claire followed. It felt, she thought, like walking on a grave. She couldn't shake the feeling that they shouldn't be there. Studying the charred walls, she looked for anything that resembled a speaker. Reyva plucked a few nails out of the burnt wood with the heel of the hammer head and dropped them in her pocket.

Mariana hadn't entered.

Stationary, she was still staring at the front doorway. The

door itself hung off of one hinge, but the front porch light and half the doorframe were still intact. Claire said gently, "Mariana? You okay?"

She expected her to say something about the tragedy of all the kids who had died here and how the place truly did feel haunted. The rain had washed away every hint of smoke in the air, but Claire still remembered the taste. It lingered in her mind, overlaid with the scent of rain-soaked forest. Or maybe Mariana was thinking about last night, about what she'd told them about her family and her life and how she'd had to move. It must have been hard to share that, after making the conscious choice to suppress it. *Harder still to go through it*, she thought. Claire wondered if Mariana wanted to talk about it more. Instead of any of that, though, Mariana said, "Doorbell."

"Sorry?"

"Old doorbells were wired. Thin wire. And if there's a bell, even better." She began to tear at the charred, softened wood around the doorbell.

Claire joined her, and soon Reyva and Jack were there, helping tear apart the wall. Softened by fire and then rain, the battered wood broke easily in their hands, exposing the doorbell.

Sure enough, thin wire led from the doorbell through the wall.

With Mariana leading, they traced it through the wall inside to the bell itself. It was an old-fashioned kind of bell, a brass bowl with a mallet that would hit the bowl when the doorbell was rung. "Perfect," she murmured. "Ecstatically perfect." She yanked the doorbell off the wall. The weak wood gave easily. Shreds of wallpaper fluttered to the floor. "Can I borrow your knife, Jack?"

He handed it to her.

Prying the back off, she revealed two spools, coiled with copper wire. "The coils act like a magnet, to make the mallet hit the bell. Unraveled, though—they're wire. Lots of it."

All three of them looked at Jack. "Will this work for snares?" Claire asked.

"Oh yeah," he breathed, eyes wide. "Absolutely."

Using his knife, Mariana extracted the coils and pocketed them. She then, with the help of the others, pulled out the additional wire that ran from the bell to the button. Together, they harvested as much as they could. Finishing, they surveyed their bounty.

"Anything else we need here?" Reyva asked. "I've got a few nails for fishhooks."

Probably, Claire thought, but most important thing was to get the net in the water and the snares set as quickly as possible. Also start a fire and boil more water. Also set up shelter for the night, in case it rained again. Also make fishhooks and line. Also think about a signal fire and lay out another SOS. Also . . . "This is a good start."

Jack and Mariana picked up the net. Reyva walked in front, while Claire trailed behind. She yanked out dandelions on the way, as many as she could find, for fish and dandelion stew, hopefully. When they reached the trailhead, she glanced back at the derelict tennis court, the burned-down house and sheds, and the cracked airstrip.

She thought of the wild man and wondered where he was— also, *who* he was.

Could he be the missing boy from Jack's story? But if so, why hadn't he been found in all this time? It didn't make sense. They weren't *that* far from civilization. Yes, it was a serious hike, but it wasn't a twenty-year hike. More likely he was a hermit or a homeless man who had retreated to the woods a few years ago, not a boy who had failed to find his way home for two decades.

She wondered if the wild man had ever seen Jack's ghost. Not that she believed in ghosts. *If I did, this place would be crawling with them.* A kid had died when this camp closed. More had died when it reopened.

It might not be haunted, Claire thought. *But it's definitely cursed.*

THIRTEEN

Squatting on the dock, Claire tied knots in the tennis net to repair the worst of the rips. Enough of the net was intact that it *should* work to catch fish. Maybe. She hoped.

Look at me, all hopeful, she thought. She wondered how long it would last.

Dad always said, "Just cheer up," as if it were as simple as that. "Smile," he'd say. "You'll feel better." And Mom would say, "Just try, sweetie. You'll have fun, you'll make friends, you'll be happy if . . ." *If* you didn't mope in your room, *if* you didn't worry about every little thing, *if* you didn't obsess over catastrophes that might or might not happen . . . *if* you became an entirely different person. One time, Claire had tried to explain how it made her feel when they told her she needed to change. Her parents had been the ones to end up in tears, and she'd spent an hour consoling them instead of vice versa. Not her most successful conversation.

At least here, not a single person had told her she needed to cheer up. *Hey, I've discovered a silver lining to being in a probably-going-to-die, life-or-death situation,* she thought. *Yay?*

She glanced over at her friends. Jack wasn't nearby—he had volunteered to find a sapling to use with the net—but Reyva and Mariana were both here, hauling rocks onto the dock. Their plan was to attach the net to half of the sapling, position it so that the net dangled in the deeper water off the end of the dock, and then anchor the other half of the sapling on the dock with a lot of rocks.

"So explain to me why," Reyva asked with a huff as she deposited another rock onto the dock, "the fish will swim into the net instead of around?"

"Because fish are dumb." Mid-knot, Mariana paused and examined her nails. "Chipped another one. That's three so far."

"A tragedy," Reyva said.

"I didn't say it was a tragedy," Mariana snapped. "Just a fact. You know, it's irritating how you keep on thinking the worst of me." Hearing the edge in her voice, Claire froze mid-knot. She had been consumed in her own thoughts. Had she missed noticing tension rising between the two of them? Last thing they needed was to snipe at each other.

Halfway back to the rocky shore, Reyva halted. "I don't think the worst of you."

I should say something, Claire thought. But she didn't know what. It was the strain of the lack of food and the constant supply of fear. It made you feel like your skin was raw. That was why they were acting this way.

"Then why the mocking?" Mariana demanded.

"Because it's easy."

Claire rose to her feet. If they fell apart . . .

But Reyva wasn't done. "You're smart, beautiful, and confident, and that makes you easy to mock."

Mariana gawked at her for a second, then laughed. "Aw, love you too!"

Together, they went for more rocks.

With a smile on her face, Claire sank back down and resumed tying knots. She felt as if a knot inside her rib cage had loosened. They all needed to stick together, and then they'd have a chance.

Waving toward the woods, where Jack had gone to find their pole for the net, Mariana asked, "Hey, what do you think Jack thinks of me? Intimidated by the smart or by the beautiful?"

Content that they weren't arguing, Claire didn't listen to Reyva's answer. Finishing the final knot, she looked out at the water. It was beautiful here, as her parents had promised. Peaceful, even, now that the gunman was gone. She thought again of the wild man by the cave. It was unlikely he'd bother them, now that there were four of them.

She remembered suddenly that they hadn't told Jack about the wild man. Probably should clue him in, just in case he ran into him in the woods.

Speaking of which, how far into the woods had Jack gone?

She'd assumed he'd be sensible enough to stick near the shore. Yes, he was outdoorsy and all that, but it was still safer to stick together. She couldn't see even a hint of his orange T-shirt in between the trees. "Jack?" she called.

Leaving the net, she crossed to the tree line.

"Jack? You okay?"

For another second, there was no answer.

He's dead, she thought.

Then his voice: "I'm fine!"

He was too far away for comfort. "We didn't tell him about the wild man," Claire said to Reyva and Mariana. She immediately began imagining various scenarios in which the wild man stumbled across Jack. It wasn't an unrealistic worry—they hadn't warned him well enough about the man with the shotgun, and he'd nearly been killed. She didn't want to make the same mistake twice. And she knew she wasn't going to be able to stop worrying about it unless she did something. "I'm going to warn him so he doesn't get surprised."

"Good idea," Mariana approved.

"Be right back." With a wave, Claire headed into the woods in the direction of his voice.

The birds were chirping, which she took to be an excellent sign. She didn't remember ever being as hyperaware of birdcalls as she was now. She wondered if she'd always notice whether there were birds or not after this.

She was pleased that her brain didn't immediately chirp, *If there is an "after this."*

As she walked, she practiced stepping softly on the forest floor. The pine needles and the moss didn't crunch, she noticed. Only the dead leaves, and even they weren't so bad since the rain. They crumpled beneath her feet.

She noted the poison ivy, steered clear of that, and watched for more blueberry bushes. Pausing at a patch of ferns, she knelt to look for fiddleheads. A few young fronds were growing beneath the full lacy spread of adult ferns.

Gathering them, she thought she heard a voice, specifically Jack's.

Is he talking to himself? she wondered.

Listening, she tried to make out individual words, but it was too muffled to be intelligible. Oddly, it didn't sound as if he was talking to himself. There were pauses between words, as if he were waiting for someone else to speak.

Stuffing the fronds into her pockets, she rose and walked as quietly as she could toward his voice. She saw a hint of his orange T-shirt through the trees. His back was to her. She didn't see anyone with him.

Carefully, she stepped heel-slowly-to-toe between the trees.

"I can fix this," Jack was saying. "You gotta trust me." A pause. "Please, it's not too late. I'm talking to you, right? So that means it can't be too late. Just . . . trust me, okay?"

What does that mean? Fix what?

She inched closer, trying to see through the tree trunks, to tell if he was alone—and a twig snapped beneath her foot.

He spun around. "Who's there?"

Claire popped forward with a wave. "It's me. Claire." She winced at herself. Of course he knew her name. Could she sound any more awkward? "Didn't mean to startle you." Crossing the remaining distance, she tried to both act casual and scan the area for anyone else. "Were you talking to someone? It sounded like you were."

He laughed as he picked up his pack, which had been lying on the ground beside him. He slung it over his shoulder. "Just talking to myself. I talk to myself all the time. Whole conversations. Ha-ha!"

She didn't see any hint of anyone else. No movement between the trees around them. Just the breeze through the leaves. "I came to tell you. There's someone else in the woods—a man who looks like he's been here for decades." Continuing to scan the trees, she described the wild man.

Jack shook his head. "Sometimes the national forest draws some weirdos. The park rangers try to flush them out, but . . . Anyway, yeah, definitely will keep an eye out."

Guess that wasn't who he was talking to, she thought.

Unless he's lying.

She glanced at the ground, trying to look casual, as if she were just examining the moss and dried leaves. There weren't any obvious signs like footprints that didn't match either hers or Jack's. Maybe an expert tracker would have been able to tell if there had been anyone else here, but she couldn't. "Did you find a tree for the net?"

He patted a leafless tree next to him. It was skinny, about three inches in diameter, with only a few twig-like branches, and it had a curve to it that would allow them to angle the net into the water. Surprisingly, it was still standing. She'd thought after this much time, he'd have had it felled. But maybe it had simply taken him a while to find.

"Need help?" she offered.

"Sure." He kicked at the roots. "It's rotted. Should fall easily."

Together, they stood side by side and shoved at the young,

dead tree. Its roots shifted in the mossy earth. He kicked again as it tilted, freeing the crumbling roots from the ground. A second later, it crashed down. She checked the woods again, half expecting someone to burst out at the noise.

"You grab one end, and I'll grab the other," he said.

She picked up the end with the leafless branches, and he picked up the end with the rotted roots. It wasn't heavy, but it felt solid enough that it should work. It was thick enough that it wouldn't snap if a fish pulled against the net, she hoped, and long enough to hold what was left of the tennis net.

"You ever talk to yourself?" Jack asked.

"Trick question," Claire said. "Everybody does." She tried to keep her voice normal and casual, so he wouldn't guess the hundred suspicious thoughts running like rabbits through her mind.

"Yeah, you think so?" He sounded relieved.

She knew that feeling well—you think you're the only one who's had a certain thought or has a certain habit, and then you discover you're not alone. It was such a rush of relief. Was that what was happening here? Was he relieved she understood, or was he relieved that she believed his lie? "Absolutely. Some of my favorite conversations have been with me."

But I don't usually sound like I'm waiting for myself to answer, she thought.

He laughed.

She liked his laugh. It was warm and deep and reminded her of hot chocolate. She could see herself liking him—in fact, she'd been starting to, before this. It was nice that he wasn't trying to take charge, even though he clearly knew more about the woods than they did. It was nice that he was helping out, volunteering to help them set up the net even though he hadn't been here long enough to feel as hungry as they were. She appreciated that he'd only fallen apart for a little while after being shot at and then had rallied even in the face of everything they'd told him in very short order. But she did *not* like that she was half certain that he was lying to her.

She could, of course, just be feeling paranoid. He might very well have been talking to himself, in which case she was being terribly unfair to someone who was in as much of a precarious situation as she was and who was only trying to help. She should remember innocent until proven guilty. She had no proof that he'd been talking to anyone.

They carried the sapling to the shore and threaded it through the top of the net. Claire tied rocks to the bottom of the net so it wouldn't just float. Then all four of them helped lay it on the dock and push it into position. Once enough of the net dangled into the water, Reyva and Mariana used the rocks to weigh down the opposite end of the tree.

Catching her eye, Jack said, "Don't worry. It'll work."

She smiled back but kept watching him.

After the net was secured, they refilled the toolbox with lake water and built a fire. It was trickier to find dry wood, but at least there wasn't the wind from the other day. Once they had the tinder bundle and enough sticks in place, Jack asked, "Uh, you aren't expecting me to have a lighter, are you?"

"Nope," Reyva said. "Mariana, would you do the honors, please?"

Mariana unwrapped a fresh stick of gum, sliced the wrapper into the correct shape, and then lit it with her battery.

"Whoa, that's awesome," Jack said.

She flashed her thousand-watt smile at him. "We might not have been able to recognize blueberry bushes, but we aren't useless."

Claire thought that was a massive understatement. Mariana and Reyva were two of the most competent, resilient, and amazing people she'd ever met. She thought of everything that Mariana had been through, with her father's screwup and all the upheaval it had caused. She was so fierce, even though she was grieving her home, missing her faraway friends and family, and coping with all the anger she had to be feeling about what her dad had done that turned her life upside down.

"I never thought you were," Jack said, with a lopsided grin that reminded Claire of a wink. His eyes glued to Mariana, he sat down next to her. "You knew how to keep the boat from porpoising. You're full of surprises."

"I am," she agreed.

Their heads close together, Mariana and Jack nurtured the tinder bundle. He handed her twigs, and she fed them to the fire. The flames leapt from stick to stick, chasing along the bark. Smoke curled skyward. Claire wondered whether she'd tell Jack where she was from. She didn't think Mariana would trust him too quickly with the full truth, but she didn't know.

Claire scooted closer to Reyva and murmured, "Do you think she's seriously into him?"

"I think she's under stress, and he's a safe outlet," Reyva said in just as soft a voice. "What do you think? Are we rooting for them to get together?"

"I think survival trumps romance right now, with anyone."

Mariana laughed as Jack whispered something to her. It was a light, airy laugh, not one that Claire had heard her make. "Fake laugh," Claire murmured to Reyva. "Might mean she's not that into him?"

"Mm," Reyva agreed, still speaking under her breath so only Claire could hear. "He thinks he's funny, and she doesn't. Relationship probably doomed."

Claire thought she sounded hopeful, but maybe that was her imagination. She wondered whether Reyva had doubts about Jack too, or if Claire was the only one who wasn't 100 percent thrilled he'd joined them and even less thrilled that Mariana was acting so friendly with someone Claire didn't trust.

As they watched, Mariana laid her hand butterfly-light on his knee, then pointed out at the water. She'd asked him a question. He whispered his answer. *Maybe I just don't like the way Jack is changing the dynamic of the three of us,* Claire thought. She'd just gotten used to being part of a trio with Reyva and Mariana.

"Any interest in checking the net?" Reyva asked Claire.

"Lots," Claire agreed.

They headed out to the dock, leaving Mariana and Jack to flirt by the fire. Claire wondered if she felt jealous—after all, he had lake-blue eyes and a nice laugh and had paid attention to her before in the woods—but no, all she felt was a spiral of worry. Glancing back at them, Claire asked Reyva, "What do you think of him?"

"I don't, really," Reyva said.

"Mariana seems to like him well enough."

By the fire, Mariana was gazing into his eyes as if she thought his every word was fascinating. Her hands, though, were busy unspooling the wire from one of the coils she'd liberated from the old doorbell. *She's good at multitasking*, Claire thought. *Flirting and electrical work, simultaneously.*

If she'd met Mariana in any other context, Claire thought she would have been jealous of her. As Reyva had pointed out, she was smart, beautiful, and confident. Here, though, Claire was grateful for her. And impressed. And a little anxious—what if Jack wasn't who he seemed to be? Or what if he was, and Claire ruined everything with her paranoia? Maybe all he wanted was to be friends with them. And she was about to sabotage that.

"She likes that she understands him," Reyva said. "I think, it's like he's a car engine to her. She knows what makes him work, and given how much has been out of our control here . . . Anyway, what do *you* think of him? You two seemed friendly coming back from the woods."

"I think . . ."

The words clogged in her throat. All the times she'd voiced her fears, her doubts, her worries. All the times she'd ruined a moment. All the times she'd acted weird and lost friends for it, like Angie and Priya, or simply failed to make them, like Sonia, driving away people with her nonstop negativity or—even more often—being afraid she would.

But Reyva was waiting for her to answer, and Reyva . . . was different. They'd crawled through a cave together. They'd run from a killer together. They'd talked about their fears, at least a few of them. Surely that was, as Mariana would say, bonding enough for Claire to speak. She thought of her parents telling her to just try, though she was certain this wasn't what they meant. . . .

"I think he was talking to someone," Claire said, "in the woods. I think . . . he's a liar."

FOURTEEN

Reyva's eyes went wide.

Quickly, Claire added, "I could be wrong. He said he was talking to himself, and I didn't see anyone. So maybe he was." She couldn't tell if Reyva believed her or didn't. Honestly, she wasn't sure which she wanted—for Reyva to agree or to talk her out of it.

She didn't *want* Jack to be lying to them.

Did she?

Was she so consumed by seeing danger everywhere that she let it poison everything? She waited for Reyva to reply, so tense that she felt as coiled as the wire.

Reyva gripped Claire's arm hard. "Fish!"

Startled, Claire turned, following Reyva's gaze, and peered into the water. Sure enough, several feet from dock, a silvery fish about as long as Claire's arm was writhing in the tennis net. She spun back to face Reyva. "Fish!"

Waving at Mariana and Jack, Reyva called, "Fish! There's a fish!"

Punching the air, Mariana leapt up. "Yes!" She tugged Jack

with her, and they ran onto the dock. Skidding to a stop next to Reyva and Claire, she asked, "Are you serious? A real fish?"

"No," Reyva said. "A plastic fish. Of course a real fish!"

"Not possible," Jack said. "We just put the gill net in. No one catches fish that fast." He peered into the water. "Whoa. Lake trout! Serious beginner's luck."

Mariana hugged both Reyva and Claire. "Do you know what this means?"

Hugging them back, Claire felt tears prick her eyes. "Food. Actual food."

"*And* it means that Reyva *is* capable of expressing emotion." Mariana hugged them again. "I heard actual excitement. Joy, even. I'm so proud! You're lowering your walls."

With a laugh, Reyva swatted her. "You are absurd."

Kneeling, Jack reached toward the net. Claire immediately went for the rocks that held the pole. The others held the sapling steady. As she moved the rocks, they lifted the tree, bringing the net slowly toward Jack.

"Steady," he said. "Keep it steady."

The tree shook as the fish flailed.

Claire held her breath. If it wiggled free . . .

Jack pulled the net toward him. When the fish was over the dock, he said, "Set it down." Reyva and Mariana lowered it. The fish flopped, twisting and writhing.

Mariana did a little dance. "Yes! Glorious food!"

Swiftly, Jack grabbed one of the rocks that had been holding the net in position and brought it down hard on the fish's head.

Mariana abruptly quit dancing. "Wish I hadn't seen that."

"What did you expect?" Reyva said. "It would just go peacefully to sleep?"

"Honestly would have preferred that," Mariana said. "I was one of those kids who thought that it was odd that 'chicken' the animal and 'chicken' the food were called the same name. My aunt Ana had to sit me down and break the truth to me. Rough day. Almost turned vegetarian, but, you know, *bacon*."

Jack drew his knife out.

"Oh, whoa, you're going to just right here—" Mariana began.

He flipped the fish onto its back, inserted his knife by the tail, and sliced neatly all the way up to its gills.

Mariana turned away. "Yep, he is."

Claire didn't want to watch either, but she felt like she should learn. Kneeling, she forced herself to watch. Reyva had no hesitation—she shoved her face forward to see as Jack slit along the fish's throat, perpendicular to the first slice, and then yanked out the intestines.

"Key, as I said before, is don't pierce the intestines," Jack said. "Basically, that's all the squishy stuff that doesn't look like what they serve in restaurants."

"Good to know," Claire said. "Thanks."

He slid the blade along the fish's spine to create two fillets and sliced again to remove the bones. Claire made mental notes on each incision. Luckily, it didn't look very hard. Just slimy.

Joined by Mariana, Reyva took the fillets to the fire. Jack carried the intestines to shore and deposited them on a rock—"Bait for the fishhooks," he said—before washing his hands in the lake. Claire watched him out of the corner of her eye. Maybe he *had* been talking to himself. Nothing he'd said or done besides that had seemed the least bit suspicious. Really, he seemed like a nice guy. Earnest.

He glanced at her. "What? Do I have fish guts on me?"

"No. Sorry. I just . . ."

He waited for her to spit out whatever it was she wanted to say. The problem was she didn't know what she wanted to say. *Can I trust you?* was the real question.

"Nothing," she said.

Maybe she really shouldn't be so suspicious. Maybe she should get to know Jack, the way she'd gotten to know Reyva and Mariana. Maybe she should give him a chance and not let her paranoia ruin what was probably their best chance at survival. She wished she hadn't said anything to Reyva and had just kept her suspicions to herself until she was more certain one way or another. First opportunity she got, she'd talk to her. Tell her to ignore what she'd said.

She joined Reyva and Mariana by the fire. Reyva had stuck the fillets onto sticks and was holding them over the flames. Perching herself on a rock, Claire wondered how she would be able to speak to Reyva without Jack overhearing.

Scooting closer to Claire, Mariana said softly, "You're wrong about him. He's stuck here, just like us, and he's trying his best."

Okay, so Reyva had clearly talked to her, in the moments while Claire and Jack were on the dock. *Great*, she thought. *Now I've really made a mess of things.* Everyone was going to be angry with her now for causing problems where there weren't any. She'd been accused of that before—a school bonfire had been canceled once, because she'd worried out loud about safety in the hearing of a teacher, and the gym had been closed when she'd thought she'd smelled a gas leak. In both cases, if she'd kept her mouth shut, everyone would have been happier. Before Claire could figure out how to reply, Jack hopped over a rock and plopped down beside them.

Cheerfully, as if no one would ever dream of talking behind anyone's back, Mariana said, "So, we mastered fishing. How about snares? If there's a way to specify that the snares only catch non-cute animals, that would be ideal."

"She only wants to eat really ugly bunnies," Reyva said solemnly.

"Or bunnies with bad personalities." Mariana held out the uncoiled wire to Jack.

He took it and knelt by the fire. "Okay, first step . . . we want about three feet of wire per snare." Using his knife, he cut off a three-foot strip. He held it out. "Who wants to try?"

Claire took it. "I will."

He cut a length for himself. "Step two, make a small loop at the end. Twist to hold it in place."

He demonstrated, and Claire mirrored it back to him.

"Push the opposite end of the wire through the slipknot to make a noose. . . ."

"Can we not call it a noose?" Mariana said.

Reyva rolled her eyes. "It's literally a noose."

"Bunny neck loop?" Claire suggested.

Mariana glared at her. "A hundred times worse."

"What's next?" Claire asked Jack.

"Well, that's basically it," he said. "You can tie it onto a branch so that it hangs over a game trail, or you can secure it to the ground with a post. . . . Okay, so we don't have a post, but we can tie it onto a skinny tree, or wedge it under a rock?"

"You're our hero," Mariana teased.

While the fish continued to cook, Claire watched Mariana flirt. She wondered what was wrong with her that she couldn't just be happy to be alive and to have food and friends.

"It's ready," Reyva said.

Reverently, she held the two fillets in front of them. Claire breathed in the smell of fresh-cooked trout and nearly felt dizzy. It smelled amazing. Reyva handed one stick with a fillet to Mariana and held the other out to Claire.

Mariana plucked a bit of the flaky white fish from the stick. "Ow, ow, ow!" She popped it into her mouth and then breathed around the fish. "Hot."

Claire and Reyva laughed.

Blowing on the fish, Claire took a chunk and placed it on her tongue. She didn't know what she'd expected it to taste like— she'd never really liked fish before. She usually thought it was kind of like eating rubber bands, chewy and tasteless.

Not this.

This was as sweet and soft as a fresh croissant from a bakery. It melted on her tongue, and she felt as if flavor was exploding in her skull.

"This is amazing," Mariana said. "You have to try it." She held a piece out to Jack.

He held his hands up. "I'm not the one who's been starving. You guys eat it."

"Gallant *and* heroic," Mariana told him, and then shot a significant glance at Claire. Mariana popped the piece of fish into her mouth. "Thanks," she said to Jack.

The three of them shared the fillets, and they were gone far too quickly.

With a happy sigh, Reyva leaned back next to her. "Is it wrong that I'm happy?"

Mariana grinned at her. "Absolutely not wrong. New, maybe. Warn us if you're going to break out in song and dance. Or if you're going to do something even more rash, like smile."

Leaning back against a boulder, Claire licked her fingers.

Across the lake, the sun was dipping closer to the tops of the trees. The nearby clouds were dyed rose. It was virtually windless, and the lake was still, reflecting the trees and the sky.

"Can I see that wire?" Jack asked Mariana.

She passed it to him. Using his knife, he sliced off several pieces, a couple of feet in length, and handed the rest back to her. She coiled the remainder up and tucked it in her pocket.

Jack stood up. "You guys rest. I'm going to set a few snares."

"Thank you, my hero!" Mariana sang.

He blushed and retreated from the fire.

The three of them watched as he trooped into the woods. His footfalls crunched on the dead leaves, audible even after he disappeared behind the thick trees.

"Think it's okay that he's going off alone?" Claire asked.

"Absolutely fine," Mariana said with a wave. "The man with the gun is long gone."

After less than a minute of not-so-patiently staring at the woods, Claire stood up. "I'm just going to go check—"

"—on what Jack is up to?" Reyva asked. "Good idea."

"Oh, stop it, both of you." Mariana swatted lightly at Claire's foot. "Leave the poor boy alone. He's fine. Everything's fine. Someone's got to be expecting him back; they'll come and save us. This is almost over. We can relax."

Claire felt a shiver.

"We have to trust each other," Mariana said. "That's the only way through this."

"Let her go," Reyva said. "It doesn't do any harm for her to at least make sure he's okay."

She hesitated a moment, not sure if she should try to explain or apologize or what. But she couldn't think of what to say, and Reyva and Mariana were both shooting looks at each other that felt laden with an unspoken argument. She'd never meant to fight with either of them. She wished she could rewind and start over. If she had a do-over, she wouldn't let herself get carried away by her imagination—*call it what it is*, she told herself, *my paranoid anxiety.*

Without saying anything more, Claire headed into the woods. She really did just want to see if he was okay, she told herself. She didn't suspect Jack. He'd been nothing but helpful. *And I'm repaying him by spying on him*, she thought.

I'll apologize to him, and then I'll explain to Reyva and Mariana. I'll fix this.

But she still walked as lightly as she could over the pine needles and the moss.

His orange T-shirt was easy to spot through the trees. He was kneeling by a rock. Closer, she watched him from behind a tree trunk. He was setting a snare, exactly as he'd said he was going to do, tying it onto a branch so that it dangled over a fallen log.

Not talking to anyone.

Now she felt extra guilty.

She took a deep breath. She owed him this apology.

His bag was lying a few feet away, and it caught her eye. It occurred to her that he'd never really shared what was inside it. *Stop it*, she told herself. She'd *just* decided that she wasn't going to be suspicious anymore. Only together would they survive this. He'd already proved how valuable his knowledge was. She'd be making a massive mistake if she caused a rift now, when they were all learning to trust one another.

Claire stepped out from behind the trees and cleared her throat. "Hey."

Jack jumped.

"Whoa, Claire! You scared me!"

"Sorry. Just . . ." She wished she hadn't revealed herself and had just gone back to the fire after she saw he was okay. She was messing all of this up. "I owe you an apology." She was going to go for it. Get it all out in the open so that they could move on.

"For what?" he asked.

"I thought you were talking to someone, earlier in the forest," Claire said. "And it made me not trust you. But you've been nothing but helpful. Without you . . . we'd still be starving. Now, thanks to you, we've got food. We've got hope. So I just . . . wanted to say I'm sorry."

"Cool. Um, okay. You didn't really need to apologize. It must have sounded super suspicious." He stood and crossed to her.

She laughed, awkwardly, at herself and at the fact that they were alone in the woods. "Yeah, well. I know you said you were just talking to yourself." *Why did I add "you said"?* she asked herself. *I don't suspect him anymore.*

"I was," he insisted.

Behind him, she saw a bit of movement. She opened her mouth to shout a warning, then realized it was Reyva and Mariana. Reyva pointed to his bag. Mariana held a finger to her lips.

What were they—

Oh.

They believed me, she thought.

The idea made tears prick in her eyes. She was probably wrong. She was probably being paranoid and suspicious and anxious and all the things she hated about herself. But Reyva and Mariana were trusting her anyway, as they had from the day she'd met them.

She had to keep Jack's attention on her, or there would be a lot more explaining to do.

"Then what were you talking about?" Claire asked. "Because it definitely sounded like you were talking *to* someone else. I heard you say, 'I can fix this. You have to trust me.' Not exactly what someone talking to themself says. You can see why I was suspicious."

He smiled at her and moved closer.

She resisted taking a step backward, reminding herself that she had to keep his attention on her, at least until Reyva and Mariana had the chance to check his bag.

"I was talking to myself," Jack insisted. "I was telling myself to trust my feelings." He took one of her hands. His fingers felt rough and dirty, and she was aware that hers were greasy with fish, dirt, and ash from touching the boards at the burned-down Lake House.

"Um, what are you doing?" He was even closer, and her heart felt like it was beating as fast as it had inside the cave. He was definitely in her personal space. She felt herself tense like a rabbit.

"Explaining," he said.

"Oh?"

Reyva and Mariana were almost to the bag, but Mariana had stopped to stare at them. Claire wanted to pull back. She didn't want to be flirting with the boy who Mariana so obviously liked. The whole idea behind apologizing was to eliminate any drama between them. But then he said, "I came here thinking it was because of Mariana, but I didn't realize it was *you*."

What?

Mariana's mouth dropped open.

Reyva rolled her eyes but didn't let it slow her. She pulled the bag toward her, and leaves crunched. Jack began to turn at the sound.

Quickly, Claire reached up and cupped his cheek in her hand. "Me?"

"So you see," Jack said, "I wasn't talking to anyone. I was talking to myself, telling myself that you were the one I came to see and that I shouldn't doubt what I felt. I should act." He leaned closer, and Claire's eyes widened.

He was not going to kiss—

He pressed his lips against hers. With one hand, he pulled her waist up against him, and with the other, he tangled his fingers in her hair.

It felt a bit like eating the fish. Soft. Squishy. A lot of flavor.

His eyes were closed.

Hers weren't.

And so she saw the moment that Reyva found the satellite phone in Jack's bag.

FIFTEEN

Claire stepped back.

Slowly, with a lazy smile on his face, Jack opened his eyes.

Behind him, a few yards away, Mariana said cheerfully, "If you were just talking to yourself, then you won't mind if we borrow *your phone* for a while."

His smile dropped off so fast that it was impossible to imagine it had ever been there. He pivoted to see Mariana and Reyva standing over his backpack. With a sparkling smile, Mariana wiggled the phone in the air.

Reyva crossed her arms. "You want to explain this?"

"Don't bother asking," Mariana said sweetly. "He'll only lie."

Jack took a step toward them. "Give my phone back." He'd gone pale, and a vein in his neck was popping up. "You don't know—"

"I think I can guess," Mariana said, sounding harder than Claire had ever heard her. "This was a game to you. You were playing hero. You thought you'd show us how to survive in the Great Outdoors and make us think you were saving us, all the while knowing you could call for help at any time. Only question is: Were you going to make a move on all three of us, or just pick and choose depending on your mood?"

Reyva plucked the phone out of Mariana's hands. "Doesn't matter. Call for help, and then we never have to see his lying face again."

"Wait—" Jack said.

As she punched the first number, the phone began to ring. Reyva looked up at him. "Who's calling, Jack?" she asked. Her fingers hovered over the buttons.

"Give me the phone," he begged. "Please."

Mariana grabbed it out of Reyva's hands and answered, "Hello? Please help us! We're stranded at the Lake House. The summer camp burned down. The program director is dead. Please, send help! Save us!" She then gave it back to Reyva.

Reyva held the phone to her ear and said, "What she said. Send rescue. We need help."

Claire wanted to cheer for them. They were both—

Jack stepped behind Claire and gripped her upper arm. She felt his fist at her throat. Cold metal touched her skin. "Tell your friends to give me the phone," Jack said, his lips inches from her ear.

Claire froze.

It was his knife. The one that had gutted the fish so quickly and smoothly. She couldn't see it without tilting her head, and she didn't dare move. She'd never felt a knife at her throat before, but she knew instantly that's what it was. "Reyva.

Mariana." Her voice came out as a croak.

Reyva started forward. "What the hell are you doing?"

He pressed the blade harder against Claire's skin. She sucked in air and tried to pull back from the blade, but he was behind her, holding her still.

"Give him the phone," Mariana told Reyva.

Claire felt her pulse beating against the blade. Why was he doing this? He wanted his phone back, but this was beyond extreme. He wouldn't kill for it, would he? Why? "You don't want to do this," she said to him.

"Give it to me," Jack said. "And I won't."

"Give it to him, Reyva," Mariana said. "Someone knows we need help. We did what we needed to do."

Reyva's eyes were narrowed and shooting so much rage that Claire was half surprised they didn't spark. "Release her, and you can have the phone."

From the phone, Claire heard a voice, muffled. It was too far for her to hear actual words, but it sounded like a man's voice. Reyva began to lift the phone to her ear.

"Not negotiating," Jack said. "And not joking. Give me the phone now, and *then* I'll let her go." Keeping the hand with the knife on Claire's throat, he let go of her arm and reached out past her with his other hand.

Reyva stepped forward, the phone held out.

The second she was close enough, he grabbed it and held the phone to his ear. He didn't move the knife from Claire's throat. "Dad? Dad, are you there?"

It made sense that his father would be calling him. But it didn't make sense that he felt the need to threaten her. His dad could come save them all. She didn't understand the drama. Just admit he'd wanted to impress them, or whatever the reason for hiding the phone—

"Where are you?" Jack asked.

Pressed against him, she was plenty close enough to hear the response, buried under a whirring noise as if he were close to a propeller or an air conditioner: "It won't let me leave."

"Hey, you're supposed to let her go," Reyva said. "That was the deal."

Jack ignored her. "What's that noise? Are you still on the boat?"

On the boat . . .

Claire felt her eyes widen. Mariana looked confused, but Reyva looked just as shocked. He *could* have meant a different boat. But what were the odds? Flatly, she said, "The man who tried to kill us . . . is your father." The same man who'd shot at Jack and stolen his boat.

The knife shook as Jack said, "Shut up." Then into the phone: "Come back. We can fix this. I know we can. I have the girls here. No one's coming for them. Their parents think they're fine. I told their parents not to expect to hear from them for at least a week—camp policy for preventing homesickness. Just as you said to say. They bought it."

Claire felt as cold as the knife.

"You—what?" Mariana asked.

At the same time, Reyva asked, "What have you done?"

Jack ignored them. "Please, Dad. You just have to come back. It'll be okay. Follow the plan."

"Let them go, Jack," his father said through the phone. "They're innocent."

"No one's innocent. And the world will be better off without three more useless girls who can't do anything for themselves. No one will miss them."

"Jack—" his father began.

"Come back, make the trade, and you'll be free."

Both Mariana's and Reyva's eyes were on Claire, and she read every bit of their panic. She tried to clear a spot in her head to think. She didn't understand what he was saying: Make what trade? To who? Free of what?

A few words were lost under the hum of the motor, but Claire heard: "—not yours to judge—deserve to go back to their families."

"What about me?" Jack said. "I deserve my family too!"

"Listen to me carefully: I don't want you to save me."

"I'm not losing you, Dad," Jack said. He was crying. Claire felt his tears land on the back of her neck. They slid down her shoulder blades, beneath her shirt. "I've got them right here. All you have to do is come back to the Lake House. Come on, Dad. Please."

"Stop," his father said. "Just stop. I can't— Listen to me, Jack, it's too late for me. I killed Mackenzie. I involved you in all of this, even though it was the last thing I ever wanted to do. I couldn't stop myself. Do you understand? I'm already lost."

Mackenzie. That must have been the dead woman in the woods, the program director. He was admitting that. It wasn't just suspicion anymore. Claire wanted to ask why he'd killed her, what was going on, but she didn't dare speak with the blade trembling on her throat.

"You didn't do it," Jack sobbed. "It wasn't you."

"My eyes looked into hers, and my finger pulled that trigger. I wasn't strong enough." His voice faded in and out beneath the roar of the boat motor. "I'm so sorry, Jack."

"Don't talk like that. You *are* strong enough! This is you I'm talking to right now! We can fight together! I know we can."

"I was weak. So very weak. I thought"—she lost more words to the roar of the motor—"please . . . forgive me for involving you. I should have fought harder to not—never wanted—only now—you."

"Dad, please, we can end this. Be free. Just come back. Dad—"

"You can't save me, but I can save you."

"No!"

Crack.

The shot rang through the phone and simultaneously echoed from across the lake.

Jack dropped the phone and the knife, then fell to his knees. Claire sprinted to Reyva and Mariana. Reyva pulled her behind them, and Mariana wrapped her arms around Claire. All of them stared at Jack.

"Was that . . . ?" Mariana whispered.

Claire's brain felt as if it were spinning: *He shot himself. That was a gun. He's dead. We heard him die.* She sucked in oxygen.

There wasn't enough air. Her rib cage felt tight, as if it were squeezing her lungs.

Jack lifted his head. "This is your fault."

Words felt clogged in Claire's throat. Shaking her head, she wanted to say . . . She didn't know what she wanted to say. She could still feel the ghost of the knife on her skin. *He shot himself,* she thought again.

"If you had come sooner, it never would have taken him. It was supposed to be one of you." He gripped the handle of his knife as he stood. "It still can be. This isn't over. I can get him back."

Claire had never seen so much desperation in someone's eyes. His charming face was twisted. She felt like a rabbit, caught in the sights of a rabid bear.

"Run," she croaked.

He was close behind them.

She heard his footsteps pounding over the branches and leaves.

Unlike the man with the gun—*his father,* she corrected herself—Jack wasn't impeded by anything. He was hurling himself through the woods, shouting that he needed them, it wasn't too late, they had to fix what they'd done.

Her side ached, and her legs burned. She tried to watch every step, but she felt as if she were careening across the slick leaves. She caught herself on a tree before she fell. Her brain screamed: *He'll catch us! He'll kill us!*

"Can you take him?" she puffed to Reyva.

"Thanks for the vote of confidence," Reyva said, "but no."

She glanced behind them and saw Jack shoving his way through a screen of vines.

"You're a champion," Mariana said.

"On flat ground without a knife and with a referee, yes, I could take him. Now? Here? With him seriously pissed off? Maybe. But it would be a risk. Come on, keep moving!"

Pushing off the tree, Claire lurched forward into a run. She felt for her pocket, its contents bouncing with each stride. "I have the Swiss Army knife." That was about all she had. She wished she'd thought to scoop up his pack. Or to bring theirs. All their supplies were back at the dock. Everything. She'd even shoved her phone in there, after the battery died.

"It's, like, a one-inch blade," Reyva shot back.

Mariana jumped over a fallen log. "Reyva's right." She kept running. "We can't send her into a knife fight with a boy who's got nothing to lose."

"Come on!" Reyva called to Claire. "Just need to put some distance between us and him!" She put on an extra boost of speed, plowing through a bush.

"Then what?" Claire asked, struggling to keep up.

They had no idea where they were heading. She should have paid attention to the direction—were they going farther from the lake or closer to it? North, south, east, west? With the thick trees and the gray clouds above, she couldn't see the sun.

And then the rain started.

A few drops as if the sky were clearing its throat, and then it spilled out in a torrent, just as hard as before. In minutes, they had to slow to a walk. Water streamed down from the sky. Wind shook the trees.

"What the hell—" Mariana said, shielding her head with her arms. "Where did this come from?"

Claire glanced back and felt a spurt of hope. It was impossible to see Jack in the thick rain. *This is our chance*, she thought. *We can lose him in this.* They could hide, and he'd pass them by. Then they could double back and . . . She didn't know what yet. One step at a time. First they had to get away.

Water streamed down her face. Her clothes felt plastered to her. The ground seemed to suck at her feet. She blinked, trying to see through the gray streams of water.

Ahead was another collection of boulders. The Maine woods were littered with them, and she was grateful for that. She caught a glimpse of an overhang with dark shadows beneath it. They could hide from the rain there.

She tugged on Mariana's and Reyva's sleeves. Pointed in that direction. With their arms up to shield their faces, they slogged toward it. She felt as if she was fording through a river as they made their way toward the rocks.

Almost there.

Just as they reached the rocks, they heard a howl. Knife in his hand, Jack catapulted himself over one of the rocks. "Stop!" he yelled. Reyva's fist shot out and caught him on the chin. He reeled back, and the three of them pivoted and fled away from the boulders as he lunged forward again.

With Mariana in the lead, then Reyva, then Claire, they fled through the rain.

Claire glanced back over her shoulder to see Jack behind them, only a few yards back. She turned forward in time to hear Mariana scream and see her disappear. Reaching for her, Reyva also tumbled into rain-choked nothingness. Before she could stop, the mud slid beneath Claire's feet and she flailed as she slid off the edge of the cliff, following her friends.

SIXTEEN

Claire half fell and half slid down the slope. Branches smacked her, and she threw an arm in front of her face. With the other arm, she tried to grab at roots, vines, rocks, anything to slow her descent.

But it was too steep. Too slick with mud and wet leaves. She was going too fast. She screamed so loudly that her throat hurt. The rain slammed down on her, and she skidded to a stop at the bottom of the cliff.

Flat on her back, looking up, she saw Jack silhouetted far above them.

And then she blinked to clear the rain from her eyes, and he was gone.

A split second later, the pain hit: everything hurt from the top of her scalp to her feet. Her entire body felt as if it had been pummeled with a dozen fists. "Reyva? Mariana? Are you okay?" She tried to sit up, and pain shot through her head. A wave of dizziness made her squeeze her eyes shut.

When she opened them again, the dizziness had receded, but her skull still throbbed. She touched the back of her head. With all the rain, she couldn't tell if she was bleeding.

I could be, she thought. *For all I know, I've cracked my skull. I could have a concussion. Or internal bleeding.*

Her lungs felt tight. She could have punctured them in the fall. Was that why it was so hard to breathe? Claire gasped in air like a fish on land, while rain poured down her face. *I'm dying,* she thought. "Reyva?"

"Claire?" It was Mariana. "Reyva?"

"I'm here," Claire said. Or thought she said. She wasn't certain her lips formed the words. *I am* not *dying,* she told herself. She tried again: "I'm here."

She got shakily to her feet.

Got to move, she thought. *Got to find them. Got to get away.*

She spotted Mariana, leaning against a tree. Careful not to slip on the muddy leaves, she crossed to her. "Are you okay?" Claire asked. Her own voice sounded distant inside her head, as if she were underwater. *I am drowning,* she thought as rain continued to crash down on her.

"Maybe? Yes? Ow?"

There was too much water. She needed to swim to the surface. Maybe then there would be enough air. If only she could get enough air. Just one deep breath. "Where's Reyva?" The words popped like bubbles.

Reyva's voice came with a groan. "Here."

Gulping in shallow gasps, Claire hobbled in the direction of her voice. A few yards away, Reyva was curled on the ground, her black hair tangled with thick brown mud. She was cradling one arm against her torso.

Immediately, Claire knew. "Broken?"

"Just above my wrist," Reyva said, teeth gritted. "Tried to grab a branch. Heard it snap. I thought it was the tree that broke, but no. Me."

Mariana joined them. "Maybe it's sprained. It might not be as bad as you think."

"I've broken bones before," Reyva spat out. "It's broken." Curling over her arm, she moaned. She squeezed her eyes shut.

Broken.

Broken.

The word thrummed in Claire's head like a drumbeat.

We're never going to survive, she thought. *We're going to die here, in the woods, in the rain, and no one will ever know. No one will ever find us.* She pictured their bodies strewn against the trees as limp and lifeless as the murdered woman's. *It's hopeless. Jack could have helped us, but he . . . he . . .* He'd held a knife to her throat, the metal cold on her skin. He'd chased them. He was still chasing them. He was going to catch them. Kill them.

Her head spun. Her heart thumped.

Count, she ordered herself.

Sixteen times two is thirty-two, sixteen times three . . . Grand port de bras, tendu front, demi plié, tendu front, developpé to arabesque . . .

But it was too late. The images of what could happen wouldn't stop. Reyva, broken, eyes open and sightless. Mariana, crumpled on the leaves. Claire felt the blade against her throat again, and she clawed at her neck. She needed oxygen. Why couldn't she breathe?

She heard the others calling her name. "Claire! Claire, are you okay? Claire, breathe! She's hyperventilating. Is it asthma? Is she choking? Is it her heart? Is she having a heart attack? I don't think she can hear us. Claire, can you hear me?"

She couldn't answer.

She couldn't suck in enough air.

A curtain of black rose up over her eyes.

She woke. Seconds, minutes, hours later?

Rain still fell on her face. Mariana peered down at her. "Claire?"

"I'm sorry," Claire whispered.

"Are you okay?" Mariana asked.

No, she wanted to say. "I'm fine."

"Truth," Reyva ground out. She was cradling her arm against her chest. It was broken, Claire remembered. Reyva was hurt. *And I made everything worse*, Claire thought. She'd scared herself so badly she'd collapsed. Again.

"I'm broken," Claire whispered.

Mariana examined her. "Where?"

"My brain," Claire said. "I . . . lose it. Sometimes. My thoughts grab me and won't let go. Sometimes I spiral down so fast that I plummet. Sometimes darkness eats me whole, and I can't stop it no matter how hard I try."

"Okay, so you lose it. Have you found it for now?" Reyva asked. "Because we have to move."

"Reyva . . . ," Mariana began.

"He didn't come down the cliff, but he could be finding a way around," Reyva said. "Wish he'd fall and break his neck."

"His father just died," Mariana scolded.

"And he held a knife to Claire's throat," Reyva said, moving to stand. Mariana scooted to one side of her, but Reyva shook her off as she got to her feet on her own. "Help Claire."

Claire didn't need help, but she let Mariana brace her as she stood. "I'm okay now," she said. The can't-breathe sensation had passed. She could take a full breath. Her chest ached, and her muscles felt drained, but she wasn't going to black out again. "I'll be fine."

"Let's go," Reyva said.

Holding on to one another, they shuffled and stumbled away from the cliff. Claire sent frequent glances behind them but didn't see any hint of Jack.

Maybe he'd given up.

Or maybe he'd be after them again.

He's going to catch us, she thought. *He's going to kill us.* Weakened from the fall, they wouldn't be able to stop him. She didn't think she could run again, and she knew Reyva shouldn't. They kept going for as long as they could, hobbling deeper into the forest as the rain pummeled the trees, the ground, and them.

An unending litany ran through her head as she stumbled along: *You're useless, you're pathetic, you're weak, and now they know. They've seen, and they'll never unsee. You've lost your friends. You've ruined everything . . .* Still, though, it was Claire who judged they had enough distance from the cliff, and it was Claire who found them a place to hide. Scanning the area, she spotted the decaying husk of the trunk of an enormous old tree. Half its side and innards were eroded away. She guided the others to it, and they all ducked inside.

Snug, it was at least drier inside, out of the steady pounding rain. The drops hit the forest so loud it sounded like fists on flesh. Shuddering, Reyva leaned back against the crumbling wood.

Eventually, the rain slowed.

One plus of the rain was that it had certainly wiped away all their tracks. If Jack had tried to follow them, they wouldn't have left any traces. *We're safe here*, Claire thought. *For now.*

And she breathed.

She couldn't look at the others. They'd seen her break down at the worst possible moment. It was sheer luck that Jack hadn't found them while she'd been falling apart. Sheer luck they weren't all dead because of her.

They can't trust me, Claire thought. *I can't trust me.*

She was a mess, and she always made everything worse. Who would want to be friends with anyone like that? It was no wonder she spent most of her time alone. It was better that way, for everyone.

She waited for one of them to speak, to ask her what had happened, to tell her how she'd failed them exactly when they needed her to keep it together. Lifting her eyes, Claire looked for the blame or, worse, pity in their faces. But they still weren't looking at her; they were gazing out at the rain-choked forest, watching for Jack, or rescue, or yet another surprise.

"I'm sorry," Claire said to their backs.

"Yeah, you said that already," Reyva said. "You're okay now, right?"

"Sure, it's passed now, but—" But it could happen again. And it shouldn't have happened at all. Neither Reyva nor Mariana had freaked out. There was no excuse for Claire not to be able to hold it together, for the sake of her friends, at least until they were safely away.

"Don't apologize again," Reyva said.

Biting her lip, she managed not to. *I'm sorry*, she thought. *I should have warned you. I should have recognized the signs. I should have been able to stop myself. I should have been strong enough.*

"One of you is going to need to splint my wrist," Reyva said. "Every time I so much as twitch it feels like a steel rod is being rammed through my arm. You need to immobilize it."

Mariana nodded. "We can do that. Right, Claire?"

Both of them looked at her expectantly, as if she hadn't humiliated herself, as if she hadn't failed them, as if they still thought she could help and wasn't a liability. They were looking at her as if nothing had changed between them at all.

Tears pricked Claire's eyes, and her throat felt clogged. No blame. No pity. *I don't deserve it*, she thought. "I should have been able to keep myself together. Sometimes . . . I can't."

Mariana squeezed her shoulder. "You'd just had a knife to your throat."

"But sometimes it happens for no reason at all," Claire said. "My brain just keeps spinning and spinning and won't stop." She held a fist to her head as if it were the enemy. "I didn't want you to see me like that. I didn't want you to know . . . I'm weak."

She waited for them to agree. Or for them to pity her.

"Broken," she finished.

Loudly, too loudly, Reyva said, "Bullshit."

All of them glanced out at the rain as soon as the word burst out of her. They waited, but no one jumped out between the trees in response. They heard nothing but the drumbeat of drops on the trees, rocks, and ground.

Reyva said, quieter, "I don't know who told you that broken means weak, but that's bullshit. You are the smartest, most capable person I've met. And just because your body doesn't behave the way you want it to all the time does not mean that you aren't strong."

She stared at Reyva and then at Mariana, who nodded fiercely.

They weren't going to . . . They weren't angry? Or disappointed? Claire took a ragged breath and then another. She looked at Reyva's arm. "Let's splint it."

"Great," Mariana said. "So . . . how do we do it?"

And just like that, they were past the moment that Claire had been dreading since she'd boarded that boat with the two of them. Her secret was out in the open, and they were miraculously moving on.

"You'll need to find two pieces of straight wood as long as my arm from elbow to fingers," Reyva said. "And then something to tie them together around my arm."

Claire noticed that Mariana still had her flannel shirt tied around her waist. She nodded at it. "That'll work, if you don't mind, Mariana."

Mariana unwrapped it. "Happy to sacrifice it. Maybe whatever is left over can work as a sling? After we have the splint attached?"

Claire nodded. "Good idea."

Reyva made a sound that was almost a hiccup.

Kneeling next to her, Mariana said, "Reyva? Are you okay?"

Lips pressed tight together, Reyva nodded.

"Are you crying?" Mariana asked.

"Just rain," Reyva croaked.

"It's okay to admit you're having a normal reaction to pain," Mariana said. "Didn't you listen to a word you literally just said to Claire?"

"Yeah, okay," Reyva gritted out.

Claire patted her shoulder, very lightly so as not to hurt any part of her. "We'll get you fixed up. We can do this." She felt an overwhelming need to prove she wasn't a deadweight. As broken as she was, she could still help. She nodded at Mariana. "Stay with her?"

"Of course."

Stepping out into the drizzle, Claire breathed in deeply. She'd never expected to find friends who would just accept her like that. Completely and unquestioningly. She looked up at the sky, wondering if the stars would be out soon. If she saw one, she'd wish for all the universe to keep them safe. *I'd do anything to get them out of here*, she thought.

The wind was moving fast, shifting the clouds away and showing patches of matte gray. It was near sunset. Or maybe sunset had already happened. Without open sky, she couldn't tell. Either way, they wouldn't have much time before it was too dark to see anything.

On the plus side, there also wasn't much daylight left for Jack to be able to find them.

She'd never hoped for darkness before.

She stepped around the fallen tree, looking for a chunk of wood that was straight enough and solid enough to work. If she'd had Jack's knife, she could have sawed down a thin tree or a branch, but as it was . . . She very much hoped that Jack and his knife were nowhere nearby. *Please let us get through the night.*

Keeping an eye on the woods, Claire selected a stray branch that seemed straight enough. It took her a few more minutes to find a second one—it felt strangely good to be focused on a task instead of, well, everything. She examined her second-choice branch. The bark was soaked, but that couldn't be helped.

By the time she returned to their alcove, Mariana had torn strips from the bottom of her flannel and was testing out various ways to knot the sleeves to create a sling, modeling it on herself. Reyva was giving instructions—or, more accurately, criticism. "Yeah, that's not going to work. . . . Are you aiming for a strait-jacket? Because I still need to be able to use one of my arms. . . . Okay, that's better. . . . No, definitely not like that."

"I can fix any carburetor you want," Mariana said, "but tex-tiles aren't my thing."

Claire scooted next to them. "Will these work?" She showed them the sticks she'd found. "How do we do this without hurting you?"

Reyva sat up straighter. "Probably can't."

That wasn't reassuring.

"We'll get out of here and get you to a hospital," Mariana promised. "And then we'll both write sappy scribbles in pink ink all over your cast about how awesome you are and how the three of us will be best friends forever and ever. We'll even dot the *i*'s with hearts."

Reyva managed a wan smile. "Don't you dare."

Carefully, Claire laid one piece of wood under Reyva's arm and one on top. "Mariana, you know knots. I'll hold, and you tie?"

"Um, sure?" Mariana said.

"Just do it tight," Reyva said. "The more immobile my arm is, the better." She winced as Mariana wrapped the first strip of flannel around. "Don't cut off circulation."

"Sorry!" She tried again.

"Better," Reyva grunted through gritted teeth.

Mariana tied three strips, and then she used the rest of the shirt to put it in a sling, tying the sleeves around the back of Reyva's neck.

When it was all done, they lay back within the hollow trunk.

The rain had fully stopped now, but night had fallen and shrouded the forest in darkness. This was as far as they'd be able to go for now. Claire shivered. Any elation she felt after finishing the splint faded away fast. She couldn't help but think of all the problems they faced, all the new and exciting ways they had to die, and the odds that were stacked against them. She thought again of how she'd passed out at the base of the cliff. How was she supposed to do this?

"We should try to sleep," Claire said. Maybe in the morning, one of them would have an idea for how not to die. *Or maybe we'll wake up dead*, she thought. It was funny, but it wasn't. She wanted to laugh, but if she started, she was afraid she wouldn't be able to stop.

She scooted down, trying to get comfortable. She was soaked again. And sore. But the crickets were coming out, after the rain. She listened to them chirp and tried not to think about Jack and his father, about her parents and whether they thought she was safely at camp, about how there might not be anyone coming to rescue them, about how they'd lost the bulk of their supplies . . .

Mariana said softly, "When it came out what my dad had done, I thought that was the worst that could ever happen to me. I thought I'd die from embarrassment. And then when my parents insisted we move, I thought *that* was the worst they could ever do to me. But Jack's father . . ."

"Don't you dare feel sorry for him," Reyva said.

"I do," Mariana said.

Reyva snorted.

"Sort of." She sighed. "It's just . . . he's dealing with the mess his parent made too."

"But he made very, very bad choices in how to deal with it," Reyva said.

"I know."

"Very bad."

"*I know.*"

Claire half smiled. "If we see him again, you can tell him

how much you sympathize while Reyva and I hit him with a large stick."

"I like that plan," Reyva said.

Her smile faded. Because they didn't have a plan. Not really. Unfortunately, all they had was one very small goal: make it through the night.

SEVENTEEN

That was, Claire thought as she blinked open her crusty eyes, *the most uncomfortable night ever.* She'd woken what felt like every five minutes, whenever the forest creaked or Reyva moaned in her sleep, and whenever a dream felt a little too real.

She kept hearing the shot, both through the phone and echoing across the lake, and she kept feeling the ground slip out beneath her as they fell down the muddy slope. But fortunately, she didn't feel the familiar shortness of breath that signaled an attack. Her heart rate stayed steady.

Claire was grateful when dawn crept over the forest, because then she didn't have to pretend to be trying to sleep anymore. Crawling out from the decayed tree trunk, she checked for any sign of Jack or the wild man or any other surprises, but the forest seemed quiet around them. A squirrel skittered up a tree, and a woodpecker tapped a rotted branch.

She peed several yards away from where they'd slept, watching the forest the whole time and pulling up her shorts quickly afterward. She missed her toothbrush and toothpaste. Her tongue felt as if it had been coated in rotten peanut butter. She scraped it against her teeth and tried to just be grateful they were all still alive.

Scouting the area, she did discover one blessing: the rain had left plenty of water to drink. It had pooled in the curves of rocks, on leaves, and on every surface throughout the forest. It wasn't *easy* to drink, but she managed a few mouthfuls before returning to Mariana and Reyva.

Both of them were just waking up.

"How's the arm feel?" Claire asked Reyva.

Reyva gave her a look. "Fantastic."

Claire decided not to pursue that. She didn't need Reyva to say she was in pain to know she was. "Anyone want to talk about what happened? With Jack?"

Mariana shuddered. "No. Rather talk about anything else. Favorite movie? First childhood memory?"

"Sorry," Reyva said. "But we have to talk about what we're going to *do*. Now. Claire, you can't tell me you haven't been thinking it through."

She had been. Of course.

"So what's the plan?" Reyva asked.

Both of them were looking at her as if she had answers. Not as if she was a problem to fix. It took her breath away, especially after they'd witnessed one of her episodes. Their trust. It was extraordinary.

She took a deep breath. *Work it like a puzzle*, she reminded herself. *A chicken, a fox, and a bag of feed on one side of a river . . .* "First, we take inventory. What do we have to work with?"

They all had wet clothes and mud-soaked shoes.

In fact, they were all wearing a phenomenal amount of mud. But what else?

Claire dug into her own pockets. She had a limp and soggy mass of dandelions and fiddleheads that they hadn't had the chance to boil, her Swiss Army knife minus the broken blade, and . . . that was it. Mariana had her phone, which was about as useless as a slab of plastic, as well as the double-A battery from her nail dryer and her pack of gum, which were much more useful. And she had the second coil of wire from the doorbell. Reyva had a couple of the nails they'd planned to bend into hooks.

Together, they had the supplies to create snares or fishing line . . . if they had the time for either trapping or fishing. *Which we don't*, Claire thought. Both activities required staying in one place, which wasn't the best idea when you were being chased. They had to stay on the move. Still . . . it wasn't nothing. The wire in particular had potential. *If we survive long enough to use it*, she thought.

"Okay," Claire said. "We have to establish our priorities."

"Get rescued," Mariana said. "Go home. Never see another tree again. Unless it's a palm tree."

Claire ignored that. Those were end goals, not immediate priorities, and she knew Mariana knew that. "Reyva, is the splint okay?"

"Don't love it," she said. "Won't die of it."

Good enough. "We ate yesterday, so we won't starve yet—"

"Love how she says 'yet,'" Reyva said.

"—and there's rainwater. If we can find places it's collected, like hollow stumps or concave rocks or whatever, then that's another problem down, for now."

"What about Jack?" Mariana asked.

She didn't *think* he was nearby. But she could be wrong. He could be anywhere, and she had no idea what kind of tracking skills he had or how determined he was to find them. Barely anything he'd said had made sense, so she couldn't expect him to act rationally either. "We'll take turns keeping watch next time we have to sleep, and we'll all be alert while we're awake."

"Okay, so what's our biggest priority?" Reyva asked.

"Hypothermia," Claire said promptly. "We're soaked. Our clothes, our shoes. We need to get dry, and to do that, we need a fire . . ."

". . . but the whole forest is soaked," Mariana finished for her.

"And if we do manage to light a fire, it could make Jack an immediate problem," Reyva said. "A fire will be visible."

"Less visible during the day, but you're right—we'll need to be careful," Claire said. "We need to get a fire going and get dried out as quickly as possible, and then put as much distance between us and our fire site as possible."

It wasn't a thorough plan, but it was at least a start of one. She looked from Mariana to Reyva and back again, waiting for their reaction.

Mariana scraped her fingernails against the inside of the trunk. "Seems flammable." She held out a wad of dry, fluffy wood innards. It would make a beautiful tinder bundle. "We can start with this."

Claire exhaled. They could have bickered with her. They

could have fallen apart under the stress of their situation. She felt herself want to smile. *Maybe we're stronger than that.*

While Reyva continued to break off bits of dried wood from the interior of the tree, Mariana and Claire scoured the nearby area for other dry or close-to-dry bits of wood. They piled all the wood bits they'd found, along with branches that didn't seem as saturated, near their alcove.

"As soon as we've got it going, the fire will dry out whatever sticks we put near it, and then we can burn those," Claire said. It wasn't going to be quick, but it *was* necessary. She really, really hoped Jack was nowhere nearby.

"You think it's a weakness that you see all the negatives, but I think you're wrong," Mariana said. "You're the one who sees what we need to do, who keeps coming up with solutions. I'd be a mess now if it weren't for you. So would Reyva. You're the one who found our shelter last night, even after you fell off a cliff and blacked out."

Claire shrugged and felt herself blushing.

"You see problems," Mariana said, "but you also see solutions."

No one had ever put it that way before. She looked away, blinking, as her eyes filled up. Of course, Claire wasn't entirely sure she believed her, but it was still nice of her to say. She filed the words inside her heart, to think about later. "Thanks. Um, we should start the fire."

"You got it, boss." Mariana unwrapped a stick of gum, split the gum between the three of them, and then used the wrapper and her battery to start the fire.

Boss, she thought.

It was a sickly fire at first, but they coaxed it larger.

Shedding their clothes down to their underwear, they draped shirts and shorts over the top of the fallen tree, where the heat would rise into it. Reyva kept her shirt on, since it was impossible to remove with her splint. Shivering, they crouched together next to the fire, with Reyva the closest to dry both her and her shirt. Claire laid her socks on a rock and scooted them closer to the flames. Mariana had her shoes upside down next to the fire. Plus there was the future firewood, drying out.

They didn't speak for a while, intent on keeping the fire alive, keeping watch for Jack, and making sure their drying clothes didn't burn. Claire spread out the fiddleheads and dandelions in the spaces between the clothes. When the greens got crispy, she split them three ways.

Helping herself to her share, Claire nibbled on a fiddlehead. It wasn't terrible. A bit like eating hot lawn clippings, but whatever. She touched her shirt. It was damp, steaming a little. Not yet dry. They waited longer. Mariana flipped her socks again.

She wondered what the others were thinking about. Food? Home? Or about the shot that rang out over the lake at the end of the weird conversation between Jack and his dad. She wished he'd just explained whatever was going on. They could have worked together and used the phone to get help for both them and his father. Now, though, what were their options? "As I see it, we have two choices: either we find Jack and try to get the phone from him—"

"Not loving that idea," Mariana said. "We're down our best

right hook, and he still has that knife."

"—or," Claire continued, "we try to hike out of here, like we originally planned."

"But minus all the supplies we planned to have," Reyva said.

"Yeah." And there was another problem, one that affected both plans. She hesitated for only the barest of seconds before saying, "Also there's the minor issue of the fact that we're lost."

Neither of the others had thought much about that. But she saw the moment that they both realized how true it was. With the thick forest around them, it was hard to see the sun, much less know which direction led to civilization.

"One problem at a time," Mariana said.

Claire nodded, even though she couldn't help but think of all the problems.

Pulling out her phone, Mariana waved it in the air. "Besides, I've got a possible solution. No GPS without coverage, I know, but there *is* a compass app."

"Dead battery," Claire pointed out.

"My battery isn't dead yet. Low, yes. Dead, no. It's worth a try." She pressed the power button, and to Claire's surprise, the screen lit up. "See? I wasn't just carrying it as a security blanket."

"Huh," Reyva said. "Guess it still has some juice left."

That was odd. All the phones, including Mariana's, had definitely quit working before, exactly when they'd needed them. "But in the cave . . ."

"Must have gotten wet and then dried out," Mariana said.

After all that rain? How was that possible? It should have gotten *more* waterlogged, not less. Regardless, Claire was grateful it was working now. "Go to the compass."

"I think I filed it under 'useless apps,' unless I deleted it. . . ."

The phone beeped.

"Okay, *now* I'm nearly out of battery." She tapped the screen quickly. "North is—that way." She pointed toward the trees, and then she shut the phone down, to conserve the last of the battery. "Okay, that's good, right? We know that's north. Which direction is the lake?"

None of them knew.

It depended on which way they'd run from Jack, and that had been such a wild flight that they could have gone in any direction. Their only goal had been *away*.

"Right. Yeah. So, problem not solved," Mariana said. "Never mind."

Claire felt Reyva watching her. "It's impossible, isn't it," Reyva said. "Us. Surviving."

She waited for Mariana to speak up and say something optimistic and encouraging. But she didn't. Instead she just flipped over her socks, drying them as if she were cooking a fish. Her eyes were brimming with unshed tears that clung to her eyelashes like raindrops on a leaf.

And Reyva was still looking at Claire.

So Claire said, "It's not impossible."

Just not likely, she thought. She didn't say that part out loud, but she didn't have to—she could tell they were all thinking it. Oddly, the shared sense of doom made her feel a bit better.

Whatever happened, she knew now, she wasn't alone.

EIGHTEEN

Squinting up at the white sky, Claire tried to guess what time it was. Noon? Earlier? Later? The clouds washed out all trace of the sun. She could check on Mariana's phone, but it wasn't worth draining the battery just to know. She felt her shirt and decided it was dry enough. Socks were still damp but not terrible.

Mariana also began gathering up her clothes, and then the two of them helped Reyva dress. Claire noticed the sunken circles under her eyes and the way Reyva tried not to hiss when she accidentally jostled her arm. She was in a lot more pain than she was admitting. *If it helps her to pretend she's fine,* Claire thought, *I'm not going to take that away from her.*

"We find a stream and we follow it to the lake," Claire said. "It worked before."

The others nodded.

Mariana dumped dirt and wet leaves on the fire and then stomped on it. Smoke curled up and dispersed as it rose up toward the whiteness of the clouds. Whether it dispersed fast enough to avoid notice . . . *We just have to hope it did,* she thought. And put as much distance between them and it as possible.

Claire double-checked to make sure they'd gathered what meager few things they had, then checked again, then checked once more until she felt calmer.

All we have to do right now is find the lake, she told herself. *One problem at a time.* If they found it, they could follow the shore and determine where they were in relation to the Lake House—then they could use the dock as their landmark and walk in the opposite direction of the camp, all the way to safety.

If, if, if.

Slowly, haltingly, carefully, they began their hike. None of them felt like moving quickly, and none of them felt like talking. Claire listened to the birds and wondered if their songs were really cheerful or if they were full of warnings.

Today the very air felt full of warnings.

Claire picked her way over and around the branches and brambles. Everything ached from the fall yesterday, and she'd seen for herself the bruises that had blossomed on her arms, legs, and hips. Mariana had had a vicious black-and-white flower of a bruise on her ribs. And of course there was Reyva's arm . . .

Why had Jack turned on them? Was it a desperate kind of grief? After the horror of what had happened, had he needed to lash out at someone? No. That wasn't it. It was *before* the shot that he'd made the decision to hold a knife to her throat . . . why had he done that? What had that whole conversation with his dad been about? "Can we talk about Jack?"

"Drugs," Mariana said instantly. "He's on drugs."

"Or he owes someone money," Reyva said. "Or his dad did. He planned to hand us over to whoever it is as payment."

"And that person would try to . . . what? Sell us? Ransom us?" It sounded highly outlandish. On the other hand, Jack had said something about "trading them." And there was someone who Jack's dad needed to be "free" of. She didn't have a better explanation. "If that's true, then it means there's someone *else* out there, whoever Jack and his dad are afraid of."

"'Kay. So long as we steer clear of Jack, his dealer or loan shark or whatever won't have any reason to target *us*," Mariana said. "I refuse to add another fear. Got enough, thanks."

"What about the wild man?" Claire asked. "How does he fit in?"

"Why does he need to fit in?" Reyva asked.

"Both Jack's father and the wild man were outside the cave when we emerged," Claire said. "Was that a coincidence? What about the dead program director? Why did Jack's father kill *her*? And let's not forget, we don't know who burned down the Lake House or why." She was warming to her topic. There was so much wrong with this place, but she didn't know how it all tied together—or even *if* it all tied together. Reyva could be right, and they could be unconnected. But she wanted all the pieces to click together into a satisfying puzzle. One that she could declare solved. Finished. Over.

"Maybe the fire was part of some kind of insurance scheme," Mariana said. "It's obvious the camp didn't have much money. Look at the state of the tennis court. This wasn't the golden paradise that my parents promised."

Claire nodded. She'd had that thought too, even before they saw the cage in the underground bunker. There was something off about the state of the Lake House, even without the fire. A recently reopened camp should have undergone some refurbishment, or at least basic maintenance. She remembered the lack of information online. The Lake House hadn't even had a website. Whoever owned this place had barely been trying to reopen. *Evidence that this was all just a failed insurance scheme?* she wondered.

"Do we know who owned the camp?" Reyva asked. "Jack was tasked with bringing us here—that sounds like the kind of summer job you could get through nepotism."

"Okay, try this," Mariana said as she ducked under a low-hanging branch, "Jack's father owned the camp. He set the fire to get the insurance money, and the program director found out it wasn't an accident and threatened to expose him and so he killed her? He thought she was his sole witness since she was the only one who had survived the fire. Everyone else, dead. Lots of sympathy. Lots of attention. And lots of insurance money to set himself free. Whatever that means."

"Then we show up," Reyva said. "And we discover the program director in the woods before he can get rid of the body. Boom, three more witnesses. Now he has a problem."

Claire nodded. "He thinks he has us where he wants us when we're down in the bunker. He closes the trapdoor, piles lots of rocks on top so we can't escape, then remembers there's another exit. He waits for us there in case we make our way through the cave, which we do." She skirted around a moss-coated fallen branch.

"The wild man who lives in the woods sees all these suspicious things and follows the killer to the cave," Mariana continued the story. "He sees us emerge and, because he's kind of confused to begin with, blames us for everything that's wrong with his life. Then sees the man with the shotgun and decides he's the bad guy instead, which, you know, accurate."

"Meanwhile, Jack's worried about his dad," Claire said. "He's found out about the money his dad owes. Maybe he suspects that his dad has done something he shouldn't have at the Lake House, but he loves his dad and wants to save him."

"He was surprised by the burned-down house." Thoughtfully, Mariana held a branch back until both Reyva and Claire had passed, then she released it. It snapped back, spraying pine needles. "I don't think he expected that."

"I don't think he expected to be shot at either," Claire said.

"The shot didn't hit him," Reyva pointed out. "I think his dad just wanted to scare us. Or maybe his dad wanted us to trust Jack?"

"Jack hatched a plan to trade us for his dad," Claire said. "But we caught on—"

"*You* caught on," Mariana said. "*I* just thought he was cute, confused, and lost."

"And when you two discovered the satellite phone, it all fell apart on him," Claire said. "His dad, consumed by guilt and regret, decided there was only one way out. . . ."

Reyva hissed as a branch slapped her arm. Stopping, she drew in breath, while Claire and Mariana hovered next to her, ready to help if needed. "I'm okay," Reyva said. "But if we're right about this, then Jack might still want to trade us to get rid of the loan he just inherited from his father. He won't follow us because he blames us. He'll follow because he needs us. We're not safe."

Claire had never really thought they were safe, so this wasn't news.

"This is a lot of conjecture. The kind that's based on watching a whole bunch of TV crime dramas," Mariana said, helping Reyva navigate over a fallen tree trunk. "We don't actually know anything."

"Probably never know," Reyva said.

Mariana shrugged. "I can live with that."

Just so long as we live, Claire thought.

"You can say it out loud, you know," Reyva said.

With an overly dramatic sigh, Mariana said, "Go ahead, Claire."

Claire couldn't help but smile. "Just so long as we live."

They fell silent again, concentrating on the hike. Every step felt hard-won. The moss was slippery from the rain, and the bushes and vines seemed to tug at their feet. Listening for any hint of a stream, they walked through the forest with no idea of whether they were heading in the right direction or the opposite.

Eventually, Claire heard the burble of water over rocks. She picked up her pace, hurrying toward it at a near run that made everything ache. She glimpsed the water soon, sloshing over moss-covered rocks. Kneeling next to it, she rested, waiting for Reyva and Mariana to catch up.

Dunking her hands in the water, she felt the crisp coolness run over them. She splashed water in her face and rubbed away some of the muddy grime. When she opened her eyes again, the forest looked hazy. She blinked and rubbed her eyes harder.

In the haze, she saw a shape: a dog?

A wolf.

She froze, not daring to breathe.

The wolf studied her. Was it a wolf? She squinted at it. It looked as if it were wreathed in a black-smoky fog. Maybe a mountain lion. Yes, the tail—but then she thought she was mistaken again because as she stared, she saw only the trees and rocks and fallen branches.

My imagination, she thought.

Or a hallucination.

She didn't feel short of breath or nauseous or dizzy. This wasn't her brain betraying her, at least not in the usual way. *We need to eat,* she thought. *And rest.* And not be in this forest any longer.

Reyva and Mariana caught up with her. "Excellent!" Mariana said. "Downstream?"

"You okay, Claire?" Reyva asked.

"Yeah. I thought I saw . . ." She realized the birds had gone quiet again only because they abruptly resumed their songs. She shivered and stood. If she was already so hungry and tired she was hallucinating, before their journey had really begun . . . Her legs felt wobbly, but she took a deep breath and steadied herself. "Let's find the lake."

They reached the lake before nightfall and collapsed on the shore. Calm, the water lapped on the pebbles. The low sun cast a path of light across the water.

"Will you hate me if I talk about food?" Mariana asked.

"Yes," Reyva said.

"We can try to fish . . . ," Claire began to say, then trailed off. As badly as she wanted food, she couldn't imagine moving. She felt as if every bit of energy had been sapped out of her. For the last few hours, all she'd thought about was reaching the lake, and now they were here . . . but home felt farther away than ever.

We aren't going to make it, she thought, then she squelched the thought. They'd made it to the lake. That was enough for now. Tomorrow she'd think about what came next.

Scanning the horizon, she saw the dock—a speck to their left. It was far enough away that it looked only a few inches long. She wasn't sure what the math said about how far it was, but it was a significant haul. She wondered if Jack had returned there, but as hard as she stared, she couldn't see any hint of movement near the dock or anywhere along the shore.

"So tomorrow we keep going that way." Mariana waved her hand in the opposite direction of the dock. "If we follow the lake away from the dock, eventually we'll reach civilization."

"Don't talk about moving either," Reyva said. "No food. No moving."

Claire closed her eyes. She was fairly certain she could sleep exactly like this, except for the fact that her stomach felt like a yawning void. Plus at least a thousand rocks were poking into her back. "We need food."

"Cheeseburgers," Mariana said. "Pizza. Burritos. Tamales. My great-aunt makes the world's best tamales. To die for. When I'm back in LA and you come visit me—note the word *when*— we'll get her to make a whole plate for just the three of us. No sharing with any of my cousins. Or neighbors. Everyone loves her tamales."

"You *still* think we're going to survive this?" Reyva said softly. "Look at how far we have to go. Can't even see the boathouse from here. It's days away."

"Tomorrow we'll find food," Mariana said. "You'll feel better after you eat."

Reyva said nothing.

Claire propped herself up on an elbow to look at Reyva. Her broken arm was cradled against her chest, and she had a cut on her cheek that hadn't been there before. It was speckled with dried blood. *She has to be in tremendous pain,* Claire thought. Yet Reyva wasn't complaining. *She hasn't given up. I can't either.* She had to keep pushing for as long as she could, for Reyva and for Mariana. "Give me the nails and the wire."

Wordless, the others handed over the supplies.

Claire pounded one of the nails with a rock until it bent. She held it up. It looked somewhat like a fishhook. Sort of.

"You'll need bait," Reyva said.

"Whole forest full of nice fat bugs and slugs," Mariana said, waving her hand at the dark-cloaked trees. "I'll find you some. Whoa, can't believe I just offered to do that."

"No splitting up," Claire cautioned.

"I'll stay close," Mariana promised. She heaved herself up with a groan and shuffled to the edge of the trees. She began rooting through the dead leaves with the toe of her shoe.

Claire wound the wire around the head of the nail, squeezing it as tight as she could. The other end she wrapped around an oval rock. She felt Reyva watching her.

"Do you think we're being hunted?" Reyva asked quietly.

She thought of the wolf or mountain lion she'd seen—or not seen—in the murky mist. *Just a hallucination,* she thought. She couldn't start imagining additional dangers when they had more than enough real ones. *Focus on the real. One problem at a time.* "I think Jack's father is dead and that Jack only has a knife. One of him, three of us."

That wasn't an answer, and both of them knew it.

If Jack were desperate . . .

His father had clearly gotten in over his head, with whatever scam or deal he'd bought into. It stood to reason that Jack would now be overwhelmed.

Claire glanced into the forest. She could see Mariana moving between the trees, bending over and then straightening. "Both Jack and his father were afraid of someone else," she said. "Someone worse." They'd talked about it, a drug dealer or a loan shark or some other kind of criminal, but they hadn't talked about *where* that "someone worse" was. That was a key detail.

"You think that someone else could be here, near the Lake House."

"I think I have an overactive imagination and sense of paranoia," Claire said. "And I think we don't know the full story." She wondered how much wire she'd need to cast the hook in the water.

Reyva struggled to sit up. "Fishing can wait. We should keep moving."

Claire wanted to tell her to lie down again. But she noticed that once again, the birds had gone silent. Prickles ran up and down her neck. Reyva was right—they could wait to fish until they were certain they were safe. She tried not to wonder if they'd ever be able to be certain.

Slowly, quietly, she stood up and held a hand out to Reyva to help her up. When they were both standing, she called softly toward the trees, "Mariana," as she tucked the makeshift reel into her pocket.

Mariana emerged from between the trees. She was carrying what looked like a pile of slugs in her cupped hand. "Everything okay?"

"I think we need to keep moving." She didn't have a good explanation for why, but Mariana didn't ask, and Reyva already understood.

Keeping to the shore, they continued on, with the dock behind them.

NINETEEN

The three of them walked until it was too dark to see, and then they slept like rabbits, in a tangled, exhausted heap, beneath the cloud-choked sky. Claire had nightmares where she kept running and running and couldn't escape. She woke in a start to discover it was still night. When she drifted off, she woke again, this time to a cry from Reyva—awakened by the pain in her arm.

When dawn came, Claire wasn't convinced she'd slept at all. She sat up on the shore and looked across the lake. They'd made some progress at least—they were beyond the sight of the dock, she was glad to see, but that left nothing in the view but water and forest and the cloud-choked sky.

It felt a bit as if there was nothing else in the world.

She should have felt alone, but she couldn't shake the sense that they were being watched. She thought again of her conversation with Reyva: the conviction that there was someone else out there, someone worse. It wasn't rational, she knew. Whoever Jack and his father feared could be miles away. There was no reason for anyone else to be in these woods. But the certainty was there, knotted in the base of Claire's stomach. *We're not alone*, she thought. *And we have to keep moving.*

She hugged her knees to her chest and tried not to think about how hungry she was, how sore she was, how tired she was. It wasn't a hunger she'd ever felt before. It felt as if a creature were inside, gnawing at her innards.

Standing, Claire felt dizzy. She waited until the moment passed, and then she toddled to the edge of the water. Bending over, she scooped water in her hands and splashed her face. She wanted to drink it, but reminded herself that she'd have to seek out rainwater to be safe.

"We need food," Mariana said behind her, softly. "Especially Reyva. I think . . . She's in a lot of pain, even though she won't admit it."

She'd guessed that.

"Did you finish making the fishing line?"

She pulled it out of her pocket—a stone with a wire wrapped around and a curled nail hook. Joining her at the water's edge, Mariana held her hand out. "We can take turns trying."

Claire nodded.

Mariana reached into her pocket and produced a wad of leaves. She unwrapped it to reveal a handful of partially crushed slugs. "Thought they might be useful." She impaled one on the curved hook. Then she stared at it. "In retrospect, sleeping with slugs in my pocket was one of the grosser things I've ever done. Maybe never tell anyone? Or speak of it ever again?"

"I'll look for other bait, in case fish don't like slugs," Claire offered.

She walked along the rocky shore as Mariana tossed the nail with bait into the water as far as she could throw. It landed with a light splash and sank beneath the surface. "It might need to be deeper to catch anything of significant size," Mariana warned.

"At this point, I'd eat a minnow," Claire said.

"Just so we're clear," Mariana said, "I don't actually know what I'm doing. The only kind of fishing I've done is off the side of a boat in the ocean. Before we moved." While Mariana fished and talked, Claire scoured the shore for anything else she could find. "You know, my parents kept talking about all the new experiences we'd have, moving to a new place, and they never once talked about all we were leaving behind. I've been pretending to be fine. I've been lying for months."

Claire located a few worms, another slug, and a treasure: a dented can with an illegible label. She carried it back reverently, with the bait inside.

"Guess I inherited my skill from my dad," Mariana scoffed. "It was easy to lie to Jack when we suspected him. I don't like how easy it was. Am I just a liar too? Is that, like, what I am?"

"You told us the truth," Claire pointed out. "You didn't have to do that. And it was right to suspect Jack."

Mariana sighed. "I just don't want to make the same mistakes my parents did, you know?"

"You won't," Claire said.

"You're thinking I'm going to make up all new mistakes that are unique to me, aren't you?"

Claire grinned. "Yep."

"Guess I won't worry about it, then." Mariana shrugged. "So

long as I'm original." She tossed her hair as she flashed a smile at Claire.

Reyva was now awake. She insisted on taking a turn at fishing one-handed, while Mariana switched to foraging at the edge of the forest. She collected a handful of fiddleheads, as well as five blueberries. Seeing them, Claire felt more hopeful, even though there were only five.

"How are you feeling?" Claire asked Reyva.

"Peachy."

"We'll eat a little, then we'll hike again."

"You don't have to look at me like you're afraid I'm going to fall to pieces," Reyva said. "I can handle this."

"That makes one of us," Mariana said cheerfully.

Claire studied Reyva, trying to gauge the amount of pain she was in.

"If I get a bite, I'll ask for help pulling it in. Promise," Reyva told her.

That was progress, of a sort. Reyva wasn't the type to ask for help, or even let anyone see she needed it. *She must hate that she's hurt*, Claire thought.

Changing the subject, Mariana added three more blueberries to the stack. "Most looked unripe. Almost picked them, but not sure if they'd make us sick."

"Anyone seen any sign of . . ." Claire trailed off, not sure what she was most worried about: the animal she'd half seen in her hunger delirium, Jack with his knife, or the person Jack's father had feared, whoever that was. ". . . anything?"

"Saw a squirrel and a bird. Very exciting."

"Good. That's about the level of excitement I can handle." Claire started along the shore in the opposite direction from the way she'd gone before, looking for anything they could use. Like a pizza that had washed up on shore—that would have been nice. Or French fries. *Or sweet potato fries*, she thought, *with honey-maple dipping sauce*. Daydreaming about sweet potato fries, she scanned the ground for anything that wasn't a rock or a stick.

Reyva called her back. "Hey, Claire, why don't we start moving? If we see a better fishing spot—someplace deeper—we'll try again?"

Sounded sensible.

They split the blueberries and pocketed the fiddleheads. Claire stored the worms and slugs in the can, and they started walking. Same direction as yesterday: away from the dock, toward help and safety, hopefully.

There was no sun—every trace of it was obscured by clouds—but it was still a pleasant day. She felt almost cheerful for the first hour. By the third hour . . . she wanted to lie down and never move again.

As they continued, the shore became more difficult to walk over. Instead of pea-size pebbles, there were jagged rocks that they had to climb over. None of them particularly wanted to go into the shadows of the woods again, so they kept clambering over the shoreline.

She heard the trickle of another stream that tumbled through the forest and spilled out into the lake. It spread out into a delta between wet rocks. Careful where she put her hands, Claire climbed over the rocks, keeping her feet out of the water—and realized that the sharp points she was barely looking at in the gravelly water were shells. "Reyva? Mariana?"

There were dozens of them, half buried in the sandy gravel of the streambed. Water curled around them and spilled over them. Most were coated in silt, but all were unmistakably live mussels.

Her hands shook as she touched them.

She'd never *liked* mussels. Slimy things. But she knew they could eat them. Jack had said so. Freshwater mussels. Safe from red tide bacteria.

"I'll build a fire," Mariana said, crossing over the stream.

Claire plunged her hand into the stream and dug them out. They'd have to heat them up to get the shells to pop open, she knew that much. Maybe sticking them next to a fire wasn't how a five-star chef would do it—better to sauté them in white wine or boil them in broth. But just plain heat should work too. And then they would eat!

They'd saved some of the wood scrapings from the fallen log, and Mariana started the fire with her gum wrapper and battery. *That should continue to work until we run out of wrappers*, Claire thought. *Or the batteries die. Or . . .*

"Claire," Reyva said.

Claire fixed her eyes on her.

"You're breathing fast," Reyva said. "Tell us how to help."

She almost hadn't noticed this time. Her brain had begun to spiral so quickly, without anything specific to set it off. But then, she didn't always need a trigger that anyone else would recognize as significant. That was part of what made it so difficult to explain to others, or to herself. "Counting helps," she said. "Puzzles. Math. Sometimes I run through the Fibonacci sequence or Pythagorean triples or even just the times tables. Or I recite ballet combinations."

Coming around her other side, Mariana said, "Okay then. Fibonacci . . ."

Together, they went through the sequence until Claire's breathing steadied. And then Claire began to talk. It spilled out of her—all the times it had happened, at home, in school, at the supermarket. Sometimes, like now, she could prevent it, but other times . . . Like after the cliff, as they had seen. She told them about how others had reacted, especially her classmates and supposed friends at school. She told them about how her parents always acted like she needed to be fixed, how they saw her as fragile. She told them about how she kept her distance from people, not wanting to deal with their judgment, their pity, or their advice. She talked about how it made her feel, when the attacks happened, and how she felt afterward—all the things she'd never told anyone else.

While she talked, they used a rock like a griddle and tucked the mussels near the flames. When Claire ran out of words, her friends did the best thing they could have done: they both hugged her—a tight bear hug from Mariana and a one-armed squeeze from Reyva with a pat on her shoulder. They didn't try to tell her what she should feel, or do, or how to fix it. They merely showed her that they had listened. And that was perfect.

Side by side, they all watched the shells, waiting for them to cook. A few more minutes passed, then a few more. "Anyone know how long they take to cook?" Claire asked.

One of the shells popped open by a few millimeters, then another.

"I think that's how long," Reyva said.

Grabbing a stick, Claire used it to scoot the cooked mussels away from the fire. While they cooled, she emptied the bait out of the can, filled it with lake water, and set the fiddleheads to boil. Mariana dug out more mussels and positioned them around the fire.

Once the mussels in the first batch were cool enough to touch, Mariana opened the shells for Reyva, and all three of them ate. "I take back every doubting, pessimistic thing I ever said or thought," Reyva said as she swallowed another.

"I don't," Claire said. "But this is good."

When the fiddleheads were done, they ate those as well, and they drank the water.

"You ever tell anyone how bad it is sometimes?" Reyva asked Claire. "All the stuff you told us—does anyone else know?"

"My parents know," Claire said.

"And they don't help?" Mariana asked.

Her parents did try. They believed they were helping. Even this summer . . . Sending her here was their latest attempt to help her. "I don't think they know how," Claire said.

"We don't either," Mariana said, "unless you tell us."

She looked at both of them and wanted to cry. "I'm glad we met."

"Definitely wish it had been under different circumstances," Reyva said.

They laughed, briefly, quietly. And Claire couldn't help

thinking that if she'd opened up to others, maybe it would have been like this sooner. Not everyone was Priya or Angie or her parents. Maybe she wasn't doomed to be alone in her room for the rest of her life.

I have friends, she marveled. *Real ones.* She hadn't realized how thoroughly she'd given up on ever having that, before Mariana and Reyva. Before this, close friends were things that other people had, non-broken people. She'd convinced herself she couldn't.

When everything was cooked and devoured, they stamped out the fire and continued on until nightfall.

We lived another day, Claire thought. Right now, that felt like a victory of gargantuan proportions. As the stars popped out overhead, they chose a fallen log to sleep against and hid themselves beneath pine branches.

This time, Claire slept through the night without waking.

In the morning, they continued on.

"We're going to make it today," Mariana said. "I can feel it."

"Kind of still all looks the same," Reyva said. Claire, glancing up at the clouds that blanketed the sky, had to agree. It looked as if someone had smeared cream cheese across the sky. Where was the sun? She felt like she hadn't seen it in days. Reyva continued. "But sure, today sounds like a good day to go home."

"You know the first thing I'm going to do once we're back in civilization?" Mariana said dreamily.

"Get me to a hospital, then go to the police?" Reyva said.

"Well, yes, but after that."

"Tamales?" Claire guessed.

"As if they'd have anything close to my great-aunt's tamales here," Mariana said. "I'm thinking shower and food. Not sure which order yet. Maybe simultaneously."

They talked about what kind of food you could eat in the shower as they walked along. Fruit, yes. Pastries, no. Soup, no. Pizza, only if you ate it really fast. All of them kept their eyes out for more mussels, more blueberry bushes, and more fiddlehead ferns.

It was almost . . . *It is nice,* Claire thought.

She'd thought she'd never have friends like this, ones who trusted her, who saw her as she was—and saw her at her worst—and still liked her. They even liked her *because* of the things she was convinced no one would like. They'd stuck together, and they were succeeding, together.

We've nearly done it, she thought. *It's almost over.* What had seemed so impossible at the start was now within reach. She felt a rush of relief so strong that tears popped into her eyes.

And then as they came around a curve of the shoreline, she halted in her tracks.

Reyva and Mariana kept walking until they noticed that Claire had stopped.

Claire felt as if the air had whooshed out of her lungs. She felt dizzy. Blinking, she tried to unsee what she was seeing—ahead of her, in front of them, was the Lake House dock.

"Did we . . . did we get turned around?" Mariana asked, her voice small.

Reyva shook her head.

Claire said, "We walked away from it. The dock was behind us. And we followed the shore. We couldn't have gotten lost following the shore."

"We must have gotten turned around," Mariana said.

"There are three of us," Reyva said. "One of us would have noticed if we suddenly turned one hundred eighty degrees around."

"We were all tired. All hungry. Not thinking straight," Mariana said. "We could have woken up one morning and simply headed back the way we'd come."

"It didn't look the same," Claire argued. "We would have passed things we recognized."

"Seriously?" Mariana said, waving her hand at the forest. "It *all* looks the same! We absolutely could have circled back. How else do you explain why—"

Reyva said flatly, "It's an island."

"What?" Mariana stared at her. So did Claire.

"Think about it," Reyva said. "We walked away from the dock. Didn't turn around. Kept to the shore. And we're back where we started. It's an island."

It wasn't an island.

Was it?

No one had ever told her it was an island.

If it was . . .

Why hadn't any of them known? Their parents—her parents had never said it was an island. They'd said it bordered a national forest. Very remote. That was all. Claire sank down onto the rocks.

The lake lapped peacefully beside her.

The dock didn't waver. It wasn't a mirage or a hallucination.

"Could it be a different dock?" Mariana asked. "We don't know it's the same one."

It looked exactly the same.

Mariana pulled Claire back up onto her feet. "At least let's make sure. Come on."

They trudged toward it, and the closer they got, the clearer it was. They saw the blue sparkle of Mariana's abandoned suitcases, the site where they'd tried to light their first fire. Closer still, they saw the jars and the toolbox, still full of water.

Stopping, Mariana and Reyva both scooped up jars and began glugging water. But Claire walked past them without even a glance. She walked onto the dock, to the very end, and stood there, looking out across the lake. Water lapped beneath her.

Back where we started, she thought.

She glanced up at the sun, low in the sky, and then shivered. "If we were walking around an island in a circle . . . why didn't we notice that?" Yes, they would have realized if they'd accidentally turned around and backtracked, but they *also* should have realized they'd switched cardinal directions. You couldn't circle an island without changing your orientation to the sun. "We should have noticed the sun in the wrong position."

"It's been cloudy . . . ," Mariana said.

"But it still rose and set," Claire said. "What's wrong with the sun?" She heard her voice rising higher. "What's wrong with us? What's wrong with this place? There has to be an explanation."

"It's an island," Reyva said. "That's it. That's the explanation."

Mariana ticked off the reasons on her fingers. "Hunger. Pain. Exhaustion. It's been cloudy. We're not master navigators. We just assumed that if we followed the shoreline, we'd reach civilization. It was a logical assumption."

Claire turned back to face the trail that led to the Lake House. She didn't think that was it, that they'd somehow mixed up east and west and hadn't noticed for miles and miles that they'd been walking in a circle around an island. There was something *wrong*. Wrong about the house, wrong about the cave, wrong about the forest and the sudden storms and the birds that fell quiet.

She cried out loud at the sky, the lake, and the forest, "Why won't it let us leave?"

TWENTY

They'd walked for days—days!—not knowing there was absolutely zero hope they'd reach their destination because the whole place was a *goddamn circle*! Claire wanted to scream, wail, cry. "I should have noticed."

"None of us noticed," Reyva said.

"It was cloudy," Mariana repeated. "We're exhausted. I was barely able to put one foot in front of the other half the time."

Claire shook her head. Still . . .

"It's no one's fault," Mariana said. "Maybe we should have used the compass, but we were following the shore. Seemed simple enough."

"We shouldn't have needed a compass! We have the *sun!*" Claire waved her hand at the sky as if it had betrayed her.

"Claire . . . ," Reyva began.

But Claire didn't want to hear it. She knew exactly who was at fault here. *Me. It's my fault.* "I should have noticed," she repeated, more emphatically. "How could I not realize we were walking in a circle?"

"You were kind of concerned with the not-starving part of it," Mariana said. "We all were. Don't blame yourself. As Reyva said, none of us noticed."

"But you trusted me!" Claire said. She heard her voice break, and she swallowed hard. It meant so much that they trusted her and believed in her, and now . . . It felt like a knife jabbed into her rib cage. She didn't know whether to scream or cry. "Anticipate the worst, that's what I always do, yet somehow I failed to even consider that we were on an island!"

"On the plus side," Mariana said, "we're not lost. And we're reunited with our stuff." Setting aside the water jar, she unzipped her suitcase and marveled at the clean clothes.

"Yay," Claire said, slumping over the railing of the dock and glaring into the water. She noted that the tennis net was still submerged. And it didn't have any fish. So much for their beginner's luck. "We're back where we started, but worse off. We're hungrier. Reyva's injured. And we still have no idea how to get home. Can't follow the shoreline. Can't swim to shore, not with Reyva's arm. And there's no boat."

It was ten times worse than before, because all that beautiful, light, fluffy hope she'd been feeling had vanished like water vapor into the air. She should have never let herself feel it.

"Come drink some water," Mariana said. "You'll feel better."

Unlikely, she thought, but she trudged off the dock to join Reyva and Mariana by the site of their first fire. She picked up a jar, sniffed it, then drank. It was lukewarm from the sun and tasted faintly swampy.

As she swallowed, she noticed that not everything was where they'd left it. The site of their fire was now more of a firepit, lined with a circle of rocks. A stack of firewood was tucked beside one of the boulders. Just beyond the tree line, she saw branches lying at an angle—a rudimentary shelter.

She lowered the jar from her lips.

"Put it all back," Claire said. "Leave everything where it was."

Mariana looked up from her suitcase. "Sorry?"

"This is Jack's camp. We have to erase any trace that we've been here." Claire tucked the jars back where they'd found them. Grabbing a branch from the edge of the forest, she swept at their footsteps, erasing them as best she could from around the camp.

Mariana scanned the area. "He's not here now. I say we use what we can—"

Reyva plunged into the forest and checked his makeshift shelter. "No backpack. He must have the satellite phone with him."

Of course he did. It would be his most important possession, his way out whenever he chose to use it. "Plan A, hiking to the boathouse, obviously won't work, so how do you feel about plan B?"

"What's plan B again?" Mariana asked.

"Get the phone from Jack," Claire said. "Call for help."

"No right hook," Reyva reminded her.

Mariana picked up a branch from the woodpile and grinned ferally at both of them. "I don't need a right hook to hit him with this."

"We hide, wait for him to come back, and then surprise him,"

Claire said. "If we catch him off guard— Or better still, we wait until he's asleep and then grab his bag. If we're careful enough, he might never even know we're here."

"Love it," Mariana said.

They devoted themselves to eradicating any hint of their presence, and then they slipped into the woods near his shelter. In this area, there were plenty of boulders littering the forest, so they had their pick of hiding spots. Crouching down, they kept an eye on his camp, the dock, and the trail to the Lake House.

And they waited.

They didn't have to wait long.

Claire heard the crunch of leaves from the trail and put her finger to her lips. She breathed shallowly and held as still as possible as she peered around the rock and through the underbrush.

A few seconds later, she saw him: Jack, still in his orange T-shirt, his pack slung over his shoulder. He was carrying a dead rabbit, but aside from that macabre detail, he looked as ordinary and innocent as he had the day he'd brought them here.

He got in over his head, she thought.

What his father had done—whoever he owned money to—whatever kind of mess he'd gotten involved in—it wasn't Jack's fault. She didn't *know* that, of course, but it felt true.

He was just trying to deal with the consequences.

And doing it badly, she thought. *Very badly.*

After all, he clearly hadn't used his phone to call for help, or he wouldn't still be here. She wondered if he was still hunting them, or if he'd stayed because he was hiding out from whom-ever his dad had crossed.

Or maybe he's just hiding from the consequences of his dad's actions: murder.

She'd never hidden from anything as serious as that, but she understood the urge to hide when you didn't want to face the judgment of the world. Certainly she'd done it often enough—hiding what she thought, what she felt, and who she was—and she knew Mariana understood too. Mariana hadn't wanted to talk about why her family had had to move from California.

Of course Claire wasn't about to pop out from behind the rock and have a heart-to-heart with him. He had held a knife to her throat, after all. Not a sensation she was likely to forget any time soon. But she hoped that Mariana didn't hit him over the head *too* hard.

Ideal would be no violence at all. If they waited long enough, he'd eventually fall asleep, and they'd steal the phone. Done and done. After that, all they'd have to do would be to keep them-selves in one piece until rescue arrived.

They watched him squat by the shore and skin the rabbit—Mariana looked away—with the same knife he'd held at Claire's throat. When he finished, he tossed the intestines into a pile and turned his attention to the fire.

He drew a metal stick out of his pack—a fire starter, Claire recognized. And he'd said he didn't have anything useful with him. *Liar.* Maybe they could steal that too. Just take his entire bag. She wished she'd thought to grab it the first time they'd run from him.

He lit a fire quickly and fed it, then speared the rabbit on a stick and began to cook it. The scent of smoke and cooking meat drifted toward them, and Claire heard her stomach rumble. She pressed her hands against her stomach and tried to will it to stay quiet.

"We go now, and we get the phone *and* the food," Mariana whispered.

"He hears you coming, and it's all over," Reyva whispered back.

They stayed put, but it was hard as they watched him tear the meat off and eat it. She'd never thought she'd *want* to eat rabbit, but at this point, cuteness would be no protection.

He washed his hands in the lake, his back to them, and Mariana glanced at Claire as if to say, *I can take him.*

Claire shook her head.

It was too far from their hiding spot in the woods to the shore. They wouldn't get a second chance at catching him by surprise. Right now, he had no idea they were anywhere nearby. They couldn't waste the chance with impatience. They needed to stay hidden so that—

Wielding a stick the size of a baseball bat, the wild man burst out of the woods only a few yards away from them. He leapt over the rocks and was swinging before Jack had time to react.

The wild man clobbered him in the side of the head.

Jack collapsed like a leaf falling from a tree.

Claire felt frozen, staring in shock. Muttering to himself, the wild man examined Jack. He placed his grimy hands on Jack's neck, as if feeling for a pulse, then nodded, seemingly satisfied.

Not dead, Claire thought. She hoped.

He hauled the boy up and over his shoulder. As he passed the fire, he extracted the carcass of the rabbit with one hand, holding Jack steady with his other. All three of them stared from their hiding place as he began trudging up the trail, casually chewing on rabbit bones.

"What. The. Ever-loving. Hell," Reyva said.

"Did he kill him?" Mariana asked. "He's not dead, is he?"

"He still has his pack," Claire noted. He hadn't shed it while preparing or eating the rabbit. Probably kept it close to him at all times. And most likely the phone was still in there. Hopefully undamaged after his fall.

"Not an answer to my question," Mariana said. "But . . . yeah, you're right." They could all see the bag, with the precious phone, on Jack's back. "So, we follow them?"

Claire considered the dangers, their options, and the odds of failure. "Yeah, we follow."

TWENTY-ONE

Creeping up the trail, Claire, Mariana, and Reyva followed the wild man. He grunted as he walked, and Jack bounced on his back with each stride.

She had so many questions chasing through her head. Loudest: *Why?*

Second loudest: *Where is he taking Jack?*

And again: *Why?*

He kept a steady pace, and he didn't glance behind him. Given that Jack was nearly his height and that the wild man looked like a malnourished skeleton, it was impressive that he hadn't stopped to rest.

She wished she could ask the others what they thought, though how they'd know anything more than Claire knew . . . but she wished she could talk about it, if only to wonder how long the wild man had been hiding in the woods by the shore, waiting for Jack.

Had he been there when the three of them returned to the dock?

Did he know they were hiding too? Did he guess they were

following him? He hadn't looked back. Not once, even though they'd stepped on a few twigs and knocked aside a few pebbles, despite how careful they were being.

She wouldn't have been at all surprised if he knew they were there but simply didn't care. Since they'd obviously been hiding from Jack, the wild man might have reasoned that they weren't likely to rescue him.

Or maybe he didn't do much reasoning at all. Last time they'd run into him, he hadn't made much sense. Maybe he'd kidnapped Jack on a whim. Or maybe he'd mistaken him for someone else. Or maybe Jack had done something to piss him off.

Or maybe he was in league with whoever Jack's father was afraid of.

Given the man's appearance, it didn't seem likely he was working for anyone, but did Claire really know? She had to stay open to all possibilities if they were going to avoid being surprised again.

They reached the ruins of the Lake House, and Claire expected the wild man to stop, but he just kept walking across the charred lawn. Claire, Mariana, and Reyva stuck to the woods, skirting the property and the tennis court. They kept an eye on the wild man, but he didn't veer from his course: straight across and down the center of the airstrip. He didn't slow when he reached the woods on the opposite side. Hefting Jack higher on his shoulder, he plunged in between the trees and soon disappeared from sight.

Hurrying, they jogged to the place where the wild man had reentered the woods. He'd left a trail: an imprint of a footstep here, a trampled fern there, a snapped twig on a bush. Claire's eyes darted from clue to clue. Soon—*too soon*, Claire's mind whispered—they spotted him. It was almost as if he'd waited for them to catch up.

But why?

And he still hadn't turned around to look at them.

"This is freaking me out," Mariana murmured. "Where's he going?"

Reyva shrugged, then winced—her arm clearly not liking the movement.

Claire concentrated on stepping quietly through the forest. She noticed the birds were few and far between—an occasional warble, then silence. The leaves rustled from the wind, sounding like a whisper. She found herself straining to hear words that weren't there. She heard a stream in the distance. It burbled incessantly, but she didn't see it—the woods were too uneven and too thick here, with too many boulders blocking the view.

"Anyone think this looks familiar?" Reyva whispered.

Sure, it looked familiar. Everything on the island looked the same, as Mariana had said. Lots of green. Lots of ferns. Lots of boulders. Slowing, Claire stared at one particular mound of boulders, devoid of the green that crawled over the other rocks and trees. She felt prickles chase over her skin.

Okay, yes, it definitely did look familiar.

"The cave," Mariana whispered.

"Where's the wild man?" Claire asked. While they'd been staring at the familiar pile of green-less rocks, they'd lost sight of the man carrying Jack. She hurried forward, scanning the forest.

If they'd followed him all this way, only to lose him now—

She spotted Jack lying on the ground near the rocks. He was still unconscious. Or dead? She saw his chest rise and fall. Not dead. And he still had his pack. It was trapped under him, but she could see the straps on his shoulders.

She hesitated, though. This didn't make sense. Why would—

Mariana didn't hesitate. She darted toward Jack.

Springing out from behind a tree, the man jumped in front of her with his arms spread wide. "Can't have him! He's not for you."

Skidding, Mariana stopped, then retreated.

Reyva and Claire hurried to flank her on either side. "We're not here for him," Reyva said. "All we want is his pack. Give us that, and we'll go away."

They would? And just leave Jack here? Of course, if they had the phone, they could call for help for everyone.

"Who are you?" Claire asked. "Why are you here?"

"And what do you want with Jack?" Mariana asked.

The wild man laughed, and his laugh was exactly what Claire would have expected—the kind of laugh that chills your skin, a high-pitched cascade that sounded as if he hadn't heard a true laugh in years.

"How long have you been here?" Claire asked, more gently. She had an idea of the answer. She knew it was equally likely she was wrong, but she tried her idea anyway: "Arthur?"

He began to tremble. "How do you know that name?"

"Is that you?" she asked softly. "Are you Arthur?"

"Once I was, and then I wasn't for a very long time." He sank onto the ground next to Jack. Picking up Jack's hand, he stroked it like it was a kitten. Claire shuddered.

"Arthur?" Reyva whispered. "The boy who was lost in the woods like twenty years ago? Presumed dead? Subject of ghost stories? That Arthur?"

Claire nodded.

"We can't leave Jack with him," Mariana whispered back.

"We call for rescue, and they'll come for us all," Reyva whispered. "But none of us are getting saved without that phone."

Loudly, Claire asked, "Arthur, why did you bring Jack here?"

"So it won't take me," Arthur said. "It doesn't want me. Not anymore. Not if it can have better. Younger. It wants a young body, you see."

It? What was he talking about?

He's lost his grip, Claire thought. *Lived too long alone here.* But why? Why was he still here? He could have signaled for help years ago. Or built himself a raft. Or swam and hiked. In all this time, why did he never leave?

"Keep him talking," Mariana murmured. She slid sideways, walking casually. His eyes darted toward her—she froze—and then back to Claire—and Mariana moved again.

"What do you mean?" Claire asked Arthur.

"I'm not a bad man. I don't *want* to give it this boy, but you have to see I have no choice. I *can't* let it take me again. Look at what it's done to me!" He held up a bony arm and shook it. The flesh jiggled around his bone. "All I want is to be free. Free before I die. Free before the end." He hummed to himself, tunelessly, as if the repetition in the phrases led into a half-forgotten song.

Free, she thought. Jack and his father had used that same word.

Claire's eyes flickered to Mariana. She'd managed to work her way around to Arthur's side, and he didn't seem to be paying any attention to her. Her eyes were fixed on Jack's bag. She'd have to roll Jack over to pull it off him, and Claire wasn't sure Mariana could do that silently. Louder, Claire asked, "Free of what, Arthur?"

"You know. You were down there, in its cave." He shuddered.

She didn't know what he was talking about, but maybe she could draw his attention toward the cave and away from Mariana. Claire took a step toward the hole. "What's in the cave, Arthur?"

"Don't!" He darted toward her.

She stopped. "Why not? What's down there?"

Reyva spoke up. "We were in that cave. We didn't see anything."

"Because it wasn't there *then*," Arthur said. "It was in the man with the gun. But then it wasn't." He shouted at the mouth of the cave. "Why did you leave him? You had him! I was free!"

Behind him, Reyva said, "The man with the gun isn't here. He killed himself out on the lake. We heard the shot."

Eyes wide, Arthur looked at her. "Ahh . . . Ahh, yes, that would do it. I never could. I was never strong enough."

She didn't understand any of this conversation, but she did

know that Mariana almost had the backpack. Claire searched for another question to keep the wild man's attention on them while Mariana worked on quietly wiggling one of the backpack straps off Jack's shoulder. "Free of who?" Claire tried. "Who are you afraid of?"

But Arthur had noticed Mariana.

He snarled, pivoted, and charged at her on hands and feet.

Abandoning subtlety, Mariana yanked at the backpack. Jack rolled, pinning the other strap beneath him. Releasing the bag, she grabbed a stick, brandishing it like a weapon at Arthur. "Stop!"

He blocked Jack with his body. Spit pooled in the corners of his mouth. "What do you want?" he howled at Mariana, Reyva, and Claire. "Why do you torment me?"

"We aren't tormenting you," Mariana said. "We just want to go home. You're Arthur . . . Benedict? Is that right? Arthur Benedict? You were the boy who went missing from the camp, the last time the Lake House was a camp."

"What happened to you?" Claire asked in as kind and curious a voice as she could manage. If they could calm him down . . . Keep him talking. Earn his trust. She still didn't understand what he wanted, why he'd taken Jack, or what he was afraid of.

He seemed to wilt. "I was forgotten."

"You weren't," Reyva said. "You became a legend. Jack told us about you."

"But no one knew what happened to you," Claire said. "You were missing. Have you been here this whole time?" It had been two decades. Why hadn't anyone rescued him?

Years alone, lost in the woods. She couldn't imagine what that must have been like. Or maybe she could: the loneliness, the hunger, the fear. She'd had a taste of all that.

"I was forgotten," he repeated. "We ruled the summer, the five of us. One night, we snuck out of the Lake House. Broke the rules. Weren't supposed to go out at night. Weren't supposed to go into the woods without a counselor. But we did because we weren't afraid. We'd never been afraid, until that night, the night it all changed, the night I lost myself."

Claire said nothing, letting him talk.

"We found the cave. Uncovered it. Opened it. And that was our mistake. We let *it* out."

She shivered, though what he was saying didn't make any sense. It was like some kind of horrible ghost story, one you knew wasn't going to have a good ending and weren't sure you wanted to hear.

"What did you let out?" Reyva asked.

"Old," he said. "So very old."

He seemed caught in a memory. Claire didn't think he'd heard Reyva.

"An earthquake, years and years ago, released it from the bowels of the earth. It should have dispersed into the world—but it didn't. It didn't reach the surface. It was trapped in that cave for so very, very long. Trapped, caught, buried, sealed away. It festered. It twisted. It learned to *want* and *need*. And when we opened its cave that summer night, it knew it wanted one of us," Arthur said. "It would let the rest go, it promised, but it wanted one of us. So the others left me. They sacrificed me. Abandoned me. *Betrayed* me!" His hands curled into fists. His knuckles were so white that she felt as if she were seeing his bare bones.

"I don't understand," Claire said. "You got left behind, yes, but why didn't you find your own way back to camp? Why didn't you leave this island?"

"*It* wouldn't let me!" he screamed.

Claire flinched.

"Okay," Reyva said placatingly. "It wouldn't let you. We believe you."

"I shouldn't have been here for so long," he said. "They were supposed to come back. To replace me. It planted a compulsion in them, before they left the island—so deep, so hidden, so strong. They shouldn't have been able to resist. But they didn't return. And years passed. And my body . . . It's failing. So that's why it had me light the fire. To lure a replacement, since they didn't come before I began to weaken."

Claire felt as if her entire body had been doused in ice. There was only one important fire she knew of. Was he saying? Did he . . . ? "*You* burned down the Lake House."

"Yes! I had to make a big fire so someone would see, with smoke reaching up to the stars and, oh, the beautiful flames! And it worked! The man with the gun came! It took him! I should have been free! It should have let me leave."

All of them began to back away.

"*You* destroyed the camp?" Reyva said.

"All the people . . . ," Mariana said. "All the other campers . . ."

The wild man snorted. "There was no camp."

"Of course there was," Mariana said. "And you . . ." She

couldn't speak. "Kids. Like us. How could you?"

"You killed all those people," Reyva said, "because you wanted to make a big fire?"

"I killed no one! I'm no killer. It couldn't make me a killer."

"Then what happened to all the people in the Lake House?" Claire asked. "Where are all the other kids? And all the counselors? Did they escape? Where did they go?"

He gawked at her. "I told you: There was no camp. There were no campers. There was no one."

He didn't even know what he'd done.

He'd committed such an atrocity . . . and he had no idea. How many had been in that house who hadn't been able to escape? She wanted to scream and then run as far from him as possible.

"But now that the man with the gun is dead," Arthur continued, "it needs someone else. And it won't be me again. I won't. I can't!" He began to cry, huge wrenching sobs that shook his whole frame.

Mariana reached toward Jack's bag—

The wild man snarled at her.

"You were lost. But we found you," Mariana said. "We can help you. Or get you help, if you let us. All we need is his backpack. If you let us have that, we can help. You just have to trust us. We're friends. My name's Mariana Ortiz-Rodriguez."

His jaw dropped and he stared at her.

And then he pointed a shaking finger at Reyva. "You. What is your name?"

"Reyva."

"Last name. Tell me your last name."

"Chaudhari."

"And your mother's?"

"Patel."

He began to laugh again as he pointed to Claire. "You. Oh, I can guess who you are. But go on, tell me. What's your name, girl?"

She hesitated, unsure if she should tell him. She didn't like the idea of this man knowing anything about her. But what harm would it do? If they played along, maybe he'd let them have the phone. "Dreyer. Claire Dreyer."

He laughed so hard that he wheezed. "For so long, I believed they'd come back, and then I'd be free. But they didn't come . . ." He gestured at himself. "Now I see! It had them send *you*. Their children."

His eyes were glittering as he looked at each of them. What was he trying to say?

"Did he marry Julie, Sweet Julie?" the wild man asked Claire. "Did they both send you here? Of course they did. It made them—its final gift, before they left. A compulsion buried deep within their minds, dormant until you reached the age we were when we set it free. How poetic." He cackled again.

She felt her body freeze, as cold as she'd been in the rain. How did he know her mother's name? And her nickname? Every night, after dinner, her father always called her mother "Sweet Julie." She'd laugh and tell him he wasn't getting any dessert, even if he called her sweet. Sugar wasn't good for him, his doctor had said. Then he'd have to eat her up, he'd say.

How does he know that? she wondered.

And what does he mean "it made them"? What compulsion?

"All we want to do is use a phone to call for help," Mariana said. "You'll be rescued too. You'll be safe. There are people out there who will take care of you. Help you. Get you whatever medicines you need."

"You're not well," Reyva said firmly. "You need help."

Claire's head spun. Her parents couldn't have known him. They'd gushed about this place for hours before she'd agreed to come, never once mentioning a boy who'd been lost, presumed dead. A boy they'd left in the woods. If they'd lived through that kind of trauma, they wouldn't have been so very eager to send their daughter here. *Meet new friends, have new experiences . . .*

"You're lying," Claire said.

Reyva shot her a look that clearly said *shut up*, while Mariana knelt slowly toward Jack's pack. "I'm only going to make a call," Mariana said soothingly. "We don't want to hurt you. We just want to help."

"You *will* help me," the wild man said. And then he threw himself at Mariana. She fell back. Scrambling away, she kicked as he grabbed for her.

Reyva lunged forward. "Leave her alone!"

He clamped his hand around Mariana's arm and began hauling her toward the mound. "You *must* help me. It wants someone new. You have to take on the burden. It's your doom and your destiny."

Reyva charged forward, a stick in her free hand. "Let her go!" She bashed at his wrist. He howled, released Mariana, and instead grabbed Reyva's broken arm. She screamed, and her knees crumpled.

Jumping forward, Claire pounded on his back and yelled, "Stop it! Stop! Stop!"

Mariana scrambled to her feet and rammed into him, tackling him from behind. He fell face-first, but when he hit the ground, he rolled and popped back onto his feet.

Claire immediately rushed to Reyva. "Are you okay?"

Reyva cried, "Watch out!"

He grabbed Claire's hair, twisted her around, and shoved her toward the mound. "Any one of you will do. It doesn't matter which." He propelled her up the rocks, toward the mouth of the cave. She didn't know how such a malnourished man could be so strong. But his grip was like a vise, and pushing against him felt like pushing against a brick wall. She lost ground.

She felt her foot slip over empty air. Panicking, she threw her weight against the wild man, but he pushed back, forcing her toward the hole.

"Claire!" Mariana cried.

Like some kind of action hero, Reyva charged up the rock and, cradling her broken arm against her, leaned back and kicked, hard. Her flat foot hit Arthur's stomach. Air whooshed out of him. As he stumbled, Claire spun around—trying to wrench herself free. He spun with her, and his feet hit the hole.

Shocked, he released her and tried to grab on to the rock. In a split second, she saw the fear in his face, and then he was gone, falling into the earth as if the cave were swallowing him. She heard him scream, heard a thud, and then silence.

The birds were silent too.

TWENTY-TWO

"Did we just . . . ," Claire began.

Kill someone, her brain finished. She couldn't say the words out loud. Backing away from the mouth of the cave, she shook her head as if that would erase what just happened.

"He might not be dead," Mariana said. "He could just be hurt."

It was so quiet. So very quiet. He wasn't screaming anymore. The wind wasn't blowing. The birds weren't chirping to one another. Just silence, closing in on them.

She silently repeated Mariana's words: *He might not be dead.* Maybe they hadn't killed him. Maybe they weren't murderers. Claire gulped in air. There wasn't enough oxygen. It had fled, sucked away with the wind. The silence was roaring in her ears.

"It was an accident," Reyva said firmly. Cradling her arm, she winced. "What he did . . . or tried to do . . . that wasn't. He *chose* to attack us. We just defended ourselves."

"Are you all right?" Claire said.

"Fine." And then she amended that. "Actually, in tremendous pain." She crumpled to her knees.

"Mariana, the phone?" If they called for help, they would be saved, Reyva would get help, Jack would get help, and the wild man . . . It had been self-defense. He'd attacked them. And he'd set the fire.

He hadn't known what he was doing, she thought.

That didn't make it okay that he'd killed all those people. He may not have known what he was doing, but they were still dead.

At what point had he lost his grip on reality?

"Do you think any of that was true?" Claire asked. Her voice was shrill in her ears. She inhaled, swallowed hard. *Breathe*, she ordered herself, and then managed in a steadier voice, "Do you think he really knew our parents?" He'd said her mother's name and knew her nickname. But how could it be true? She knew her parents. Maybe they didn't always understand her, but they were definitively and objectively *nice*. They wouldn't have abandoned a friend in the woods. They wouldn't have left him there to have *this* happen to him.

"You can't believe anything he said," Reyva said. "You're the one who called him Arthur. He could have latched onto that story of a missing kid—it's an urban legend around here."

"Rural legend," Mariana corrected as she struggled to roll Jack off his bag.

Reyva was right. Claire had brought up the name Arthur. He hadn't volunteered it; he'd just latched onto it. He might not have actually been the missing boy from all those years ago. He might not have had any idea who he was.

Except he knew "Sweet Julie," she thought.

And he knew he'd burned down the Lake House.

They'd stumbled onto two separate crimes: the burning of the Lake House by the wild man and the shooting of the program director by Jack's father. *Truly horrific luck*, she thought.

But it was almost over. Her heart rate was starting to slow, and the forest wasn't spinning around her. Mariana at last succeeded in extracting the phone from Jack's squashed pack and held it up as a trophy. "Got it!"

Claire felt like crying. Soon, they'd be saved! It wouldn't matter who the wild man had been or whether he'd known their parents, because they'd be safe and all of this—and all of *that*—would be the past.

"Dial," Reyva ordered.

Hands shaking, Mariana punched 9-1-1.

It didn't beep. It didn't ring. Nothing happened.

"Try again," Reyva said, her teeth gritted.

Mariana examined the phone, turning it over. "It's cracked. Must have happened when Arthur was dragging him over the rocks. Or when he dropped him on the ground."

Claire scooted closer to see. It wasn't just cracked; it was crushed. And she felt all her elation crash down around her. *I should have known it was too good to be true.*

"Can you fix it?" Reyva asked.

"If it were a car, yes, but a phone?"

"You have to try."

"Of course I'm going to try!" Mariana said. "It depends what's wrong with it. If the battery is just knocked out, then easy. But if it's more serious . . . It's not like I have any tools. So it might take a little time." She dropped cross-legged onto the forest floor and scowled at the back of the case.

Claire didn't know if Jack had time. Or the wild man. If he was only hurt and not dead, there might be a chance to save him, if help came soon enough. It was possible that they hadn't killed him. *I don't want to be a murderer,* she thought.

While Mariana tried to pry the back off the phone with her fingernails, Claire climbed back up the boulders to peer into the mouth of the cave. It was a darkness that felt thick. She couldn't see any differentiation in the shadows. Just a blackness that seemed so complete that it looked solid. *We should go down there,* she thought. *Just to check. He could be injured—*

A hand reached out of the cave.

Bloody, with dirt clinging to it.

"Reyva! Mariana!" Kneeling by the hole, she called, "Arthur, are you okay?" And then she saw his face. She screamed. Scrambling away, she stumbled down the rocks.

"Claire?" Mariana rushed forward.

Shaking her head, Claire continued to retreat, unable to speak. She felt bile rise into her throat as the wild man clawed his way out of the cave.

Seeing him, Reyva swore, also backing away.

His head was bashed in. Half his skull, crushed. Blood oozed down his neck, and his neck was at an improbable angle.

He wasn't alive. But he wasn't dead either.

"Not possible," Mariana breathed.

No one could survive wounds like that. His neck was broken, and his skull was crushed. Yet he crawled out of the ground as if out of a grave.

"What are you?" Mariana yelled at him. "What do you want?"

Blood oozed out of the wild man's mouth as he spoke. "I want to live."

They stared. Claire felt frozen.

He couldn't be speaking. But he was, his words garbled by the blood in his throat. Red tears leaked from his eyes as he hauled his battered body out of the hole.

Reyva spoke. "*Run.*"

All three of them turned and ran, with Mariana clutching the broken phone to her chest. As they passed Jack, he pushed himself up to sitting. Groggily, he said, "What the—"

Claire shouted at him. "Run!"

Jack stumbled to his feet, then swayed.

She hesitated for a moment and then backtracked to him. "Come on." She draped his arm around her and tugged him with her. He didn't budge.

The dead man lurched toward them. His legs were bent at unnatural ankles. *Broken*, she guessed. He couldn't run. He shouldn't be able to walk. But he was, inexorably, coming after them.

Mariana hurried to Jack's other side. "Let's go, knife boy."

With Reyva leading the way, they barreled through the

273

forest, pulling the woozy Jack between them. He stumbled as they rushed him forward. "What's . . . going on?" he managed. His words were slurred.

"Wild man is Arthur, the missing boy," Claire said. "He's dead, and he's chasing us. He's the one who burned down the Lake House and killed all those people."

"It was abandoned," Jack said.

"What?" Claire said.

"There was no camp. It closed years ago."

Claire jerked to a halt. That . . . How . . . Why? No, that wasn't possible. They'd been sent here to the Lake House for "summer enrichment." Their parents had talked about it, complained about checks and paperwork, and arranged transportation. Jack himself had taken them across the lake, talked about other campers and counselors. Of course there was a camp!

"You can explain it all to us," Reyva said, "later. Keep moving, Claire."

Claire glanced over her shoulder. The dead man was losing ground behind them, but he hadn't stopped. She wondered if he would ever stop. He wasn't alive. Or was he? What was he?

I want to live, he had said.

She shuddered and sucked in air. *Count*, she ordered herself. She began counting her strides: *One, two, three, four . . . twelve, thirteen, fourteen . . .*

They'd left an obvious trail when the wild man had carried Jack to the cave and they'd shadowed him—trampled grass, muddy prints, broken twigs. They followed their own tracks back to the Lake House. Claire was certain the dead man was following them just as easily. *Two hundred eighty-six, two hundred eighty-seven . . .*

Suddenly, Jack sagged.

"Whoa, stay with us, knife boy," Mariana said. She smacked his cheek lightly. His eyes looked glassy, not focusing on anything in particular. He groaned but straightened his knees.

"Concussion?" Claire asked.

"Yeah, think so," Reyva said, peering at him. "Seen it in the studio. He needs a hospital."

"So do you."

She didn't respond to that. "We have to keep moving."

Mariana and Claire propelled him forward, following Reyva. She kept counting steps, focusing on that, not on what was following them. Together, they hobbled across the airstrip. Without the roots and brambles, it was faster going, only slowed by Jack. She ached to run and flee as fast as she could, as far as she could. She didn't know how far would be far enough.

"We can't just go to the dock," Claire said, over Jack's head. "He'll find us."

"You think he's intelligent, whatever he is?" Mariana asked.

"He can talk. I think we have to assume worst case." Able to think. Able to reason. Able to find them, if they went anywhere obvious. "We have to lose him in the woods."

Glancing back, she saw the dead man limp out of the forest behind them.

"Come on," Reyva said. "Gotta move faster."

Picking up their pace, Claire and Mariana half carried Jack the length of the airstrip, to the burned-down Lake House, while the dead man lurched behind them.

"Leave us alone!" Mariana shouted over her shoulder.

"I only need one," he said in a gurgly voice. "One, and the rest can go free. You will leave this place joyfully, unburdened by thoughts of the one you've left behind. Like your parents before you."

"No!" Claire shouted.

"You cannot escape me," he said. "I will send storms. I will cloud your minds."

They hobbled faster, until they were almost dragging Jack between them. His feet stumbled under him, trying to keep pace. Claire gritted her teeth and did not let go. If he fell, she was certain he wouldn't get up again.

The dead man called after them, "You will not suffer, for you will not remember. And I will live. None will be harmed!"

Except the one left behind, Claire thought.

It can't be true. This can't be happening. She was stuck in some nightmare, and soon she'd wake up, wet and cold in the woods.

"Why not . . . why not leave me?" Jack asked.

"Not leaving anyone," Claire said to Jack.

"Unless you're volunteering?" Reyva asked.

"Reyva!" Mariana said.

"What? Just asking."

Jack's words came out slurred, as if he were untangling his tongue while he spoke. "But I . . . attacked . . . you. Why are you t-trying to save me?"

"No idea," Reyva said.

"Maybe because we're not monsters," Mariana spat.

"I'm not a monster," Jack said.

"Debatable," Mariana said. "You tried to give us to whatever he is."

"To save my father," Jack said. "You . . . you . . . you would have done the same."

"We are literally *not* doing the same right this very second," Mariana snapped. "So focus, summon your inner strength, and *move!*"

Behind them, the dead man said, "Only one." He wasn't shouting, yet his voice rolled over the airstrip. Claire noticed that all else was still. No birds. Not even any wind. "You will never leave this island. You will never be free of me."

She shivered through her sweat. He couldn't keep them here, could he?

"This can't be real," Mariana said. "We're asleep in the woods, and I'm having a nightmare. This has to be a nightmare."

"If it is, we're all in it," Reyva said.

"That's exactly what you'd say if you were part of my nightmare," Mariana said. Her voice had a shrill edge, as if any second she was about to start screaming. Claire felt the same way.

"Not a nightmare," Jack said. "Real."

"Then what *is* that?" Claire asked.

"Ancient spirit," Jack said, struggling over the words, as if his tongue was in the way and he didn't know how to move it properly. "Always been here, but buried in a cave, until some fools let it out a couple decades ago. Got one of them. At least that's what my father told me. He discovered it when he was hunting on the island. Not supposed to hunt here. But Dad didn't like rules. He found Arthur Benedict. And then he brought a cage to hold him. Maybe force the evil out."

Claire thought of the cage in the bunker, with the shackles. She'd suspected from the smell that it had been used recently, but she'd thought dog or wolf. Not possessed man. He must have escaped.

Jack's words mashed together, but she could still understand him. "But then it took my father. Made him kill his girlfriend, Mackenzie Williams. She'd come here to help him."

Claire's mind flashed to the body in the woods—they'd assumed it was the camp's program director, but they hadn't known for certain, she realized. None of them had ever met her. In fact, now that she thought about it, Jack himself had been the one to tell them about her, on the boat ride here. If he'd been lying . . .

"I didn't know," Jack said. "I didn't know he killed her. I didn't know he wasn't free when he told me the plan. I thought Dad wanted . . . He tried. Tried to fight it. To resist. But he couldn't. . . . I thought I could bargain to free him. When you came—"

"You wanted to trade us for him," Claire said, remembering the phone call. "You wanted it to possess one of us instead." She stumbled over the word *possess*. It was absurd. Yet . . . very hard to argue about possible versus impossible while being chased by a dead man.

"I thought I could save him, if I followed its instructions, if I pretended there was a camp and helped it. . . . I thought it would leave him, if it had you, but instead . . . I was wrong. There's no escaping it. We're going to die."

It began to rain. Suddenly. Impossibly.

They could escape in the deluge, Claire realized. If the spirit had sent this storm, it had made a mistake. Veering away from the trail and heading past the tennis court, she ordered, "This way."

The others went with her without arguing.

Together, they plunged into the forest.

The rain continued to pour down as they forded through the trees. Claire didn't look back. Maybe they could lose it in the storm.

They had to try.

The journey seemed endless—the green ahead of them, the rain pounding down on them—but they kept going, deeper and deeper into the forest, away from the Lake House. Claire's side ached, her legs ached, her head ached. She felt every bit of hunger gnawing inside her, warring with the fear.

It was the fear that threatened to choke her. She tried to think about it logically, and rationality skittered away. None of this should be possible. It didn't make sense. Except that it did. Every little thing she'd tried to explain away about this place . . . the fire, the cage, the cracked tennis court and unmaintained airstrip, the odd weather, the way they'd walked in a circle and hadn't noticed.

At last, Reyva halted. "Can't. I can't anymore."

The others stopped too.

"Did we lose him?" Mariana asked.

"Don't know," Claire said. She scanned the forest. She didn't see anyone. With the rain, she couldn't hear any birds. "Maybe?" Or maybe he'd come lurching out of the shadows.

"Maybe we should go a little farther," Mariana said. "Like, as far as we possibly can."

Beside them, Jack swayed.

"Whoa, what's wrong?" Claire said.

"Dizzy," he managed, and then he collapsed. She half caught him on the way down, as did Mariana. He hung limply between them, as if he'd melted.

"I think we have gone as far as we possibly can," Reyva said grimly.

"We need shelter," Claire said.

Mariana pointed to an outcropping of rocks. "There?"

It would do. They hauled him as best they could, aiming for what looked like an alcove. They stuffed him under the ledge and all of them squeezed together. Rain poured down in a sheet in front of them. Stray drops spattered them within the alcove.

Claire shivered.

"He's breathing," Mariana said.

"He could have internal bleeding," Reyva said. "Definitely has a concussion." She winced as she adjusted her arm. Claire couldn't imagine how much pain she had to be in, but there was zero she could do to help either her or Jack. And Jack very obviously needed help. "If we don't get him to a hospital soon, he could die. Can you fix the phone?"

Mariana stared down at the cracked plastic. "Let's see what's wrong with it." Bending over it, she unscrewed the back casing with her fingernail and pried it open.

There were wires pulled out of wherever they were supposed to be, but that wasn't the major problem. Inside the phone was a circuit board—and it was smashed. The case had splintered, and shards of broken plastic had pierced the innards. It was ruined beyond repair.

All three of them stared at it, and Claire felt her last wisp of hope evaporate. She'd been trying so hard to stay . . . if not positive, then at least determined. But this? It was too much. She buried her face in her hands, unable to look at either Reyva or Mariana, and she, for the first time ever, wished her mind would spiral and take her into the oblivion of unconsciousness.

But it didn't, and the rain continued to fall.

TWENTY-THREE

The rain died at dawn.

Looking out, Claire realized she could see the lake through the trees. They were near the shore. She emerged from beneath the shelter of the rock overhang and listened to the birds calling from tree to tree. She wondered if that meant they were safe.

She wondered if she'd ever feel safe again.

She shivered. She was soaking wet yet again, her clothes stuck to her skin. Jack was either asleep or unconscious. So far, he was still alive. But for how long? How long would any of them be able to stay alive with *that* out there?

Reyva and Mariana emerged on either side of her. She couldn't bring herself to look at them. If she did, all of this would feel real. "So," Mariana said, "do we want to talk about what just happened?"

"Not particularly," Reyva said.

"If we believe what Arthur said . . . ," Mariana began.

"If we believe he *is* Arthur," Claire said.

"Or was," Reyva corrected her.

"Whoever he is, he can't be dead," Claire said. "Dead people don't talk and don't walk." Now, with the rain over, the clouds dispersing, and the birds twittering again, it seemed clear they'd all leapt to an impossible conclusion. It was far more likely that his wounds weren't as bad as they looked. Head wounds bled a lot, after all, and as for his twisted legs . . .

"Claire." Reyva said her name firmly. "He was dead. His skull was bashed in."

Except for that unescapable fact. She knew that. She'd seen it with her own eyes, and both Mariana and Reyva had seen it too. "It's just . . ."

"I know," Reyva said.

Mariana continued. "*If* we believe him . . . then years ago, our parents were at summer camp here. They snuck out of the Lake House and discovered a cave. Opened it. Went inside. And they released something evil."

"Sounds like a ghost story," Reyva said.

"Whatever we're dealing with? It's not natural," Mariana said.

Claire shuddered harder. Mariana was right.

There was no way to know how close he was. He was familiar with this island, and they weren't. How long would it take for him to hunt them down? And where were they supposed to go? It was an *island*. No boat. No bridge. No hope.

"Our parents left their friend behind, to be possessed by an ancient evil spirit. They did it to save themselves," Mariana said. "He was the reason the camp was shut down."

"You think our parents left him behind?" Claire said.

"I think exactly that," Mariana said.

Reyva's frown deepened. "It said it only needed one. One

body to live in."

No. This couldn't be what had happened. There had to be another explanation, didn't there? Because the current story relied on believing their parents had done something unforgivable. "You believe that our parents sacrificed their friend to save themselves? And *then* thought it was a great idea to send us back here?"

Mariana snorted. "Do I believe that my parents could have made a mistake in their own lives that negatively impacted *my* life? And that they wouldn't notice or care? Yeah, I think I can imagine that."

"But to send us here," Claire said, "knowing what they did."

Maybe Mariana's parents could have, but Claire couldn't believe it of hers. She knew they cared about her. Maybe they didn't understand her, but they cared. They must not have known what they were doing. Hadn't the wild man said that? He'd talked about a compulsion. Her parents wouldn't have knowingly sent her into a trap—put her in the path of an ancient, evil spirit.

I'm positive this wasn't in the camp brochure, she thought.

If there ever was a camp.

How could there not have been a camp? Jack had said there wasn't and hadn't been for years, but what was a lie and what was the truth? She couldn't tell anymore. All of it made her feel sick.

"We can ask them when we see them again," Mariana said decidedly. "And we *are* going to see them. Right?"

That was the million-dollar question.

Trying to unravel her thoughts, Claire walked forward

through the trees into the sunlight on the shore. She lifted up her face to feel the sun on her cheeks.

Breathe in.

Breathe out.

She ran through ballet combinations in her head, trying to center herself in the moment: *developpé to arabesque* . . . Mariana was right—whatever had happened years ago with their parents and the missing boy was not the issue. They had a much more immediate problem.

Just need to tackle one issue at a time, she told herself. *Think through the puzzle.*

She sat on a rock by the lake. The water lapped at the pebbles peacefully, as if it had never stormed. Hugging her knees to her chest, she tried not to think about how hungry she was.

Maybe they could have found a way to survive here if it was just them on the island. Maybe they could have figured out how to fish, how to snare rabbits, how to build a shelter, how to do it all. *But we aren't alone*, she thought.

And the thing that lived on this island wasn't going to let them thrive. Whatever it was, whatever its story, there was no denying that it was after them. The sooner she accepted that, the better their odds. Just because none of this was possible didn't mean it hadn't happened.

She took a deep breath. Inhaled. Exhaled. Again.

"What does it want?" Claire said, thinking out loud. "It wants to live. It needs a body to live, apparently. A young body. Arthur got too old, and now it wants a replacement."

"Yep," Reyva said. "It tried possessing Jack's father for a while, then he managed to kill himself—guess it didn't have complete control. But he wasn't who it really wants anyway. It wants one of us."

"Only one," Mariana said. "It said it will let the rest go. Obviously the answer is no. Not leaving either of you behind." Looking back, Claire smiled at her. She felt the same way. So, from the expression on Reyva's face, did she.

We stick together, Claire thought. The spirit from the cave wanted to break them apart, wanted them to sacrifice one of them so it could live, but they weren't going to allow that. They'd sworn to stick together, and that was what they were going to do. They could survive this—together.

Of course, there was one obvious solution that didn't involve sacrificing any of the three of them.

Claire didn't want to be the one to say it.

Someone had to say it.

"Jack," Reyva said.

"No," Mariana said.

"You still like him?" Reyva said. "After what he did? And what he tried to do?"

"I don't, obviously," Mariana said. "But . . . Look at Arthur, what that *evil* did to him. It took his mind, his future. It took him away from his family. It destroyed him. We can't knowingly do that to someone else. Maybe our parents . . . Maybe they didn't know what they were doing when it happened. They were scared. They weren't thinking. I can make a lot of excuses for them—I have a lot of practice at that. Maybe they didn't know what fate they were condemning him to. But we know."

Claire nodded. "We're not going to make the same mistake they did."

Reyva sighed. "You're right. We can't leave anyone to *that*, even Jack. But . . . that doesn't leave us with many options."

Or any *options*, Claire thought.

Careful of her arm, Reyva lowered herself onto the ground next to Claire. "You asked about my greatest fear: it's being powerless. Admittedly, I never imaged this exact scenario, but . . . I hate this. Hate feeling helpless."

Mariana sat on the other side of Claire.

Putting their arms around each other, they leaned closer together and watched the sun glitter on the lake.

Listening to the birds, they foraged along the shore. No mussels this time, but they drank rainwater that had collected on the rocks, scooping it into their mouths with their hands.

Mariana located a blueberry bush, and they stripped it of every berry, even the bitter still-partially-green ones. Splitting their meager harvest, they ate them all. Claire felt the berries slosh inside her, barely making a dent in her hunger. Her innards churned as if they didn't remember how to digest food anymore. Straightening, she felt her head swirl and put her hand on a tree trunk to steady herself. Light-headedness wasn't a good sign.

"We should check on Jack," Claire said. "See if he's regained consciousness." He'd need water and food too, if he woke enough to swallow them.

"So we're decided?" Mariana said. "We aren't leaving him

287

behind to save ourselves?"

A bird took flight, and Claire saw a flash of cardinal red. Other birds were calling to one another, and a squirrel rustled in the branches of a nearby pine tree. The lake was peaceful today, its surface smooth, with only an occasional ripple from the wind. It looked far too idyllic for terrible life-or-death decisions. But was there really any decision to be made?

"I'm not my parents," Reyva said.

"I never want to become mine," Mariana said.

Claire still couldn't imagine her parents leaving a friend. Maybe they hadn't known what they were doing. Maybe it had been an accident. Or maybe the spirit had clouded their minds. Regardless, now that she knew the truth, there was no real other choice to make, if she wanted to be able to live with herself. She knew she'd never be able to look Mariana and Reyva in the eye again if she chose to consciously and willingly leave anyone behind, even Jack. "We're decided."

"Glad we all agree," Reyva said. "Because I see something." She pointed with her good arm up the shore.

Squinting, Claire followed her finger to rocks jutting out into the lake. Impaled on the rocks, upside down . . . "Jack's boat?"

"Please, oh, yes, please, let it be real!" Mariana cried.

All of them hurried toward it. Claire felt hope pounding so hard in her throat, but her brain whispered: *The spirit is not going to let you leave. It can make storms. It can capsize you. You can't escape by boat.*

She tried to argue back: Here was a *boat*! A way off the island! It was a gift, a miracle, and she shouldn't be looking for ways to deny it.

They reached it. It had been flung up onto the rocks, probably in one of the recent storms. If they'd been in this boat when the water had tossed it to shore . . . She shuddered, thinking of how they would have been tossed with it, their bodies thrown against the rocks and trees. She wondered if the capsizing had been natural, or if the boat had been targeted. She wondered what had happened to Jack's father's body—had it sunk into the lake, or would they find it along the shore? She hoped that Jack wouldn't be the one to find it. No one deserved to see that.

Reyva slowed. "Look."

The side of the boat had been torn apart.

No, Claire thought. *No, no, no!*

They hadn't been able to see it from a distance, but the impact had shredded the hull. The fiberglass had been gouged so badly that it looked as if a wild tiger had ripped through it. She touched the edge of the hole gingerly. It wouldn't, couldn't, float like that. Hope burst like a bubble.

Mariana dropped to her knees and stared up at the damaged boat. "You know, for a minute there, I thought the universe had given us a gift." She sounded close to tears.

"Me too," Reyva said, putting her good hand on Mariana's shoulder.

It couldn't be over. *I won't let them give up*, Claire thought.

She examined the boat. Maybe they could fix it? With what, though? And how? It was missing a huge chunk. Even if they could flip it over and get it back in the water, it would instantly sink. "We could build a new boat," she mused. "Use the engine."

"Can't exactly order parts from my car parts dealer," Mariana said.

"Not a fiberglass boat. A raft. There are trees here. Vines. We can lash the logs together like Huckleberry Finn, using Mariana's knots." Claire ducked underneath the part of the boat sticking off the rock. Near as she could tell, the engine was still intact. "Until *it* causes another storm and tosses us onto the rocks, of course."

"You think you're a pessimist, but you're not," Reyva said. "You're a planner. A puzzle solver. Come on, Claire, talk us through what you're thinking."

I'm a puzzle solver, she thought, turning the words over in her head. She liked that a lot better than "paranoid mess." *I've hidden who I am and been ashamed of who I am for so long . . .*

But I'm not weak. Maybe I'm broken, maybe I can never be "fixed," at least not enough to please everyone, but I am not fragile. I am not powerless. I am strong, no "despite" or "except for" or any other conditionals. I am enough exactly as I am.

I can figure out this puzzle, and we can survive this.

Thinking, Claire bit her lower lip. "It's evil. Whatever 'it' is. Old and evil. I felt that in the cave." The sense they all had that something else was there . . . that something was wrong . . . Now that she'd seen the dead man, she could believe they'd felt the residue of whatever was animating him. It explained why they'd all felt so certain they weren't alone. It had a power that they could barely comprehend. "I don't think we can stop evil with evil. And that's what giving it Jack would be."

"Yeah, we already agreed we're not going to do that,"

Mariana said.

"It said it can send storms," Claire continued, "and we saw proof of that. If we try to escape across the lake, it'll drive us back to shore, if not sink us." It controlled the island, which meant they couldn't play by its rules. If they did, they'd lose.

"So we can't give it what it wants and we can't escape it . . . so, what do we do?"

"We stop it," Claire said. The words felt wild and unruly in her mouth. She wasn't certain she was allowed to say a sentence that implied such optimism, but what other choice did they have? All the other options were beyond terrible.

Reyva smiled. "Knew you were going to say that."

"How?" Mariana asked Claire.

"I don't know if it can be killed," Claire said, "but it was trapped once. Before our parents found it and released it. That means . . . it can be trapped again."

TWENTY-FOUR

Kneeling, Claire drew in the pebbly sand with a stick. "We know the cave has two exits: the trapdoor and the hole in the woods. Luckily, Jack's father took care of the trapdoor for us." She'd seen it, piled high with rocks. Short of welding it shut, it was more secure than they could have made it. Dead or alive, no one would be able to shift all those rocks from within. "So that just leaves the hole."

"Bury it," Reyva said.

If they had shovels . . . Even then, it would be too slow. The dead man would never wait patiently while they buried him. Also, the amount of dirt they'd need to fill the hole . . . They'd basically have to fill the cave itself. No, it wouldn't work. "It'll escape while we dig. Or attack us." They had to find a way to block the hole. Rocks, maybe, like Jack's father had used for the hatch, or maybe they could fashion a lid out of scraps . . .

"Cause a cave-in," Mariana suggested.

Now *that* had possibility. If they could collapse the exit . . . She liked that idea. A cave-in would be much faster and much more effective than any shoveling they could do and more permanent than any lid they could lift.

Next question was how. She'd never caused a cave-in before. It seemed to her that it would require an explosion. Her eyes landed on the damaged boat and its perfectly functional-looking engine. "What could make a boat engine explode?"

"Fuel vapor build-up," Mariana said automatically. "Not incredibly common, but it's why you have to maintain outboard motors like that. Even more of an issue in older models. If fuel vapor builds up and then there's a spark . . . Boom."

"Can *you* make it 'boom'?"

Mariana thought about it for a moment. "This kind of outboard motor is water-cooled, so if we run it out of the water . . . and if I block the vent valves . . . Yeah, I think I can figure it out. I mean, I know how to *not* blow up an engine, so I'd pretty much just do the reverse. But this all depends on us getting the motor near the cave entrance without *it* noticing. Also, how do we get *it* to go nicely down into the cave and stay there until we're all ready?"

Good question.

"Bait," Reyva said.

Claire nodded. That was the simplest, most-likely-to-work option. "One of us goes down there, pretends they're going to sacrifice themselves for the sake of the others. That'll attract its attention."

"I'll do it," Reyva said immediately.

"That is super sweet and noble," Mariana said. "But you can't climb with your arm." She waved her chipped nails at Reyva's broken arm.

Reyva scowled at her splint as if it were its fault. "Not letting one of you do it."

Mariana raised both her eyebrows. "I don't think that's fully your decision. And it's not like we're *really* planning to sacrifice anyone. Right, Claire?"

Definitely not going to do that. If she wasn't willing to hand over Jack, whom she didn't even *like*, she certainly wasn't willing to give up someone she loved.

Loved.

The word stopped her for an instant. She turned it over in her head. Yes, she loved them both. They'd seen who she was—all her secrets and insecurities and weaknesses and fears—and they hadn't turned away. They were the best friends she'd never had and never thought she'd find.

She wondered if they felt the same way about her.

It didn't matter if they did or not. She wasn't going to let anything happen to either of them. *Even if I have to be the one to stay behind*, she thought.

Claire felt the truth of that, and then she buried it, hoping that neither of the others would guess that she'd considered it. That was one thought she wasn't going to share with them. She was instead going to hope very hard that it didn't come to that.

Out loud, she said, "Whoever goes down there can set snares. Catch the wild man's ankle, and then climb out before he can escape. You saw how he was dragging his leg. A snare could work. Mariana, do you still have that spool of wire?"

Reaching into her pocket, Mariana pulled it out with a flourish. "Ta-da."

"Excellent," Claire said. "So I set up the snares—"

Reyva huffed.

Claire ignored that. "—and Mariana rigs the engine to explode above the cave opening."

"Terrible plan," Reyva snapped. "Much too dangerous. Why is it you who sets the snares and Mariana who rigs the engine? You know how much danger you'll both be in? The dead man isn't going to sit politely by while you fuss with your trap."

A fox, a chicken, and a bag of corn need to cross a river . . . This was how they could solve the puzzle. Maybe there was a better way, but it was the only solution she'd thought of that didn't require leaving anyone behind. "It has to be us," Claire said. "Mariana is the one who understands engines. It will have to be her who sets it to blow. No choice there. And since Reyva's arm is broken *and* I'm the one who helped Jack make snares, I have to be the one to climb into the cave and set the snares." Her voice faltered a bit as she said it. The idea of going back into the cave, after seeing the dead man crawl out of it . . .

But she'd do it. For them.

It wasn't as if they had much choice. If they didn't trap the spirit in the cave, they had zero chance of making it off this island. Look at Arthur. He'd lost decades. If they didn't want to share his fate, then she had to do it.

"No, hate this," Reyva said. "You aren't doing this without me."

"Your arm is broken," Mariana said. "Not to be blunt, but you can't—"

"He'll catch you, and then what?" Reyva said. She was scowling harder than Claire had ever seen her scowl. "Only way this will work is if I distract him while you two set the trap. I have to get him to chase me and keep him away from you until you have everything in position. And then I'll lead him back to your trap."

Claire had to admit it was a sensible plan. They'd need to haul the engine to the hole without the dead man noticing, and they'd need time to set the trap. Plus someone had to tell him that Claire had volunteered to stay and get him to take the bait. Except Reyva was injured, so how could they ask her to be the decoy? What if he caught her? What if she had to fight? How could she defend herself with a broken bone?

"Absolutely not," Mariana said.

Reyva glared at her. "I am not going to sit by when you two endanger your lives—"

Mariana shook her head and said mulishly, "You can't run with a broken bone."

"I don't run on my arms," Reyva argued.

"You'll jostle it," Mariana said. "You'll be in incredible pain."

And then Reyva erupted. "I'm always in pain!" Tears sprang up in her eyes, and her uninjured hand clenched into a fist at her side.

Shocked, Claire took a step backward.

Mariana reached toward Reyva. "Reyva—"

Reyva pulled away. She was breathing heavily, and tears were streaking down her cheeks. "You want to know my secret? You want to know why I am the way I am? That's it. I am *always* in pain."

Claire had never seen so much emotion in her face or heard so much pain in her voice. "Reyva? What are you talking about?"

She shook her head, wordless.

"Reyva, talk to us," Mariana pleaded.

Reyva turned to face the lake, no longer meeting their eyes. She took a deep, shaky breath, while Claire held hers—she thought of all the times that Reyva had cut herself off and swallowed her words and her feelings. She could do it again and push everything down. *She's been doing this for a long time*, Claire thought. *Months? Years?*

She should have seen it. After all, she was an expert at hiding her own problems. She wondered how long Reyva had been close to bursting. She thought of what Mariana had said the night they'd first hid from the man with the gun and the wild man, about Reyva having plenty of feelings but always squashing them down. Mariana had been right.

Softly, Reyva said, "Three years ago . . . there was a car accident. My mom was driving. She looked down at her phone—my dad had texted, and she'd been waiting to hear from him. A pickup truck ran a red light. She didn't see it in time. I was . . . I had a lot of broken bones. Seriously broken. Two surgeries on my left leg. Also one on my shoulder. And when I finally started PT . . . I pushed myself. I didn't want anyone to look at me with pity. I didn't want them to know . . . My parents, especially my mom, blamed themselves so much. I didn't want to deal with that. They're happier pretending it's in the past, and I'm their strong fighter who they didn't damage at all. They need me to ace my classes and win championships, because otherwise . . ." She trailed off.

"They don't know you're hurting?" Mariana said gently.

"No one does," Reyva said. Her lips twisted into a sour smile. "Or no one did."

Maybe there was something the doctors could do, if they knew. And maybe her parents wouldn't push her so hard. Claire began to speak. "If you—"

Reyva stopped her. "I refuse to let pain define me. Not then. Not now. The dead man will chase me, I'll lead him to the trap, and you will spring it. End of discussion." She wiped her cheeks with the back of her uninjured hand.

Both of them stared at her, and Reyva glared back, defiant.

"It's your choice," Mariana said at last.

"It is," Reyva agreed. "Don't you dare tell me I can't. Just because my body doesn't behave the way I want it to all the time does not mean that I'm not strong."

She said those same words to me, Claire remembered. *After the cliff.* She hadn't realized until this moment that Reyva had been talking about herself too.

Reyva was waiting for them to speak. Her eyes were still wet, but her glare didn't falter. She was no longer crying, nor had she wiped her cheeks.

Claire nodded. "Okay."

"All right." Reyva's shoulders sagged as she exhaled. "It's a plan, then."

Cheerfully, Mariana said, "Yay! We'll all be risking our lives in horrible ways. Very bonding." She then added, "One problem, though, possibly major: we can't blow up the cave if we can't find it. I know it's somewhere in the woods." She waved her hand at the trees. "As you might have noticed, there's kind of a lot of woods."

Reyva scowled at the trees as if they'd caused all of this.

"That's . . . not actually a problem," Claire said. "I can find it."

"You can?" Mariana asked.

"I counted my steps," Claire admitted. "Before, when we ran. I was trying not to panic so I counted from the cave exit to the Lake House. I can find the hole again." She was positive about that. She knew where they'd emerged—at the end of the airstrip—and she knew they'd run straight through the trees. Even if the rain wiped away every trace of their passage, she was confident she could find the cave.

"I bet you never guessed that would turn out to be one of your superpowers," Reyva said. Her voice was steady again, and her eyes were dry.

Claire smiled. "I did not."

"Okay then," Mariana said. "We can do this! Maybe. Yes?" She asked Claire, "Do you think your plan will work?"

Claire hesitated before answering. She turned the plan over in her head, examined it, then considered the fact that it was literally the only plan they had. "Maybe?"

Reyva began to laugh.

Claire stared at her, unsure why she was laughing or what to do about it.

Laughing harder, Reyva doubled over her broken arm, and then Mariana began to snort-laugh too, as if it were contagious. Claire felt her lips curl up at the edges, though she had no idea why she was smiling. There was really nothing to smile about. The odds of success were low, and their plan relied on too many things going right when so many things had already gone wrong. All along, they'd been making assumptions based on their idea of what had happened at the Lake House and what was happening now, and every time, they'd been proved wrong. What if they were wrong again? It could cost their lives. Or their souls. Or both.

But the sun was shining again, and Reyva and Mariana were laughing so hard they were crying. Claire gave in and laugh-cried with them.

They set to work.

First step was to remove the engine from the boat.

Easier said than done.

Mariana got beneath it and called directions to Claire: hold this, steady that, twist this . . . She disconnected the steering arm and unhooked the shift cables. Disconnected the battery and threaded the connections back out through the boat. All of this had to be done upside down.

"Bit of good news; bit of bad news." Mariana poked her head out from under the boat to talk to Claire and Reyva. "Good news: this particular outboard motor has an internal fuel tank, and it looks like it still has gas in it. Can't get a boom without gas."

"Bad news?" Claire asked.

"It's bolted to the boat, and we don't have a wrench."

Claire ducked under the boat to join Mariana in staring up at the engine. Heavy-duty bolts attached it to the back of the hull.

Mariana pointed. "See, when you install an outboard motor, you clamp it onto the transom—that's the crosspiece on the stern. Sometimes it's attached by nice, friendly screws that you can turn by hand. But for the higher horsepower engines like this . . . bolts."

Claire gazed at the bolts for a moment, then at the crosspiece that Mariana had called the "transom." It had deep gashes in it, presumably from the crash. One slash split the fiberglass less than a foot from the motor. "Break it."

"Not sure you understand how tough bolts are."

"Not the bolts," Claire said. "The boat. The transom. See?" She pointed to the deepest gash. "It's already damaged. The crash weakened it. We don't need to unbolt the motor; we just need to break the transom enough that the engine's own weight rips it off the boat."

"You want to break off a piece of the boat and bring it with us?"

"Exactly."

Mariana opened her mouth to reply, then shut it, thinking. "Okay, I need a rock."

Reyva, who was on guard duty, located a sledgehammer-head-size rock and passed it to Claire, who handed it to Mariana. Mariana began whacking at the damaged fiberglass. "We don't ever need the boat itself, right?"

"Be as destructive as you want to be," Claire told her. "But also as quiet as you can be." She glanced up and down the beach and hoped that the noise wasn't traveling far. Luckily, it was a muffled thwack. "Any sign of him?"

"Not yet," Reyva said.

"Do we have a plan if we see him?" Mariana asked.

"Hide," Claire said immediately. It was the most sensible option. Very unlikely they could fight and win against a man who was already deceased. She didn't even know if he could be hurt, but it was safest to assume he couldn't be. At least then they wouldn't be disappointed.

"And if he suspects what we're doing?" Reyva asked.

"He'll think we want to use the boat to escape," Claire said. "It's the logical thing for us to try. He won't suspect this." Frankly, she didn't think anyone would—not because it was so brilliant but because the odds of success were so low. So many, many things could go wrong, and she could envision them all, unspooling in her mind like a movie that couldn't be paused. "All we'll have to do is wait for him to notice the state of the hull, and we can continue as soon as he leaves."

Mariana ducked back out to smile at Claire. "Look at you! Being positive! I'm proud of you. Also, what do we do when the engine does break free?"

"Catch it and lower it down." Joining Mariana beneath the boat, Claire positioned herself beneath the engine so she could catch it when it broke free. She spread her legs to brace herself and readied her hands. "How heavy is it?"

"A hundred pounds. Maybe a hundred fifty."

Okay, nope. She'd be squashed. Claire quickly scooted out

from under the engine. "Maybe we shouldn't drop one hundred fifty pounds on my head."

Mariana quit pounding on the boat. "Yeah, bad idea there."

"How about we just let it fall to the ground?"

"If he's close enough, he'll hear it crash," Reyva warned. "He'll definitely come then."

"Then we hide as soon as it thuds," Claire said. "Wait for him to come, and then wait for him to leave." She wasn't going to let anything ruin this plan. Sure, it wasn't the perfect plan, but it was the only one they had. Plus it had a symmetry to it: close the cave that their parents had opened. She *did* wish it didn't involve her climbing back down into the cave and acting as bait. But that part wasn't until later. She wasn't going to think about it right now. *One problem at a time*, she reminded herself. *Got to get the engine.*

Mariana continued trying to break the boat. Keeping an eye on the stern, Claire cleared the sharpest rocks so that the engine wouldn't be impaled when it fell.

A few more thuds of the hammer-rock, and the fiberglass began to creak.

"Almost there," Mariana huffed.

"No sign of him yet," Reyva reported.

Claire grabbed a loose branch from one of the pine trees and, using it like a broom, began obscuring their footprints. She wasn't going to be able to erase every trace that they'd been here—the beach was mashed with their tracks, and she was likely to miss a few—but she didn't want it to be obvious that they'd spent significant time here.

Getting an idea, she marched to the opposite side of the boat, deliberately leaving footprints that led away from it for about five yards before reaching a stretch of rocks. She then carefully walked backward through her prints to the boat. She hoped that was enough to confuse the dead man, if he came to investigate. At least it might distract him long enough for them to slip away into the forest and hide. Hide, and hope he didn't guess their plan.

At last, the chunk of the stern that surrounded the motor began to bow.

"It's about to go," Mariana said as she darted out from under the boat. Together, the three of them scooted into the forest and crouched down amid the thick bushes.

The hull groaned as the weight of the engine pulled.

And then the engine ripped away from the back of the boat with a loud crack, taking a chunk of the stern with it, and crashed onto the pebbled shore. They waited, hidden. A bird circled above the boat and then flew away. The waves lapped calmly at the shore. Claire listened for the telltale silence.

"Maybe he didn't hear?" Mariana whispered.

"Give it a little longer," Claire said.

Beside her, Mariana shifted to a more comfortable position. Reyva stared into the forest with an intensity that made Claire wonder what she was thinking. She wondered what the others thought of her plan. It used their strengths and their resources, but would it work? She couldn't account for every single variation of what could happen, but it helped that the plan was straightforward: bait and trap.

It worked for fish.

Of course, this was a very dangerous fish.

"I'm going back out there," Mariana said.

Claire placed a hand on her arm and shook her head.

The birds were silent again.

Emerging onto the shore, the dead man lurched toward the broken boat. His head was askew, bent at an unnatural angle, and he dragged one of his legs, twisted behind him. Only tufts of his red-and-gray hair were left, matted with dried blood. Between the clumps, broken bits of his skull were visible.

They held their breaths and watched as he approached the boat. Claire saw him study the ground. She hoped she'd cleared away enough of their footsteps that it wouldn't look as though they'd been here recently or that they'd stayed for any length of time. With luck, he'd see the damage to the hull and assume they'd concluded the boat was useless—a logical conclusion since it *was* useless as a boat.

As he circled around the boat, she saw his ruined face. Beside her, Reyva hissed, and Mariana shushed her. Claire felt a scream build in her throat. She tapped her finger on her wrist, in rhythm with her pulse, and silently counted. She couldn't let herself make a sound.

Bloodstained and mud-coated, he looked even worse in full daylight than he had in the shadows of the forest. There was no mistaking the fact that he was dead. She saw the slug-like pale pinkness of his exposed brain, clumped with dirt. There was no explaining away *that*.

She saw him discover the false tracks she'd left on the opposite side. He knelt, touched one with clawlike fingers, and then, with a grunt, loped after them.

"I'm going to follow him," Reyva whispered.

"No!" Mariana whispered back. "We're not ready!"

"It's the only way to be sure this works and he doesn't surprise us. Get the engine in place and the snares set. I'll try to give you as much time as I can before I lead him to the cave."

Claire knew that was the plan, and it had all seemed fine and logical when it was theoretical, but now that the moment was here . . .

Mariana grabbed Reyva's uninjured arm. "I know you feel like you have to do this. I get it. Really, I do. But what if he sees you? What if he catches you?"

"He won't," Reyva said.

"He could," Claire put in. Maybe there was another way, a safer way, that didn't involve Reyva sneaking after a dead man fueled by a supernatural whatever it was.

Reyva smiled one of her rare smiles. "Getting caught . . . Yeah, that's not my greatest fear. You know that. You know *me*. So, you have to trust me. I've got this." And then she added, "I *need* to do this."

After a moment, Mariana released her.

"Keep your distance," Claire cautioned. If Reyva led the dead man to the cave too early, they'd fail. If she was caught, they'd fail. Lots of ways to fail. Very few to succeed.

"I will," Reyva promised.

"And when the time comes, run fast."

"Stop worrying," Reyva said. "You really think I can't run

faster than some undead asshole with a broken leg? Let me do this."

Mariana had tears in her eyes. Her face was flushed. "You don't have to prove anything to anyone. Especially us. You're amazing, pain or no pain."

"Then trust me," Reyva said. "I got this."

"We trust you," Claire said firmly. She thought of a hundred other things she wanted to say, but there wasn't time. He was receding in the distance. "Good luck."

Kissing Reyva's cheek, Mariana said, "Yeah, good luck."

With a wave to both of them, Reyva crept out of the forest and began trailing the dead man. Chewing on her lower lip, Claire watched her and worried. They'd said they wouldn't split up, yet Reyva was already halfway down the beach. What if this was a mistake? What if their plan failed? Maybe they should have thought of a backup plan. Or a different plan. Or—

Mariana thumped her shoulder. "Every second, she's risking herself. We have to move."

Claire, with Mariana, darted out to the engine. Together, they tugged the motor over, flopping it like an extremely heavy fish. "How do we get it to the cave?" Mariana asked. "Can't carry it. Not easily."

"Let me figure that out," Claire said. "You sabotage it so we'll be able to blow it." She had an idea—when she'd first searched the sheds, she'd found various maintenance equipment.

One item she'd found was a wheelbarrow.

"I'll be back," she said.

"Hey, first Reyva, now you?" Mariana said.

On an impulse, Claire hugged her. "We're only splitting up

so that we can be together away from here." *It's worth the risk*, she told herself. Now that she'd seen the dead man again . . . This was their best chance, and she was going to take it. Just because she knew the odds were bad didn't mean it wasn't worth rolling the dice.

Especially when the alternative was worse. So much worse.

Hugging her back, Mariana said, "Well, so long as it's not because you're sick of me. . . ."

"I'll hurry back," Claire promised.

Moving as fast as she could, she followed the shoreline back toward the dock. She spared a thought for Jack, hoping he stayed hidden, hoping he was still alive. If there had been time, she would have checked on him, but time was something they didn't have to spare. The longer this took, the more risk that the dead man would spot Reyva following him, or that he'd turn back to where Mariana was with the engine and Reyva would have to lead him away. Once she had to begin running, she wouldn't be able to do it indefinitely.

They had to move fast. For Reyva. For all of them.

As Claire hurried over the shore, she realized this was the first time she'd been alone since she'd arrived at the Lake House. Usually she spent a lot of time by herself—in her room, doing homework or practicing at the barre. She tucked herself away from her family and her classmates. At school, she didn't seek out other people. Not since everything fell apart with Priya. Sure, she had a friend group—others from her classes and the dance studio—but she still often ate lunch by herself, telling herself she didn't have time to join the others in the cafeteria. She had homework and tests and ballet class and practice . . . Well, a dozen excuses for why she didn't risk opening up to other people, but it all boiled down to being afraid they wouldn't like what they saw. She didn't want them discovering the real Claire, only to have to see them pull back from her. She didn't want the pity or the advice or the judgment.

But Reyva and Mariana had never pulled back. They wanted to hear her thoughts. They trusted her plan. Everything was different with them. *She* was different with them. And she didn't want that feeling to end.

I hope this works, she thought.

She reached the Lake House and jogged to the wheelbarrow. It was where she'd left it, full of random debris from the sheds, as well as several inches of rainwater. She paused to drink a handful of the water before she dumped everything out on the lawn.

She hoped that the dead man hadn't paid attention to what was here and what wasn't. With luck, he wouldn't return to the Lake House at all. Certainly he wouldn't expect them to come back here. It made more sense for him to search the forest, where there were far more places to hide.

They were taking an awful lot of risks.

Don't let him catch you, she thought at Reyva. *Please, stay safe.*

She thought of everything Reyva had already been through and how much she contended with daily, hiding her pain. She had to trust that Reyva could take care of herself. Hard not to worry, though, and imagine all the various ways this could all go terribly wrong.

Grabbing the handles, Claire guided the wheelbarrow across

the charred lawn. It wobbled on its one tire until she got the hang of it. She pushed it back down the trail and along the shore, without incident, until she saw the wrecked boat in the distance, with Mariana and the engine beneath it.

"Ready?" Claire said, when she reached her.

Mariana grinned, her relief written on her face. "You are resourceful."

"How's the engine? Will it explode?"

"I blocked the fuel lines with as much muck as I could. Vapor will build up. But I don't know how long that will take. It could go instantly once we start it, or it could be five, ten minutes. Could be it won't work at all, and the engine will burn out before it blows."

"Let's get it to the cave," Claire said. "Any sign of Reyva?"

Mariana glanced toward where they'd last seen her, before she'd disappeared from view into the woods. "No." There were a dozen emotions packed into that one word, everything from pride to fear.

"She's smart, she's fast, and she's strong," Claire said. "She'll be fine." But she too gazed down the beach and worried. Only for a second, though. There wasn't time for more.

Together, they hefted the engine into the wheelbarrow, and they began pushing it down the shore. Claire tried not to look behind them every few steps, but she couldn't help it. She glanced back over and over as she listened to the birds.

Keep going, she told herself. *Don't overthink this. Just keep going.*

TWENTY-FIVE

Pushing a loaded wheelbarrow through a forest wasn't easy. The beach was fine, the trail was tough but doable, the Lake House lawn was a piece of cake . . . but now that they were in the woods beyond the airstrip, following Claire's memory of how to reach the cave, every inch had to be fought for and won.

We're leaving a trail, Claire thought.

The wheel was crunching bushes beneath it and leaving gouges in the dirt and mud. Worse, the harder she strained to push the wheelbarrow, the deeper her sneakers sank into the ground. Soon, she and Mariana were grunting with each inch, as they tried to shove the wheelbarrow over fallen branches.

"We've got to carry it," Claire said.

"It's heavy as hell," Mariana warned, "which I suppose means that hell weighs one hundred fifty pounds." She considered it for a moment. "Actually, that's pretty much how I always pictured the Devil. Slim, fit, devastatingly handsome. Built for temptation. I did *not* picture him as an unwashed, skeletal man who reeks like old fish or as a gun-toting, camo-wearing woodsman."

Claire set down her handle of the wheelbarrow and so did

Mariana. They circled around to opposite sides of the engine while they caught their breath. "You think it's the Devil?"

"Or *a* devil. 'Released from the bowels of the earth,' he'd said super-ominously. Why? You have another theory?"

"Not really, no. I'd been sticking with 'ancient evil spirit who wants to possess us.'"

"Sure, that works too." Mariana positioned her hands beneath the engine. "Together?"

"Together," Claire agreed. They lifted. Carrying it off the wheelbarrow, they each paused to readjust their grip. It wasn't impossibly heavy, at least not shared like this. She supposed there was some sort of metaphor there, but she was too busy struggling to hold up her half to comment on it.

"You know, I always suspected there were things in the world that couldn't be explained away," Mariana puffed. "A reason for superstitions. I feel justified in my wishing on stars now. If there are devils, then why not angels?"

"Or aliens," Claire said. "You could be wishing on UFOs."

"Hah. Hilarious."

They maneuvered around a rock.

Glancing at the woods, Claire hoped the dead man didn't find them now. It would be hard to hide what they were up to. *Although he might just be confused . . .* It wasn't every day that two girls carried a motorboat engine through a national forest.

"Was a class with Balanchine really your wish?" Mariana asked. "No judgment if yes. It's just . . . I don't know. It felt like it wasn't what you really wanted to say."

For a second, Claire didn't know what she was talking about.

Balanchine? When had she— She remembered the first night near the lake, under the stars, when Mariana had talked about wishes. It felt like eons ago. "Um, no, actually. I . . . I'm supposed to love ballet. I've done it since I was five, but the last couple of years . . . I've wanted to quit." She hadn't said those words out loud before.

Mariana grunted as she readjusted her grip on the engine. "Why haven't you?"

"Because then my parents, my teachers, everyone would ask why," Claire said. She'd have to explain that it wasn't her anymore—that she only did it because it was what she'd always done, because she knew how to do it, because it was expected— and then they'd ask, if ballet wasn't her, what was? She didn't have an answer to that.

"You're afraid of judgment."

"Along with cliffs, quicksand, nuclear war, school shooters, cancer, drunk drivers, brain-eating parasites, brown recluse spiders, and now apparently ancient evil forces that reside in the earth, which I didn't even know was something that I needed to be afraid of." She didn't think Mariana had any idea what it was like to live with a thousand fears, but for once, she wasn't worried about how someone would react. She thought of the time Priya had laughed—*laughed*—when she'd tried to explain, and all the times her parents downplayed or dismissed her feelings. *Just don't worry so much*, they'd say. Or *try not to think about it*. She knew Mariana wouldn't do that.

And she was right.

"I don't think you should be afraid of being who you are,"

Mariana said. "Who you are is pretty awesome."

"That's"—*not true*, a voice in her head whispered—"very sweet."

"It's true," Mariana insisted, as if she'd seen Claire's thoughts. Maybe she had guessed from Claire's tone. "And you should know that before you climb down into that hellhole." She glared at Claire in an imitation of Reyva. "Tell me you believe me."

"Mariana, you're—"

"Say 'I am awesome and amazing, exactly as I am.'"

Claire laughed.

"Say it."

"Okay, okay." She took a breath. "I am awesome and amazing." Mariana raised both eyebrows, waiting for her to finish. Feeling herself blushing hard, Claire said, "Exactly as I am." It felt both cheesy and also kind of wonderful to say.

"Now, believe it."

She wanted to believe Mariana—after all, here was someone who had seen her fully, at her lowest low. *Maybe I can believe,* she thought. *At least a little.* "If we survive this . . . ," Claire began.

"Don't say 'if,'" Mariana said.

But Claire said, "*If* we survive this . . . how do you think it'll change us?" She knew that was thinking ahead too much, but she couldn't help worrying about it. Now that they *knew* pure evil existed and the dead could walk, what was this going to do to her nightmares? How was she going to move forward, knowing that such things existed in the world?

They maneuvered the engine around a tree and over a fallen log before Mariana answered. "I don't think it will. Not in essence. I think it will just make us *more* of who we are—which, as I said and you said, like, a minute ago, is awesome and amazing. And you should say '*when* we survive' because I'm not giving up on us, ever."

Before Claire could come to any conclusion about how any of that made her feel, they'd reached the cave. They laid the engine down and shook out their arms. She stretched her arms across her chest.

"So how do we set it off?" Claire asked.

"Just like a lawn mower. You pull the starter cord, and it'll work," Mariana said. "The vapor should build up on its own. With an engine this old and with no water to cool it . . . it should be quick, but as I said, I have no idea. And I should warn you that it's entirely possible it won't explode at all."

"It will explode," Claire said.

"You sound unusually certain."

It *was* unusual of her to feel so certain. But . . . Mariana had rigged the engine. "You did it. I trust you." Claire didn't have an explanation beyond that.

Mariana took Claire's hand, laced her fingers in hers, and squeezed. "All my life . . . everyone's underestimated me. My parents. Teachers. Even friends and cousins. They haven't *seen* me. But you trust me with your life."

Claire squeezed back. "You're trusting me with yours."

"Absolutely."

Once they'd positioned the engine near the mouth of the cave, they piled loose branches on top of it to obscure it from view.

"Ready to trick the Devil?" Mariana asked.

Claire peered into the hole. "I imagine that's not a sentence you ever thought you'd say."

"Nope." She handed Claire the spool of wire. "But then I didn't know what to expect from this summer. Couldn't have predicted that I'd meet you and Reyva. You know, I think on the whole that balances out a confrontation with ancient evil."

"Does it, though?"

Mariana grinned. "Well, almost." Then her grin faded. "I hope she's okay."

"Me too," Claire said.

Both of them gazed at the forest around them. Claire wondered if Reyva was still trailing the dead man or if he was chasing her. And she wondered if Jack was okay, hidden in the alcove. She didn't think the dead man had found him, but that didn't mean he was safe.

Better do this quick, Claire thought. *She won't be able to run forever.*

Sitting cross-legged on the ground, Claire unspooled the wire and took out her Swiss Army knife. Trying not to think about Reyva or the dead man or anything but the task at hand, she measured out lengths of wire and made slipknots the way that Jack had taught her.

She listened and was reassured to hear birds singing in the trees. Surely if Reyva and the dead man were near, they'd quiet. *We have time,* she thought. *We can do this. If we're fast.*

As Claire worked, Mariana began trying to obscure their tracks around the cave. It wasn't possible, though, to unbreak branches or uncrumple ferns. Without looking up from her wire, Claire said, "It's okay if we've left a trail. He's supposed to know I'm down in the cave."

"You sure?" Mariana asked.

She wasn't sure, but she did know that Reyva was out there, risking herself for them with every second, and they had no idea how much time they had left. Not much, she suspected. She needed to set the snares, and Mariana needed to hide. "I'm sure," Claire lied.

Mariana stared at her for a moment before saying, "You have a tell when you lie."

She hadn't known that. Did she blink? Or dart her eyes sideways? "What's my tell?"

"You say words that I know Claire would never say," Mariana said. "Like 'I'm sure.' Or 'I'm not worried.' Or 'It'll all be fine.'"

"Hah. Very funny. You're right—I'm not sure about any of this, but I don't think we have much choice. I'm not going to let it take either of you."

"We won't let it take you either," Mariana promised.

They stared at each other for a moment.

As nice as it was to hear that she and Reyva felt the same way, Claire wasn't certain that any of them would have a say in the matter. Either their plan was going to work, or it wasn't. There weren't too many options in between. Standing up, she looped the snares over her shoulder.

"You ready?" Mariana asked her.

"Nope."

"You going anyway?"

"Yep."

She thought of the days she'd spent here with Reyva and Mariana. She thought of her parents, back home, probably worried sick. She thought of Jack and the man who'd once been Arthur and how he must have felt when his friends abandoned him. She tried *not* to think of the odds. And then she climbed into the hole. Mariana's phone was tucked in her back pocket so she could use its flashlight to set the snares when she reached the bottom. She didn't want to waste the battery on the climb, so she descended into darkness.

It felt, she thought, like descending into hell.

She kept her eyes up, on the sunlight above, as she climbed down, feeling with her toes before trusting the rock with her weight. Dirt coated her, and she breathed in the stale air again. It felt as if it were clogging her throat.

She had to stop. Force herself to breathe evenly. Inhale and exhale. *There's air here*, Claire told herself. *Don't freak yourself out.*

The only enemy here was her own mind. The true enemy was up there, chasing Reyva. At some point, Reyva would run out of energy and time, or the pain would get to be too much, and she'd have to bring him back here, hoping that Claire and Mariana would be ready with the trap.

And so I have to be ready, Claire thought.

She kept climbing.

She didn't remember it being so far the last time. It had been kind of a blur. She wished she'd counted as she'd climbed, then she'd have some idea of how far it was down. It felt like she was climbing into nothingness. She felt as if the darkness was closing all around her. The sliver of light from above was shrinking. *What if it winks out?* she thought.

Stop it, she told herself. *That's the sun. You won't lose the sun.*

He could obscure the sun.

That's how they'd lost their way before, she was sure of it. He'd brought the clouds and the rain, and they'd circled the island without even knowing it. She wondered what else he was capable of and then told herself not to let her imagination run wild.

He had limits, she was certain—otherwise he would have captured them already. *We can do this*, she thought. *We can outsmart him. We can win. There are three of us, and one of him.*

Together, they could do this.

She had to keep thinking that. She wasn't alone, even though she was alone. She pictured Reyva in her mind—the way she'd resist smiling, the way she sometimes burst out laughing, the way she could guess what Claire was thinking, the way she understood. And Mariana, who knew how to cheer them up, who knew how to open them up, who'd brought them together. Both of them were so strong.

And together, we're stronger, Claire thought. *Stronger than* it.

Her feet stretched for the next rock, and she felt pebbles beneath her. She lowered herself and felt with her feet. It was solid ground.

She took out Mariana's phone, powered it up, and turned on the flashlight. For an instant, it dimmed, and she thought with dread that it wasn't going to work, but then the beam brightened. She laid it on a rock so it shone across the cave and got to work.

The key would be to lay them everywhere so that wherever the wild man went, he'd step in one, dragging his broken leg, but she had to leave a route for herself to escape.

So, a pattern.

Claire began to lay the snares, tying the loose end of wire around boulders, wrapping them so they were tight and using cracks in the rocks to secure them. She laid them in a spiral pattern, memorizing exactly where each one was, before covering them in a thin layer of dirt.

She was nearly done when she heard Reyva's voice. Her heart began to beat faster. Tucking the last snare into her back pocket, unset, she scooped up Mariana's phone. Holding it to her chest, she danced across the spiral, avoiding the hidden snares, and positioned herself on the opposite side of all the traps. He'd have to cross them to reach her.

Taking a deep breath, she then did the bravest thing she'd ever done:

She didn't hide.

She stood right out in the open, where anyone—or anything—could see her.

TWENTY-SIX

Claire's mouth felt dry. Her hand holding the phone shook, and the light danced over the rocks and the roots. She felt chilled, and not from the lingering dampness of her clothes. She heard the sound of dirt and pebbles tumbling down from the cave opening.

She couldn't see the wild man yet, but she felt . . .

She couldn't describe what she felt. Enveloped. As if the darkness was eating at the light from the phone and wanted to consume all of her.

She would have told herself not to get carried away, that it was her overactive imagination, except she knew this time, it wasn't. The darkness truly was coming to consume her. She forced herself to stand still.

Don't run. Don't hide.

It was the hardest thing she'd ever done. She'd always been the kind of person who hid, who tried to choose the palatable thing to say, who tried to disguise what she wanted and what she feared—all the while never letting herself get close to anyone, out of fear of, as Mariana had said, their judgment. But now . . .

there was no more hiding. Not from Reyva or Mariana. Not from herself. Not from the evil that lived here.

"I'm here," she said out loud. "It's time to keep your promise! Let the others go, and you can have me."

He'd take the bait. She was sure of it. He'd done it before with their parents and Arthur. He'd do it again. He'd stop chasing Reyva and come after her.

Claire stared up at the hole, and then she saw his feet, climbing down. He was coated in dried mud and blood, and she could see the bone poking through flesh in the wild man's broken leg. It didn't slow him, though. He continued to climb down.

As her heart thudded in her chest, she tried to remind herself that this was what she wanted. *It's going to work*, she thought.

He was mumbling to himself, wordlessly, happily. The darkness around her seemed to swirl, and she thought she saw shapes in it: a wolf, a bear, then the branches of a tree swaying in the wind, impossible under the earth—and then only nebulous shadows again. She started to shake as he climbed painfully slowly down the rocks, muttering meaningless syllables in a singsong voice.

Then worse: the words began to make sense. "Keep them all," he was saying. "Yes, yes, yes. All four. Put the spares in the cage and never fear again."

That was, of course, the flaw with her backup plan that she'd tried so hard not to think about: he had to keep his promise. If he didn't plan to do that . . .

All it means is plan A has to work, she thought.

Her brain whispered: *And if it doesn't?*

Count, she told herself.

She started the times table in her head. Simple, with two, like she had way back in second grade, when everything was easy and there wasn't an undead horror hunting her. *Two times one is two, two times two is four, two times three is six . . .* Faster. *Three times five is fifteen, three times six . . .* He continued to climb, spiderlike, down the rock face to the cave floor.

She kept herself motionless, her breath even, as he reached the ground. He straightened, turned, and looked directly at her with cloudy eyes. She raised the light to his face in time to see a smile stretch his lips until they cracked and bled.

Then the light died.

She was plunged into darkness and all her hard-won calm fled. She felt a scream building in her throat. Whispers circled around her, and she felt wind on her neck.

Don't move, she told herself.

Don't move. Make him come to you.

He had to drag his feet through the snares, catch them on the wires, and tangle himself in her traps. She had to make him cross the cave.

She listened as hard she could. Only her own breathing. "Where are you?" she whispered. She couldn't make her voice louder than that.

"Here."

His voice sounded as if it was everywhere.

What if she'd miscalculated? What if the spirit wasn't in the wild man anymore? What if it was all around her? *No*, she thought. *It needs a body to live.* She wasn't going to invent new things to be afraid of. There was plenty real to fear already.

All she could do was act on the information she had. No inventing new fears. Maybe there was evil in the cave—she'd seen the shapes in the shadows—but it still craved a body. She had to hope it wouldn't leave the one it had until a new vessel was in its grasp.

She heard a scraping sound. That was him, the dead man, dragging his broken leg over the cave. Any second he'd be caught on a snare . . . She just had to wait. A little longer.

She thought of Mariana and of Reyva, waiting for her, worrying about her, and depending on her. She wasn't going to let them down. She was going to get out of here, rejoin them, and they were going to get off this island together.

She clung to that hope, knowing it was unlike her, but still, she seized that shining bit of optimism and held it close.

And she heard the moment that he was caught in a snare. A grunt. A thud. "What have you done?" His voice curled out of the darkness.

Claire flew into motion, dancing through the spiral by memory, knowing where she'd laid the traps. He'd have come straight for her, so she circled around the edges, skipping over the rocks. She didn't speak. She didn't scream. She kept her feet light, landing on her toes. She counted her steps and knew the moment she'd reached the rock face.

Without hesitating, she began to climb.

"What have you done?" he howled.

"Come on, Claire!" Mariana called from above.

Climbing faster, Claire yelled back, "Are you okay? Is Reyva there?" She imagined everything that could have gone wrong on the surface—

"Save your breath," Reyva called. "Climb!"

She heard scuffling behind her. He couldn't be free already! She climbed faster, reaching for higher and higher handholds. Her feet scrambled behind her. She heard a howl and pebbles below her.

He *was* free.

And he was climbing too.

It should have worked! She'd littered the cave with snares! He should have been tangled in multiple wires by now.

She felt as though his howls were rising up to grab her. Gritting her teeth, she moved as fast as she could. Hand over hand, foot pushing, propelling herself upward.

The sliver of sun seemed impossibly far.

She was aware that the dead man was climbing behind her. Her mind displayed all the things that could go wrong: she could lose her grip, she could climb too slowly, he could catch her, he could possess her and stop Reyva and Mariana from escaping. He'd use the cage, keep them as spares for when her body failed.

"You can do this, Claire," Mariana called.

"Just a little farther," Reyva said.

She listened to their voices, and they drowned out the spiral of doubt as they urged her upward. Focusing on them, she concentrated on one hand after another.

She felt a brush of wind on her ankle.

She screamed. He was close! He'd almost touched her. Another inch, and he would have had her. Tears filled her eyes. No, no, no!

I'm not going to make it, she thought.

He was too close.

"Start the engine!" Claire called.

They had to blow the motor. He had to be trapped down here. If he escaped . . . There was no other plan. This was it. It wouldn't work twice. They'd never trick him into the cave again. She didn't know of any other way to stop him. Arthur had never escaped, and the spirit had no intention of letting the three of them go. They had to trap him now.

"But you're not clear!" Mariana said.

"Just start it!"

She'd been willing to be possessed to save them; of course she was willing to be blown up. So long as it stopped him. So long as the others went free. She'd do it. If she had to. Only if she had to. Until then, she was climbing—toward them.

Mariana had said she didn't know how long it would be until the engine blew. It could be minutes. But they wouldn't have minutes. He was right behind her.

"Not until you're safe!" Mariana called.

"I'm almost there!" Claire called. She could see the light above. "Just do it! Please!"

She heard him, directly behind her.

"Claire, flatten," Reyva ordered.

She flattened herself against the rock face. She felt the whoosh of wind as a rock sailed down past her, then another. She heard a *thunk* and a grunt—one had hit the wild man.

Gritting her teeth, she kept climbing. The sun above her was broader now. She saw the silhouettes of Reyva's and Mariana's heads.

"Start it!" Claire called.

They couldn't wait any longer. The fuel vapor had to build up. A minute or more. She'd either make it in a minute . . . or he'd have caught her. Either way, there was no time left.

She heard the roar of the motor starting.

Her arms and legs ached so badly they shook, but she didn't slow. Her hand shot up into the air, and she felt one of her friends grab it. With Reyva's help, she scrambled up, crawling out of the hole as fast as she could. She turned and saw the dead man's hand reach out of the hole.

"Mariana!"

"It's running," Mariana said. She pushed the engine closer to the mouth of the cave. Both of them scurried around to join her, and they shoved the engine toward the hole, then directly over it, blocking it.

Then they began to run.

They almost made it.

Behind them, the engine exploded.

TWENTY-SEVEN

Claire blinked her eyes open. Blue swirled with green as her vision resolved itself: sky and trees. The trees seemed to be reaching to pierce the blue. She realized she was lying on her back. She didn't remember lying down. Her ears were ringing. She tried to listen for birds, but she heard nothing but a roaring like the sound of the sea.

No sea, she thought. *A lake.*

A lake house.

The Lake House.

She remembered it, burned down. All her memories rushed back, and she sat up quickly. She knew who she was, where she was, but not what had happened after she'd blacked out—the engine had blown, but had it caused a cave-in? Was the spirit trapped? Were her friends okay? "Reyva? Mariana?"

"Here," Reyva croaked.

Her voice sounded far away, as if underwater. Claire tapped her ears, as if that would clear them. She squeezed her eyes shut and then open again.

The first thing she saw was Reyva next to her, curled in a C around her arm. Claire crawled to her. "Are you okay?"

"Yes." Then: "I'm not sure. But I don't think anything new is broken. You?"

"I think I'm okay." She raised her voice louder. "Mariana?"

Reyva joined her, calling, "Mariana?"

Rocks were everywhere, and a skinny tree had fallen. Everything looked different, askew. Holding her breath, she turned slowly to face the mouth of the cave . . . and she saw that the mound of boulders had collapsed in on itself. "I think we did it," Claire said, hushed.

The cave was buried.

It was buried.

Their plan had worked! They'd caused a cave-in, and the rocks had tumbled into the mouth of the cave and sealed it more thoroughly than she could ever have dared to hope.

She thought she'd feel joy—but where was Mariana?

Claire pushed herself to her feet and swayed. Closing her eyes, she waited for the dizziness to pass. When it did, she looked again.

She spotted Mariana on the ground a few feet away.

"Mariana? Are you okay?" Stumbling to her, Claire knelt next to her. Mariana wasn't moving. Claire touched her shoulder, and Mariana didn't respond. "Mariana?" She heard the fear in her voice, felt it squeeze her throat.

And then she saw Mariana's chest was rising and falling.

"She's breathing." She exhaled in relief, and her vision swam again.

Mariana was coated in dust and had a streak of black soot on her cheek. Worse, her eyes were still closed. "Mariana, wake up. Please."

Reyva crawled over to join her.

"Are you sure you're all right?" Claire asked Reyva.

"Peachy."

"Can you stand?"

"Probably," Reyva said. "Not in the mood to rush it."

Claire glanced at the mound. *It really worked*, she thought. The explosion had caused a cave-in as they'd planned. Yay? She turned back to her friend.

Suddenly, Mariana coughed. She curled onto her side, coughing, and then moaned. "Ow. That was loud. And explode-y. Did we do it? Did it work?"

She's alive, Claire thought. *She's okay! We're all okay.*

"Think so," Reyva said.

"Are you hurt?" Claire asked Mariana.

"I'm okay. You?"

"Fine." The ringing in her ears was beginning to fade. She got to her feet and helped Mariana and Reyva stand. The three of them shuffled toward what used to be the cave. It had collapsed in, with rocks and earth filling the hole.

The birds were singing.

"I think we did it," Claire said tentatively.

Mariana wrapped her arms around both of them, careful of Reyva's sling. "We did it!"

They stared at the rocks for several very long minutes, but nothing stirred. Claire began to breathe easier. She felt bruised, especially on her right hip and thigh—she must have landed hard on that side—but nothing broken and nothing unbearable. Both Mariana and Reyva seemed okay. Alive. Wonderfully alive.

"Now what?" Reyva asked.

"We need to make sure no one ever opens it again," Claire said. Like their parents had, beginning all of this. Starting forward, she began gathering up the pieces of the engine. She winced as she moved. "If we can make it look like nothing ever happened here, maybe no one will guess there's a cave."

Mariana fetched the wheelbarrow, and they picked up all the pieces of boat engine they could find. After that, they wiped away as many of their footprints as they could. They worked slowly but methodically and didn't stop until they were satisfied they'd done the best they could. It still looked like something had happened here—there was no way to erase the way everything looked torn up—but given time, the forest should swallow it.

With one last look at the cave, they trooped out of the forest and back to the Lake House. They deposited the wheelbarrow with the parts in one of the sheds, so it would look like it belonged with the house.

Claire considered the shed with the trapdoor. The rocks would keep the lid shut from the inside, but what if someone came across it and was curious? She voiced her worry out loud.

"We could knock the walls down," Reyva suggested.

She liked that idea.

With Reyva directing them, Claire and Mariana shoved at the charred walls. It didn't take much before it collapsed in a heap, further burying the trapdoor and the rocks.

When they finished, they retreated beneath the charred tree on the lawn and surveyed their handiwork. "It'll do," Reyva said.

"It has to," Claire said.

"Now can we leave?" Mariana asked. "Unless you wanted to stay. Build a summer home. I'm sure this is a lovely place—you know, when it's not inhabited by evil."

They returned to the dock.

Claire walked out on the dock to check the net, while Mariana and Reyva started a fire.

"We'll make it huge," Mariana said. "A signal fire, like Claire wanted in the beginning. Someone's guaranteed to see it, sooner or later, right?"

Peering into the water, Claire saw a shadow wriggle in the net. "I think we have a fish!" You couldn't call it beginner's luck anymore. She didn't feel like a beginner. In fact, she felt as if she'd aged ten years since they'd arrived on the island.

At least ten, she thought. *Maybe a hundred.* She wouldn't go as far as to say she felt like a different person. . . . *I don't want to be a different person.*

And the thought stunned her so much that for an instant she didn't breathe.

She didn't want to be different.

She turned that idea over in her head, like it was a shiny jewel. Less hungry would have been good. Less bruised. But not different.

Breaking through her thoughts, Mariana cheered, "Yes! Fish!"

With Mariana's help, Claire pulled the net in. The fish flopped on the net, and she stared at it for a moment as it flailed. Murmuring an apology to the fish, she picked up one of the rocks that held the net and hit the fish on the head. It quit moving.

Before she could talk herself out of doing it, she pulled out her Swiss Army knife and cleaned the fish: a slice up its belly, then gill to gill. "Ew, ew, ew," she said as she pulled out the guts. She sliced the fillets from the spine.

And then she stared at all of it and wondered how she'd just done that. The Claire from a few days ago never would have been able to. She supposed it was nice that all those survival shows her parents watched had come in handy—they must have sunk in. She'd known to be careful to not pierce the intestines, and the result sort of looked like what you'd buy in a fish market.

By the time she'd cleaned everything up and gotten the net back in the water, Mariana and Reyva had the fire going. They set water to boil, slid the fish fillets onto sticks, and held them over the fire.

"We can't tell anyone about the cave," Claire said. For one thing, no one would believe them. For another, it would only make it more likely that someone would decide to dig it up.

"So what do we say?"

"I was thinking we go with what we thought originally: the house was burned down in an insurance scam. When the man with the gun's girlfriend discovered the truth, he shot her and then fled. He then shot himself out of guilt." Except for the insurance scam, which would obviously be conjecture anyway, it was the truth.

"So we lie?" Mariana said. "Like my father did to his company. Like all our parents did when they talked up this place. You want us to lie to everyone?"

"Not to each other," Reyva said.

Claire looked at both of them and managed a smile. "Never that."

They built the fire up as high as they could, until the flames licked the sky. Lying on the rocks, they listened to it crackle and watched the fire writhe and dance. But as high as they built it, it was still another day before they heard the hum of a boat motor across the lake.

Mariana jumped up and down, waving.

Reyva shouted, "Over here! Help!"

Claire joined in, both jumping and shouting, "Help! Help! Help!"

After what felt like an unbearably long time but in reality was less than thirty minutes, the boat angled in to bump against the dock, and a woman in a park ranger uniform—khaki shirt, olive pants, and a National Park Service hat—jumped out and tied onto a mooring. All three of them ran onto the dock.

"You kids aren't supposed to be here," the woman scolded. "This island is protected. No trespassing allowed."

But Claire could only cry.

We're saved, she thought. *We survived.*

Both Reyva and Mariana started talking at once, saying how they'd been abandoned here with no way off. They'd been told there was a camp, but there was no camp. And the woman's demeanor changed as she looked them over. She saw Claire's tears and Reyva's arm and took in the state of their clothes and hair and makeshift camp, then her concern switched to alarm as they told her about the man with the gun and the dead body in the woods that they'd thought was the program director but couldn't have been.

"Dead body? Where?"

They pointed to where they remembered finding her.

"And the man with the gun? Where is he now?" The park ranger was scanning the woods, as if she expected him to pop out and start shooting, which Claire found somewhat comforting. At least the park ranger believed them.

"We heard a shot out on the lake," Reyva said, "and later found his boat washed up onshore." She pointed down the beach. "We think he must have killed himself. At least, we haven't seen him since. And the boat is all torn up."

"Please," Mariana said, "we just want to go home. Can you help us?"

Clucking over them sympathetically, the park ranger helped them load their packs into the boat. She examined Reyva's arm in the flannel-shirt sling and promised to get all of them to a hospital to get checked out.

"Who told you there was a camp here?" the park ranger asked. "Who brought you here?"

Claire opened her mouth to answer.

Closed it.

Frowned.

She couldn't remember. Glancing over at Reyva and Mariana,

she saw that they looked just as confused. "It . . . must have been the man with the gun?" Mariana said.

Reyva nodded. "It must have been."

How strange, Claire thought. It should have been a detail she'd remember. "Our parents sent us to camp. They'd been here when they were kids, and they thought it was still here."

The park ranger snorted. "They definitely should have checked, because this place has been closed for decades. Come on, let's get you out of here. The police can take it from here."

They climbed onto the boat and put on life jackets. As the boat pulled away from the dock, Claire looked back at the island and then up at the sky.

No storm stopped them.

The sky stayed blue, with birds circling overhead.

TWENTY-EIGHT

Only Reyva was hurt.

On a doctor's order, a nurse at the tiny local hospital whisked her off for X-rays and a cast, while another doctor checked out Claire and Reyva. They were, the doctor concluded, in remarkably good shape for having been lost on their own for so long. They should be proud of themselves, they were told—three teenagers with no wilderness training surviving on their own was remarkable. ("See, always underestimated," Mariana said.)

The police talked to them.

A local reporter wanted to talk to them but was shooed away.

They were allowed to shower and change into clean clothes, and they were given trays of hospital food. Mariana requested extra applesauce. Claire ate the pudding first. Focused on the food, neither of them talked beyond a few words about how it all tasted. When Reyva rejoined them, she had a white plaster cast from her hand to her elbow.

"I asked for black," she told the others. "But my choices were white or pink."

"Ooh, I should have been the one to break my arm," Mariana said.

"And . . . I told them about the chronic pain," Reyva said. "I promised to tell my regular doctor when I'm back in Boston. I don't know if there's anything they can do, but . . . I am not going to hide it. Well, totally going to keep hiding it whenever I feel like it from whoever I want. But not everyone and not always."

"I think that's good," Claire said. "Brave."

"Yeah," Reyva said. She then smiled one of her rare smiles. "Learned it from you two."

Claire thought about her parents and what exactly she was going to tell them. What did they remember? What would they believe? *At least I'm alive and safe and able to tell them anything*, she thought.

The park ranger had informed their parents that they'd been found and rescued and were fine. And the second they were all checked out, clean, and fed (and their phones were charged again), they called their parents. Claire had never been so happy to hear her mom's and dad's voices in her life. She gave a short-ened explanation of events.

"You're sure you're okay?" Dad asked for the dozenth time.

"I don't understand how this happened," Mom said, muffled since they were both on speakerphone.

Claire hesitated. Here was the sticky part. She wasn't sure how her parents were going to take it. She didn't want to sound as if she was blaming them, but . . . they *had* sent her to a defunct camp. And if the dead man had been telling the truth, it was their terrible choice that had doomed Arthur, whether they remembered it or not—which led to everything else that had happened to her and her friends. "Do you remember a boy named Arthur Benedict?"

"No," Mom said. "I don't . . ." Then she paused. "What was the name again?"

"Arthur Benedict. You forgot him," Claire said. "But it wasn't your fault."

"Everyone has forgotten what they've forgotten," Dad said jovially. "You just sit tight. We'll be on our way in a jiffy." It would be a many-hour drive from Connecticut, but that was okay. She could eat everything in the hospital cafeteria between now and then. Or they could venture out and find pizza. It was a tiny town, but it had to have pizza. She fantasized about that for a moment before she realized her parents were talking again.

And then: "Arthur Benedict," her dad was musing. "It does sound familiar. Can't think why, though."

"Do you remember sneaking out of the camp one night and uncovering a cave?" Claire asked. "It was against the rules, but you did it anyway because you were fearless."

They were silent.

"No, I don't remember that," Mom said. "We never . . . Or did we? Honey?"

They truly didn't remember. *He didn't lie*, she thought. It had been part of the dead man's promise: to make her parents forget and allow them to have happy lives after that summer ended. She exhaled heavily, more relieved than she thought she'd be. She hadn't liked thinking that her parents had sent their daughter to the Lake House knowing the danger. It was better that they'd genuinely forgotten and had instead responded to some deeply implanted compulsion, embedded without their knowledge or consent, dormant until their daughter was old enough to serve as a viable host. *Okay, maybe that's not "better,"* Claire thought. She'd have hated to have her mind messed with. "Don't worry. I'm sure—"

"There *was* a boy named Arthur," Mom said. "Remember, honey? Red hair? He used to follow us around all the time. Called me 'Sweet Julie.'"

Claire shivered.

"Whatever happened to him?" Mom asked.

"He left camp early," Dad said. "Must've had some family thing."

"Right," Mom agreed.

But she didn't sound certain.

Claire squeezed the phone, listening to her parents half remember. The truth was buried inside somewhere, repressed for all these years. *This could have been me,* she thought.

Her mom changed the subject. "Did you have any . . . episodes?"

Claire hesitated again, then said firmly and clearly, "Yes. But I handled it."

"Oh, my sweetie—"

But Claire, for the first time in her life, cut her mother off. "I handled it," she repeated. "It's a part of me; it doesn't define me. Or limit me. I'm—I'm fine. Like I am."

In fact, so many of the things she'd thought of as flaws . . . weren't. Okay, maybe they weren't all strengths exactly—she wasn't ready to go *that* far—but they were all part of who she was, which was, as Mariana had insisted, awesome. *I am awesome and amazing, exactly as I am*, she thought. And for the first time, she believed it.

She wasn't going to hide anymore. Not from her parents. Not from her friends. And if she someday wanted, like Reyva, to talk to a doctor about her attacks, then she would. Either way, it didn't mean she was anything less than capable, brave, and whole.

"I'm fine," she told them.

Her parents were silent for a moment, and then her dad said, "We're proud of you, Claire. And so very sorry for the mix-up with the camp. I really don't understand how we could have made such a mistake." Her mom echoed that, apologizing yet again.

At last, they hung up, with promises that they were starting their drive right now and would be there as soon as they could. She was to stay put, and everything would be all right.

Returning to the others, she collapsed into one of the hospital lobby chairs.

Both Mariana and Reyva had finished with their parents as well. "My mom is pissed at my dad for sending me to a camp that doesn't exist," Mariana reported.

"Mine remembered sneaking out with Arthur," Reyva said, "but they were positive he chickened out before they got very far and went back to camp."

"Not sure how much mine remembered," Mariana said. "I kind of distracted them when I told them I wanted to finish high school in California." She flashed a smile at her friends. "You inspired me, Reyva."

"You told them that?" Claire said. "That's great!" Also brave. Reyva high-fived her.

"What did they say?" Claire asked.

"They said we could talk about it," Mariana said, still smiling. "I've got an aunt and uncle who'd probably say yes, if my parents asked. I could live with them. Visit my parents every holiday. They said they'd had no idea I was unhappy—they thought I'd wanted to start over too."

Both of them congratulated her, and she talked more about moving back to California. It wasn't a perfect solution, Mariana admitted. She'd miss her parents, but it would let her return to her high school, her extended family, and the home she loved.

"We're proud of you," Claire said.

Reyva nodded emphatically. "What she said."

As they talked, Claire helped herself to another pudding. For now, the hospital staff was leaving them alone, busy with other patients who were in more need than three malnourished girls with bumps and bruises. They'd been told they could stay until their parents arrived, and Mariana's parents had offered to pay the bill for whatever the three of them ate—Mariana had their credit card and permission to use it. The park ranger was still present, filling out paperwork at the nurses' station.

"It's over," Mariana said with a sigh.

"Yeah," Reyva said.

"Guess it really could mess with minds," Mariana said. "Our parents are proof."

Claire shuddered. That was a terrifying power. She hoped the spirit stayed sealed in that cave forever. She'd left out an explanation of how they'd trapped it when she'd talked to her parents, not wanting to risk anyone overhearing. The fewer people who knew about the cave, the better.

She tried to focus on the positives: they were saved, they were safe, and they were all going home. But a whisper of a thought crawled into her mind and, without stopping to reconsider whether she should say it out loud, she said out loud, "What if it messed with ours?"

"It didn't," Reyva said.

"We defeated it," Mariana said. "Right?"

Claire stood and began to pace, counting her steps. Now that the idea had taken root, she couldn't dig it out. "How did we get to the island? It had to have been by boat." She remembered being on a boat and knew they'd later exploded the boat engine. But whose boat had it been? "Who took us there?"

"The killer," Reyva said.

"Do you remember that?" Claire asked. "A specific memory, not just what you think must be true. I remember being on the boat. It was porpoising, and Mariana knew how to fix it."

"Adjust the throttle," Mariana said.

"But who was driving the boat?" Claire asked.

All three of them looked at each other.

"There was someone else," Claire insisted. "We've forgotten someone."

Less than an hour later, they were back in the park ranger's boat. Yes, their parents had said to stay put, but it would be many hours before they arrived, and the doctors had said they were free to go. The tricky part was persuading the park ranger to take them back to the island, in defiance of the no-trespassing rule.

"Why 'no trespassing'?" Claire had asked her.

"It's a sanctuary," she'd answered, "for birds."

Answering *her* questions had been a lot harder. There was someone else on the island, they'd told her, but they couldn't say who—or why they hadn't mentioned this other person before.

"It wasn't until after we ate and showered and had a chance to chill," Mariana explained, "that we started to remember. Guess we'd blocked out some of our time there. Trauma, you know."

"It was a blur," Reyva said.

"Hunger can do that to you," the park ranger said, a bit doubtfully.

Claire didn't know if that was true or not, or if the park ranger believed them or not, but they all nodded vigorously.

The park ranger had looked at each of their faces, and Claire didn't know what she saw. Sincerity? Or desperation. Either way, she had agreed.

Only when they were already on the boat did the park ranger say more. "Always been something off about that island," she said. "Lots of local stories. Sightings. Odd weather. If you say there's someone else there . . . well, it's not a place anyone should stay."

Claire wondered if the locals suspected, in the back of their minds, what lurked on the island. She knew from the park ranger that they'd seen the odd weather patterns. Maybe they'd heard the quieting of the birds. Felt the way the island was always watching. As the spray from the lake hit her face, she watched the island draw closer and closer and wished they were headed in any other direction.

"Can't believe we're going back," Reyva muttered.

"Are you sure there's someone we've forgotten?" Mariana asked, low so that the park ranger couldn't hear her over the thrum of the motor. "I mean, I don't remember forgetting any-one . . . which, now that I say it out loud, makes sense."

"How did I know how to clean that fish?" Claire asked. "And whose satellite phone was that, the one you tried to fix? I know it wasn't mine or either of yours." She felt like she had all her memories—she could trace every step from the moment they walked onto the dock—but they didn't make sense when she strung them together. "Why did we chase the wild man? Think about it. It doesn't make sense that he'd have a satellite phone. He'd been lost for decades. Whose backpack was that that the phone was in?"

The spirit must have made them forget, with the plan of claiming the body of whomever it was they'd forgotten for itself.

It hadn't counted on them trapping it inside the cave . . . which meant that he was still somewhere injured and alone.

How did she know the forgotten person was a *he*? And why did she think he was injured? She felt certain of that, though she didn't know why or what injuries.

Mariana was nodding, her lips pressed together. "There was a boy . . ."

"Yes!" Claire latched onto that. She wasn't alone in thinking it was a boy. What boy? Squeezing her eyes shut, she tried to remember. It felt like the memory was a fish, wriggling away through the water. She reached for it, and it slipped through her fingers.

At the dock, they all jumped off the boat. There was police tape visible in the woods—the police had already been here and had presumably found Mackenzie Williams's body, or at least begun a search for it. Claire hurried to where their campfire had been. She spotted a shelter in the woods, branches leaning against one another. "He built that," she said.

"We hid there," Reyva said, pointing.

It began to come back.

They'd hid. The wild man had come.

Together, they began to hurry up the trail toward the Lake House, with the park ranger following them. Halfway up, Claire caught Mariana's arm. "No, we didn't come down the trail. We ran into the woods, beyond the tennis court." She remembered this part. The dead man had been chasing them . . . "And then we hid not far from the shore. Not far from where the boat was wrecked. We found it the next day, remember?"

"If we follow the shoreline . . . ," Reyva began.

As one, they pivoted and backtracked to the lake. Following them, the park ranger asked, "Are you sure you girls know where you're going?"

"We're remembering!" Claire said. The memories were coming faster, now that they were back on the island. She began to run along the shore. There was an indent in the pebbles from where they'd pushed the wheelbarrow with the boat engine.

Soon, they found the wrecked boat, where they'd forcibly removed the outboard engine. There was still the impression on the ground where it had thumped down, and Claire could see the wheelbarrow tracks.

The park ranger examined the broken boat, while Claire scanned the edge of the forest. Which way . . . They'd hidden for the night and left Jack there.

Jack. That's his name.

She remembered now!

"Jack!" she called.

Mariana and Reyva called too. Leading the way, Mariana plunged into the forest. They watched for anything that looked familiar. They'd hidden themselves with branches beneath an overhang of rocks—

"There!" Mariana cried.

They hurried through the forest to where they'd hidden Jack. Quickly, they cleared the branches, and there he was. Eyes closed. Body curled.

"Is he . . . ," Mariana began and then stopped, afraid to continue.

Claire knelt and placed her hand a few inches from his mouth. She felt his breath cupped in her palm. "He's alive." To him, she said, "Jack? Jack, wake up. Jack, it's over."

His eyes opened very, very slowly. "Did . . . did . . . did it get me?"

Claire paused before answering, listening to the birds sing above them. A breeze rustled the leaves, and the air smelled sweet as moss. "You're safe." She felt it was the truth, though she couldn't explain why she felt so certain. "We all are."

Mariana patted his shoulder. "And if Claire says it, you know it's true."

Together, they helped him stand. "Come on," Reyva said. "Let's get you home."

TWENTY-NINE

With the park ranger, they delivered Jack to the hospital. He was immediately given an IV and whisked away to be examined, all the while shouting that his dad hadn't wanted to kill Mackenzie—*it* had made him do it—and that his dad shouldn't have killed himself.

Claire hoped he had the sense to watch what else he said. She couldn't remember ever telling Jack anything about the cave. After all, for much of the time they'd known him, including much of the boat ride back to civilization, he'd been unconscious. With luck, he wouldn't even know there was a secret to be kept.

That was the best they could do.

And it's good enough, Claire thought. Despite the odds, they'd survived.

They talked to the police one more time, explaining that they'd suddenly remembered Jack—they'd forgotten in the stress of it all, they'd claimed. The police told them that they'd found Mackenzie Williams's body, and, even more, that Jack's father's body had washed to shore and been discovered by a local fisherman. His rifle sling had gotten tangled around his body, and the coroner had confirmed that the bullets that killed both him and Ms. Williams were from that gun, registered to him. The police had their own theories for why he'd shot his girlfriend and why he'd burned down the Lake House (as they believed), and Claire, Mariana, and Reyva nodded along for all their ideas—happy enough that no one suspected either them or the truth.

By the time the police released them, they were hungry again. Asking a nurse at the hospital's front desk, they got walking directions to the town's pizza place, and they strolled there, arm in arm. It was late in the evening—the first few stars had appeared—and Claire listened for the birds. There weren't as many in the heart of town, and they were harder to hear beyond the usual cacophony of cars and people. But they were there, returning to their nests for the night. She imagined that after this summer, she'd always listen for them.

Mariana bought the pizza with her parents' credit card, and soon they were ensconced in a booth by the window with the pizza in front of them. Steam rose off the gooey cheese, and it smelled more glorious than Claire could have imagined. Diving for it, they each took a slice.

Closing her eyes, Claire bit into it. *Bliss*, she thought.

Then she thought of how hungry she'd been on the island, and her heart began to race again. Running through the first twenty-five digits of pi, she steadied herself and opened her eyes to see her two friends. The sight calmed her more than anything else she could think of.

"Okay," Mariana said. "Greatest wish. Reyva, do you want to start?"

"Not our greatest fear this time?"

Mariana waved a hand airily. "Already faced that. Greatest wish, and it can't have anything to do with the Lake House."

"I wish we'd ordered more pizza," Reyva said.

Claire looked pointedly at the only half-eaten pizza. They weren't in danger of starvation today.

"I'm planning ahead," Reyva said. "Like Claire does."

Fair enough. Claire took a sip of soda and thought about how nice it was they hadn't had to boil their beverages. "What's the first thing you're going to do when you're home?" she asked Mariana.

"Visit my car," Mariana said without missing a beat. "Then check the mail, to see if the parts I've been waiting for have arrived. Then I'll leave a message for my parts dealer, asking why the parts haven't arrived yet. And *then* I'm calling you two, and we're going to talk all night long while I start packing for California." She said the last bit with relish.

"My parents have phone rules," Reyva said.

"You're going to break them, because your parents sent you to a camp that doesn't exist to play host to an evil spirit, even if they don't exactly remember that last part. Just the sheer fact that they sent you to a defunct camp and didn't check to make sure you weren't abandoned on an uninhabited island without food, water, or shelter means they totally owe you."

Reyva brightened. "Good point."

"Honestly, that probably explains why mine were so on board with the idea of me moving in with my cousins," Mariana said. "Wonder what else I can ask them for. . . ."

Claire grinned. She had every intention of forgiving her parents—she'd seen firsthand how the spirit could mess with the mind—but maybe she'd forgive them *after* they agreed to let her visit Reyva and Mariana as often as she wanted.

Mariana pointed at Reyva. "You're dodging the question. What's your greatest wish?"

"More pizza is a reasonable wish," Reyva said. "To never lack pizza again. Also, to never break my arm again. Never have to sleep outside, soaking wet. And never have to be afraid like that ever again."

That was an entirely reasonable wish. Claire took another bite of pizza. The cheese pulled off the sauce, and she tore the mozzarella with her finger so the final bites wouldn't be cheeseless. Ah, cheese. She'd missed it. You couldn't forage for cheese in a forest.

"I'll accept all that," Mariana said. "Claire?"

Claire thought about what to say. She thought about the fear, the hunger, the cold. She remembered it all now, or at least believed she did. She'd run through her memories several times and couldn't find any more holes or inconsistencies. Finding Jack had erased the last bits of fog from her memory.

She looked at Mariana and Reyva, both of them waiting for her to answer, and she knew that whatever she picked to say would be okay. They'd seen her at her worst. So she went with the truth:

"I don't have to wish," Claire said. "I met both of you."

"Aw," Mariana said.

"Very sweet," Reyva agreed. "But I'm still taking that slice." She scooped up the largest remaining slice and shoved a quarter of it in her mouth.

Pulling out her phone, Mariana said, "Can't believe I didn't think of it sooner. . . . We need a picture. Come on." She scooted around the booth, squeezing in with both Claire and Reyva.

Jostled, Reyva yelped as she nearly dropped her slice. She glared at Mariana as Claire wiped a splatter of sauce from Reyva's cast.

"Scoot closer and smile," Mariana ordered. She stretched her arm out with the phone aimed at the three of them.

They all squeezed together and smiled. She took the picture, then checked it and showed them the result. *We look happy,* Claire thought. *And tired. But mostly happy, together.*

"Now we have a new tradition," Mariana declared. "We have to take a photo of us together every summer."

"With pizza," Reyva said.

"But absolutely no islands," Claire said.

"Agreed," Reyva said.

"We could try camping," Mariana said. "Now that we're experts and all."

Both of them looked at her. "I'm going to assume you're joking," Reyva said.

Mariana laughed. "Sort of? But this time we pick a place that isn't cursed. . . ."

It wasn't a terrible idea, actually. "Grand Canyon?" Claire

suggested. "Canadian Rockies? Yellowstone?"

"Or we could go backpacking through South America or Europe? Ooh, how about Southeast Asia?" Mariana suggested. "Ask your parents while they're still feeling guilty. Maybe they'll say yes."

Claire had no idea what her parents would agree to, but right now the details didn't matter. They'd stuck together, and they'd survived. *I've lived through my greatest fear*, she thought, *and gotten my greatest wish*. Anything was possible.

Squeezed together on one side of the booth, Claire, Mariana, and Reyva talked and laughed and dreamed about the future as they polished off the rest of the pizza.

On the island, near the ruins of the Lake House, deep inside a sealed cave, the body of a dead man clawed at the rock and earth in the darkness. Snares clung to his ankles, tight, but the spirit within didn't feel them. It felt only fear that it would never escape.

And fury that it had been outwitted by its prey.

ACKNOWLEDGMENTS

I have zero survival skills—I'm the friend you want with you in a bear attack and/or zombie apocalypse because you'd be able to escape while the bear or zombie or zombie-bear munched on me—but I have always wanted to write a survival book.

Blame it on one of my all-time favorite TV shows: *Alone*, which airs on the History Channel. It's a survival show where the competitors have to survive alone in the wilderness with ten items, their wits, and an absurd amount of camera equipment. So my first thank-you is to all the people involved in that TV show. Thanks so much for the inspiration!

This book was also inspired by the incredible friendships forged between teenagers. So often you see friendship between teens—especially between girls—depicted as vapid or catty, when the truth is the absolute opposite. I firmly believe that the intense bond that can develop between teenage girls is one of the most powerful and beautiful forces in the world. More powerful than any evil, ancient or new. So this book is for all the friends out there, giving one another strength.

I'd like to thank my phenomenal editor, Kristen Pettit, and

my awesome agent, Andrea Somberg. *The Lake House* would not exist without the brilliance of these two magnificent women! A huge thank-you, as well, to Lisa Calcasola, Jessie Gang, Mikayla Lawrence, Catherine Lee, Gwen Morton, Vanessa Nuttry, Linda Schmukler, Clare Vaughn, Jessica White, and all the other amazing people at HarperTeen for bringing this story to life! You all rock!

Thank you to my readers for following me deep into the woods of Maine. I am eternally grateful to you for choosing to share your time and your hearts with Claire, Reyva, and Mariana! Books don't exist without readers, and I wouldn't exist without books.

And thanks and so much love to my wonderful husband, my fantastic children, and all my family and friends! You are as essential to me as food, water, and shelter.